What the critics are saying

"LUCAVARIOUS will knock your socks off with its sexual tension and intriguing characters. Ms. Burke has outdone herself." - *Michele Gann, The Word On Romance*

"Humor, suspense, fantastic characters, great story!" – *Flora Bell, Sensual Romance Reviews*

Ellora's Cave Publishing, Inc.
PO Box 787
Hudson, OH 44236-0787

ISBN # 1-84360-446-9

Lucavarious edited by Martha Punches & Karen Williams.
Cover art by Darrell King.

LUCAVARIOUS

Written by

STEPHANIE BURKE

Chapter One

She could feel them gaining on her, getting closer every second. The fading darkness of the woods no longer protected her, no longer held her within its cold black embrace. The crash of their headlong chase gave her feet new life as she renewed the exhaustive pumping of her legs.

"Just a bit further," she panted, encouraging herself as she raced onward towards the glowing purple orb that marked the boundary between the pack lands and *him*. She slipped and almost fell to the leaf-covered ground as her soft slippers flew from her feet, but ignoring their meager protection, she paid no attention to their loss and struggled onward.

Then, for a moment, there was complete, utter silence. The change had begun. They were transforming into their secondary bodies, and that frightened her more than any thoughts of *him*. If they caught her, all her plans would be ruined, her deathbed promise useless.

Turning again, she continued her flight into the approaching dawn, towards the glowing shield that was now her only goal, her only hope.

She felt its power first, felt it pulsing and growing. The smell of it was foreign to her, different from the power with which she was accustomed, stranger than anything that she could have imagined.

But thoughts of those differences spurred her onward. Again she lost herself in the rhythm of pounding feet and straining muscles. Looking back over her shoulder, she noted that she could barely make them out, dark shadows streaking across the land behind her.

With a frustrated sob welling in her throat, she turned and almost ran straight into that wall of energy and power. Jolted by its glowing presence, she paused in front of it, just looking at it, tasting the air around it, basking in its energy.

"Dark!" a voice wailed.

Dark snapped back to herself, turned and then gasped in shock. They were almost upon her. She had no choice.

Praying that she would not be killed despite the invitation, and struggling against the urge to turn back, she crossed her arms over her face and plunged through.

There was a snapping sound and she suddenly felt as if there were electric jolts shooting through her body. Her ears popped and a pale glowing light burned her eyes where she peeked through the barrier of her arms. Tears of pain welled up and flowed down her cheeks. The air was forced from her lungs as she opened her mouth to let out a cry of distress, then just as suddenly, she was forced through the barrier. Gasping for breath, she fell to her knees, inches away from the purple shield, and lowered her head to the soft ground.

"Dark!"

She spun around to see pale yellow eyes glowing at her from beyond the other side of the dome. Massive jaws and razor-like teeth snapped ineffectively at the barrier, unable to break through. Even so, her heart raced as she scrambled further away on trembling knees and torn hands from the wall of the protective dome.

"Dark!" another sinfully seductive voice growled as she pulled herself to her cut and bleeding feet and again raced towards the castle. Those voices had the power to mesmerize. She didn't want to be caught in that trap.

"No!" the voices chorused together as she reached the castle steps. But she paid no attention, even as the two calls coalesced into a howl of anger and rage. She had a date with the devil and it was an appointment she was determined to keep.

* * * * *

The room wasn't what she'd expected. When speaking of the Vampesi, one thought of nothing but darkness, cold power, and dampness. But this room, this circular room was almost...*pleasant.*

Totally encircled by long dark draperies, no light could enter the room from any angle. Even the brightest rays from the sun would be absorbed into this absolute darkness.

She took a cautious step forward and sank into plush carpet so thick and luxurious it almost made her ashamed of her dirty bare feet and tattered sleeping gown.

As she stepped further into the room, a constant dull ache in her abdomen made her clench her teeth against the discomfort and curse the fates that added this latest issue to her existence.

Gritting her teeth, she looked around the room and finally noticed a large desk in the rear, centered perfectly, but nothing else. Turning, she visually circled the room, searching for some sign of life.

"Lucavarious!" she called, a sudden fear making her voice loud and authoritative.

"Wolfen-child," came the light reply.

Her attention snapped to the center of the room again, as if for the first time seeing the wide high-backed chair that sat there, faced away from her.

"We have business to discuss," she said, trying to interject braveness into her voice.

"Do we?" questioned the amused voice. It was dark and dangerous, far more seductive than the voices of the two she'd just avoided.

"The contract, Lucavarious; it must be fulfilled."

"Really, Wolfen-child?"

"Don't play games with me!" she screamed, losing patience. The ache was gnawing at her, the night was catching up to her, and anger was slowly threading its way into her voice.

"Games, Wolfen-child?"

"Damn it, Lucavarious. Show yourself."

Slowly the large black chair began to rotate and a small dim light seemed to glow around it. Dark felt her breath catch as she awaited her first glimpse of the monster that she had come to see.

He was…not what she expected.

Long tendrils of curly black hair dropped carelessly over his forehead and into his eyes. He stared at her with pale black eyes from beneath long lashes. His steepled fingers framed a set of full, well-formed lips. His nose was straight and wide, giving him a feline look. Even his hands were different, the little finger of each one crowned with a noticeably longer nail painted pure onyx, each sharp nail pierced with a small silver hoop.

Around both wrists were several silver bangles that tinkled and sang with the movement of the chair. One leg was casually thrown across the arm of his chair, a silver toe ring gracing one perfect toe, the other folded neatly beneath him.

As if to contrast all of the blackness that surrounded him, he wore a loose-fitting shirt and pants of a near-blinding white.

"Not what you were expecting, Wolfen-child?" he asked as he tilted his head to view her at a different angle. A faint howl grabbed his attention and he turned to face the drape-covered windows.

His ear was also pierced, she saw. A large diamond pierced the top of his ear while several tiny silver hoops jingled with his movements. So much for the myth that silver poisoned the Vampesi. The man was a walking silver mine.

"You are not what I had expected," she finally conceded. He was much more than she expected.

"Not bad for a 400-year-old man?" he laughed as he agilely leapt to his feet. "Friends of yours?" he asked, tilting his head in the direction of the mournful howls.

"About that contract," she changed the subject. "You have to honor it."

"I *have* to do no such thing." He laughed as he turned his pale black eyes back on her.

"You signed this!" she cried, slapping a tattered piece of parchment on the desk in front of him, her sudden anger making her forget her fear of crossing the room to face him.

"I signed that with your parents, Wolfen-child, not with you. Where are they?"

"Dead."

"And your entourage?"

"They tried to prevent this meeting."

"How?"

"Poison," she breathed, knowing that he meant her parents.

He hissed a long deep breath and the room noticeably chilled. She shivered as the temperature dropped several degrees. "I am sorry, Wolfen-child."

"They made me promise to come," she added.

"When?" he again asked, meaning her parents.

"T-Tonight."

He noticed the gleam of pain and the sheen of tears in her eyes.

"And them?" he asked, tilting his head towards the window.

"They are nothing!" she cried as she jerked her eyes to his. He didn't need to know that some of her parents' top advisors had wanted to stop this contract. And she had to act quickly. Dawn was fast approaching. She could feel it singing in her blood. She had to hold off until then. Then she would have the advantage.

"They are the Wolfen Clan, Wolfen-child." He settled an amused look upon his face. "Can you not hear their complaints?"

"I don't know what you're talking about!" she screamed, the cramps gripping her again. Crossing her hands over her stomach, she tried not to show him any signs of her distress.

"The children of the night," he laughed, quoting a long-lost book of fiction. With a flourish, he leapt to the ledge that encircled the room and tossed aside the curtain. "What beautiful music they make." He threw back his head as if relishing their mournful wails coming from beyond the barrier.

"It fits somehow." He let the curtain fall back and turned to face her again. "Wolfen and Vampesi," he laughed.

"Stop it!" she suddenly screamed. Her cramps were becoming uncontrollable. Fire was licking its way through her body.

"But I thought togetherness was the whole point to this contract, Wolfen-child?"

"We have to settle it tonight, Lucavarious," she gritted out, trying not to double over. His scent was driving her crazy. His power was driving her crazy. He was making her insane.

"And why is that, Wolfen-child?" His voice suddenly became low and dangerous.

"Because I'm going into heat."

"And we both know that I am the only thing keeping them from having you flat on your back taking turns to fill your belly with their seed and stealing all of your power." The Vampesi was serious now; keen intelligence shone from his eyes. He knew what he was up against if he fulfilled the terms of the contract. There would be no keeping him in the dark.

"They are scared," she reasoned just as the first rays of the new sun touched the sky.

"They are fools," he returned as he stepped down from the ledge and faced her, inhaling her scent, forcing her to lose her train of thought.

"You have to fulfill the terms!" she screamed, finally feeling forced enough to use desperate measures.

She raced past him to the curtains and latched on tightly. "You have to fulfill the terms," she cried again, anguished over what he was forcing her to do. It was not in her nature to wish harm upon anyone, but he was forcing her hand. "If you don't agree, I'll pull this open. The sun is shining now. I swear I will pull it."

"So you'll kill me to force me to aid you?" he quipped, laughter in his voice.

"I will!" she cried and realized that she meant it. All of her emotions and hormones were out of control. A volatile mixture of anger, frustration, and shame flooded her body. She now felt things, smelled things, heard things that she had never before noticed. Like the musky scent of him, the low boom of his heart beating, how his presence filled every inch of this room.

So lost was she that she barely noticed him walking up and surrounding her small hand with his larger one, but the heat was incredible.

"Do it," he hissed as she raised her troubled eyes up to his serious black ones. "Do it now, Wolfen-child."

Her body trembled as it recognized masculine heat and for the first time, she knew why her parents spent so much time caressing and cuddling each other.

"Do it," the silken voice urged as she suddenly realized that she didn't want to harm this man.

She whimpered as she listened to that voice. She had made her declaration and he did not believe her capable of carrying it out. What kind of leader was she if she could not keep her word, even when she had no wish to do so?

"Do it."

She had no choice.

With a loud broken sob, she yanked back the curtain, flooding the small room with new light, covering his body with the only thing she believed would harm him.

With a cry, she turned to see what she had wrought and saw…nothing.

"I was born Vampesi, Wolfen-child, not created." He opened his eyes and stared directly to the east and the rising sun, enjoying the sight.

She stood there, amazed, and a bit confused.

"After all of these years, do you think that I would leave myself in a vulnerable position, Wolfen-child? If you think your people are cut-throat, you have yet to meet the Vampesi."

"I can't force you." She sighed as she looked out of the window and into the forests that surrounded the castle, drinking in his magnificent visage as the sunlight caressed it. "All is lost then."

In the daylight, the purple barrier was invisible. She had a clear view of the land that had been entrusted to her people for a thousand years, guarded by her family for almost all of that time, and knew that soon dead bodies would cover that land.

"I will honor the contract, Wolfen-child," he purred as he raised one hand to touch her face.

"What?" she asked as her eyes zeroed onto him once again.

"I will fulfill the terms, Wolfen-child. I but wished to see the true caliber of my mate."

"Why?" she asked, not quite understanding but beginning to hope.

"I need someone willing to sacrifice, to fight. You would have killed to keep your word. I admire that."

She stood there mute.

"What is your name, Wolfen-child? I have to call you something."

"Dark," she whispered absently, a great weight lifting off of her chest and her tension eased up a bit. "My name is Dark."

With a smile, he stepped back from her and turned to face the door. It opened silently and a servant entered.

"Please take my bride to a place of honor so that she might refresh herself and rest."

"Rest?" Dark asked, coming out of her daze.

"Today, you must rest, Wolfen-child. Tonight the contract will be fulfilled and you will become my mate. We have a lot of work to do if I am to get a child upon you that will unite our peoples. A lot of work indeed." His black eyes glittered with amusement as he turned his back to her and faced the open curtain again.

Stunned, Dark allowed herself to be led out of the room by the kind-looking older woman. She took one last look at the man bathed in sunlight that should have killed him, but instead stood basking in its rays.

She had kept her date with the devil, and now she was going to have to crawl into bed with him.

Chapter Two

"I want to get out," Dark muttered to the servant, who was bustling around the room. "I want to get out and I want you to leave me, *now.*"

After being led from what was known as the master's study, Dark had been taken to a large room that curiously seemed to lack windows. "Where am I?" she demanded, but the female only smiled.

The servant smiled again as the tatters of Dark's gown were practically torn from her body and she was brought to a bathing chamber. This room was one large sunken pool. There were no windows here either, giving the place the feel of a prison. Dark noted a table piled high with large towels and bowls of dried flowers. Large marble pillars surrounded the room; cream-colored, with thin black veins. The floor was made of some type of tile that was warm beneath her bare feet. An elegant prison then, but a prison nevertheless. She looked back at the muddy footprints her feet had left and let out a resigned sigh. She was woefully unprepared for this.

Still not quite believing what had happened to her, Dark let the woman ease her into a tub filled with steaming water, yet still the servant said nothing. Dark sighed a bit as the steam filled her nostrils and the hot water seeped into her pores, washing away her earlier terror of the chase and her shock of meeting the Vampesi.

Now that her initial fear and anxiety were over, her hormones had calmed to a tolerable level—although that ache that had alternately heated then chilled her body was still there, simmering just below the surface. It was like some ravenous beast waiting for her control to slip so that it could take over her body, her mind, and drive her mad.

While sitting there, her mind turned to thoughts of her future mate, the devil-man Lucavarious. She recalled all of the silver that adorned his person and let out a tired sigh. "Mama, Papa, you were wrong about the silver." She couldn't use silver as a means of equaling their relationship.

And she couldn't threaten him with sunlight. He appeared to be immune.

But the thing that galled her most was that he had been testing her all along. *She* was the hunter, *she* was the one that supposedly could see through the devious traps of the Vampesi, but she had played his little mind games and found herself lacking.

She didn't realize it, but as thoughts of self-recrimination churned in her mind, a low growl began to rumble from her throat. Her short-cropped black hair, wet with steam, began to stick in clumps to her head, outlining her oval face and exaggerating her high cheekbones. Her deep brown eyes took on a feral glow and her breath began to pant from her throat.

The water, once soothing, was now an irritant on her suddenly sensitive skin. She wanted to get out. She *needed* to get out.

"I said I would like to get out now," she growled, her senses again going on overload.

The servant, a non-descript older woman, took one look at her, blanched, and then ran from the room, shouting for Lucavarious.

"What is wrong with these people?" she nearly shouted herself, the smell of the woman's fear agitating her further.

Her golden skin began to itch, and unconsciously she ran her hands over her arms, tearing delicate skin with talons that sprang forth where nails used to be. The smell of her own blood only made her emotions jumble more. She had to get out, to escape. She was trapped.

"Dark."

The low sharp voice caught her attention. The scent was familiar to her, new, but familiar.

"Breathe deeply, Wolfen-child," he said in calm tones.

Why was he speaking to her as if she were a child? She rubbed her arms faster, trying to stop the itching that was now beginning to burn.

Lucavarious entered the bathing chamber and clucked his tongue at what he saw. His Wolfen had made a royal mess of her arms, and she didn't seem to notice it.

When his servant had exploded into the room crying about the monster that he had brought into his home, he did not know what to expect. But as he inhaled the sweet smell of her adrenaline-saturated blood and saw the wildness in her eyes, he realized that he should have expected this reaction.

When she had walked into his study earlier, he was at once taken by her young determined face; but it was the hint of wildness that intrigued him. Her large brown eyes dominated her face and her full, pouty lips promised passion in her blood. As she argued with him, he found that promise to be true — fire flowed within her blood. Her golden skin and flashing eyes stirred something in his blood he had thought lost. Now, looking at her wild eyes and heaving chest, he found that his desire for her was not a random happening. No, his little Wolfen-child had awakened something savage and dangerous in him.

"I am a randy bastard," he said to the room at large as he felt his member begin to swell within the confines of his once loose-fitting pants. There was something definitely wrong with him if her confusion and distress were turning him on. Or maybe it was her sudden air of helplessness that had awakened him.

"I want to get out," she said again, in a trance-like voice. "I don't want to sit here any longer."

"Very well, Wolfen-child," he agreed as he grabbed a towel from a nearby stack and cautiously approached the tub. "Can you stand?"

"I'm not a baby," she growled.

He saw that the changes her body was forcing her through were beginning to take their toll. She looked exhausted. There were dark rings around her eyes and her face seemed quite pale.

He knew that her physical state was taxing her strength, but this was worse than the usual drain on the body caused by being a woman in heat. This reeked of some mental trauma that she was struggling with.

"Dark," he called softly and in a flash of movement, she turned her head towards him, the beast in her making the move seem wild and savage.

"Lucavarious, you bastard," she hissed from between clenched teeth.

"I have been called worse, Wolfen-child."

"I am not a child." Her lips curled back a bit from her teeth, exposing the growing fangs that threatened to slice her gums to ribbons.

"Impressive, Wolfen," he murmured. "But if it is a show of fangs you want, that display is woefully inadequate. And I know you are not a child. Your bare breasts with their firmly erect nipples tell me that. Now do you wish to leave the water that you are currently bloodying with your attempts at self-mutilation?"

His words knocked the wildness right out of her. *Self-mutilation?*

She looked down and stifled a small scream of fright.

"What...how?" She looked up to him, a little girl lost, and waited for him to explain.

"How long have you been in heat?" he asked calmly as he pulled one bleeding arm from the tub.

"A few days now," she answered in a shaky voice.

"Hmm." He placed her arm on the edge of the tub and pulled back the sleeve of his shirt.

"What are you doing?" she asked. She knew that he wouldn't hurt her; he was going to mate with her, but his actions confused her.

"I am going to fix your arms, then I am going to help you scrub the rest of the forest from your body, then you are going to bed. I need you fresh for tonight."

That said, he raised one pinkie to eye level, the silver ring there bouncing against the black nail. As she watched, he lowered that hand and made a quick slash, opening his arm, leaving a thin trail of blood.

"Why?" she asked but he shushed her.

"Watch and learn, Wolfen-child."

Squeezing the wound a bit to encourage the bleeding, he deftly captured the sparkling red drops on his fingertip, then smeared his life-fluid over the gouges and tears on her arm.

"That burns!" she cried out, trying to pull her arm back.

"Of course it does. My blood is powerful." But still, he bent his head and pursed his lips. Gently he blew cool air on her arm, and almost instantly the stinging sensations stopped.

"Give me the other arm," he commanded as she stared in awe at her arm.

The rough tears that she was sure would need stitches were rapidly healing themselves, the flesh neatly knitting back together, leaving a long pink seam on her golden skin.

"It's healed," she said, dazed.

"Of course," he replied as he reached around her and pulled her other arm to him.

"Why?" she said, then gasped as he repeated the stinging procedure.

"Because I do not want you bleeding all over my castle. The only blood shed this night will take place in my bedroom."

That shut her up.

When her arms were healed, he reached up and produced a small sponge and a bottle of cleanser.

She started to ask him what he thought he was doing, but her words were reduced to gurgles as he gripped the top of her head and forced her beneath the water.

As she emerged with an angry splash, he again quieted her by dumping the soap directly on top of her head.

To keep soap from her eyes and mouth, she closed them both and silently fumed. She was very angry with him, but as her emotions turned towards him, the wildness in her blood receded until it lay dormant within her. It still pulled against the civil chains that bound it, but for now, it was contained.

In short order, her hair was scrubbed clean and she was again dunked to remove the suds. As he soaped up the sponge, her hands shot out to detain him.

"I believe I can handle the rest," she said in a cold calm voice, while glaring at him.

"I do believe that you are correct, Wolfen-child. I fear if I continue further, I might anticipate our mating a bit."

He looked down and she followed his gaze to his crotch. She blanched as she saw the material of his pants tented out before him.

"And no, it's not pierced. Yet."

He laughed as he used one finger to close her mouth before he rose to his feet and quit the room.

Dark finally managed to gather her composure as he closed the door behind him. But strangely, it seemed that the room had risen several degrees in temperature.

Chapter Three

"Master, there are some...*people* at the door."

Lucavarious opened his eyes and stared at the tall, red-haired servant who stood at the entrance to his inner domain.

"People, B.B.?" he asked as he stretched his long corded arms over his head, smiling at the sound the tinkling bracelets made.

After leaving Dark to complete her bath, Luca fled—walking slowly, but still he fled — to his private chambers. How on earth could that young Wolfen affect him so quickly? He had to admit that the smell of her blood was enticing, but she was so gauche in her actions, so inexperienced with real life, so damn...hot, he thought in annoyance.

But she did have a fine set of fangs.

As advanced as he was now, he no longer felt the urge to gorge himself on any willing vein that happened to be present. In fact, he was to the point where the animal blood that he kept in ample supply was enough and human blood was considered a treat. A treat that he rarely indulged in.

But the scent of her animal magnetism combined with the heady smell of her blood had taken him back to his youth, to a time when he struggled to set a good example for his people by not draining every human that served.

"People, Master," B.B. said with a sneer in her husky voice.

Ah, the lovely B.B. shows her jealousy, he thought as he sat up in his satin-draped bed. What a pity. She would obviously have to be replaced soon.

He again stretched his arms above his head and observed his private chambers. His massive bed filled the alcove that it sat in, the nine-foot pillars reaching up towards the high ceiling. Behind the impressive marble headboard was a large tapestry done in dark, winding ropes of black and red. The abstract design fit his perception of his inner self perfectly, darkness moving in ever-changing conflict, warring with what little light remained.

In the center of the chamber hung a large crystal chandelier—a relic from the days before the Supernaturals made themselves known to the mortals, the days when such shows of ostentatious wealth actually meant something. Now it was merely a fanciful reminder of the past, an antique curiosity to be displayed for his pleasure.

On the floor were several rugs made of white wolf skin, relics from the war that had nearly decimated the populous of the Unnaturals, as the mortals once called them.

"What shall I tell them?" the flame-haired woman again asked, even though her disgust was clearly showing.

"I do believe that you are speaking of my new in-laws, B.B., and you overstep your role. Please have a care to remember who and what you are, and how easily you can be replaced."

"Master," she gasped, quickly looking to the floor to show her obedience.

"So by all means, make them comfortable, B.B. Toss them some kibble or whatever it is that they eat."

"They eat human flesh, Master," she returned, a sick look coming over her nearly perfect features.

"I'm sure you would like that, my dear," he purred then bit back a bark of laughter as he saw fear in her green eyes. "No one has a sense of humor anymore," he sighed as he tossed back his satin coverlet and rose to his feet.

B.B.'s eyes widened appreciatively as she took in the full sight of her master, naked save for a small loin wrap that seemed too small to contain the bulge it barely protected.

"And please fetch my mate," he added as he watched her face flush with the beginnings of desire. Yes, she would now have to be replaced. Her hunger was beginning to annoy him.

"To your chambers?" she asked, her eyes jerking away from him to land on the wolf pelts that covered his floor.

"Yes, B.B., to my chambers. Why? Do you think that it would be in bad taste to display the skins of her slain cousins?"

B.B.'s face blanched as she pictured her master's *pet's* reaction to the skins.

"And you had better hide your lust, dearest," he continued as he pulled on a robe from the foot of the bed. "She is extremely sensitive, and we wouldn't want anything to set her off."

"No, Master," she stammered as she quietly closed the door.

"Just when I was starting to get used to her, too," he sighed as he ran his fingers through his mussed hair. "Good B.B.'s are getting hard to find."

* * * * *

Dark paced the floor of the room where she had been left to wait, absently muttering about the confining gown she wore with some reluctance.

As the day slowly ebbed into night, her nervousness increased, and with her anxiety came the renewal of the beast longing to be free. Her over-sensitized skin itched where the soft, silky material touched, and that only increased her anxiety.

She was barefoot. She absolutely *refused* to wear the tight, toe-pinching, heeled sandals that were provided with the gown. Hell, the gown was bad enough. She had never been forced to wear something so frivolous in her life.

The gown was nothing more than a long tube of white material held over her shoulders by a pair of thin ribbons. And to add insult to injury, there was a thin sheer train that attached to the back. She felt like a damn butterfly, not the powerful Wolfen princess that she was.

"I bet he's wearing his pajamas again," she groused as she paced the floor. "He gets comfort and I get to look like wounded prey in a house full of predators. Could he make me look any more vulnerable?"

And vulnerable she did look. With her large brown eyes shining with her inner struggle and her delicate features made all the more fragile with her worry, she looked like a princess in need of rescuing. Pity the only prince available was one of the dark persuasion.

The soft knock at her door gave her something else to focus on besides her helpless, womanly appearance. If it was that bastard Lucavarious, she had some words for him.

But a young, red-haired human female entered, and she looked...arrogant? What was going on here? Dark prepared herself for her newest conflict, because she had the feeling that this female hated her.

"What do you want, human," she fairly growled, the Wolfen in her showing her voice.

"Luca has sent me to fetch you," she nearly sneered.

Dark stiffened then bristled as she recognized a pet name that this creature was calling her mate. He may be a bastard and an arrogant, silver-encrusted peacock, but he was *her* peacock.

"And do you always address your betters so familiarly, human?" she asked as she took a step closer to the irritating female, chuckling as the wench took a hurried step back.

"I...I am special," she bravely continued, although the scent of her fear was beginning to fill the room, making the beast within struggle against its chains.

"Special, are you?" Dark asked as she stepped closer. The woman was so short she barely reached her shoulder, and there she stood, trying to intimidate her with her relationship to her future mate. "By what name are you called?"

"B.B.," she said, her chest puffing out with pride despite her growing anxiety.

"B.B.! God. Can't he even give them proper names?" Dark moaned. She shook her head at the poor deluded creature.

B.B. stiffened her spine and jerked away from the door, a jealous glint in her green eyes. She would show this man-stealing creature a thing or two, she thought with glee. "B.B. is a special name that Luca has given me because I fulfill an important role in his life." Her leering glance told Dark all she needed to know about this special role.

"So he sends the old whore to bring the fresh one," Dark said as she gave the woman a considering look. "If I were you, human, I would be offended to have my lover toss me over for his new plaything so publicly. But then, we are talking about humans here. You all were never considered as having much pride anyway, the way you bastardize yourselves to these blood drinkers. Well, no matter. Lead me to your, um, master, B.B., as I see that there are things that we must discuss."

Then with her head held high, she swept past the sputtering woman and into the hall, snagging B.B by one hand as she lifted her nose in the air and scented out the position of her future mate.

* * * * *

"Look and see who has come to play with me," Luca snickered as he saw the two wolf shapes slide stealthily into his chambers. "And before we were properly introduced too."

Luca sat cross-legged, levitating high on a pillow of air as he observed his visitors. The Wolfen did look exactly like their four-legged counterparts, except for their great size. Nothing in nature could create a wolf the size of a small horse and give it the ability to walk upright if need be. His two wolfish visitors had to have some reason for sneaking into his rooms, after he'd extended his warm invitation and all.

Too bad they forgot that the Vampesi could not be surprised in their own homes. He knew the moment they followed his scent into the hallway outside his door by the aura of anger and hatred that they gave off. In fact, the smell of their wild animal emotions so filled his chamber that he knew he would have to air it out before feeling comfortable here again. The room dropped several degrees in temperature, causing a fine sheen of ice to coat the crystals hanging from his chandelier. He so hated having his inner sanctum disturbed.

"Now, please tell me," he breathed on a puff of anger to the two that entered uninvited into his rooms, "Are you male or female? Well, it really doesn't matter; I'm going to kill you both anyway."

Barely suppressing his anger, he lowered his legs and landed softly on his feet. The two turned towards him, eyes flashing red-hot as their muzzles wrinkled to expose sharp fangs dripping saliva and flecks of blood.

"Oh, my in-laws. How mannerly you are," he hissed, a silver fire heating his black eyes as the temperature in the room plummeted.

"What have you done to her?" the disembodied voice echoed through the room. "Where are you holding her?"

One wolf, a black and brown female, lowered her upper body and tightened the muscles in her powerful hind legs in preparation for a leap.

"And if I don't tell you, you will probably rip out my throat and feast on my tender innards," he drawled in a sickening imitation of her voice, a sarcastic high falsetto. "Wolfen, please. I grow tired of this old song and dance."

As he spoke, a purple haze began to surround him, a pulsing visible barrier that throbbed with the beat of his heart. The robe he wore tangled around his legs, outlining their power as an invisible wind whipped around the room, icing over the furniture, growing colder with each passing second.

"Where is she?" the dark Wolfen cried out, her muzzle not moving but still she projected her voice loudly. "Nothing could have made her come willingly here to you. The others told me of how you lured her here with that black power of yours. I want my niece and I want her *now*."

That said, she leapt into the air, claws extended, teeth bared.

The impact of her hitting the shield sent her tumbling head over heels into her light brown companion, knocking them both off of their feet.

"I inform you of our coming nuptials, extend an invitation to you, open up my home to you, and this is how you repay me? With vicious attacks and accusations?" Lucavarious fought to control his anger, but then he thought, *why bother?* What rights did they have attacking him, and before he was even dressed?

The Dark Prince, silver jewelry tinkling, lifted his hands in the air and prepared to call forth another special little trick of his—a force field that would surround the two totally. Then he had three options. He could slowly fill the invisible cage with air until their lungs exploded and their eyes popped out; he could slowly draw the air from the force cage until their bodies eventually imploded, turning inside out; or he could hold them until Dark arrived to talk some sense into them.

Yeah, right.

"Before you die," he growled, blood-deep anger turning his voice rough as he fought against the urge to let his fangs show, "I should tell you that Dark came running to me in the middle of night, begging me to fulfill a contract. The contents of that contract are none of your business, but it behooved me to let you know that your niece is mating with me tonight. A couple of your people would have raped her to prevent this match from taking place. So know before you die that she came here of her own free will and now belongs to me."

Two pairs of Wolfen eyes widened in shock as they took in his words, then showed finality, accepting their fate.

"Die!" he cried out, his first set of fangs breaking free in his anger, tearing the flesh of his gums and spewing his blood across his formerly pristine white robe as they extended. Fangs, white, thin triangles sharper than a Wolfen's talons, glowed softy in the dim candlelight. The air in the force cage began to grow thin and dissipate.

"*Lucavarious!*" a voice cried from behind.

"What is it?" he bellowed as he turned to face the open door.

Dark stood there, a… well…*dark* expression in her brown eyes.

"It is what's left of my family that you are torturing there." Arms akimbo, Princess Dark looked ready to fight.

"Torturing?" he asked, his temper refocused on her, his earlier agitation with her coming back in spades. "Are you aware that these two, like the cowardly dogs they are, sneaked into my rooms and accosted my person?" His black eyes sparkled with the silver flashes of his anger. He also stopped forcing the air from the cage as he mentally girded his loins to match wits with his future mate.

"What are they doing here, Lucavarious? And what is this?" she nearly bellowed as she thrust a babbling B.B. into the room.

"I invited them so that we may begin discussing peace between our two peoples, and the *that* that you are mishandling is B.B."

"Why wasn't I informed of this, and what is a B.B.?" She was not backing down one bit on this matter. Funny, but it suddenly seemed more important than Aunt Zinia and her daughter Puaua getting the life-air squeezed from their bodies.

As for the trapped Wolfen, as soon as the pressure lessened in their chests, they watched the by-play between the dreaded Lucavarious and Dark with simple amazement. Like two spectators at an ancient game once played called tennis, their heads swung back and forth, observing the action.

"You were not informed because you were too intent on flaying the flesh from your own body and trying to prove that you are the bigger man. And B.B. stands for Blood Bank, you silly twit," he growled, the wind easing and the temperature starting to warm up with his temper, which was better than the cold rage he had exhibited earlier.

"Twit? How dare you call me a twit, you barbarous monster! *Blood Bank?* You keep this simple-minded creature as your own personal stash of hemoglobin, and you call me a twit? What's next, Oh Great Master? Free-range Humans?"

"Well, you misbegotten resting place for fleas, that sounds like a grand idea to me. Free-range humans. Come on out and pick your meal. Make sure you watch them run and jump before your selection, just to make sure the blood is healthy."

"You bastard!" Dark screamed before she stormed over to him and…

Whack.

The sound of her hand connecting with his face filled the now-silent room. Even B.B. stopped whimpering, her eyes wide with shock as she saw the Wolfen woman slap her master.

The force cage winked out of existence as Lucavarious, standing still in shock, raised one hand, bracelets tinkling loudly in the quiet room, and touched his throbbing cheek. A bright red handprint stood out clearly against his golden skin.

"You…" he began, but a sound from behind had him turning as with a cry, his second set of fangs exploded in his mouth beside the first, only these were longer sharper, deadlier.

Holding both hands at his waist, a powerful blast of purple energy lifted him to the ceiling just as Zinia, seeing an opening in his defenses, leapt for his throat.

She missed by mere inches.

Now plastered against the ceiling, his opaque purple shield holding him safely out of reach, Lucavarious stared down at the two leaping Wolfen and his irate mate. His anger abated and slowly the double set of fangs sank back into his gums. Dark, cynical amusement lit his eyes as he observed the Wolfen—his soon-to-be…relatives.

"I feel so much like one of the family," he drolly quipped as he lay on his stomach, his purple force field easily holding his weight.

"Hey, Zinia," he called as she leapt and uselessly bounced off of his shield. "Can I call you Auntie?"

Chapter Four

The barefoot bride nervously eyed the people gathered in the lower hall of the castle. Almost as if one of Lucavarious' shields separated them, they were divided.

On the right sat her two kinswomen surrounded by a company of at least five serious-faced males. They all glared at the altar, which held the joining paper, and if they could produce flame with their very stares, the parchment would have exploded into flames and reduced to ash.

And on the left sat those who only could be the disapproving members of the Vampesi. Some of them levitated, some of them surrounded themselves with shields of various hues — protection, she assumed, from the invading wolfish masses — while some of them pointedly turned their backs on her when they noticed the attention they were receiving from the bride.

Mixed freely among the Vampesi were humans. They stuck close to their Vampesi masters as if the Wolfen were getting ready to pounce and feast upon their succulent meat. *As if.* Humans, she was once told, were far too tough, stringy, foul tasting, and not worth the effort to hunt. >From the two that she had met she had added scared, shallow, and sour to the list.

And one of the worst of the lot just entered through the door in the rear. As B.B. made her hurried appearance, she paused to glare at Dark.

Never one to take insults sitting down, Dark narrowed her eyes, and a loud thundering growl erupted from her throat. Then she had to fight back a bark of laughter as what color was left in the redhead's face drained away. Damn, but letting the beast out a little bit was fun.

In response to her growl, the Wolfen, as in a phalanx, turned to the rear of the chamber, hackles raised and low warning growls in their throats. Which in turn had the Vampesi strengthening their shields, tensing muscles, and protectively moving in front of their humans.

"Oh hell," Dark muttered as she dropped her forehead and cradled that aching body part within her hand. Talk about a little fun getting out of hand.

"If you wanted to incite a riot that would in turn begin the next war between our people, there are easier ways of doing it, Wolfen-child."

That droll, sarcastic voice could only come from one person. "Lucavarious," she sighed before she lifted her head and stared at her dark prince. He was again dressed all in white, from the long tunic of some silky material to his loose trousers. Like her, his feet were bare, his silver toe ring glinting in the lights from the many candles set around the room. His golden skin glowed and his black eyes twinkled at her. He had caught her actions and was amused by them.

"Really, Wolfen-child, there are easier ways to grab my attention." He raised one long-nailed pinkie and pointed to his face where her handprint was still clearly marked. "Take this for example."

For a moment, she thought to apologize for her loss of control, but then she decided to hell with apologizing. He'd brought it on himself. "Hmmm. I wonder what I can do when my claws come in?" she asked, a faint smile playing about her lips while her eyes shot dark fire.

"Truce, Wolfen-child," he laughed after a surprised look crossed his face. "And if we are to war amongst ourselves and not our people, you really should call me Luca. All of my," he leaned down low and let his warm breath bathe her face, "*friends* do."

"Then thank God I'm going to be your mate," she returned with a smile of her own. "Now I don't have to stoop to giving you pet names."

"Speaking of pet..." he began, only to be cut off as the Sage stepped forward.

"Tonight, we join two people, two clans, two races."

Dressed in dark robes that completely covered his face and body, the Sage was the neutral party to unite Dark and Lucavarious in this mating. Everyone respected the Sage. No one really knew how old he was, but he was the keeper of the history for both the Wolfen and the Vampesi. The knowledge contained within his agile mind could start wars, but he chose discretion to gossip. That was why both races respected him highly.

"The contract, please," he intoned and reached one whitened hand for the document.

As if handling rare treasure, Dark picked up the contract, the thing that her parents had sacrificed their lives for, and for a moment held it close to her heart. It was so hard to pass it on, especially now that it felt like the last link between she and her parents. So many times she had heard them discussing each little detail, from the wording to the offering. It seemed wrong somehow to now let it go, to let her parents go, but she knew that she had to fulfill this bargain.

Hands trembling slightly, she passed the contract over to the Sage and he began to read it out loud.

"For the future, for the continuation of our kind, for life, we have given our daughter into the care and keeping of the absolute ruler of the Vampesi, and along with her, the mantle of shared leadership."

There were ugly growls from the Wolfen contingency present. The Wolfen, as befitted their nature, were private people, used to keeping their own council. This new development would place any final decision-making into the hands of their enemies. Especially if the so-called absolute ruler was to court Dark's way of thinking.

"I think there will be trouble," Dark whispered as she looked at her aunt and her followers. "You could have sent them a message after the contract was fulfilled." She unconsciously stepped closer to Lucavarious, closer to the protection that he offered.

"And miss all of the fun?" Luca asked, raising one black eyebrow condescendingly at her. "Perish the thought." With a tinkle of his bracelets, he crossed his arms and glared at the assembly.

He too had noticed the Wolfen reaction and wondered if there would be a blood- bath to celebrate his nuptials.

He looked over to the Vampesi and noticed the smug looks on their faces. He so did hate for his people to take things for granted. That left them open and vulnerable. Just wait until the Sage read the other clauses set in the contract.

"Shared leadership for both clans."

The gloating smiles on the Vampesi vanished.

"When the time is right, the progeny of this union will inherit both kingdoms and therefore responsibility of both peoples, ending the war and strife that has existed between us for centuries."

Now there was absolute silence in the room. Not a breath could be heard, not a whimper or a whisper.

"Let the games begin," Lucavarious whispered to Dark before he threw up a protective shield around her.

"Nooooo!" wailed a voice and Dark turned away from her mate to see her aunt throw herself at the couple behind the purple barrier. "He has corrupted you, Dark. The leadership should pass on to me. I am the next most powerful woman here. Your parents were insane."

"Such confidence they show in you, Wolfen-child," Lucavarious muttered as he looked from one woman to the other.

Auntie Zinia wasn't half-bad looking. She possessed the same deep brown eyes as Dark, but that was where the similarity ended. While Dark had a thick cap of cropped black hair, Zinia's long locks hung in a profusion of brown and black waves to her mid back. She looked amazingly like her brother, the now deceased Wolfen ruler. And there was passion in her blood. That was another thing that Dark and Zinia had in common.

"My parents were murdered for this contract, Aunt. I will fulfill my death-bed promise, then I will find those traitors among my people and they will know my wrath."

Her dark eyes spit fire and the beast within was again straining to be released. The cramps began low in her stomach, causing her to shake, but she stood her ground and faced down her aunt.

"Our people would never," the woman hissed, a feral light entering her eyes. "It must have been the Vampesi."

At her words, a mass *hiss* could be heard from the Vampesi. This accusation did not sit well with them. How dare those four-legged freaks accuse them of an underhanded murder? Especially murdering something as loathsome as a Wolfen.

Before Dark could growl an answer to that accusation, Lucavarious stepped in.

"Woman, you defame my people and their good name," he quipped. "We would never sink so low as to use poison. Decapitation is more our style."

The general laughter from the Vampesi front ended any immediate threat from his people, but there was still the Wolfen to deal with.

"How dare you make jokes?" Zinia's anger now focused on Lucavarious. "My brother and his mate lie dead in their own beds and you…"

"Are attempting to fulfill their last request as we agreed upon several months ago," he finished in a bored voice. "Now if you would be so kind as to take your seat, we will continue so that I might begin impregnating your niece. She is in heat and needs relief. So, sit. Sit. Good girl."

"You bastard!" shrieked two different sets of Wolfen throats.

"Oh, dear," he sighed as he looked over at his mate and noticed her fangs fighting to be free and her fingernails exploding into talons.

"How dare you tell my personal business?" she growled.

"How dare you treat me like some simple-minded animal that you can control?" That from his new aunt.

"Yes, I can see that you are related," he again sighed as he turned away from the minor threat of Zinia and faced the more dangerous threat of his mate.

"Well, it's not like you can exactly hide it," he began, turning towards Dark, but the Sage's words interrupted him.

"If you are done toying with the people, Lord Lucavarious, I would recommend that you agree to this contract and swear upon your life to uphold it."

Fighting back an impulse to take the man to task for daring to preach to him, Luca tightly nodded his consent. Raising his long pinkie nail, he slashed a small opening on his wrist. Then taking a signet ring from his pocket, he dipped it in his dark, flowing blood and stamped the paper.

"I didn't know that you had a family crest," Dark murmured, looking over at the small shield.

"There is a lot about me that you do not know," he said, as he looked down at the top of her head.

She had bent low to see the marking on the paper and in doing so, exposed her long graceful neck to his avid gaze.

Throughout this whole farce of a ceremony, Luca had fought for control. The sight of Dark waiting below for him in all of her barefoot glory was enough to make him want to drag her to the nearest closet and have his way with her. She ignited a fire in his blood and he was beginning to accept his desire for his new mate. The fact that she was falling deep into heat and her emotions quickly swung from cold to hot only made her more intriguing, more interesting to observe, to be around. He was hard-pressed to hide his reactions from both of their people and from her, but the hour was fast approaching when he would relinquish all control and bury himself into her warm soft body.

"Take this," he growled, nearly sounding Wolfen himself, as he reached for her finger. "You will have time to examine the mark later." He slid the ring, still coated with his blood, onto her finger.

Dark looked down at the ring now weighing down her finger, then up at the man who had placed it there. *Oh, God*, she thought. *I belong to that now, and he, God help me, belongs to me.* She took a deep breath and swallowed audibly as she realized that they were now intertwined until death.

"The Wolfen mate for life, you know." She stared at the ring.

"I know." Suddenly he had no cynical remarks to make. This mating was now real and almost complete.

"What do I do?" she asked, turning to the Sage.

"Offer him your throat," the kindly voice replied.

"No!" Zinia cried out. "He will drain you and solely rule all of our people."

"Will you shut up, old lady?" a voice from the Vampesi called out. "We are growing tired of the honorless accusations you throw at our ruler."

"Would you like to try and make her?" Puaua growled, flipping her long brown hair over her shoulder and glaring at the bloodsucker that dared to command her mother.

"Oh, hell!" Dark muttered as she stepped up to Lucavarious and tilted her neck to the side. "Do it quickly, before there is war."

"You trust me not to drain you and turn you into a mindless corpse?" Luca asked, amusement replacing the serious look on his face.

"Just do it, and only use one set of fangs, please. I don't want to be marked by you."

"But it's too late for that, Wolfen-child," he purred as he reached one hand up to caress her delicate neck. "You are already marked by me, and they," he gestured to the argument taking place beyond the shield, "know it."

"Luca," she gasped, trembling at the emotions his touch evoked.

"Yes, I like the sound of my familiar name upon your lips, Dark," he whispered as he pulled her even closer to him. "And I would never hurt you. On that, you have my word."

First his warm breath bathed her sensitive skin. Her hands, of their own accord, reached up and grasped his shoulders for balance as heat rushed through her body.

Then his tongue lashed out to graze her pulse point; the wet contact sizzling her already overwhelmed nerve endings. Her grasp on him tightened as her talons began to again emerge, ripping through the white material of his tunic and piercing his skin as surely as his fangs would penetrate her flesh.

"Luca," she moaned as her trembling increased.

Then she felt his teeth lightly graze her, the needle-sharp fangs dragging at her skin. Heat exploded low in her abdomen as she suddenly found it hard to breathe. Her nipples hardened where they were pressed against his chest and her eyes slowly closed.

Then there was a brief, sharp pain.

"Luca!" she cried out then sighed as the hurt receded, brushed away by the gentle lap of his tongue.

Then she moaned as she felt his soft lips surround the small wound on her neck. Electricity began to course through her body and she found it difficult to stand. Her body began to arch against his and her hips thrust against the sudden hardness that she felt rising between the two of them.

"What are you doing to me?" she managed to gasp through the liquid heat in her veins.

"I am taking you within me," he purred as he pulled away from her neck, lapping at the sweet blood that flowed from her.

Never before had he felt a sharing like this. His senses were on overload and his loins were ready to explode. The taste of his Dark was like wild honey, sweet, untamed, and hard to resist. The effect it was having on his body was miraculous. He felt his control begin to slip, but he also knew that, as promised, he would never harm her.

He could feel the beast within was ready to break out and knew that her arousal at his hands helped to ease the torment a bit. But soon arousal would not be enough. She needed a full mating soon. And as her faithful mate, it was his responsibility to see to her every need.

It might not be so bad being her mate, after all.

With a tinkling of his silver bangles, he lifted his wrist to her mouth and nudged open her lips.

"Bite," he urged her as he continued to lap at her neck.

Almost as if under a spell, she parted her lips and felt her fangs pierce her gums as they emerged. Her blood mixed freely with his as her teeth clamped down on his wrist, neatly severing his skin and loosing the dark flow of his blood.

"Mmm," he moaned as he felt her teeth penetrate—an almost sexual feeling.

Reluctantly pulling his wrist away, he captured a finger full of his blood from the already sealing wound, and stopped the sensual licking at her neck. With an almost palpable reluctance, he used his blood to seal the two tiny wounds at her neck before he bent again and dropped small kisses along her jaw line.

"No," she moaned, pulling him back closer to her, wanting to feel more of the heat he set loose in her body. She had tasted true passion and was now hungry for more. "Luca?"

"Later, Dark," he whispered as he took her in his arms and held her tenderly. They had just shared an experience that he had never felt before in all of the sharings he had experienced over the years. It was almost as if she were made just for him, attuned to his tastes and wishes. It almost humbled him—almost.

Blinking herself back to awareness, Dark pulled away slightly and looked up at Lucavarious. "Are we mated now?" she asked, her voice raspy with unfulfilled desire.

"All that's left is to do the deed," he assured her, waggling his eyebrows at her.

Blushing brightly, Dark looked at her hands and gasped as she saw his blood staining the former pristine white of his tunic.

"What did I do?" she began, but then the clamor taking place beyond the purple shield caught her attention.

"What the hell is going on?" she nearly bellowed as she saw her aunt lift a chair and toss it into the group of Vampesi.

The chair splintered on contact with a shield, but now the transforming glow was beginning to form around Puaua and their escorts.

"Stop!" Dark cried out, rushing over to the force shield that Lucavarious had put up earlier. "Don't throw that. Stop...*Do you mind?*" she asked turning to glare at Luca while pointing to the shield.

"By all means, Wolfen-child."

In the instant the shield was removed, a vase flew past her head, almost knocking her senseless.

"Stop it!" Dark bellowed as she began to wade into the middle of the fray. "Puaua, Aunt Zinia. Stop it!"

"Are you going to help her?" the Sage asked Lucavarious as he rolled up the crumpled parchment. It disappeared within the folds of his voluminous robes.

"Eventually," he answered as he crossed his legs and began to levitate a few feet above the floor. "This will work off a bit of her...tension, and that will make my job that much easier later."

"Oh, the wisdom of youth," the Sage chuckled as he stepped back and blended in with the shadows. "You will learn, my boy."

"Boy?" argued Luca as he turned to the shadows. "I am over four hundred years old."

"Boy," came the raspy voice, then all traces of the Sage were gone.

Grumbling under his breath, Luca again turned to see his mate deliver a quick kick to one of the Wolfen guards before throwing a punch at an unsuspecting Vampesi. This was beginning to be quite enjoyable.

"Lucavarious, *do something!*" Dark yelled as she turned and noticed him levitating—doing nothing to prevent the spread of violence—with an amused look on his face.

"Okay, Wolfen-child. For you on our mating night." He blew her a kiss before he lowered his feet to the floor.

"Hear me!" he bellowed, his voice now echoing the power within him. "*Hear me now.*"

So loud was his voice that the walls began to shake and everyone paused in their delivery of flying fists and flailing feet, and turned in amazement to the lone figure in white.

Almost instantly, the Vampesi snapped to attention, their eyes on their ruler, while the Wolfen turned wary eyes to the man who commanded such a powerful voice. "It is done. We are all now one people under my rulership."

"Excuse me?" Dark cried out, her eyes flashing her anger.

"*Our* rulership," he amended, nodding to Dark. "So let us now behave as family. You may beat the hell out of each other, but please, no bloodshed, bloodletting, or tearing out of throats. Have fun, but don't tear up my castle. At sunrise, I expect you all to be gone. Oh, and don't disturb me tonight. I have progeny to create."

With that, he levitated Dark with one hand, opened the door with the other and calmly exited through a sea of faces that ran the gamut from shock to disgust.

As he and his floating mate cleared the door, it slammed with a bang and almost instantly the fighting began anew.

"That was help?" Dark asked as her feet touched the ground.

The feeling of being levitated by her mate was different. At first she'd had to fight her desire to scream and fight until he released her, but then she realized that she felt as if she was being cradled by him. His power, she realized was an extension of his being.

"It got us out of there, did it not?" he asked as he grabbed her hand and pulled her towards his personal rooms.

"But we are their rulers. We should make them listen."

"Allow me to impart a bit of truth to you, Wolfen-child. Rulers rule when people allow themselves to be ruled. They want to fight and to blow off steam? I say let them. It's the best way to know someone, you know?" he said.

"And the humans? Won't they be hurt?"

"Apparently you missed the mass exodus," he chuckled. "Before the first chair flew, the humans left the battle to the idiots in there." He pointed back down the corridor. "The humans are smart, as you will learn. They are the true masters of survival."

By this time they had reached the door to Luca's rooms, and for a moment, they both stood there, as if the whole contract and mating ceremony were finally hitting home.

"Ready to become a woman, Wolfen-child?" he asked as he almost eagerly gripped the doorknobs and opened the door.

"As I ever will be," she replied.

The fighting had taken the edge off of her tumultuous emotions, but now the beast was again longing to be set free. Its attack now took the form of fierce heat coursing through her veins—a heat that was only magnified when she was in Luca's presence.

Swinging the door wide and ushering her in, Lucavarious took great delight in slamming the door shut and placing a force shield around it. There would be no poorly timed interruptions.

Tonight he would make Dark his mate in truth and help her through her first transformation.

Dark looked around Luca's rooms. There had been some changes since this afternoon's fiasco. The white rugs were gone, replaced by a few handsome red and black carpets, and the hot smell of Wolfen anger had been replaced by the sweet smell of fresh flowers and masculine musk.

Then something caught her attention, glinting against the pure whiteness of his pristine bed.

"Uh, Lucavarious?" she began as she watched him discard his ruined tunic and practically leap onto the bed.

"Yes, Dark."

"There are chains on the bed."

"I know, Wolfen-child."

"Why are there chains on the bed?"

"Why, for you, of course, Wolfen-child."

"I get to chain…you?"

"Not exactly, Wolfen-child"

"I, uh, get the chains?"

The smile on his face turned…wicked.

"Oh, fuck," she gasped.

"Exactly, Wolfen-child."

Chapter Five

Dark stood there and watched the broad naked chest reclining upon the bed move slowly up and down with his breaths. It was a beautiful chest, a masculine chest; too bad it was attached to such a bastard.

"What do you mean by that smile, Lucavarious," she raged as she stared at the chains in utter fascination. "You are not clapping me in irons."

"Don't knock it until you've tried it, Wolfen-child," he answered, leering at her for all he was worth.

"And I suppose that you and B.B. play these games all of the time, but recognize this, bloodsucker." In her anger, she marched right over to the bed and actually climbed up onto it to get into his face. "I am not one of your play toys. Got it? I am your mate, and as such, I demand to be treated with respect."

Why did he have to smell so good? Dark looked at her demon, her mate, and almost sighed in exasperation. Her heightened senses jumped to red alert at his very presence, but she knew that she had to maintain some control over herself. As her parents before her, she trusted no one, one hundred percent, including herself, and she would be a fool to offer up complete control to him now.

"And what of me, Wolfen-child? Will you treat me with respect?" He raised one black eyebrow at the end of his statement, managing to look both curious and dangerous at the same time.

"Of course," she answered, taken aback. Their duties in life might be different, but she was going to treat him equally and fairly. That was the Wolfen way.

"Really, my Wolfen-Child?" he breathed as he rose to his hands and knees and slowly crawled across the few inches separating them.

Dark's breath caught at his grace and economy of movement. Her heart pounded faster and the gnawing ache in her center increased as she watched his hard muscles shift beneath his firm dark skin. His scent, alluring and heady, filled her nostrils, and her eyes unconsciously dilated as she watched his every erotic move.

"Really," she whispered faintly as he moved so close to her that his every breath bathed her face with the essence of him, until she could feel the heat from his body begin to change and alter the ache into something syrupy sweet that threatened her sanity. "Really."

"Then, Wolfen-child," he purred as his tongue flashed out to steal tempting tastes from her lips. "Get your golden hide to the top of the bed so that I can chain you properly."

"*What?*"

His smooth, sexy voice suddenly changed into the cold impersonal tones of his usual voice as he reared back to sit upon his heels, silver jewelry tinkling and making a mockery of her returning anger.

"You heard me, Wolfen-Child. If you respect me, then protect me from being clawed to death by those uncontrollable claws of yours. I kind of like my hide intact, which it would not be if I let you run wild in here."

"Lucavarious, you, you, *man*." she cried. "How dare you claim that I have no control?"

Without a word, he pointed to the rapidly healing scars on his shoulders, the marks she made with her first brush with real desire.

"Need I say more?" he asked.

This was too much. This couldn't be happening. Where was the mating night that she had always dreamed of? Where were the romance and the loving mate who would gently initiate her into the ways of love-play, who would help ease her first transformation into her secondary body?

Non-existent. Her dreams were non-existent. Her parents were dead, her mate was a total lunatic, and the people she was about to help rule were a bunch of undisciplined savages.

"I want to start over," she said in a calm voice, and her confused emotions fed the beast within.

"Reaching our limit?" Luca asked tiredly as he moved to envelop her now stiff body within his embrace. It was hard being a mate, accepting responsibility for another. B.B.s were a lot easier. Just sip and go. No fuss, no muss, no unnecessary emotions.

"Luca, this is not what I wanted," she whispered as she instinctively leaned in closer to her mate. "I wanted so many things, had so many dreams. There was going to be a fireplace to snuggle in front of, a drink of pure water to share from the same goblet, joyous tidings from my newly combined family, my mother to tell me what to expect. I'm…"

Lost, she whispered to herself.

Luca rubbed her back encouragingly as her words filled the silence of the room. For once in his long life, Lucavarious, absolute monarch of the Vampesi, was speechless. What could he say to her that would be a comfort? What words could he offer to replace the dream man she had envisioned, or the joyous ceremony that made a farce of the sanctioned brawl still taking place in the upper chambers? What words could replace the kind, loving advice of a mother?

He buried his head in her short soft hair and tried to comfort her the best way he could. He felt a stirring in the vicinity of his chest, and the new emotions left him almost as helpless as she. He had to figure out what to do or say before they both ended up two gelatinous masses of unchecked emotions on his pristine white bedclothes.

"Wolfen-child…Dark," he murmured as he pulled back a bit from her, "I don't know what to say in this instance, but I know what to do. Can you trust me a little?"

"I have no choice. By my actions, I am pledged to you, Luca. That means I have to trust you a little."

"Then let me explain a few truths to you, Wolfen-child. I am no mother, but I do know a little about what is going to happen to you when we mate."

Lifting her glazed and confused eyes to him, she asked, "What?"

"You will experience great joy and satisfaction."

"Of all the insufferable, arrogant, stupid claims," Dark roared, all signs of defeat washed away in her rush of anger. "Great joy, my Aunt Zinia."

"That's the spirit," Luca crowed, more than happy to deal with her anger rather than her deeper emotions. "If all goes well, we might invite her in with us next time. Always wanted to try a threesome."

Dark's roar of anger could be heard throughout the castle. Laughing with glee, Luca turned and slammed her to the bed. With deceptively quick hands, he raised her arms above her head and within seconds, she was manacled to his headboard.

"Lucavarious," she growled as she struggled and pulled against the metal chains holding her fast.

"Now is that any way to call to your future lover and mate, Wolfen-child?"

"When I get my hands on you… " she raged as she reared up against the bindings.

Within her, the beast was called forth and eagerly attempted to spring free.

Her hair bristled as her low rumbling growl filled the room. Her eyes, already their large pupils dilated, widened even further until the dark brown was awash in a sea of black. Sharp talons again sprang free and helplessly scored the metal, the sound increasing the tension in the room.

"I do so love it when you go all wild on me," Luca purred, strangely excited by the wildness that dwelled within her. His breathing noticeably increased as he watched her young firm breasts heave and push against the thin white material of her dress, a dress that was now in the way of his enjoyment.

Dark grew still and watchful as Luca reached out towards her. Her hunger for this man was rising rapidly again, as it had during their one kiss, and she discovered that she liked this impassioned state. While her mind was drugged with need, she needn't think about the future; she was only concerned with the here and now.

She remained utterly still as his hands reached out and grabbed the front of her bodice.

"This has to go," he said in a low, aroused voice as his hands slowly tightened on the material, his warm skin brushing against her cleavage as he fisted his hands.

The sound of the rending cloth sent fire skittering along her nerves, and her whole body quivered, but she still maintained her silence, her large dark eyes watching his every move.

As the material parted, Luca caught his breath as he took in the aroused beauty of her. Her full high breasts were topped with deep, berry-colored nipples, nipples that stood erect and begged for the touch of his hands and mouth. Her dark, golden skin was firm and fresh, the muscles of her stomach creating a concave plane that awaited his heated caresses. As the material parted further, her slim hips and delicately muscled thighs were exposed. When the material finally gave way and dropped to either side of her, Luca himself was panting, fighting to maintain his own slipping control.

"You are strong, Wolfen-child," he managed to say through his tight throat. Sweat began to bead up on his brow and he noticed an odd tremor in his hands. Hell, the madly tinkling bangles around his wrists were a dead giveaway of his excited state.

She was glorious perfection—condensed power and strength held within a lithe, willowy body. The torn material, falling to either side of her, only emphasized the dark wonder of her, contrasting against the thin bush of hair that shielded her feminine secrets from his prying eyes.

"Your lust is showing, Lucavarious," Dark growled as she eyed the rapidly rising front placket of his pants, then deliberately licked her full bottom lip as her eyes rose to his.

"Already you are learning about the power of a woman, Wolfen-child," he answered. Only a fool would doubt that her agile hunter's mind had missed all of the heated signals she had thrown in his direction, and Luca was no fool.

I do indeed have power over him, Dark thought as she watched his whole body tighten in reaction to her simple gesture. *But it is a power that can consume me too. With this, I must be careful.*

"Am I now a woman in your eyes, Luca?" she asked as she lifted her head slightly to take in more of his delicious scents. Combined with the hot scent of man and Luca's own personal musk was mixed the earthy smells of passion and desire yet to be fulfilled. It was a smell that she was finding quite to her liking.

"You are a mere child," he huskily responded as he lifted his hands and rested them in the center of her chest.

She jumped as the cool metal of his rings brushed against her skin, but they quickly heated as suddenly the room filled with a humid, almost wet, heat.

"A child you would turn into a woman?" she asked as some unknown demon inside her urged her to part her legs a bit, just to see what he was going to do.

His reaction was more than she could hope for.

Lucavarious, the absolute ruler of the Vampesi, the scourge of the Wolfen, the cold calm calculated brash man, closed his eyes and moaned.

"You will regret this taunting of me, Dark," he growled in a low dangerous tone as his eyes opened and pinned her with their silver-shot stare.

Before she could pull away from this dangerous game as her internal beast activated her *fight or flight* instincts, Luca dropped his dark head and lapped at the soft skin between her breasts.

"Oh," she cried out as his rough wet tongue awakened more nerves, created more fire within her. She tried to bring her hands down to pull at his head, but then realized that the chains did not give enough play for her to lower her hands. She was trapped under his tender, frustrating ministrations.

But now that the taste of her was on his tongue, Luca couldn't stop. He felt his fangs begin to emerge, a pleasure-pain that added to his arousal as he dragged his hungry mouth over her skin. Her taste was ambrosia and he craved it more than the searing kiss of silver that both pained him and sent something wild soaring through his blood.

One hand reached up to cup her swelling breast and held it still for a new assault. His tongue then lashed out to taste her fragrant skin, noting the different textures between her straining nipple and the soft flesh that surrounded it. His pinkie lightly caressed her plumpness with its sharp nail, before his equally sharp first fangs gently skimmed the surface of her nipple.

"Luca," Dark said, a little frightened of this new sensation, before his mouth covered the whole of her swollen flesh.

Then all she could do was arch up into his touch as the hot wet cave of his mouth drew out desires that she had never before hoped to experience. Again she pulled at her restraints, desperate to capture and hold his wonderfully giving mouth to her, but again she was denied her wish. The restraints around her wrists tightened as the leash on her inner beast loosened and gave with each passing second.

Luca purred as he savored the taste of her, the feel of her filling his mouth. Gently he nipped at her with his fangs, a reaction that was instinctive to him, but not hard enough to break her skin. Just hard enough to make her writhe and release more of her aroused scent. His hand dropped the delicious fullness of her trapped breast to grip her free one; his fingers trapping then gently rolling that lonely nipple, giving it exquisite care.

Dark's slender body first pulled away from such awesome sensations, but the caress of the cool material at her back added another wonderful torture to her already strained senses. Again she arched into him and surprising to her, a little howl escaped her lips as she again arched into his touch.

A furnace was raging inside of her and her hips twitched uncontrollably on the bed as he feasted on her ripe flesh. A wave of liquid heat flooded her lower regions, and it startled her.

"Luca," she whimpered. "Luca, my body..."

"Is perfection," he growled as he released her nipple and blew cold air across it.

She shuddered and shifted her legs in a futile attempt to close them, to stop this heat that was tearing at her, but Luca had other plans.

"Don't close yourself to me," he growled as he felt her efforts. "Never close yourself to me, Dark."

His black eyes, now liberally shot with silver heat, bored into hers. His lips were pulled back in a feral grimace, exposing his long sharp fangs, before he looked down at the flesh his hands were gripping possessively.

"But Luca..." she started, but her own panting breaths stole her voice. He looked wild and untamed, and it called to something deep within her. She liked him this way. The beast within answered and the chains slipped a little more.

"Never hide yourself from me," he said in a low dangerous voice as he reared back on his heels and settled himself between her legs.

"I do what I want," Dark growled, as she again became the hunter, stalking her prey.

Deliberately, she raised one leg, still shielding her center, but caressing him through his thin white pants with the slow glide of her calf.

"You are asking for trouble," he again warned as he felt his second set of fangs explode through his gums, filling his mouth with the wild taste of his own blood.

"And here I am, a threat to the big bad Vampesi, all chained up as I am. Poor baby," she taunted. She knew not why she spoke these things, but it seemed that her body knew just what to do and say to push his buttons. She relaxed and waited to see what would happen.

His answer was a silent roar that made the tendons and sinew of his neck stand out in stark relief. His eyes narrowed into tiny silver slits and a slow grin spread across his face.

"Play time's over, little girl," he growled as he bent low to hover over her.

"Play time," she purred as she lifted one foot and pressed it to the bulging heat of his groin, "is over."

"Damn it," he roared before he gripped her legs and forced them to part, rather widely.

"Luca," she began, a bit of fear coming into her voice. If she had driven him to blood lust, she would not be able to stop him, and that place he was examining now was very…sensitive.

"I'm watching you drip with your want, Wolfen-child, and I like the look of it, the smell of it," he inhaled deeply a wicked light glowing in his eyes, "the taste of it."

Before she could think to protest, he lowered his head between her legs and his broad tongue gave one full lap at her richness.

"Hell," he muttered before he fell into her, devouring her, delighting in the liquid expression of her pleasure.

Never had he felt the need to totally bury himself in someone before. Never had his blood been so hot, his senses so tuned, his need so great. He lapped at her. He teased her feminine opening with his tongue, nuzzled her pleasure pearl with his nose, and all the while, drank in her essence.

Dark was a mass of quivering nerves. Her thighs began to tremble, her head to spin, her chest to heave at this new pleasure he introduced to her body. She pressed her legs close to his head, hoping to hold him close to her, delighting in the feel of his soft hair brushing against her sensitive thighs.

He approved of her actions, because a low grumbling started deep in his chest, the vibrations making her body sing as he moved to penetrate her opening with his tongue.

She made a futile effort again to pull herself free from the restraints. She wanted to feel him, to hold him closer to her. She sobbed in frustration as her attempts proved futile. The chains held her fast, a prisoner of his desires.

"You are honey," he moaned against her as he moved to capture her tightly drawn clitoris between his lips. "You are divine."

His words sent her senses reeling and pushed her tension to another level.

Her fangs exploded in her mouth as her panting increased. He was forcing her past some point of danger, to some explosion that frightened as well as attracted her. The beast lying dormant in her cried its triumph as the blast approached and her muscles tightened almost painfully. Then his lips clamped around her clitoris and he sucked.

"*Luuuuuu.*"

Her cry ended in a wail as the tension snapped, flinging her off a precipice of unimagined delight. Her inner muscles clenched and convulsed as he played her with gentle suction and a rough tongue.

Sweat exploded from her body and her fangs sank into her full lower lip. Waves of heat flushed her, caressed her with their burning touch as her lungs screamed for air. Never had she expected such joy, such delight. Luca hadn't boasted or lied. He gave her great pleasure.

She closed her eyes and sighed, still feeling curiously bereft, but sure the understanding would come. The beast inside her still strained at its bonds, but something was holding it back, agitated that release was so close at hand.

"We're not done." His low voice snapped her out of her revelry.

"Not..." she began weakly, her body still quivering, muscles still knotting and trembling.

"I have to release you, Dark. I have to set you free."

"The cuffs?" she began eagerly, but he shook his head.

"I have to release your spirit, Dark. Can't you feel it fighting for freedom?"

Her eyes widened in shock. How could she have forgotten the most important part of this ritual, the release of her true spirit? It made her forget Luca with his erotic kisses and dangerous tongue.

"How do you know?" she asked, unconsciously licking at her lips and the fangs that hung low yet familiar within her mouth.

"I know quite a lot, Dark," he answered, thankful that her father had pulled him aside and told him of this phenomenon as they went over the treaty.

"How..."

But again he cut her off. "Like this, Wolfen-child."

Quickly and with pent-up frustration, Luca ripped at the pants confining him and tore them from his body. All too soon, she was faced with what she ultimately feared and desired.

His naked arousal was full and proud, brushing against his navel with its ruby head. Thick veins creased the golden skin of his erect member and a thin mat of curly black hair accented its strength at its thick base. Luca was built in proportion to his strong hard body and showed no shame at being full and hard in front of her.

"Where do you think you're putting that?" Dark cried out. Her body may crave him, but common sense was quickly cooling her ardor. The man was just *too damn big*. He would never fit. He'd kill her with the attempt.

"Right here," he answered, before a long finger pierced the opening to her innermost body and pushed in deep.

Again her hips arched towards him, the animal in her welcoming this new possession. Against her better judgment, her body gave him a warm wet welcome. She moaned as he added a second finger.

"You will fit me because I say you will," he growled before he bent and, disregarding her fangs, thrust his tongue deep inside her mouth, possessing her as did his fingers.

Dark closed her eyes and groaned with contentment as the thick invasion of his tongue again ignited her senses. He tasted of her — of raw sex and musk, and a tiny essence of…blood?

But her body gave no time for contemplation as it instantly reacted to him.

Her nipples hardened again, begging for the brush of his lightly furred chest; her legs sought to close, to trap his teasing fingers where she needed the stimulation most; her hands sought to hold him, but the chains held fast.

She could only moan her pleasure and acceptance and arch her body against him to show that she was ready for more.

"You are so hot and wet here, Dark," he murmured as he found a new erogenous spot on her body as he slowly traced her fangs with his tongue. His wiggled his fingers, searching for her internal pleasure button and grinned as she jumped when he touched it. "So welcoming and feminine. I will enjoy plundering your depths."

It was too much. Dark pulled her head to the side, desperate to avoid his over-stimulating caresses and clamped her teeth down on her lower lip.

"Stop it," he seduced with his voice. "Don't bite your lips so. Bite me."

So saying he tilted his head and presented his shoulder for her teething enjoyment.

Dark needed no second offer. She whipped her head around and using the strength of her frustration, clamped her fangs into his skin.

He groaned loudly as he felt her fangs pierce deeply, a quick burning stab, before it mellowed into a sizzling heat. He felt his skin instantly began to heal and urged her to bite again.

Biting was something highly erotic and desired by the Vampesi. Only true mates allowed this personal touch, and with Dark, Luca found that he craved its biting heat and the flood of desire it produced in his hot blood.

And Dark was in the mood to bite. The beast inside reveled in such actions and she felt her wildness increase as her fangs penetrated the golden skin of her mate. His taste flooded her as his body worked magic below.

"Enough," Luca finally cried as he spread her legs further and settled his hips in the feminine cradle her splayed thighs made.

"Luca, I'm afraid," Dark admitted as she felt him take the dominant position.

She was afraid of this act, of the intensity between the two, of loosing her inner beast and embracing the wildness within. Her fear forced the confession out of her before she could force it back.

"Not afraid, anxious," his husky voice assured. "Here, bite me here, Dark, when the anxiety overwhelms you."

He tilted his head aside and exposed his vulnerable neck. His free hand came up to cup the back of her head, urging her closer as his other hand, still embedded within her, teased at her place of pleasure, his thumb coming up to press against her swollen, pebble-hard woman's seed.

Dark gasped as she arched her head back, her senses lost in the magic of his touch. The air surrounding her became almost too heavy to breathe and an incredible heat filled her.

"Please," she whimpered as she felt his fingers swiftly withdraw and something thick and hard replace them.

"Luca," she said again, her...anxiety taking over. Then she clamped her teeth into his neck. He said she should do it, and she damn well did.

"Dark," he cried out as he slammed his full length into her.

They both moaned as the deep, sharp, shafts of pain filled their bodies, but they groaned as the burning pain mellowed into a fierce heat.

"Oh, God, Dark," Luca moaned as he felt himself enveloped in her tight wet heat. Nothing had ever felt like this. Nothing would ever feel the same afterwards.

Dark released her biting grip on Luca's neck as the pain eased. Filling her now was a sense of elation; the burning and stretching no longer mattered.

Uncontrollably, she licked at his neck, her legs rising to trap his slim hips while her body swallowed his hardness. Something in her gave way.

Then he began to move.

Slowly, he pumped, tilting his hips as his hands came up to grip handfuls of her hair, cupping and caressing her head, each skillful movement punctuated by the tinkling of his bangles. Slowly he pulled out until only his thick head rested within her, until she whimpered her fear that he would leave her, then he eased his way back in.

"Luca," she breathed into his ear as a sense of freedom overcame her and something inside her snapped.

"Yes, Dark, yes," he purred as he increased the speed of his thrusts, moaning as he felt the full pulling caress of her innermost walls tugging at him, quivering around him.

"Luca," she called again, her voice becoming rough and raspy.

Her muscles again tightened and a deep ache began in her lower abdomen. She pushed herself towards him, thrusting her hips high to accept him, moaning her joy.

Luca felt as though a thousand heated fingers toyed with him, demanded that he give more. He lifted his head and gazed into her wide dark eyes — her wild eyes — and could not help but lower his head and take her mouth in another drenching kiss.

Their fangs clashed as Dark eagerly tilted her head to taste more of him. The small vibration caused a slight tremor in his body, straining his control. He tore his mouth free, knowing that he would not last long, and adjusted the glide of his flesh against hers so that he brushed against her erect pleasure point with each thrust.

She went wild in his arms.

Dark tossed her head from side to side as pressure began to build within her again. Her skin burned and throbbed in time to his masterful thrusts. All thinking ceased as instinct took over. Her control slipped as the tension mounted and she felt herself reaching, striving for this new release.

"Luca," she panted. "Luca, Luca, Luca, *Luuuuuuu….*" It ended in an ear splitting howl as her control snapped her body screamed its release, and the beast within reveled at its birth.

"Damn it, Dark," Luca cried out as he felt his body slam into climax. The top of his head fairly exploded as he tossed back his head and gave himself over to the pleasure in a series of short hard strokes. With his eyes clenched tightly, his brain mush, and her scream of release exploding in his ears, he didn't feel or hear her metal binding begin to snap.

His first clue to the sudden shift in power was the feel of warm soft fur against his chest.

His eyes snapped open just in time to see Dark's wrists thicken and pull at the restraints. They snapped like old dry twigs.

Hell, he thought as in a flash of movement, he was neatly flipped from her body to land on his back with a joyous tinkling of his bracelets. Before he could move, a hot massive weight rested against his chest and a warm muzzle, filled with razor sharp throat-ripping teeth, clamped around his neck.

He looked up to see Dark, his mate, in her secondary form. Her dark eyes glinted down at him with something akin to humor as a low, rumbling growl emerged from her throat. Her fur was pure black, black as night, black as his inner secrets, with no hint of brightness to lighten the effect.

As he watched her eyes, her hands shifted into powerful paws, razor sharp talons catching his hands and positioning them above his head. Her slim body faded in a slow hypnotic growth of hair, until nothing was left of Dark, his mate, and she was all Dark, the Wolfen Queen, the woman who now possessed a piece of his soul.

"*Hello, Luca.*" Her powerfully seductive voice was projected from her mind.

He gulped.

She grinned wider.

"You wouldn't eat a man who gave you two orgasms, would you?"

Chapter Six

The brush of fur against his naked chest was distracting. The humidity in the room, which at one time was staggering, now evaporated as the room returned to a normal temperature. Only the deep, rumbling growl and the sound of two beings slowly breathing broke the silence

Dark felt a glorious rush of power flow through her body. She could smell things from outside. She could hear the blood as it coursed through Luca's veins. She could taste his arousal through the thin skin of his neck. She was one with nature. Well, almost. There still was the matter of her precocious mate.

"Do you want me to let you go, Luca?" she asked, or rather *projected* to him. She had to but only think of something to say and it was broadcasted for all to hear. Part of their innate honesty that was part of the core of their society was that Wolfen could not lie.

"No," he answered in that calm voice of his. "I want you to continue sitting on me as if I were some great big overstuffed pillow for your amusement."

Clearly, he was not pleased with this sudden change of command.

"I could do that," her voice purred as she clamped her teeth a bit harder on his neck. *"Or I could rip your head from your body and play with it."*

"Fetch, no doubt," he drawled as he continued to stare at her. Both sets of his fangs still filled his mouth and he still had the urge to bite something, but he was more than shocked to find that his awareness of her was stirring to life again. Not in a sexual way, mind you, but he suddenly craved information about her, her thoughts, her personality, the way to get her off of his chest before she got herself hurt.

"Want to find out?" she snapped, annoyed that he refused to acknowledge her position of power.

"By all means, Wolfen-child. Show me, do. But while you're at it, remember the respect you promised."

Her snort was succinct and to the point.

"Don't tempt me, Lucavarious," she growled.

"Oh, but I did, Wolfen-child. I tempted and teased your luscious body until you were howling beneath me. My ears are still ringing."

"And don't call me Wolfen-child." she demanded, the feral animal in her easing her further away from her humanity.

"Then what shall I call you, Dark? The woman who moments after experiencing explosive bliss in my arms decided it would be more fun to play 'bite the Vampesi'?"

"Mistress?" she asked, amusement filling her tones.

"Hardly," he himself snorted, suddenly finding the humor in this situation. So a fledgling now trapped him, the four hundred-year-old. Didn't see that one coming.

"Say my name, Luca," she suddenly whispered, the playful part of her nature coming to full force. *"Say it and I'll let you go."*

"I'm not into power games, Wolfen-child," he enunciated. "I like my sex straight-forward, my humans iron-rich, and my mate beneath me."

"Why do you have two sets of fangs?"

That question caught him off guard.

He flexed his hands against her sudden strength and found that he would likely do serious injury to them both if he struggled, and he didn't want to harm her. Her hold on his throat held him immobile and her hind legs were close to the body part that he was most in love with. He would lie still, for now.

"That is for me to know, Wolfen-child," he taunted.

"Stop calling me that," she snarled, her eyes narrowing in sudden anger. She found it a bit difficult to control these mood

swings. The Wolfen in her wanted to react, but the human tempered those actions. It was draining and more than a little difficult to control.

"Well. I can't call you a woman, child. You are snapping at the hand that feeds you, my dear. Very not smart."

"You, feed me, Luca? You wouldn't be two bites," she laughed, his comments restoring her good humor. She loved a good debate.

"I see your point," he sighed as he lifted his head a bit and stared at the long black body that covered his.

"Besides, I like being on top." she crowed, her hot breath wafting across his neck.

"You have a taste for power, Wolfen-ch...Dark?"

"That I do, Luca." Her eyes twinkled as she looked down on him. *And I am gaining power over you*, she thought to herself with glee.

"So are you going to answer my question?" he asked, still gently testing her strength against his own with small flexes of his muscles.

"I don't know, mate," her amused voice filled the room. *"I kind of like having power over you. It's so much fun, I might take up being a bastard too."*

"Hmm," he purred, a moment before his muscles jerked and his strong legs clamped around her lower hips.

In a surprise move, he tensed his body and, taking advantage as her teeth loosened in surprise at his throat, used his lower body to neatly flip her over.

Her concentration broke at his move and suddenly she found herself flat on her back, looking up at her mate with both paws stretched unnaturally above her and her lower body trapped in a hard vise.

Before she could retaliate, she found her muzzle held closed as he jammed his head under her jaw. She was again trapped beneath him, but not at his mercy.

She had not forgotten the power of her new-found femininity. Already the beast within delighted at his quick masterful responses, but the woman decided a little revenge was in order.

"Change. Change back into your corporeal form, Dark, or I will not be a happy man."

Even as he commanded this, her body was already shifting, blurring, changing. She did not know how she could call back the beast so rapidly, but now that it was free, it was content to take its secondary place within her. With contentment, it receded to allow her humanity to resurface.

Long soft black hair quickly retreated beneath the surface of her firm soft skin. Her bones shifted and shortened as they once again took on human shape. Her muzzle quickly retracted and reformed to once again display full red lips that still held the deadly set of fangs. Her body shortened and softened until once again her lush form was lying beneath Luca, naked and flushed with heat.

"Is this how you wanted me, Luca," she purred as she lifted her hips and brushed his semi-erect hardness.

"Dark," he sighed as he lifted his head and stared into her large, deep-brown eyes.

"All that fur turn you on?" she taunted as she lapped at his throat with her tongue.

"You're playing with fire, Wolfen-girl," he gasped as her contact with his neck so recently healed from her bites and still so sensitive, shot an arrow of heat straight to his loins.

He again inhaled deeply of her scent, taking in the animal wildness of her that seemed so natural and the smell of her excitement. Mingled with this was the scent of the few drops of blood she spilled as her hymen broke. Again Dark was driving him mad with her innate passions. Did she know how scrumptious she looked, feigning the helpless damsel under him, looking up at him with her big eyes, slowly licking her full lips?

Yes, she knew. And she delighted with this new power she held over him. Who would have thought that the great Lucavarious could be controlled by his libido?

"I'm not a girl, Luca," she pouted, delighting as his eyes began to sparkle silver. "I am a woman." She deliberately arched her back up to brush his chest with her hardening nipples.

"Stop that," he cried, a confused look crossing his face. Who was in command anyway?

"But it feels good, Luca," she purred, a wicked look coming to rest on her face. "I find that suddenly I love things that make me feel good. Will you make me feel good? Hmm, *Luca*?"

She deliberately enunciated his name so that her tongue wrapped around the syllables. She even managed to bat her lashes at him and keep a straight face.

Luca broke out in a hot sweat as he watched his mate turn from innocent to seductress before his very eyes. Was it getting hot in here? The temperature in the room soared as the humidity rapidly increased. Helpless, he lowered his head and lapped at her lower lip with his tongue, taking in her rich flavor.

"Will you, Luca?" she asked as she again wiggled her hips at his now full erection. "Make me feel good?"

"Dark?"

Her answer was for him to suddenly thrust deep inside her. She tossed back her head and hissed her pleasure as lightning shot through her body. She was again losing herself in sensation. But secretly inside, she crowed with glee.

She had found the key to equalizing their relationship a bit. The way to get to Lucavarious was not through games of strength or cunning, but through his libido. No one had ever, she assumed, dared to strike him through his strong sexuality, until now. And as the Wolfen on a whole were highly sexual creatures, it would be no hardship for her to twist the screws on his control to her advantage.

No trouble at all, she thought as he began to swivel his hips just so.

There were some advantages to being mated with Luca.

* * * * *

"She's trying to kill me," Luca sighed aloud as he settled himself into his bath.

"More, harder, faster, deeper," he groaned as the hot water settled over his abused flesh.

"Whatever happened to timid virgins?" he asked the ceiling as he looked heavenwards for answers. "I thought that virgins were supposed to be docile."

He shook his head at his own sorry state as he viewed his weakened body. Time to take inventory.

There were bruises that pained him on his bottom, caused by her lack of control with her claws, no doubt. The damn things always popped out when she got excited, and they usually popped out on him somewhere.

His chest was a bit sore, possibly from all of the biting that went on. Sure he healed quickly, but she needed to learn to give new skin a chance to heal before she tore into it again.

His bangles tinkled merrily as he ran his hands through his hair. Yup, it was still there. But he was given to wonder because of all the yanking and pulling that went on. Who knew that the Wolfen had uncontrollable urges to scalp the men that pleasured them? From now on, he was holding her hands down.

His back hurt. He now knew that he needed to stretch well and limber up before having coitus with Dark. She wanted him to move in all sort of weird positions while maintaining maximum thrust and control. This was worse than battle training.

And his penis. He looked down at the poor piece of flesh he had once treasured and sighed at the abuse he had deliberately put it through. Not that it was complaining mind you, but its needs seemed to concur with hers and their combined desires were killing his body. He was four hundred and twenty-seven years old. Much too old for bedroom acrobatics. He wished someone would remind his libido.

But she's in heat, his id screamed at him. And it feels good to help your mate. Very, *very* good.

His ego said nothing but sighed because it knew that he would be forced to prove his worthiness yet again,

His superego cowered in fear.

Ignoring the parts of his psyche and trying his best not to analyze his reactions to this situation, he settled back in his bath and moaned at the warm comfort it offered. He had finally managed to put her to sleep, but who knew how long that would last?

After she had dropped off the first time, he just knew that he was assured at least an hour of uninterrupted rest, but she had snapped to attention the moment he untangled himself from her body. And that was almost five hours ago.

As he relaxed, he felt the sun begin to ascend in the east. He had been awake for a total of two days now and knew that soon he would have to retreat and revitalize. But he would force himself to stay awake for as long as she needed him. No matter how he had to force his body to perform.

But damn, he loved being needed, especially with the type of help he had to give.

His id rested, assured that more pleasure was coming, and he smiled, secretly delighted that he, old man that he was, was able to keep up with his young nubile mate. But then superego forced a question to his conscious that couldn't be ignored.

How long do the Wolfen stay in heat anyway?

* * * * *

Dark purred with contentment as she snuggled deeper into the warm tangled blankets that still held her mate's scent. If she lifted her nose, she could catch his scent mingled with the heat of water and the clean smell of his soap. She had exhausted him, poor baby. Not that he would admit it.

Lucavarious was a font of knowledge and skill, but even he had to have a breaking point. Not that she wanted to break him, just test her power a bit. And boy, had she practiced.

It was amazing. She could fight him and he would just subdue her until her anger had passed or let her rage out her anger until she felt like a fool arguing with a brick wall. She could ignore him, but he knew just what to say to garner her attention and force her to acknowledge his existence. She could try to baffle him with knowledge and he would twist her words, creating elaborate mazes of logic that often left her in a surprised daze. But if she batted her lashes, licked her lips, and posed herself just so, all of his control fled and he was almost putty in her hands.

He had finally managed to quiet the ravenous beast within her and soothe her into a well-needed rest, but now she lay there and contemplated her new life. It wasn't going to be easy.

She felt some grief over the loss of her parents, but like all of her people, she accepted the inevitable and moved on. Her parents would be missed, but they would leave no gaping hole in her soul. They had lived long and well.

Her aunt and her cousin would present a bit of a problem, though. Even though Luca demanded that they quit the castle at daybreak, she knew that her aunt felt cheated. Zinia wanted to rule the Wolfen now that her brother and his mate were out of the picture, but Zinia was too much of a hothead. Her father even suspected her of siding with the rebels that were just starting to stir up trouble between the two powerful peoples that ruled this planet. That was one of the reasons they had insisted on this match between the Vampesi and the Wolfen.

"War will demolish us all, Dark," her father had told her once as she balked at the idea of being a Vampesi sacrifice. "And there is a connection between our two people. One can not exist without the other."

"What did you mean by that, Father," she sighed out loud. "How are we connected?"

Now she would never find out what great truths her parents had uncovered. When she had felt a searing pain in her chest on the day of their deaths, she had known that it was her parents calling out to her. In her bedclothes she had raced to their sides, but she arrived too late. Her mother already lay on the floor, burdened no longer by the troubles of this world while her father sat quietly on the floor by her head, gently stroking her long black hair.

"The contract," he told her in his deep mellow voice. "You must fulfill the contract, my daughter. You are my heir and the match between you and he must be carried out immediately."

She could see his body spasm in pain, but his eyes and his voice remained clear.

"Father," she cried, tears falling down her face as she took in this tender scene, the last thing she would remember of her parents. She knew that even if her father were to survive, he would never be the same for he would grieve unto death for her mother.

"Poison, Dark. I never thought to check for poison. You must take the contract, which our murderer will surely come here and search for, and you must flee to him. He will understand what has happened."

"I can't leave you, Father," she cried, dropping to his side, but his low snarling growl stopped her.

"Do you disobey me, Daughter?" he snapped. His eyes hinted at barely suppressed wildness as he stared at his daughter. He tightened his hold on his mate as he glared at her. Tears gathered in his eyes; tears for the suffering his mate had to endure before death came and stole her away; tears that he could not protect her from this great evil; tears for what his daughter now had to face alone.

Her whole body trembling under his rebuke, Dark dropped her head and a small whimper escaped her. "No, Father. I will not disobey you."

Almost immediately, his rumbling growl stopped and he lowered his head as if it were too heavy a burden to hold.

Dark cried silent tears as she watched her father, once so vital and strong, wither before her eyes. How could this poison so quickly devastate his large muscular body? How could her invincible father be defeated?

"Take the contract and go, Dark. The Wolfen are counting on you, daughter. Without this union, there will be no future, for either of our people."

He then gestured to the tiny bit of parchment that hung unobtrusively in a plain frame on the wall. That bit of paper had hung there for as long as anyone could remember. Was that the contract?

With trembling hands, she forced herself to her feet and made her way to the frame. Pulling it from the wall, she turned it over, expecting to see a hidden compartment or a clue where the contract was.

"Inside, Dark," her father urged, his voice sounding weaker by the second. She could feel his life force leaving the room, separating itself from her as the time of the end approached.

Carefully, she peeled the wood back from the frame and the parchment tumbled to the floor. What everyone thought was just old decoration or a faded bit of memorabilia, was actually the contract. How long had it hung there, ignored by the people who came and went out of the Alpha male's house constantly? How long ago was this begun?

"It is old, Dark," her father continued. "It was started by my forefather in hopes of bearing a daughter. Every leader has had the hope of bearing a daughter since. In four generations, you are the only female born to my line. The contract will be fulfilled through you. You must go to Lucavarious, Dark. Take the contract and go now."

"But Father," she cried ignoring the parchment as she again dropped to her father's side, "I can't leave you."

Again his low growl halted her words.

"The only thing that I now live for is you, daughter. You must fulfill the contract or my death is meaningless. You mother would have given her life in vain." He forced himself upright as he lectured his daughter. Tendons stood out in his neck and a pain-induced sheen covered his massive body. Already the glaze of death began to cover his liquid dark eyes and the color drained out of his deeply bronzed skin. "Go, Dark. Go now and leave me. Go and save our people as you were destined to do."

"Father," she acknowledged as she again dropped her head in respect. Her tears had begun to dry up. Her father was lost to her, as was her mother. The only thing she could now do was to keep that deathbed promise.

"I love you, Dark," he sighed as he again slumped over her mother, his mate, and awaited death. "Your mother was my life, but you are my heart."

"Father," she again cried, but this time when she crept to him on all fours, he accepted her approach. "I love you, Father."

"This eases my passing, Dark," he managed in his weak voice. "For I have loved you from the second of your conception."

Carefully, lips trembling in fear and anguish, she raised her hand and rested it on her father's head. He grumbled his acceptance of her touch and she crept closer to nuzzle her face into his neck, noticing that his skin was becoming cold and hard.

"Father?" she whispered as a sudden cramp caught her off guard. Ignoring her physical discomfort, she moved in closer to her father, trying to heat him with her own body.

"I love you, Dark," he said again as his hands tightened their grip on her mother and he weakly buried his chin into her short-cropped hair.

Then his chin slid away.

"Father?" Dark cried, looking up at his still face. "*Father?*"

71

He was gone.

Uncontrollably, her head snapped back and a loud howl of rage and anger exploded from her throat. Tears ran unchecked down her face and her whole body tensed as the loud keening wail filled the still night air.

Unbroken, the cry continued until there was no breath in her body, until her lungs felt ready to collapse, until the very heavens knew of her rage and grief. The animal inside reveled in the release of the pain, but the woman plotted revenge.

Abruptly, the cry was cut off as her suddenly heightened senses picked up the smell of the intruders.

"Get away," her mind screamed as she scrambled back from the husks that were once her parents, and groped on the floor for the parchment. Once it was in her possession, she fled through the front door and out into the night. That's when she felt them, smelled them, *knew* that they were watching.

Turning, she sprinted west, towards the place of the setting sun and the purple haze that was silhouetted against the night sky. Away from her small village and the people who dwelled there, she ran. Away from her pursuers, the murderers of her parents, the honorless bastards, she ran. Towards a dark demon of the night, she ran.

A tapping at the door caught her attention and pulled her from her dark remembrances. Cautiously, she lifted her head and tried to scent who was at the door, but she could smell nothing through Luca's force barrier. Apparently, he wanted no one seeing, hearing, or smelling what they were doing.

"Luca," she called, but received no answer. Her mate was either ignoring her or had fallen asleep.

But just the thought of him awakened the sleeping beast within her, and almost instantly she was anticipating another round of bed-play. The man had skills and had trained her body well. If he couldn't keep up with the demand, it was his own fault.

Just before she leaped from the bed and headed for the bathroom anticipating water sports, that light tapping at the door started again.

"Oh bother," she snarled as she turned from thoughts of a more pleasant pursuit and started for the door.

She winced at each step, the night's sexual excesses making themselves known, which only added to her annoyance.

Muttering under her breath, she limped to the door and shouted through the thick wood, "Who is it and what do you want?"

She was not in a good mood. Sexual frustration and physical discomfort, well, they were both new to her. The animal inside her snarled and Dark felt the need to do the same.

"It's me, B.B., Master. Do you have a need of me?"

B.B.? How dare that…that…*human* come sniffing around her mate?

Her anger lent her strength as she gripped the handle and wrenched the door open.

Luca's force shield snapped and an angry cry was heard from the bathroom as the door bounced on its hinges.

Naked, Dark stood at the entrance to the room, her anger at an all-time high as all her new emotions coalesced into rage. A rage focused on the small red-haired woman who now stood cowering at the door.

"What is it?" Luca shouted as he ran in from the bathroom, naked save for his silver adornments and a tiny white towel. "Who is at the door?"

With a wicked smile, Dark allowed her fangs to emerge and a low growl filled the room.

"Why, Luca," she answered as she leaned towards the pale-faced woman. "It's dinner."

B.B.'s screams filled the castle.

Chapter Seven

"We don't eat members of this household."

"Oh, so that's what we're calling it now?"

Luca sighed as he raised his eyes skyward and prayed for an answer from the great unknown.

Dark sat at the desk in his study and glared at the pacing figure of her mate. Even though he looked kind of cute with that befuddled expression on his face, she refused to let her anger lessen.

Today he was dressed in his customary pristine white and his bangles tinkled and sang as he ran an exasperated hand over his face. How many pairs of drawstring pants did that man own? Was he color blind? His wardrobe needed severe help. Had the man ever heard of fashion? Maybe B.B. liked him in easy-access clothing?

That thought had her fuming again.

"We are calling it nothing, because that is what is going on. Damn, I don't have to justify myself to you, but I have never done anything improper to that woman."

Dark crossed her arms over her chest and glared at him.

"I mean it, Dark. I have no reason to defend myself for any of my actions, but you, Wolfen, have a lot to answer for. Do you know that woman is so scared that I had to call upon other valuable servants to look after her? She has taken to her bed with shakes and, uh, an irritable bowel." His face twisted with disgust as he revealed that last bit to her.

"Good." Dark's answer was direct and to the point. "She had no business creeping to the door and offering her dubious services to you."

"That's her job, Dark." Luca sighed, and again for the hundredth time wondered why he hadn't replaced B.B. when she'd first started acting funny. But he decided that maybe it was hormones that were causing her problems. Now he figured that it was sheer stupidity. Rather sad, really.

"So find her a new job, Lucavarious. I refuse to be a woman on the side to my mate. I told you once before that the Wolfen mate for life, and for better or worse, you are it." She sniffed as she again examined him from his bare feet to the top of his curly black hair. "And don't you ever wear shoes?"

Luca sighed and tiredly sank into a nearby chair. This was a bit too much to take. First he was mated to a veritable sex machine, then she scared the hell out of his food source. Didn't she know that blood flooded with adrenaline and fear tasted awful? Now she was complaining about his wardrobe. Would the tortures never end?

"When it is necessary, Dark, I will wear footwear. But it makes my toe rings uncomfortable. Besides, I like the feel of the marble floor beneath my feet."

"But it's cold," Dark argued as she looked down at the narrow slippers that he supplied along with another one of his joke dresses. It had to be a joke. No woman would want to be caught dead in this creation of white lace and ribbons. It was an affront to her very nature to look so, so, *fragile*. This ankle length number was just as bad as her mating gown.

"It is not, Dark," he contradicted. "Maybe you were too preoccupied by our beautiful and amazingly serene ceremony, but the floors of this castle are heated. It's built over natural hot springs so I can walk around in the buff if need be and I'd be comfortable."

"Hmm," Dark mused. "Very wise, Vampesi. Anything else I should know?"

"That humans live in this castle and are not generally considered dinner," he quipped as he raised eyebrow.

"But you drink their blood, Luca. Doesn't that put them at the top of the menu?"

"No, Dark. As a rule, the Vampesi don't drink much human blood. It's against the rules."

"Whose rules, Luca?" she asked, curious to know more about her mate.

"Mine," he stated firmly in a voice that refuted any contradiction. His tone implied that you disobeyed this rule on the threat of a very painful, drawn-out death. "On the whole," he began again, "our blood is supplied through animal or synthetic means. Human blood is largely unnecessary, although I kind of like the idea about free-range humans. Only a few have B.B.s of their own."

"But you take from that...female," Dark answered, bringing them back to the original purpose of this conference.

"Only because she volunteered, Dark. We do not force humans to become a meal. They know what they are getting into and they are rarely used in this manner. I have had B.B. for almost a year and I never even sampled her blood...much."

"Then why do you have her?" Dark groused. If that female was unnecessary, she was out the door.

"To set an example, Dark," Luca sighed. "I need to let my people know that human blood is unnecessary and that they don't have to rely on humans for nourishment."

"Well," Dark began, "that is still no excuse for that hussy to be throwing herself at you. And she did it as if I wasn't even in the room. She's lucky that she has no other problems besides a case of watery bowels." She narrowed her eyes and glared at her mate.

"Dark," Luca groaned as he leaned his head back against the chair and folded his legs beneath him. "I could never betray our vows. You are inside me now, and betraying you is like betraying myself. Even if you are a stubborn bi...woman." He cracked open one eye to see how she would take his deliberate slip.

She glared at him.

"Aren't you hungry or something, for other than B.B.'s flesh?" he asked. "How about breakfast? You can get the hell out of my hair for a few moments and I can get some rest."

Dark's first reaction was anger, then she realized something. Luca was trying his best to rid himself of her. Why?

"No, Luca dear," she purred as she rose to her feet and began to stalk across the room towards him. "I'm going to sit right here and learn all that there is to learn about you. It's fascinating, really." She bit the inside of her jaw to keep from laughing as his body slumped a bit in his chair.

"I'm not that interesting," he replied, an almost desperate look on his face. He squirmed back in his chair as far away from her as possible. She was getting that look in her eyes again and that didn't bode well for his abused body.

"Oh, yes, you are," she purred as she pushed his chair back and settled herself on his lap.

He groaned as she wiggled her bottom into the space left by his folded legs and turned to drape her legs over the arm on his chair. In this position, she twisted her chest to rest against his and ran a small soft finger over his cheeks. Her smile was wicked and she slowly licked her lips, as if he were some choice morsel that she was ready to devour.

Against his will, he felt his lower body begin to tingle and tighten as his traitorous blood left the places that it was needed—like his brain—and rushed below his waist. He looked first down at his enlarging member as it rose up to brush against her hip, then at his mate whose knowing expression was too experienced for the newly plucked virgin that he knew she had been.

"How long will you be in heat?" he asked as a small wail made its way into his deep voice.

"Oh, for weeks yet, Luca," she answered as she bent to lap with her tongue at the silver hoop that hung from his ear, stifling a giggle as his body stiffened even more. "Who really knows how long I will be this hot. But I'm sure you can keep up with the demand."

"Mercy," he sighed softly before his lips slammed down on her slick damp ones, drinking in her essence and savoring her taste. He thrust his tongue between her lips and moaned at the feel of her soft tongue tangling and mingling with his.

"Maybe later," she purred against his lips, then pulled away and clamped her teeth on the tightly drawn skin of his neck. She smiled as his whole body began to quiver beneath her touch.

When a cleared throat interrupted their growing kiss, he didn't know whether to leap with joy or growl with anger.

"If you are done mauling my niece, there are a few things that we must discuss."

"Aunt Zinia," Dark wailed. She was about to break him. What was so darn important that her aunt had to interrupt now?

"I thought I told you to be gone at daybreak," Luca said as he easily picked up Dark and set her on her feet. With fluid grace, he rose to face Zinia, his new auntie. He wanted to find out why she dared to disobey his direct order. "I didn't expect to see *you*," emphasis was on the 'you', "around and creating trouble."

She sniffed as she tossed her brown-streaked hair over her shoulder.

"So in other words, you and your people will obey me only when I am around to see that my words are heeded. Not very smart, Aunt, letting me in on your strategy so quickly in the game. It doesn't bode well for your, or should I say, *my* people?"

His sarcastic tone and thunderous expression exposed how he felt about the matter. For once, he made no effort to control his temper and the room began to chill with his anger.

Zinia took a deep breath, then confronted her new "leader." There were a few things that she needed to discuss with her niece and this barbarous bastard wouldn't stand in her way.

"Because I love my people, Vampesi, I have come forth. I need to know what the Vampesi are doing to protect the Wolfen from all-out domination. I do not trust you, bloodsucker, not at all. I should have been made ruler, but now it is too late to look back. So I will make myself one of your advisors so that I will know that you are looking out for our best interests."

"Sort of like a liaison?" Luca queried, his expression still dark.

"Yes, that, and like I said, one of your advisors."

"I have no advisors," Luca growled as he again took his seat and examined the woman standing before him. Her scent was similar to his Dark's, but different in some indescribable way.

"No advisors?" Zinia cried out, scandalized. "Whatever happened to democracy? Or are you just a dictator, never considering the needs of your people?"

"That is enough, Aunt," Dark stated in a loud, controlling voice.

Before Luca could defend himself or ignore her words, his fierce little mate was leaping to his defense. Interesting, he thought as he sat back and watched the short hairs on the back of her neck rise with her anger. Very interesting, indeed.

Surprised, Zinia turned towards her niece — surprised that she spoke so forcefully. "It is never enough, Dark. How are we to survive if we have to depend upon his whim?"

Good one, Luca thought as he turned his head to his mate and waited for her reply.

"That's what I am for," Dark said in an authoritative voice. "I will see to the needs of my people. It was I who was chosen, Zinia, and I who will succeed my father. It was his wish."

"Will you stand for our people, Dark? Will you stand when you are on your back with this…man?"

"You may call me Luca, Auntie," the man in question interjected. "We are all family here." His black eyes sparkled in amusement.

"You may call him Master," Dark growled, her fangs exploding in her mouth. "Or you may call him Lucavarious, but you have not earned the right to call him *Luca*."

That surprised Luca. His eyebrows shot up almost to his hairline as he examined his mate. She was ready to attack in defense of him. This was something new. He had never had anyone stand up for him, and it made him feel...funny.

"Already, he has turned you against us," Zinia cried out, righteous indignation flaring in her brown eyes. "I guess a few moments of having something stiff between your legs has warped your sense of right and wrong."

"Watch yourself, Zinia. You have overstepped your bounds and I will gladly show you the error of your ways." A loud growl now filled the room, Dark making her place as alpha female in this unusual pack known. No one would challenge her authority. *No one.*

Taken aback by Dark's new intimidating nature, Zinia took a step back and raised her eyes to her niece's. Brown eyes fought with brown eyes, each vying for supremacy, each correct in their beliefs and convictions.

Zinia was the first to look away. She knew that the right of succession passed to Dark as her brother wanted, but she was still not happy about it.

"I suggest you leave my home, Aunt. If you want to speak to Lucavarious or me, you make an appointment. Otherwise, you will not show your face around here until you are invited. Is that understood?"

Her aunt nodded shortly and quit the room. The slamming of the door in her wake sounded like a primitive gunshot in the quiet of the room.

"*Your* home, Dark?" Luca asked, one eyebrow raised in amusement as he observed his mate with her hackles raised.

"Shut up, Vampesi," Dark growled as she turned to him, anger still alight in her eyes. "Yes, this big stone barn is now my home, come hell or high water. And I have more important things to do here than spar with you or play Lord of the Manor. Your place is to provide me with sexual fulfillment and stay the hell out of my way. I have a job to do, and you will not keep me from it."

"Sexual fulfillment," Luca cried out in amused indignation. "Provide you with sexual fulfillment?"

"That, and to stay the hell out of my way, Lucavarious."

"What did I do?" he asked, totally bewildered at the sudden shift of moods in his mate. It had to be hormonal. But Dark was paying him no attention.

Her new emotions, still so unstable and ever changing within her, needed a release. And the closest safest target was her mate.

"Never you mind about that," she growled as she swung her head towards him and bared her teeth. "This is now my home and now I have to clean it up before it's fit for my occupancy. That redheaded bimbo is out of here. If you need blood, you take it from me. I need to see where the humans stay and where they work. I also need to know more about the Vampesi who live around here. I have a sudden need to know more about my people and you are just too abnormal a Vampesi to get good information from."

"Abnormal?" he wailed. Was that a wail?

"And another thing, I'm hungry. You had better have some real food in this house or your precious B.B. is on the breakfast menu."

"*Abnormal?*" Yup, it was a full blown wail.

"If you can't participate in a conversation and make sense, Lucavarious, I suggest to you again that you shut your mouth. Things are going to change around here, starting today. This is a shared power thing, Vampesi, and you'd do well to remember it."

With that, the door slammed a second time and Luca was left alone.

"All I wanted was a little peace and quiet," he said to the now empty room. "I just wanted some time to rest and recuperate and now I'm here with a stiff dick, a headache, and a need to yell at someone. But there is no one left to yell at. Am I not the master of this house? But that Wolfen just reduced me to vibrator with fangs. It's just not right."

So saying, he too rose to his feet and slammed out of the room. He needed sleep and he was going to damn well ignore the world while he got some. Women were strange creatures and better dealt with on a full stomach, with a clear head, and an owner's manual to figure them out.

And in the darkest recesses of the castle one low voice said to another, "We missed our mark, but never fear, there will be plenty of chances left before that bitch starts to breed."

Chapter Eight

Luca sighed in relief as he made his way to his sleeping chambers. Dawn had broken, the new day had started, his household was in an uproar, and now he desperately needed sleep. The new sun was tugging at him, draining his strength and sapping his patience. He had managed to face the sun for one full cycle and now his body had had enough.

With nothing but the thought of a long peaceful sleep on his mind, he opened the door to his chambers and saw heaven in an alcove. His bed, his gloriously huge bed with its fresh pristine linens beckoned to him from the doorway. Pillows. Pillows, big fluffy ones, waited to cradle his aching head in comfort. The turned-back sheets almost made him giddy with delight as he dragged his tired body across the floor. Closer and closer they loomed as he placed his hands on the firm mattress and slowly crawled across the surface.

Rest. Blessed sleep. Sweet oblivion was at hand.

With a hedonistic sigh of delight, he dropped facedown into the waiting arms of the luring bedsheets. Tears almost filled his eyes as he burrowed deep into his pillows, groaned a long painfully happy groan, and closed his eyes. So grateful was he for being horizontal, he almost forgot to place a force shield around his bed.

Muttering a few choice curses under his breath, he waved one hand, bangles tinkling, and created a large lavender force shield that completely covered the opening of his sleeping alcove. The deep purple shield prevented any from entering or seeing anything that went on within and was a sign for any who entered that he did not wish to be disturbed.

Never had he been so tired in his life; well, except for maybe the time when his father forced him to face the dawn at the age of seven, or when his mother first pierced his ear with silver at eight. He remembered that she had used gloves to hold the poisonous metal as she jabbed the stud through first his right then his left ear. He didn't understand at the time why his loving mother, with tears in her eyes, had done such a thing to him.

He spent the entire night, and the next three bent over in pain and trying to force it to a tolerable level. He had no problems facing the sun then; in fact he welcomed the intense pain that the daylight brought. It was a distraction from tearing agony taking place within his body.

Four months later, as his mother replaced the studs with a set of small hoops and inserted the second set of studs, he barely flinched.

Now after dealing with his new mate and his new in-laws, he felt as if he had gone through a battle with the Wolfen Clan of old. Quite well he remembered the old fighting warriors who took no prisoners and fought with an animal-like stealth. He was twenty-seven when one of the old ones killed his father. Soon after, his mother, recognizing that both species were slowly committing genocide, devised a plan with the old ruler, and told him something that he found it hard to believe—something that he now knew was truth.

The contract was born, and every new generation of Wolfen leader awaited the birth of The One while living with an uneasy truce with the Vampesi. Every new generation, he waited with his mother for the birth of a female born first in her line. Every new generation, hope died a little as yet another son was born.

By the time he knew of Dark's conception and birth, he had almost given up hope of ever fulfilling this contract. He now sported more silver than most humans laid claim to and continued with his father's sun treatments until he could face the dawn and not be burned to a crisp. In fact, one of his true regrets in life was that his father never got to share a sunrise with him.

But he quickly put those sentimental remembrances aside. He was born for a purpose, raised to that end, bred to be a leader among Vampesi. He existed for a purpose, and now that purpose was coming to fruition. But only half of the job was done.

When he felt rested, there were a few things that he had to explain to his mate. Among these important life lessons was the fact that he did not exist to provide her with sexual pleasure.

If he let her continue with that thinking, men everywhere, Vampesi and Wolfen alike would suffer a fate worse than death. They would lose rank and power in their own households. They would all be reduced to—dare he even think it—sexual ornaments, playthings, *boy toys*.

Give a woman an inch, she would take a mile. Give her control over your body through sex, well, he knew man's weakness. Once they had you by the balls and whipped into submission, you would turn into a mindless slave willing to drain your own mother for another slice of paradise. He could not—no, he *would* not—let that happen to him or to any other man under his rule.

So thinking that, his mind steady and clear, he gave himself up to the arms of Morpheus as he drifted off into a deep sleep. And he dreamed of Dark, her eyes wide and black with her passion, her nails digging with a sharp pleasure/pain into his back, her teeth piercing the delicate skin of his neck. Oh what wondrous dreams he had!

* * * * *

Men. Who needs them? They only provide one service, and then you still have to train them, Dark fumed as she tore into her breakfast of rare steak and fluffy scrambled chicken's eggs with cheese. She was on her third plate and in no way felt satisfied.

"Where are all the Vampesi?" she asked the servant standing in the dining room waiting to serve her. "I thought that all of the blood drinkers would be positively haunting this castle today. Did my family eat them all?"

"Uh, no," the young man answered as he stifled laughter.

He was rather tall and had long brown hair pulled into a tail at his nape. His bright blue eyes told of his good humor and his rather handsome, honest face instantly caused one to relax in his presence.

"Well, where are they, Human? Or am I not to know out of fear that I will stake them through the heart as they sleep?"

"Well, that wouldn't work either, ma'am," the man replied. "Well, maybe on a turned Vampesi, but not a born one."

"Wait." Dark stopped with her fork half way to her mouth. "You mean there are really two types of Vampesi running around here?"

"Yes, ma'am," he answered again, amusement lighting up his blue eyes.

"Luca said something to that effect earlier, but I thought he was just bragging," she mused as she placed her fork back on the plate. "So, how come there are two types of them?"

"Well, the short story is that certain humans were turned for a reason, the long story is that we are all related in some distant way."

"What is your name?" she asked, her attention drawn to this informative Human.

"Vincent," he answered as he gestured to the plate on the table. "Are you done?"

"No, Vincent, I am not," she replied as she picked up her fork again. "But you can explain that rather cryptic concept."

"Well, the Vampesi, at one point, were nearly hunted to extinction. They are fiercely loyal and kind of…"

"Snobs?" she asked as he seemed to search for words.

"Well, I would say elitist snobs, but the regular type of snob will do."

Dark bit back a bark of laughter at his droll expression as he said that.

"They almost died out because of it," he continued when she gained control of herself. "They had been drinking off of humans, as the old legends say, but there is good and bad in every people. Some of the worst would go around creating blood slaves for themselves and commanding them to seek out their masters when called. But in truth, no Vampesi can exercise mind control over another. The bad ones would go around sleeping and drinking off of humans, and when those humans were caught, they cried rape and told stories of how the big bad monster came into their rooms and raped them of their blood and virtue. No one wanted to be caught sleeping with a man who will get you burned at the stake."

"I can agree with that," Dark said. "But that doesn't explain how a Vampesi can be created."

"That's the good part," Vincent informed her with glee. "A created Vampesi is none other than a man or a woman who managed to steal a bit of Vampesi blood in return."

"You mean it wasn't given?" Dark asked, an astonished look on her face and her breakfast thirds forgotten.

"Elitist snobs, remember? Who would willingly admit that the lesser species managed to steal something as precious as their blood from them? They let the stories of evil Vampires stealing blood from innocent maidens spread to save them embarrassment."

"Oh, I see," Dark mused. "Rather evil and devious than inept and gullible."

"Something like that," Vincent laughed. "But when the humans drank the Vampesi blood, instead of making them like the Vampesi, they became..." he looked at her and waited for her to come to the obvious conclusion.

"Vampires." she exclaimed, understanding making her sound shocked.

"Give the lady a prize." Vincent laughed. "You are right. They became Vampires and got real pissed because they had none of the Vampesi powers. They needed blood more than the average Vampesi and they could be easily killed as they slept. The only reason the Vampesi blood didn't kill them outright is because Vampesi and Human are related in some way."

"Related how?" Dark asked. She knew she was now receiving valuable information that she never would have learned from Luca. He was too secretive to let good stuff like this slip out.

"Well, that I don't know. But I do know if you gave Vampesi blood to anybody but a human, they would go mad and die a rather painful death. There aren't many Vampires left in the world. Most were destroyed at the beginning of the Great War, but there are still a few out and about. And you can kill them with a stake to the heart. With a Vampesi, you never get that close."

"So tell me, Vincent, why are you here, serving the Vampesi? I thought you would be afraid of the bloodsuckers."

"Afraid? Never! Lucavarious takes good care of us. In fact, there was a time when the Wolfen could not tell the difference between a human and a Vampesi. Thousands of us were slaughtered when the war began. The Vampesi offered us shelter and safety from that destruction. In return, we offered blood when necessary, and it's not that necessary — only in times of extreme stress and physical injury. Other than that, they leave us alone and pay us for a job well done while offering us protection."

"The days of the war are well past, Vincent. You have nothing to fear from the Wolfen," Dark said quietly. She didn't want even this human to think badly of her people.

"Oh I know that," he assured as he patted her hand. "But if it ain't broke, why fix it? The arrangement has worked well for years and Luca is a competent boss. Heck, we have the run of the castle and we get paid for living here. It's a good arrangement. And if you are wondering where the rest of the Vampesi are, they went home. This castle belongs to Luca and he doesn't like to be crowded. Besides, he is the only Vampesi awake during the day to appreciate our work." Vincent laughed at that again as he observed his new mistress.

"You mean the others aren't awake during the day?" Again Dark was surprised. It looked like her parents' information was correct to some degree. That information just didn't apply to Lucavarious.

"Oh, no," Vincent said as he shook his head. "Luca is the only one. The only one who wears silver, too. I think the others are allergic to it or something, but I'm not sure. Heck, some of them don't even have fangs."

"What?" That brought Dark almost out of her seat.

"Yup. Some of them don't even have fangs. To let them drink from you was a painful and messy experience. But Luca figured out a way around that one too. Next time the clan gathers, look at their hands. As a rule, they all grow their pinkie nails long so that no one knows who was born with fangs and who was born without. Another one of Luca's ideas. He didn't want any member of his race feeling superior over another."

"So they get to feel superior over Wolfen and Human," Dark groused, again angered by Luca's seemingly too arrogant behavior.

"Well, not quite." Vincent grinned as he picked up her plate of cold food and started towards the kitchens.

"What do you mean?" Dark called out to him as he left the dining area.

"Well, they hold us Humans as being vastly superior to Wolfen." He laughed as he left the room.

For a moment, Dark was stunned into silence. Then she called out, "Well, you aren't all that, you walking rack of ribs."

Her eyes twitched in amusement as she thought about all that she had learned. She was too grateful for the walking sack of meat to be offended.

"And you had better remember your superiority the next time you close your eyes. The Wolfen have excellent night vision, funny man, and we could catch you and have a snack before you knew what hit you."

His boisterous laughter was her answer as it rolled from the kitchen.

She had made an acquaintance, and hopefully, a friend.

Chapter Nine

Today was a good day to explore, Dark thought as she wandered through the halls of the castle. With her stomach filled and her head ringing with knowledge, she set off to explore her new home.

Now, where to begin?

Turning away from the dining area, she realized that she had only been on one floor of this massive place. There was Luca's study, the sleeping chambers, the dining area, and the chamber where the wedding ceremony had taken place, but all of that was separated into wings on the first floor. She wanted to search the second story of this stone mausoleum and see what she was now required to live with.

So with those thoughts in mind, Dark set off to find the stairs to the second floor.

"Where is a human when you need one?" she groused as she walked along the quiet halls. "Where is Vincent when I actually need him? For that matter, where do B.B. and the other humans stay?"

After her meal was completed, it seemed that all life inside this place had disappeared. Silence greeted her footsteps as the soft soles of her slippers scraped against the smooth marble of the floor.

The walls were hung with several portraits of beautiful people from Earth's past and quite a few mirrors. There were also several vases of fresh flowers scattered around. All in all, this castle would make a comfortable home. But where was the good stuff hidden?

The curious animal within her urged her to explore deeper into the castle. Not wanting to go against her true nature, Dark lifted her nose and scented the air around her.

There was something fascinating up ahead, and her senses screamed for her to investigate it.

Muttering to herself, she wandered around a corner she never approached before and stopped short at what awaited her.

The well-lighted corridors left no room for shadows and left no room for doubt.

She had just wandered into an indoor garden of Wolfen delights.

Rushing forward in haste, her mouth dropped open as she saw the wondrous vaulted ceiling made completely of glass. She sighed in pleasure as she felt the glorious warmth of the sun showering down upon her, beckoning her deeper into the almost tropical splendor of the room.

Tentatively stepping forward, she inhaled the rich scents of fresh grass. Lemon grass, wolf's bane, peppermint grass — it all exploded, a glorious taste sensation within her as she inhaled and tasted the fragrant air.

Amaryllis and day lilies vied for the brightest color while a blanket of violets provided a startling contrast between the reds and yellows. Roses were set off to one side while a huge Lord Baltimore dominated a sunny corner. Morning glories trailed a lavender curtain up and over a hanging trellis while small daisies and forget-me-nots circled a bench just beneath.

A small fountain bubbled in the background, providing a soothing white noise, while extremely tall, decorative crystal balls flanked the comfortable-looking seat.

The humidity touched her bare skin, setting off nerve endings and causing her nipples to tighten as she realized that the feel of the place reminded her of how Luca made a room feel when he was primed and ready for action. Was he responsible for the sudden temperature changes, or was it her own imagination, an extension of her inner feelings?

Deciding to debate the issue later, she softly stepped amidst the bountiful beauty that nature seemed to have blessed this room with, and walked over to the bench,

It was cushioned with a large purple cushion that showed its age by its worn spots and smelled suspiciously of Luca.

Tossing her head back, she inhaled deeply before she threw her arms out as if to embrace the life in this room and turned in a small circle, for once not minding the loose gown that allowed the fresh-scented air of the place to wrap around her legs and further fuel her senses.

Laughter bubbling up in her throat, she walked over to the bench and prepared to throw herself down upon it.

"Please remove your shoes," a voice intoned.

"*Eeeeeek.*"

Startled out of her placid state, Dark jumped and turned, landing in a crouch, teeth bared, the hair at her nape standing on end, and sharp talons exploding from her fingertips.

"Calm yourself, woman," the gruff voice commanded, as the sound of Dark's nervous breathing shattered the peace of the room.

"Sage?" she asked quietly as she slowly uncoiled her body from *flee-or-fight* position and again stood straight and tall.

"Remove those shoes," the voice repeated as the robed figure moved into Dark's view. "And yes, I have been called such, but how wise I am has yet to be seen."

Nodding her compliance, Dark bent and removed the slippers from her feet and tossed them onto the bench. She sighed in pleasure as the soft, damp, warm grass tickled her toes. Now *this* was living. The beast within concurred as her senses settled down and again the wonder of this room filled her.

"So what have you learned thus far, child?" the Sage asked.

"That there is more to be seen than meets the eye," she answered truthfully.

She had met with the Sage many times over the past years when her parents conducted ceremonies or needed some obscure fact checked, so she felt comfortable in speaking honestly with him

"And that I have a lot to learn."

"Very good, Dark," the Sage praised. "You were ever a bright child."

She almost flushed with pleasure at his comment, but managed to hold her joy inside to be savored later.

"But don't get too complacent, woman. You spoke true when you said that you have a lot to learn."

She nodded, taking his words to heart.

"What are you doing here?" she asked as she took a seat and invited the Sage to sit with her. The bench was as comfortable as she had imagined and the smell of her mate was well intertwined with the old fibers of the cushion.

The Sage declined her invitation but answered her just as truthfully.

"This is one of my favorite places to meditate when I visit Luca. We spent quite a bit of time together here when he was young."

"That man has never been young, Sage," she groused as she again remembered this morning's episode.

"Luca is an old soul," the Sage agreed, "but he is one of the few here who keeps his word. Darkness and mystery cloak you, Dark. You must be on guard at all times."

"Excuse me?" she asked, a perplexed expression on her face. "I am in danger?"

"Life is danger, woman, I just say be on guard," the Sage said from within the folds of the voluminous robes. "From the moment we are born, we start to die. Just be careful that no one helps you on your journey."

"This has to do with my parents, doesn't it?" she demanded, her eyes flashing black in sudden anger. She had declared revenge on those who had stolen her parents away, but she thought that she would be able to investigate the crime a little later, thinking that her mating ended any direct threat to her.

"All things are connected in some way," the Sage said in his usual cryptic manner.

"Now you sound like that human, Vincent. 'All things are as one and we all are related in some way'." She sighed in disgust and ran one hand through her short, mussed hair. "I have to avenge the murders of my parents, and it looks like I will have to begin my hunt earlier than I planned."

"Be careful what you hunt, woman. Be careful to choose the right prey and the right reason."

"Then why would someone seek to harm me now, Old One?" she asked as her mind struggled to sort out her problems. "Nothing can be gained by my demise now. If I am killed, then Luca will rule over both of our peoples alone. No one wants that, including, I believe, Luca."

"You will learn, Dark, that there are more reasons than one to do you both harm. Be wary, woman, and watch the people closest to you. The only one that you can trust now is your mate, because he wants nothing from you."

"Nothing?" exclaimed Dark, a bit of anger in her tone. "I wouldn't call the partial rulership of the Wolfen a big nothing."

"Did he ask for it, or was it asked of him?"

That shut her up. She knew that the contract had been around for ages and that her parents put a lot of time into updating it and adding clauses for her protection, but never had Luca come wanting to fulfill its terms. The terms were set for him many centuries ago. He just followed its dictates out of...loyalty. Would he be as loyal to his mate as he was to a document that predated him and whose writers were long dead?

"So my mate has a few redeeming qualities," she groused. "I guess I can trust him for now."

When she looked up, the Sage was gone and she was again alone in the room.

"Damn. I need to find out how he does that," she mused as she settled comfortably on the bench to think about all that she learned.

Everyone was being so helpful to her and that made her wonder...why? This sudden fount of information seemed suspect to her. Everyone trying to be so helpful and divulge secrets that were centuries old was just a bit too easy. The only one who hadn't tried to drown her in opinion-formulation-information was Luca. The Sage was right in saying that he was the only person who would not benefit from this mating, the only one who hadn't cared one way or another. She would place her trust in him for now, but she remembered something that her father had once told her.

"Dark," he had said. "Never trust anyone one hundred percent, not even yourself."

Good advice years ago and good advice this day.

* * * * *

Luca turned over in his sleep and popped his thumb in his mouth. It was a habit that he had had for years, one that even the threat of crooked fangs could not cure him of. While he was awake and active, the thought to stick that appendage into his mouth never crossed his mind, but while he was asleep, his guard eased up a bit and that offending digit would find its way into his mouth.

But now the feel of his flesh in his own mouth in this *between sleep and wakefulness phase*, brought forth images of Dark.

He loved the feel of any of her various body parts in his mouth. Her nipples were hard/soft fruits that tantalized the senses. Her tongue was soft and hot and flavored with her special womanly spices, her sharp teeth a temptation to prick his tongue with. Her toe...Her toe? That woke him up.

"I will not put that woman's feet into my mouth," he growled as he jerked to an upright position.

"No one asked you to," came the sharp reply from outside of the shield.

"You can hear me?" he asked and he raked one hand through his sleep-mussed hair. "Of course you can hear me, your blood is in my body now," he groaned as he answered his own question. He had forgotten about all of that.

"So? Lots of women's blood is running through your body, Lucavarious. Are you telling me that they all can hear you inside that blasted bubble that you keep around you?"

Hmm. The little woman sounded angry. This did not bode well for him or his head. At the rate he was going, a headache would be the norm for him.

"No, dear," he nearly growled at her, "only the woman that I have bound myself to can hear me. But you can't break through the barrier. That 'blasted bubble,' as you so eloquently put it, is unbreakable, even by smart-assed Wolfen women who eavesdrop on a man's private words."

His sarcasm was sharp this night.

"*Women*, Lucavarious?" came her droll reply through the purple shield. "I thought they were ready-made sex dolls equipped with warm running blood designed with your every wish in mind."

"Jealous?" he quipped and smiled as her muffled roar filled his ears. Score one for the bloodsucker.

With a negligent wave of his hand, he vanished the barrier and got his first look of the night at his mate — his *irate* mate.

She stood in an aggressive stance, her arms akimbo and her toes tapping as she glared at him with dark narrowed eyes. She wasn't too happy with his direct hit. Too bad. He was rested now and ready for battle. Make him a walking sexual object, would she? He would make sure that he had the last laugh.

"And to think that I was this close to trusting you, you, you fanged walking pig with more jewelry than an Old World whore. How dare you even insinuate that I am jealous of that red-haired mattress with feet?"

Her breath huffed as her still-uncontrollable emotions took a turn for the worse. The beast within growled and roared while her eyes spit fire at the man who was the beginning and end of her most recent set of problems.

"You seem to assume a lot about the people that you know nothing about, Wolfen-child. And you know what they say about people who assume, don't you?"

She stood there and sputtered as Luca rose up and casually began to pull his clothes from his body. Her breath caught as she again was exposed to the perfection of his form. His bare, golden expanse of chest muscles flexed and contracted as he bent to untie the drawstring that held his pants on his narrow hips. They fell with a soft rasp and he stepped free of them, leaving his lower half as bare as the day that he was born.

Dark hungrily examined every exposed inch of his skin. His large man-staff lay dormant along his thigh, leaning to the left, and was surrounded by a thin fall of silky curls. His thighs were still thick and corded with muscle and tapered gracefully to well-formed knees and thick muscular calves. His ankles were nice, too. The man was just too beautiful naked.

Stalking over to the bed, she grabbed a blanket and tossed it at him.

"Look, Luca, I didn't come here to argue or play sensual one-up-manship with you," she sighed as she realized that she was letting her jumbled emotions get the better of her. As much fun as it would be to taunt and tease the man until he acted somewhat normal, she had interrupted his sleep for a very important reason. "I want to discuss something important."

"Your walking vibrator with fangs awaits your every command, Lady," he drawled, but he tossed the blanket aside and made for the robe that, as usual, waited on a chair near the bed.

"Now pray tell me, what is so important that you must postpone our little game just when I'm coming out on top? It must be important for you to forgo the usual jibes and jabs that you use to express yourself in such a mature manner. So, Dark, your vibrator is all ears."

"Luca, I want to talk about my parents' death."

That caught his attention. He abandoned the tie to the robe he was struggling to tie just so, and walked over to her.

"Has anybody threatened you here? Has anyone dared to attempt to harm you?"

Again he spoke in the tones of the Ruler, his deep voice sounding sharp with concern and his black eyes glowing with a silver glint. His hands cupped her shoulders protectively as he pulled her to nestle within his arms.

Instinctively, Dark pushed her face into Luca's neck inhaling his scent and nuzzling closer. *His neck is my favorite place to bury my nose,* she decided after a moment. With his arms softly caressing her back and his heart beating under her ear, she felt safe and protected.

"No one has done anything to me Luca," she sighed at last as she stepped back a bit to look up into his eyes. "But after speaking to the human Vincent and having words with the Sage in the garden, my instincts tell me that this must be laid to rest. The danger isn't over, Luca. I know that someone wanted to halt our mating by killing off my parents and now that we are mated the danger should be past, but what if it isn't? I won't feel comfortable until I know who did the deed and why."

Luca was silent for a moment, absorbing everything that Dark had to say. Yes, it was time to "clean house" so to speak. He refused to have any under his rule who would stoop so low as to use poison to murder another. And he wanted to lay to rest finally this tragedy for Dark so that they could get on with the business of mating, arguing and child-producing. He rather enjoyed their arguments; they kept his wits sharp.

"Well, if your instincts are correct, then we have a viper in our midst, and I am not referring to your tongue," he joked, just to see the feral light of anger flare in her eyes.

"If you won't take this seriously…" she began, her eyes expressing her anger, but he cut her off.

"Oh, but I do take this seriously, Dark. The guilty will pay with extreme pain and agony before they go off to meet their makers, this I swear to you. And if anyone lays a finger on you, there will be hell to pay."

"Luca," Dark exclaimed, her body stiffening in pleased surprise. "Do you care for me so much?"

"No," he denied quickly as he felt a flash of something warm shower over his heart. "I just know a good lay when I find one. I'll be your vibrator, baby, if you will be my mattress with feet."

"Lucavarious. You bastard."

Chapter Ten

"What? Did you think that I wouldn't want to help you, Dark?"

"Well, that thought did cross my mind, Luca," she said as she stepped back and glowered at her mate. "Why are you being so helpful all of a sudden?"

Luca gaped at Dark. No words could pass through his lips and the incredulous expression seemed permanently affixed to his face.

"All of a sudden?" he finally grated out. "Where is the suddenness in it, woman? Did I not agree to fulfill the terms of that blasted contract that you held onto like a shield of honor?"

"Because you wanted to," she heatedly pointed out.

"And I settled the first family dispute."

"By allowing them to try and kill each other," she nearly screamed.

"And I have done a pretty damn good job of keeping you satisfied, Wolfen-child."

"So you have one thing that you are kind of good at, Luca. But other men have been able to make that claim, bloodsucker. So try another one."

By this time, Dark had both hands pressed to her hips and her eyes spat dark fire at her mate. She was aggressively leaning forward with her eyes narrowed in her suddenly returned anger.

The beast within her delighted at the challenge, loved butting heads with the alpha male, testing his strength. Her inner hunger began to grow as a sudden shaft of desire shot through her. How long had it been since she had last faced sexual devastation at this man's hands? If she had to ask, it had been too long.

The light of anger in her face changed into the light of fierce passion as she examined her man.

Luca almost took a step back once he saw the rapid play of emotions shift across her face.

First, there he was, doing an admirable job of defending himself to his ungrateful little flea-bag of a wife, when all of a sudden she started looking at him as if she wanted to lick her chops.

What had gotten into her? He was enjoying matching wits with her and now she was…looking quite aroused.

"Damn, you're still in heat," he summarized finally as he tightened the belt on his robe, as if the white cotton material would protect his, uh, virtue.

"What of it?" she almost purred as she began stalking her prey, uh, mate. Her eyes were now twinkling merrily as she anticipated the chase. She was hoping that he would run. He only made it better when he put up a fight.

"Nothing, nothing at all," he assured her quickly as he felt an answering jolt of sexual heat flood his senses. This was amazing. He should be spent now, but here he was, contemplating having her flat on her back, or in some variation of the act.

"Then why are you backing away?" she asked as she lifted one foot and kicked her shoe away. "Why are you running, Luca? If you're scared, say that you're scared and I'll go easy on you."

"Scared?" he sputtered, then his lightning-quick reflexes caught the second shoe that she kicked in his direction. "I am not scared of a little lost puppy trying to cut her milk teeth on my hide."

With some disdain, he tossed the shoe aside, but couldn't stop his eyes from wandering down to examine her feet. Gosh, she had pretty toes.

"Then stop running away from me, Luca. I promise not to hurt you. Much."

Luca blinked and realized that the whole time she had been talking, he had been backing away from the bed. Now he stood next to a padded chair in the corner where his robe had rested. Disgusted with himself for letting his control slip, he decided it was time to take back the power, to take back the night.

"Running, Wolfen? Never. Positioning you for an attack is more my style."

With a wicked grin, he let the robe part as he untied the sash at his waist. His silver bangles tinkled as he casually tossed aside the white cotton and stood before her in all his naked splendor. The temperature in the room increased dramatically as his male flesh began to fill and rise with his growing lust.

It was time to teach the little woman a lesson. Class was now in session.

"First off, Dark," he said in a deep rumbling growl, "it is time to remove that ridiculous get-up that you are wearing. It doesn't suit you, not at all."

"With pleasure, Luca," she returned. "I didn't pick out this stupid piece of fluff anyway. I will be happy to rid myself of it, even if it is for you."

But she didn't remove her dress in the traditional way. She sighed with pleasure as she felt her nails expand into the dangerous talons that all enemy of the Wolfen dread. Then with a smile on her face, she gripped the fabric of the top of her dress and slowly rent the material from collar to waist.

"I'm impressed," he breathed, as the humidity almost became oppressive. "But I can do better."

With a wave of his hands, the material parted down the front to fall as a useless rag at her feet. Then with another wave, Dark was lifted and carried across the small space separating them. She landed softly on her feet, facing the seat of the large white chair.

"Very cute, Fang," she whispered as the hot yet gentle force held her in place. "So what are you going to do for an encore? Mount me from behind and make like a dog in heat?"

Her eyes glittered at the thought and her limbs began to tremble. *Please let him try it like that,* she thought and the animal within her concurred wholeheartedly.

"Can you read minds now, little Wolfen?" he asked as he stepped behind her.

She could feel the heat pouring off of his body and pooling in her stomach. His unique scent seemed to fill her nose, thrilling her senses and making her hunger for a more physical touch.

"I have no idea, mate," she answered. "I am new to my powers as of yet and haven't explored them all. But I can guess what you are thinking, Luca. It's written all over your face. You have the hots for my body and that desire is about beyond your control."

Maybe she should not have let him know that she was on to his secrets so soon, but something inside her was pushing him, wanting him to react, and waiting for what he would do next. This was a very exciting game and she threw herself into it fully.

"Well when you find out," he murmured as he stepped so close that only millimeters separated them, "be sure to let me know. I need to get as far away from your crazy ass as possible. Only the demented would toy with me when I have you in this position."

He punctuated this remark with a teasing finger that ran down her sleek, delicately shaped back and stopped just at the rising fullness of her bottom.

She shuddered under his light touch, that hot, heavy feeling stealing into her limbs. She gently tested the strength of his force field, smiling as it allowed her to move her hands forward and brace them against the back of the chair. Her smile grew as she realized that she could not move them back to their previous position. Lucavarious had her good and trapped, and she decided that she kind of liked it. It was thrilling,

Peering at him over her shoulder, Dark dropped one sultry eyelid into a wink full of wicked promise. Even where she stood, she could hear his deep gulp and fought to hold back a triumphant smile. He was hers for the taking.

Luca was now faced with one of his greatest fantasies and one of his worse nightmares. This woman, his mate, was toying with him. She was beginning to learn about the power her sensuality had on him and he found that he didn't like it. Sure, he kind of lost reason around her, but only when things turned sexual. Any other time she was an amusing bit of fluff. She had to be fluff.

But she was too damn intelligent for him to discredit her that way, he admitted to himself. Where any other woman would have gone running and screaming from his castle to avoid his very presence, his little Wolfen bared her teeth and growled back when he snapped. And now, instead of shying away from the dark pleasures that he envisioned, she winked and eagerly joined in. Damn, he was in love.

"No, I'm not," he growled out suddenly.

"No what, intelligent, resourceful, more than just a cute little face, thumb-sucking deviant? What?" Dark asked as humor vied with the confusion written on her face.

"Quiet, you," Luca commanded, his cheeks darkening with the beginnings of a blush. "The only things I want coming from your mouth are moans of pleasure and pleas for more," he gritted out as his fangs burst from his gums, filling his mouth with a sweet pain as the taste of his own blood sent his passion spiraling.

Then almost gently, his low moan filling her ears, his hands reached around to cup her full breasts, one in each hand.

Dark gave up on thinking as the sweet fire filled her body. His touch was magical as he rolled her painfully hard nipples between his fingers. Her back arched, trying for a closer contact, but then Luca stepped close enough for the hot hardness of him to brush against her bottom.

"Do you like this, Dark?" he asked as he pressed his body close, conforming to her shape so that not an inch separated them. "Or can this bloodsucking deviant do better?"

Without giving her a chance to expand on her earlier comment, Luca dropped to his knees behind her, licking a wet path from her neck to her rounded buttocks.

"Wh-what are you going to do?" she asked, breathless as the wet trail he left upon her skin almost sizzled with the rising wet heat in the room. Her eyes shone brightly as she looked down at her lover, her mate as he pushed his head between her legs.

"Are you woman enough to take me, Dark?" he asked as he licked his lips and rested his head comfortably on the seat of the chair.

"I don't believe that we're having this conversation." Dark almost moaned as the picture he made reclining there between her spread legs burned its way into her brain and her memories.

"Believe it, baby," he returned, seeing her anger and confusion plainly written on her face.

He reached up and ran one teasing finger through the damp curls that guarded her secrets from his eyes. She was hot and wet for him. That made him feel...

With a growl of frustration, he reached up with a second hand and parted her, exposing her to his view.

"You are beautiful." His words slipped past his lips without thought as he gazed at Dark and saw himself buried there, his manhood, his fingers, and his tongue.

Dark choked on a strangled moan as she tried to break free of his hold to run her fingers through his tousled curls.

"Let me loose," she growled, her voice becoming deep and dangerous as he played her with curious fingers. "Let me go."

"I think not," he countered as he lifted his head and blew a puff of warm air against her wet secrets. "I kind of like you like this, Dark. Better than any leash or choke collar."

"Luca," she began but was cut off as his tongue lashed out and caressed her swollen nubbin, sending shock waves careening through her being.

"Don't speak," he whispered before his teeth clamped gently around her small bud of desire.

Her growling response changed into a wringing moan as the tip of his tongue began to flicker over the sensitive skin of her clitoris. She gurgled as he applied a light suction while keeping his tongue in constant motion.

Luca moaned as he felt her body tense up then shudder as he assaulted her with his skills. He loved to feel her body's wet reaction and thrilled to know that he was the cause.

"More, baby," he murmured against her as his lips released their tender treasure. "I want to drink you in."

Dark felt her knees began to shake at his erotic words. Luca had been an excellent lover before, but now there was intensity to his actions that some deep part of her answered with abandon. Luca was trying to prove something to her and to himself, but what?

Again thought fled as his hands cupped the sensitive skin of her derriere and pulled her closer to his mouth for this oral ravishment, his delighted groans and her mewling cries filling the room.

But Luca had only begun. He released Dark and again pulled himself up behind her, making sure he let his curly locks feather over her heated skin.

"Come back here," she growled, her eyes completely black as she felt his abandonment. "Finish what you started."

"I'll finish it, in my own good time and when I damn well feel like it," he growled as he enveloped her frame in a full body embrace.

Dark purred as she instinctively rubbed her body against his, loving the feel of the soft down of hair that covered his body brushing against her. She wiggled her bottom, bringing his hardness closer to her heated core, trying to urge him to join with her.

"No, my sweet Wolfen," he growled as his teeth clamped onto her neck, his fangs scraping but not quite biting. "Not yet."

Then his hands reached around to cup her breasts again, shaping and lifting their slight weight and savoring the softness of her skin.

"Soft, so damn soft," he murmured as he brushed his face against her shoulder before clamping down on the skin of her neck again. "So soft and so strong." The loving words slipped out before he could stop them.

"Yes, strong and soft," Dark cried out as his fingers found and plucked at her nipples. Her nails began to penetrate the padded back of the chair as her desire rose. The slight ripping sound only served to drive her deeper into her sexual haze. Her senses were on overload. All she could smell was Luca, his personal scent, his lust. She wanted him and she wanted him now.

"And so hungry," he continued as his tongue laved away the slight imprints from his sharpened teeth.

One hand left the enticing flesh of her breasts to travel slowly across the muscled plane of her stomach. There he scraped his long pinkie nail over her side, touching hidden nerve endings and making her legs tremble. He lingered there for a moment, wringing every shudder and shake from her as his other hand continued to administer pleasure to her breasts, then let his fingers crawl down until they reached the thin soft curls that hid her wet woman's slit.

"Yes," Dark breathed between her clamped teeth as her head fell back on her shoulders, exposing her neck to his prickly caresses. "Yes, touch me there,"

"Here?" he asked, playing with her as his tongue curled around her neck, his fangs following with teasing nips that made her gasp and shake.

"Luca..." she growled, again fighting against the hold of his force field.

"Maybe here?" he asked as his fingers fluttered over her swollen pleasure pearl to trace the small crease where thigh connected to pelvis.

"No," she breathed, her breaths now panting as he traced her delicate ear with his talented tongue.

"Then here," he said and without preamble, he thrust one finger deep inside her.

Dark's body stiffened as if struck by a bolt of lightning. She let out a strangled cry as his thumb began to caress her throbbing woman's seed.

"Yes, must be there," he murmured as he leaned over and captured her lips in a deep, soul-burning kiss.

Dark bucked against his hand as he added another finger to the first, stretching her, pleasuring her, caressing her from the inside. It was too much; it was not enough. She now hungered, a deep hunger that demanded to be appeased.

'Luca," she growled as she felt her fangs explode into her mouth.

Luca moaned as he felt the sudden eruption of her fangs from her gums. He savored the sweet sharp taste of her blood as her fangs extended to their full length. Moaning in delight, he caressed them with his tongue, loving the *mewling* sound she made when caressed like that.

Uncontrollably, his second set of fangs exploded from the top of his gums, his full mature set begging to be released, but he fought the urge. Tearing his mouth away, he began a vigorous thrusting of his fingers still sunk into her scalding wet heat. His body unconsciously mimicked the movements of his hand.

"Yes, Luca, like that," Dark cried out, and his control broke.

Leaving the fullness of her swollen and sensitized breasts, Luca reached down and grabbed her right thigh, forcing her knee to the seat cushion.

"Yes, now, my mate. Now," he gritted out as he fitted himself to her opening, his hand leaving her to grip her waist to hold her steady.

"Luca," Dark wailed out as the first thrust united them as one in body and spirit.

"Damn, you are killing me," Luca groaned as her inner walls stretched and clamped onto his hot hard flesh.

"More," Dark cried out as she wiggled her bottom against his hard stomach. "Now, damn it."

Eager to comply, Luca braced one knee on the chair beside hers, and very slowly pulled himself free of her clinging heat.

"No!" she gasped as she felt him leaving her, but with a growling cry, he thrust himself home again, filling her deeper than before, touching places that begged for his caresses.

"Oh, Dark," he panted as his whole body tightened at the rush of sensation that enveloped him. "Good, baby, so damn good."

"Yes," Dark whimpered as she arched her back, bringing him still deeper.

"I'm gonna...Dark," he cried out as his hips began to pound at her, turning her bones into mush and making her body sing with joy.

Luca closed his eyes in unholy delight as he slowly gave in to his body's demands to conquer her, to tame her, to make her his own. His hand left her hip to again caress her stomach. When the heel of his hand pressed a certain spot below her navel, she screamed at the added sensation. But when he let two fingers reach down to encircle her feminine knob, she reared back and a blood-curdling yowl exploded from her throat.

He felt so good, so big, so hard. He was pushing her higher and higher. Her muscles tensed as each breath brought a fresh stab of desire. She was drowning as her nerves began to vibrate, making her skin tingle from head to foot. She inhaled the air, rich with the smell of their straining bodies, opened her mouth and tasted the passion that grew stronger between the two of them. Tighter and tighter she was wound, her body tense to the breaking point, then in a flash of wildfire that ran from her streaming eyes to her quivering legs, Dark felt her body shatter into a million shards of white-hot light.

"Luca," she howled as her nails ripped plugs of material from the soft chair back. Her body snapped back as crushing waves forced her inner muscles to contract around his marble hardness.

His control snapped. Like a madman, he pounded furiously into her, seeking to find his release as her inner walls convulsed around him.

"Damn," he started to mutter with each stroke. "I love this. I love you. No I don't. Shit. Hot, so hot. You're burning me, Dark. Oh Hell. *Dark.*"

At his mumbled words, Dark, still recovering from her first mind-blowing release, felt her body tighten again around his pounding flesh. She whimpered, her head falling forward in surrender as sensation again built and her body tensed. She had no strength to fight as this new orgasm began to build inside her. If it were not for Luca's force field, she would have collapsed into a boneless heap in the chair. But his magical strength held her upright, an offering to his pleasure as he expelled his misgivings and confusion within her, a willing sacrifice as new waves of release tore through her.

"Yes!" Luca screamed as he felt her body again milking him just when his climax hit him in full force.

"Luca!" Dark cried, tears filling her eyes as pleasure once again rocketed them both to another dimension.

"I've died," Luca panted as he felt his hot seed explode in spurts into her receptive womb. "I've died and been reborn in your fire."

Tiredly he sagged against her, trusting his shield to hold them both. The temperature in the room, which had been downright muggy, eased until comforting warmth surrounded them.

Finally, with a sigh, Luca wrapped his arms around Dark and vanished his shield. Dark slumped in his arms as he carried her the few feet to the bed—still rumpled from his day's rest—tears trailing down her cheeks.

His chest tightened at the sight. "Did I hurt you?" he asked, real concern showing on his face as he hovered over her.

"Mmm. Can we do that again?" she purred as her eyelids lifted, and he was struck by the total satisfaction he saw there. Her beautiful dark eyes were glittering with happiness. His breath caught at the sight and he immediately collapsed onto his back beside her.

"Luca?" she asked as she reached one arm over to caress his damp chest.

"I am not in love," he muttered. "I don't know what love is. How can I be in love if I can't tell love from heartburn? What is heartburn? How do I know what that feels like? I've never had it. I've been around the human's too much. I need to pierce something. Maybe a nipple? No An anklet. I need an anklet. One with lots of tinkling bells that ring when I walk. How can I be in love? I don't know what love is."

His eyes began to look desperate as he turned his head to view his amused mate.

"Suck on this, Luca," she said, taking his hand and lovingly caressing it with her fingers.

For a moment, his eyes lit up and his mouth popped open. Could she be offering him a breast to nurse until he worked his problems out, like a good mate should? Or was it something else? Would she straddle his face and....

His thumb plopped into his mouth.

He had thought that she was going to use his hand for balance, he thought wryly as he glared at her.

"Well, all of your disjointed ramblings were giving me a headache and I need a nap. We'll talk again later after I've rested. Not all of us can comfortably sleep the day away, you know?"

With that, she turned her back to him and snuggled down into covers that smelled exactly like him.

"Will you do that shield thingy with the alcove?" she asked as she closed her tired eyes and enjoyed the pull of well-used muscles as she made herself comfortable. Luca was a lot to handle in the sexual department. He had overwhelmed her that time, and that was good. His mind was confused. If she kept him in a constant state of confusion, they would continue to get along just fine.

Her eyes closed as a faint purple flash filled the room and they were both encased within the protective shield.

Yup, getting along with Luca was easy, now that she knew the secret.

Beside her, Luca fumed as he furiously sucked at his thumb. How could he be in love, especially with that selfish shrew? He gave her the best hours of his life and she rolled over and went to sleep. If he had had her in the bed, he would have made her sleep in the wet spot. He was not in love with anyone, especially her. He was not in love.

Chapter Eleven

He was in love.

That was the only reason he could think of for his recent behavior. He calmly watched as Dark ransacked his office, wearing his clothes no less. Even though he had to admit, the comfortable drawstring pants and tunic, tied at the waist, mind you, never looked so good.

But she was disrupting his whole routine. He sighed as she took up more than her fair share of desk space and used his favorite quill to scratch on a sheet of his finest paper. She was composing a list of all who had a motive for killing her parents, and she placed his name at the top of the list.

"Please tell me again why my name is on that accursed list?" he asked as he bodily lifted her out of his chair and reclaimed his seat for himself and all of the other browbeaten men of the world.

"Because you are the most unlikely suspect," she again explained. Really, he could be so thick sometimes.

"Because I had no motive; that gives me the perfect motive?" he asked as he pinched the bridge of his nose. Another headache was forming and this one seemed to want to stick around a bit.

"Exactly, Luca!" she exclaimed, exasperated with him. She stood there and glared at him for taking the most comfortable chair in the room, but deciding that it wasn't worth the argument, she walked around the desk and took another chair.

"You are the last person anyone would suspect. Besides, everyone knows that the Vampesi are a dishonorable lot. You don't need a reason to murder at will."

She lifted her nose into the air and sniffed as she dared him to say anything.

"Well then, may I point out the oh-so-honorable actions of one certain Aunt Zinia? You remember her, don't you, Dark? The woman who would have killed you at the ceremony to claim your role as leader? Or the goon squad she sent running after you the night we met? I must remember to ask her where she received her training. With tactics, excuse me, *honorable* tactics like that, we Vampesi need to take lessons."

His eyes narrowed at her as the sarcasm rolled off of his tongue. Prejudiced little thing, wasn't she?

"That was not my aunt's doing, Lucavarious," she declared as she glared at her mate. Well, she had to say something but she couldn't actually defend those particular actions. But there was one thing that she was sure of. "My aunt didn't send those men after me."

"Perfect motive and opportunity, Dark. You would be a fool to discredit that so early in the game."

"Oh, I never said that she wasn't on the list, Luca. I just said that she never sent those men after me. That's not her style. She would have chased me down alone or with her daughter if she was going to stop me that way."

"Well, you should know your own family, I suppose. But remember, Dark, blood tells. I wonder if our children will be egomaniacs with more arrogance than the whole race has a right to claim?"

He sneered at her as he said that. He was again well rested and ready for anything that she could throw out.

"With you as their father," she replied with a saccharine smile, "that will be the least of their problems. They will have to worry about being humorless megalomaniacs with relationship issues."

"I am not humorless," he returned with some heat. "I called your flea-bitten relatives *family,* did I not? That, if I don't know what else it was, was humor."

"You bastard," Dark cried, with amusement sparkling in her eyes.

"Everyone seems to be under the impression that my parents were not mated. On the contrary, they were mated fair and true. I just have no idea why everyone insists that they weren't."

Before Dark could reply to that, a discreet knock sounded at the door and Luca took the opportunity to prevent Dark from retaliation.

"Enter," he gleefully called out, holding back a laugh at the disgruntled look on her face. Looked like she was about to let him have it, so the knock couldn't have come at a better time.

"Master?" a timid voice called as the door cracked open and a thatch of red hair showed clearly through.

"Oh, for crying out loud." Dark breathed as she leaned back in her chair and prepared to watch the show about to take place.

"You should have a care, B.B.," Luca sighed as he eyeballed his mate, wanting to gauge her reaction.

"Oh, I care for you, Master. If you have a need of me I am here."

She paused as a loud growl filled the room, then completed her announcements in a rush.

"But that is not why I'm here. There is a message, a request for an audience, Master."

"Who is it?" Luca asked in his imperious tones. The Ruler had returned and the teasing, long-suffering mate disappeared in a flash.

"Oh, who else can it be?" Dark grated out as she narrowed her eyes on the red-haired woman. "Show my aunt in."

"But it…"

"Show her in, human," Dark growled, her voice sounding dark and savage.

Before Luca could say anything, the door slammed on a frightened squeak and the sound of her footfalls racing away could be clearly heard.

"That is no way to improve Human/Wolfen relations, Dark," Luca said as he wryly eyed the closed door. "You could have at least given her time to explain."

"I gave her time to see to her own neck, Lucavarious. For that you should thank me."

With a sigh, Luca slumped back into his chair. He would have to replace B.B. and soon, for her own well-being. He couldn't understand this jealousy thing that Dark possessed. Did he not tell her that he would not violate his marriage vows? Was it not stamped in blood? Did she not wear his family seal ring on her finger, albeit tied with string to make it fit, but did she not wear it?

Shaking his head at the mystery of women, he turned to the stack of papers awaiting his attention on his desk. If Auntie was going to pop in, it might be a while before he could catch up with the business of the realm, so to speak.

There was silence, but for the sound of her quill scratching on paper for a few moments, then the door was flung open with a bang.

Both Luca and Dark jumped in their respective seats, Luca ready to encase the intruder in a force cage and Dark ready to claw their eyes out with her suddenly unsheathed claws.

"Luca," a voice boomed, and a tall man dressed all in black filled the doorway with his presence. "How long has it been, cousin?"

"Oh, hell," Luca sighed as he relaxed in his chair. Today was not his day. His aching head began to throb.

"And who is this delicious morsel that you have locked away in your dungeon? Hmm, very tasty too. Mind if I sample?

"Touch her and die," he growled out, the room growing uncomfortably hot with a sharp dry heat.

Dark was about to answer the mannerless stranger that had exploded into their midst, when Luca made that comment.

She turned startled eyes to him as he half rose in his seat. His eyes were flashing silver, a sure sign that his patience was being taxed and that she had but a moment to prevent this idiot from becoming locked in an airless box of his making.

Rising to her feet, she quickly yet calmly walked behind his desk and placed one hand on his shoulder.

"Introduce me to the imbecile before I have to hurt him."

"Imbecile?" the man whined as he took a cautious step forward. You would have to be a fool to miss the signs of killing anger pouring off of Luca, and he was no fool.

He tilted his head to the side and examined the woman who was beginning to defuse Luca's dark temper. She was a cute little thing, but there was something about her that he couldn't place.

The temperature in the room began to return to normal as Luca turned to face Dark. He realized that he had risen to a murderous rage at the thought of that man placing his fangs in his woman. That was…unlike him,

"Dark, this is my burden, Omnubius. Burden, this is my mate."

"Burden?" the man wailed as Dark examined him closely.

He was tall, taller, in fact, than Luca. His hair was a strange mixture of brown, black, red and gold and hung to his waist in a long straight fall. His skin was almost as dark as hers, if not darker, and his eyes were an odd shade of green. His black clothes, tight black leather pants and a silk shirt, strangely, fit him. His black leather coat dragged the ground and was lined in deep purple silk. Some might consider him attractive, but he was just okay-looking in her book.

"Since we are mates, Luca, do I have to share this burden with you? It seems a bit much to ask of me."

Dark noticed right away the arrogant way Omnubius carried himself and knew that he thought that he was God's gift to women. This one would be difficult to control. He even had the nerve to wink at her after she made that statement. If he was a cousin, then her thoughts had been confirmed. The whole family was stark raving nuts.

"Are you going to let your mate talk about your loving cousin like that, Luca?" he asked, a laugh escaping him. "I mean, after all we have been through together?"

"Dark, meet the family bones, fresh from the closet. I want to introduce you to possibly the only one of his kind, a Vampire made from the blood of my family's line."

"Vampire?" Dark asked, eyes going wide. "A real Vampire?"

"Well, he ain't Vampesi, and that's for sure," Luca retorted as he took his seat, calm once again. His bangles tinkled as he ran a hand through his thick curls. "So what do you want, Nubius, and make it quick. I have business to attend to."

"Is that any way to treat an honored guest?" he asked as he waltzed into the study and took Dark's chair. "And I have been planning this trip for some time, too. And then, how could you become mated and not let me, your only living blood relative, know about it?"

"You are related to me only due to the fact that some stupid ancestor let you steal a bit of blood from them. That is all we have in common, Nubius." Luca sighed as he rested his head on the back of his chair. "That is the reason I tolerate you. Who knows what trouble you might cause being unmonitored."

"I am affronted and shocked by those disparaging remarks," Nubius cried out, feigning heart pains as he slammed both hands across his chest. "I am hurt by your ungracious words, Luca. How could you? After all, we grew up together, kind of."

"Dark," Luca said as he opened his eyes and took in her stunned gaze, "I guess I should explain. The same year I was born, some relative of mine decided to feign being human and slept with this trickster. Needless to say, he helped himself to the goods and made off into the night. When my parents were killed, he stepped forth and helped name the ones responsible. I have no idea why he stayed."

"Because I long for these quaint family get-togethers Luca." Nubius laughed. "Besides, I have come home to stay. I missed you, cousin."

"Home?" Luca said, his voice low and dangerous.

"To stay?" Dark added as she again took in this man. "What female would be stupid enough to sleep with you and expect you to stick around?" she gaped, not meaning to blurt out what she was thinking but shock moved her tongue for her.

"Who said that it was a female, doll?" he purred as he waggled his eyebrows at her.

Her mouth dropped open in shock as she gaped at him.

"Home?" Luca again asked, ignoring their little aside for the moment. Was Nubius planning on staying?

"Home is where the heart is, dear man, and my heart is here, with you. Now, please let me in on why you mated so quickly. Is she knocked up? And what about the contract with the Wolfen? Did the daughter keel over or what?"

"She is just fine and dandy, you leather-clad male prostitute wanna be," Dark growled out as again the foolish man said something to make her temper jump.

"That is her? But where are the fangs and the fur?" Nubius asked, blinking up at her innocently. "Does she at least have a tail?"

"I'll show you fangs and fur," Dark growled, her voice deep and dangerous as she started to stalk around the room to get to him.

But Luca's laughter stopped her charge.

"And what is so funny?"

Luca was indeed amused by something. He had his head tossed back, laughing so hard that tears ran down his face.

He continued to laugh as the other two stared in confusion at him. He gripped his stomach and doubled over, laughing harder, until he had to pound on his desktop in hilarity.

"Well, cousin? Your mate is about to bite me and you sit there braying like a hyena. What is so funny?"

"I think...I think I may have to keep you around," Luca gasped as he wiped the tears from his face. "If she's ranting at you, she'll be too tired to start in on me. You two are funny."

There was silence as everyone in the room glared at him, but Luca was enjoying himself too much to care.

Then the door banged open again to be filled by the dark-haired figures of Zinia and Puaua, followed by a trembling B.B.

"Well, hell, the more the merrier,'" Luca chuckled as he watched the newbies enter the room.

"We are here, as we informed you we would be," Zinia began, but was cut off by B.B.

"Master, I thought you knew that they were coming. The Mistress said..."

"Out," Dark cried out in exasperation. This is what she got for not listening to full messages. Was it too archaic to kill the messenger?

"But Mistress, you said..."

"I know what I said, woman. I just can't call you B.B. Just go away. And if anyone else sends a message, tell him or her to wait. I have a feeling we are going to be busy for a while."

B.B. scurried from the room and again Zinia began another demanding speech.

"If you will clear the room of all peasants, we have family business to discuss."

"Auntie," Luca exclaimed, coming to his feet and walking over to the woman. "It's been ages."

"Cut the crap, bloodsucker. You know why I am here. There is a murder to be solved."

"Murder?" Omnubius' eyes lit up at the word. "There is trouble afoot and you didn't call me? Why are you calling that woman Auntie and who was offed? Murder is my specialty. Just call me Sherlock Jones."

"Zones," Dark corrected. "Sherlock Zones, and that is my aunt who can't recall protocol," she said, pointing ungraciously to Zinia.

"Phones," Zinia countered. "Sherlock Phones, and I remember protocol, I just thought that it would not be practiced in a Vampesi home."

"It's Holmes, and it was Dark's parents who were killed — poisoned, actually," Luca added as he took in the now grim faces of the Wolfen and the interested one of the Vampire.

"Have no fear; I will ferret out the killer," Nubius declared as he jumped to his feet.

"No, thank you. We have all of the Vampesi help we need," Zinia snorted as she glared at Luca. "If we can get him to take us seriously enough."

"Oh, my mate is taking it seriously, Aunt. He even put his name on the list of suspects."

"He did?" Puaua asked, finally stepping up from behind her mother.

"I did?" Luca asked as he again turned to his mate.

"Why?" this from Zinia who was now looking less aggressive and more concerned by the second.

"Because I am the most unlikely suspect?" Luca asked as he turned to gauge Zinia's reaction.

"Good thinking, Vampesi. You do have a brain," she nodded in emphasis at that point.

I will never understand the female thought processes, Luca sighed to himself as he saw Puaua nodding in agreement.

"Who is this enchanting goddess in our midst?" Nubius suddenly asked as he rose to his feet.

In a daze, he approached Puaua, neatly stepping around her mother to take her hand and gaze into her dark eyes as if he were in a trance.

"Unhand my daughter, Vampesi," Zinia exclaimed, arms akimbo.

"Vampire," he corrected, his eyes still locked with Puaua's, which seemed to take on a pleased light of their own. A blush began high on her cheeks as she gazed at the handsome man who noticed her.

"Vampire," Zinia growled as she turned to glare at Luca. "You let these unsavory characters defile your home?"

"Well, he is my cousin, uh, by blood, so to speak, Auntie. Please treat him with the same kindness that you have shown me."

"Dark," Zinia nearly screamed as she turned to her wayward niece. "Do you see him making goo-goo eyes at her?"

"And she's making them right back, Aunt, if you would care to stop snipping at my mate and pay attention to your own daughter."

"Well, I never," Zinia sniffed as she again turned to glare at Puaua and Nubius.

"Well, she did at least once," Luca drawled and Dark turned her angry eyes onto him.

"Behave, mate," she hissed as she watched amusement fill his eyes and a smirk touch his lips.

"Beautiful enchantress," Nubius crooned, "if you growl and bite for me, I'll be your bone."

"Oh, brother," Dark moaned. "That was terrible."

"Yet effective," Luca noted as Puaua rubbed her cheek against his hand and giggled up at him. "How come you never giggled at me?"

"Because I'm too busy trying my best not to kill you, Luca," she answered.

"Oh, yeah," he replied. "I forgot about that."

"Do something," Zinia nearly screeched as Nubius led Puaua off to a side wall for a bit of private conversation. "I come here to seek help in solving a murder and ensuring the protection of my people, and my daughter is kidnapped by some male prostitute claiming to be your cousin, and a Vampire to boot. What are you going to do about this?" She tapped her foot angrily as she glared at the man who was now the outlet for all of her anger. The man who now had the power of life and death over her people.

"I am going for a walk. No, no don't bother to come with me. I'm sure you all want to get...uh, acquainted again. Omnubius is harmless and he is a very good detective. He might give you an angle that you never thought of. No, don't thank me. I can see how grateful you are."

As he spoke, Luca eased his way around the table and towards the door.

"Dark, please stay and explain our strategy. I shall return, love puppy. Just entertain our guests as you see fit. You are a capable leader, I think, and I am perfectly comfortable leaving you in charge, uh, here. Until later then," he exclaimed as his hand reached the doorknob and he quickly exited the room.

The Garden had to be empty this time of night, and if it wasn't, it was a good night for a walk in the forest. A long walk.

He quickly padded barefoot down the hall, his tinkling bells announcing his presence to all those in residence, including sending a warning to the two who were secluded in a secret alcove.

"There will be trouble," one voice said in a whisper as they observed the closed door.

"Not necessarily," the second voice countered. "We might be able to take care of business and divert the blame. It is to our advantage. Take heart, comrade. We will have our day."

Chapter Twelve

Luca sat on his favorite cushion and inhaled the scents of Dark, the heady scent that permeated the air around his bench and blended in with the smell of the flowers that grew here in lush profusion. He dropped his head and closed his eyes and began to think.

Why was life so complicated? All he needed to do was to knock up his woman and rule her people. Now his home was filled with visiting Vampires, wild Wolfen women, and more confusion than he had ever experienced in his life. And he was beginning to enjoy it.

That was one of his problems. The other problem was Omnubius.

He had literally grown up with the Vampire and knew that Nubius only turned up when something was about to go down. Did any of this have to do with Dark and her parents, or was there a deeper threat? If that was the case, he had better figure out what was going on quickly, or he would be dealing with the mass anarchy that was slowly beginning to take over his home and throughout his realms.

And finally, what was going on between him and Dark? He was ready to take off Nubius' head for his typically inane yet totally joking comment about sampling his mate. This flash of anger was very uncharacteristic of him. He usually had better control and a better sense of humor about things. But the thought of any man with his hands on Dark made him...

Damn. *He was jealous.*

It was okay to care about Dark; after all, she was going to be carrying his heir, but to feel this deep wrenching emotion... It was something that he had never experienced before and could hardly put a name to. He wasn't sure he could cope with it. It had almost scared him, and for him to admit that meant that, even to himself, it had to be something serious. It could be love.

"So that's why I could smell you so clearly here," a deep husky voice said and drew his attention back to his surroundings.

Dark, as barefoot as he, carefully picked her way across the grass that appeared black velvet as night filled the glass room. The moon cast shadows that played a game of reveal and conceal with her features. The white tunic and pants almost glowed with life of their own as she slowly walked towards him.

"That was a dirty trick, Luca," she laughed as she stepped so close that inches separated them. She looked down at his tousled hair and resisted the urge to run her fingers through it, balling her hands into fists at her sides. "Leaving me in there with all the warring factions like that."

"I gave you a taste of leadership at its finest," Luca chuckled as his hands automatically and possessively went around her waist to pull her between his spread legs. "It's called delegation."

"Well, if that is leadership, I am suddenly a Vampesi princess. It was pure madness in there, Luca, and it was mean of you to leave me with those crazy people."

"Threw you to the wolves did I?" he chucked as she snarled lightly down at him.

"Your cousin is still in there making kissy faces at Puaua while my aunt is ready to declare war on the Vampires. Do you realize that he almost admitted to sleeping with a man just before hopping in on my sweet cousin? He is so…"

"Unnatural?" Luca offered as he gave in to the urge to press his head against her stomach and inhale her rich scent.

"Yes," Dark said as she sighed at the feel of her mate touching her. She ran her fingers through his curls like she longed to do, relishing her rights to do that. "Unnatural is the perfect word to describe that leather-clad freak show."

"Hey," Luca protested, lifting his head and opening his eyes to look up at her. "He is of my blood line, Dark. Unnatural he may be, but he is no freak show. Show a little respect."

"Like the same respect that he showed me?" she asked as her hands tightened in his hair, causing him to wince a little.

"Well, I thought it was funny," he said after a moment, kind of enjoying the sharp tugging of his hair. "Besides, Nubius will grow on you. He turned up at the right time too. He is kind of the troubleshooter in the family. That's the reason no one has hunted him down in all of these years and cut off his head. He is good at what he does. You have to be a good snoop to steal Vampesi blood, good at planning and carrying things out. Nubius is excellent at doing just that."

"I know he'd have to be," she said as she relaxed her hold on his hair and resumed stroking his scalp. "Vincent told me about the Vampires and the blood thing."

"So you have met our ever mysterious Vincent," Luca laughed. "What do you think of him?"

"He was pretty nice, I think. A little arrogant but nice."

Luca grunted as he again laid his head against her stomach. This was strangely comforting and relaxing. He enjoyed being in her presence. Was that love?

"What was that *grunt* supposed to mean?" Dark asked as she wrapped her arms around his head and snuggled him closer to her.

"It means that he should be on your list of suspects, Dark."

"That puny human, poisoning my parents? I don't think so, Luca. No human is a match for a Wolfen." She snorted with laughter as she made this declaration.

"Now who is letting her arrogance show?" Luca asked as he pulled back from her, serious once again.

"Why would a human want to hurt any member of my family, unless it's that red- haired woman you keep."

She took a step back and glared at her mate. This man was being unreasonable and difficult. A human plotting against the Wolfen? What would be the advantage?

"Maybe the humans didn't want this match, Dark. Remember, the Wolfen murdered many a human by accident and I am told that human flesh is considered quite tasty by some."

"That was years ago, Luca. Besides, they would have more to fear from the Vampesi or the Vampires if that were the case. You guys still live off of human blood."

"Not unless it is absolutely necessary, Dark," Luca said as he stood and towered over her. "We exist on synthetic blood and nutrients that are easily made and stored. Do you see any humans running in fear of us? No. Because we were the ones to come to the humans' rescue when your people were using them for lunch and a light snack."

"That's unfair, Luca," Dark said angrily, her brown eyes turning black. "That happened years ago. Wolfen do not hunt humans anymore."

"But it was bad, Dark. I know because I was there." His eyes turned inward for a moment as he began to recount what had happened almost four hundred years ago.

"The screams a person makes while being devoured alive is something that you never forget. There was a time when any human walking in the woods at night was fair game. The Wolfen could not tell Vampesi from human and really didn't care to differentiate between the two. I saw my fair share of humans being slaughtered and murdered senselessly. The war was hard on everyone, Dark, but the humans were brought to the brink of extinction. It will take them a long time to forget."

"I had nothing to do with that, Luca," Dark said quietly. She had no memories of these atrocities but she remembered well the stories that were told of the Vampesi. "But I recall walking into your bedchamber and seeing two Wolfen furs lining your floor. That was unnecessary."

"Of course it was necessary, Dark," Luca snapped as his eyes began to flash silver. "It was very damn necessary for my peace of mind. Those were the two bastards that murdered my father and later my mother."

Dark sucked in a deep breath as she reexamined her life-mate. What could she say? She refused to bear the responsibility for some others' actions, yet she wanted to comfort him in some small way.

"I sympathize with you, Luca," she finally said as she stared right into his piercing eyes. "Yet I don't know how you feel. The murderers of your parents are gracing the floor or storage area in your home. The monsters that killed an innocent man and woman, my parents, are still running free."

For a moment there was an intense stare-down, neither one wanting to back down, then Luca took her hand.

"I am sorry that this happened to your parents, Dark. Your father was an honorable man and your mother was lovely. They did not deserve to be murdered in this way. But we will find their killers, Dark. We have help now, in Nubius, and we will ferret out the killers and they will pay."

Dark nodded and looked away. She was placing her trust in her mate. He had experienced what she had and would help ease the grief that filled her heart, the thirst for vengeance that at times consumed her soul.

"So what is going on in my study?" Luca asked in an obvious attempt to change the subject. "They had better not have broken anything, Dark, or I will hold you personally responsible."

Luca didn't like to see black thoughts fill her mind. He had enough demons for the both of them. Her main job was to bear his children and not worry her pretty little head about the things in the past that could not be changed. It was not good for fertilization.

"Auntie is going home but will return tomorrow with a list of possible suspects. She is also checking who was chasing me the night that we met. She is still angry about Puaua and Nubius hitting it off so well, but she will accept his help if I command it. But she did say one mating with undesirables was enough for any family," she chortled.

"Who said anything about a mating?" Luca asked, waggling his eyebrows at her.

"Nubius wouldn't dare compromise her virtue," Dark growled, suddenly the fierce protector of her people. "If he did, it wouldn't matter if he has slept with men in the past because he would never be able to poke another woman again."

"Woo-hoo. Savage warrior." Luca laughed as he took in her defensive stance and dark, angry eyes. She looked ready to go to battle over her cousin's virtue. Must be hormones.

"Don't joke, Lucavarious. He might hurt her."

"Omnubius has never harmed an innocent, Dark," he assured her as he pulled her stiff body into a warm embrace. "But if she is not so virtuous, well, that is another matter altogether."

"He had better not mess with her, Luca. Or he leaves a eunuch," she growled into his chest as she wrapped her arms around his waist.

"He is the best detective that we could have, Dark, and if he can help us, all the better. That leaves us more time to fulfill the terms of our contract."

Dark said nothing, but decided to enjoy the moment. For once she and Luca weren't arguing and she wasn't looking around for an object to cosh him over the head with.

"Is that all you want to do with me, Luca?" she asked, looking up at him from beneath her lashes. "I can think of so many other things that we can do here in this garden. It's rather quite…nice, you know."

"I know," he said, amazed that his body was hardening again against her stomach. How many times had they done…it… in the past two days?

"And there is that contract…" she trailed off.

Luca sighed as he again took stock of all his body's aches and pains. His back felt like someone was twisting his spine in figure eights and using the muscles there for bongo lessons. His thighs complained every time he moved and even worse, his hips felt bumped out of joint. His skin was oversensitive in places she loved to scratch and bite; not that he was complaining all that much, but the worst was what was left of his manhood. Was it possible to get calluses on one's penis, he wondered as that stupid body part again showed off and rose to the occasion? When would it learn? Hell, when would *he* learn? This woman was dangerous, and his body was too slow to comprehend what his mind was yelling at him.

He sighed as his body prepared itself for its suicide mission.

"How long will you be in heat?" he asked, almost desperately.

"Oh, another month or so. Then we will know if I'm pregnant or not. But I have to warn you, when a Wolfen woman carries, we get very sexually aggressive."

Luca gulped.

"Yup, our sex drive increases dramatically. It has been said that Wolfen women often cause injury to their mates before the whole thing is done and over with. Some women have been known to crave sex while they were in labor, but I think that that would be too uncomfortable for the baby, don't you? Luca, are you all right? Suddenly you don't look so good."

* * * * *

Omnubius sighed with pleasure as the door closed on the Wolfen women and he was left alone in the study, Luca's study.

Taking a seat in Luca's favorite chair, he sighed again as he lifted his booted feet onto the desktop. He crossed his hands behind his head and sighed with true pleasure. Luca always knew how to live.

He ignored the door opening a crack and the person who entered after carefully checking the area. The room was empty so the person who called for him entered without fear.

"So, did you see her? Is she not as despicable as I have said?"

"Yes, you were right about that, but I never expected her to be so cute."

"Keep your mind on your business, Vampire. Now that you have met her and have seen the one she is trying to protect, what do you propose that we do?"

"I think, gorgeous, that you should stop being jealous and let me do my job. I know what must be done and I am just waiting for something before I play my hand."

"What are you waiting for, Omnubius? You know that she probably murdered her own family and you know who's next on her list. You have to do something."

"I need proof, Red," Nubius said calmly as he opened his eyes and observed the red-haired woman standing in front of him. "I can't justify my actions to him without having solid proof. He may be family by blood, but I am still under his rule. If you think that he would hesitate to kill me in a heartbeat, you are wrong. Give our boy more credit than you are giving him now."

"But, Nubius, you can see the danger that we are all in. If she has her way...Damn that contract. If it wasn't for the contract, things would continue like they have been."

"Calm yourself, B.B.," Nubius sighed as he dropped his feet to the floor and rose to his full height. "I know what this means to you, and believe me, she will be stopped, Wolfen or not. But you have to let me do things my way. I need her to trust me, and then I can take what I need from her. But until then, keep your eyes peeled. I don't need Luca getting suspicious. It would be the end of all of this if he were to find out what is going on under his roof. He would not be a happy bastard, not at all."

Reassured, B.B. nodded then turned for the door.

"If you need anything, Nubius, and I mean anything at all, just let me know. You know where I am."

She quietly strode to the door and disappeared down the hall, her footsteps silent on the hard marble.

"Now, how do you kill a Wolfen?" Nubius said out loud as he strode to the window of his cousin's curious round room and stared out into the land, the people that he longed to become a part of. "Poison is too trite, draining their blood too dangerous for a Vampire, and beating them to death too obvious. A slit throat seems to be the best option here," he mused as he looked down to examine the long pinkie nail that grew on his right hand. "Yes, one quick slice and the rest is history. Too bad she is so damn cute with that black hair and all. I have always been partial to dark hair. Who knows, maybe I'll get laid before I have to do the deed. At least that gives me memories."

Silently he stood in the window and felt dawn approach. Soon he would have to take cover in the chambers that Luca always left prepared for him, to protect him from the burning rays of the sun. Soon his plans would come to fruition, thanks to the one that had called him there. Soon, the halls would run red with Wolfen blood and the truth would be revealed. He just hoped that "soon" would give him enough time to complete all that needed to be done.

"Damn, it's hard being a Vampire," he sighed as he turned to seek his sleeping chamber. "But it's also a hell of a lot of fun."

Chapter Thirteen

"I want to see where this synthetic blood is made, Luca."

Dark looked across her plate at the dining room table to her mate, who sat sipping from a brass goblet.

The midday sun was shining brightly overhead and she had just finished tucking into a rather large lunch. Being with Luca worked up an appetite. Besides, she decided that he needed a break. He was starting to look decidedly wan and that wouldn't do.

"Why?" he asked as he peered over the edge of the metal cup at her. "Think I have a human bleeding facility hidden on the second floor? Equipped with several torture devices to draw the best blood from humans fed a special high iron diet, no doubt."

"Nothing like that, Luca," Dark said as she frowned at him, her eyes flashing annoyance. "I just wanted to know more about you. That's all."

"Well then, feel free to ferret out all of my little secrets. That is, if Vincent hasn't given them all away by now."

He had noticed the special attention that the human had showed his mate and was a bit annoyed by it. His first inclination was to simply rip the man's eyes from their sockets, but then he regained control over his emotions. If this was love making him react like an untried youth, then this love thing was the pits.

"Only you know all of your secrets, Luca." Dark sighed as she rolled her eyes towards the ceiling. "Otherwise I would know by now why you have two sets of fangs and are addicted to silver."

"I am addicted to silver because it hurts so good going in," he purred at her, hoping to catch her off guard and start another fight. She was being too unpredictably conversational and he didn't like it. With a spitting, snarling Dark, you could anticipate her next move. The biddable Dark was just too unpredictable. "And my second set of fangs is for me to know about and you to find out."

Take that, he thought as he fought against the urge to poke his tongue out at her. It may be childish, but boy, it felt so good.

"What is it with you and pain anyway, Luca?" she finally asked, disregarding his attempts to make her angry. She was burrowing too close for comfort, inside that metal organ he called a heart and he didn't like it. He would probably like it even less if she didn't take the bait, so therefore she ignored his barbs. It annoyed him more.

"Pain and pleasure are relative terms, Dark," he explained after it was obvious she was going to ignore any open invites to a fight. "The pain takes you to a higher plane of existence, and then you get a greater understanding of yourself and your world. That becomes the pleasure. Knowing that you controlled it to the end, that you conquered it; it changes you."

"That is sick, Luca," she cried out as she turned up her nose in distaste.

"On the contrary, Dark, do your fangs bursting free from the prison of your gums cause pain? Yet don't you relish the ability to do so, for the change it brings is greater than any discomfort that you feel? Does it not hurt to have talons exploding from your fingertips, but does it also not bring comfort, knowing that once you get past the pain, your body will transform into something that is spectacular?"

He took another sip from his goblet as he stared at her, watching her compute all that he had told her, and comparing it with what she knew to be true.

"I guess I never thought of it quite like that, Luca," she said after a moment. "But I'm talking about all of those pierced body parts of yours, and you are thinking about piercing something else too. Where do you draw the line, Luca? Just how many holes does your body need?"

"Enough to satisfy me," was his quiet answer.

"But Luca," she began, "when will you be satisfied?"

"Maybe never, Dark," he said as he placed his goblet on the table with a click. "Maybe I will never experience enough pain to purify my soul and grant me greater understanding. But know this. In the next few days, I will add yet another silver adornment to this body, this shell that I exist in. So tell me, babe," he asked as he leered at her. "Where should the next one go? The penis or the nipple? Your call."

He broke out into laughter as she snorted and rolled her eyes again.

"What? Afraid that your walking, talking vibrator will stop dispensing pleasure?" he laughed as he watched her snarl at him. "I hear that it can be better that way."

"Show me the blood-makers, Lucavarious," she groaned. "And if you pierce my penis, I'll have to hurt you. The only holes you are getting there are the ones that I bite there myself."

"Oh, baby," he howled as he rose to his feet. "Talk dirty some more. It turns me on."

"Oh, spare me," Dark groaned as she, too, rose to her feet to accompany him. "You have the sickest sense of humor, Luca. No wonder the humans disappear during the day. No one wants to be around you."

"But you love me," he purred as he took her hand and led her out into the hall. "You know you do."

"Who said anything about love, Vampesi?" she asked as she sniffed and tossed her nose in the air. "I just happen to lust after your body. You have great thrusting ability in your hips, even though you don't look like much."

"Hey," he growled.

But she turned her back to him and imperiously demanded, "Which way?"

Silently he pointed the way as he fumed.

She didn't love him, huh? Well, if he was going to suffer true love, she was damn well going to suffer with him.

With that determination, he pulled her down the hall to a door near that garden room. After staring at her for a moment, he waved his hand and there was a grating sound as a portion of heavy, solid, stone wall slid back, exposing a narrow staircase that led up to a dark maw.

"After you," he nearly growled as he urged her through the doorway.

"Cold, dark and dank," she muttered as she stepped inside and heard the sound of the stone wall dragging itself back into place. "Just like you, Luca. You must have designed it yourself. It shows."

He muttered under his breath something that sounded like, "Ill-mannered broad," but she couldn't be too sure.

Confidently, she led the way up the staircase, her Wolfen eyes automatically adjusting to the dark and her sense of smell finding…fresh air?

"Luca? What is up…?"

"Keep going," he sighed as he placed one hand on the small of her back to keep her moving. "All of your questions will be answered soon."

Dark gasped as she walked into a room filled with lights, large open windows, and…and…and…machinery?

"I don't understand," she said as she stepped further into the room.

Along one rear wall was a bank of small computers, cheerfully gurgling and grinding as information processed. A large silver-metal door, obviously of the refrigerated kind, stood against the next wall. There was a small glass window that was frosted over and gave no clue as to what was inside.

"What's not to understand?" he asked as he stepped into the sterile environment. "We are synthesizing blood. What did you expect? Pedestals and Grimoires filled with magical spells? Step into the new age, Dark. The days of hunger-wracked Vampesi flooding the streets at night in search of hapless victims is so passé. We develop our own blood here. Besides, have you seen what the humans were putting into their bodies before the Great War? AIDS, drugs, tattoo ink. You'd have to be a fool to want to ingest some of that stuff."

That kind of left Dark stupefied. She turned towards him and shook her head.

"Damn, there goes another great story. If you keep killing all of the myths, Luca, I'm going to start believing that you aren't the monster that we thought you were."

"Don't do me any favors," he snorted as he walked over to check on a computer sheet.

"So what do you synthesize blood from?" she asked as she trailed after him.

"Cow's blood," he answered as he made a few adjustments.

"Cow's blood?" she asked, interested but respectful.

"Yes, cow's blood from very special cows. They are fed a strict diet of nutrients before a sample is drawn. Then we use the platelets in the blood to make up plasma. The plasma is enriched with hemoglobin and other things that our blood lacks, and flavor is added. I prefer Wolfenberry myself," he said as he turned from the computers and leered at her for all that he was worth.

An unexpected blush lit her features and she quickly turned towards the windows, inhaling the fresh air.

"So why the secrecy and security?" she finally asked when her hormones dropped down to a normal level; well, normal for a Wolfen female in heat.

"Here, we make enough blood to supply all of my people in this region. Using computers, we send out the recipe, as it were, to my people who cannot be reached or accessed easily. If someone were to tamper with this computer or this supply, it could be detrimental to my people. We would have to revert to the old ways of depending on humans for the blood that we need to sustain us, and no one wants that to happen."

She nodded her understanding. By doing this, Luca had protected both his people and the humans and maintained peace between the two.

"It is a clever plan, Luca," she said. "When did you start it?"

"I didn't. My mother did," he answered quietly.

"Your mother?"

"She was a great woman and believed in peace. She implemented this plan just before the great wars of the 2000's began. I was almost thirty years old and went along with her plan despite my misgivings. I made sure to set an example after the wars were over and my people began to regroup. It was one of the reasons that my parents started that contract. To maintain the peace with Wolfen as we had with the Humans."

"And look how well it's working," Dark laughed as she crossed over to him and took his hands in hers.

He automatically smiled down at her, loving the way she moved, the way she smelled, just everything about her. *Love?*

No, *like*. He *liked* it. He liked it a whole lot. Who the hell was he kidding? He was falling in love.

"For now, mate," he nearly growled as he accepted his sorry state and sighed deeply with acceptance. Nothing he could do about it now. Nothing but make sure that she fell with him. He would see to it. He was not going down alone. She was going down with him, kicking and screaming if need be. Actually, he kind of liked the kicking and screaming part.

"Let us adjourn to the study, Dark," he said before he could lower his head and take her succulent lips in a kiss that would further test the endurance of his beleaguered body. "We have a list of suspects to complete."

He silently chuckled as he saw the flaring heat in her eyes dim as reality again intruded.

"Yes, Luca. Time to get some work done."

* * * * *

"Who's there?" B.B.'s quiet voice splintered the oppressive silence that filled the sleeping chambers of her master and his mate.

She had gone into their room to change the sheets and repair any damage that they had wrought during the night. But someone had beat her into the room and was now in the master's bathroom.

"Again, I say, who's there? No one is supposed to be in here, save those who personally serve the master."

"B.B.?" a low male voice called out. "Is that you?"

"Vincent?" she asked, relieved when she heard the familiar voice. For a moment, she had feared that someone was trying to do the master harm, and that she could not allow.

"Yes, B.B., it is I. I have come to place a few special flowers in the bathing chamber, in honor of our new mistress."

"That was sweet of you Vincent," B.B. said as she continued with her duties, stripping the bed and placing fresh white linens on the firm mattress. "But I could have done it for you."

With her back to the door, she didn't see the shadow race past or feel nothing more than a prick as something stabbed into the back of her neck.

"Ouch," she gasped, slapping at the area where a bug must have bitten her. "I hope that woman doesn't have fleas or something."

"Fleas?" said a voice right beside her, causing her to jump and turn as she grabbed for her heart.

"Vincent. Make some noise when you approach me like that. You almost gave me a heart attack." As it was, her heart was racing as she drew in a deep calming breath.

"I'm sorry, B.B.," he said as he stepped back and placed a balancing hand on her shoulder. "I truly meant no harm. And to make up for it, try some of this."

"What is it?" she asked as he withdrew a small flask from the pocket of his pants.

"Special wine. I mixed it up myself, knowing that our new mistress would not partake of the master's libations. I left a bottle of it in the bathroom in hopes that it will please them both."

"You are too nice, Vincent," B.B. laughed as she took the flask and downed a healthy draught. "It is delicious."

"Have all you like," he said as he smiled serenely at her. "I have more than enough. I have enough for everyone in the castle."

"Suddenly, I don't feel so well," B.B. breathed, as instead of slowing down her heart, the wine seemed to speed it up. Her breath began to rasp in her chest as she collapsed back onto the freshly made bed.

"Vincent?"

But then she could not see him. The room was blurring and swirling all around her. Her stomach lurched as she tried to pull herself up, but she only succeeded in rolling off of the bed into the tangled linens that lay at her feet on the floor.

"Vinn," she slurred as she fought her way to her knees. "What...you...do...me?"

"One problem out of the way," a voice above her said quietly as she felt a hand on her neck. "And this one is about gone. That stuff is effective. Now we have to find a place to take out the trash."

Nooooooo. B.B. silently screamed as she felt herself hefted over a strong shoulder and carried off.

Now she could hear nothing, see nothing, feel nothing. Her body was paralyzed with more than fright. She could not move a muscle.

Please, God, she begged. *Please protect me. Please wake me up. Please let me be dreaming.*

"Bury it with the others," a low voice commanded, and in vain, B.B tried to move, to wiggle, to show some sign of life.

Please, God, she prayed again as she felt the cool night air against her skin. *Please touch me and know that I still live.*

She could smell the night air, fresh and sharp against her body. She could hear the call of the owl and the panting breaths of the person who carried her as he struggled with her dead weight.

Oh, God, not dead.

Then she was placed on something hard and cold and she began to struggle and scream within. Her heart felt as if it would explode through her chest, and her brain began to seize.

Move! She screamed to the body that now betrayed her. A hand, a foot, a finger. Anything.

Then she felt the sad sigh as the person crossed her hands over her chest and whispered a prayer.

Please don't do that, she mentally screamed. *Don't do that to me. Please don't bury me! I'm not dead. I'm not dead!!*

But as the first fall of gravelly soil caressed the skin of her thighs she began a horrible wail that could be heard only by her.

Noooooooooooooo. I'm alive. I'm not dead. I am alive.

Chapter Fourteen

"Well, I am just about out of ideas," Dark sighed as she settled more comfortably in her chair.

She peeked over the desktop at Luca, who sat contemplating paperwork that he had put off for far too long.

"What are you doing?" she asked as she noticed him scribbling away, an almost content look upon his face.

"I am preparing a list of all the rents and taxes due," he said as he lost himself in the figures before him. "That way I can tell how the population has increased and how much help each region will need for the winter. You know? Road repairs, building repairs, barn repairs, that sort of thing."

"You handle all of that?" she asked, a bit of awe telling in her voice. The Wolfen had always admired the well-organized properties and neat roads in all Vampesi land. She had no idea that it wasn't because he demanded the work from his people as any absolute ruler had the might to do. He actually paid to have these things taken care of. Something else positive to add to his growing list of glowing credentials.

"What did you think I did, Dark? Whip the peasants if they refused to hop to? Or maybe I would stake a few out for some hungry Wolfen to come upon and devour?"

His eyes glinted with dark humor as he peeked at her from beneath his lashes. Yup, the scowl was in place and his mate was glowering at him. This was fun.

"Well, of course I did," she finally returned. "With your swelled head, I'm surprised you don't demand virgin sacrifices to be delivered to you with your evening meal."

Flipping through some papers, he intently scanned them before seriously looking up at her with serious eyes. "Not this quarter."

With a snort, Dark adjusted her body in the chair and rather daintily rolled her eyes at Luca.

"What? Not what you wanted to hear?" he asked, a smile in his voice.

"What I want to hear," she said, "is that you have discovered who killed my parents and why. There still might be some threat, Luca, and I want to know if we are in danger."

Luca's lips spread into an engaging grin. Something suddenly made him very happy.

"What?" she asked as her mouth automatically spread into a matching smile. He looked so happy that the grin was contagious.

"You said *we*," he chuckled as he shuffled his papers together and set them aside.

"Yeah, so?"

"You are trying to protect me," he pointed out, his grin turning into a full smile that bared most of his teeth.

"So?"

"You care," he said, then neatly lifted her papers from in front of her. "So, what have you got?"

"What?" For a moment she was dazed by his words. Of course she cared. If something should happen to him before they conceived, the whole contract would be null and void. Besides, she was beginning to enjoy his company. Luca could be witty and intelligent, if he tried hard enough.

"What have you found?" he asked again, slowly, as if he was speaking to a lackwit. "What clues to this mystery have you uncovered?"

"Well," she began, snapping herself back to the present, "I have discovered that you would benefit most from my parents' death, but only if you killed me, too. And since you had ample opportunity to do away with me and you haven't, you aren't the killer."

"I am so pleased that you think me capable of murder, but only for the greater good," he quipped as he shook his head at her reasoning. He would never understand the line of thought that women engaged in.

"Anyway," she said loudly ignoring his sarcasm, "my aunt would benefit from my parents' murder, but I don't think that she could follow through with it."

"And why not?" Luca asked as he looked down at the meticulous notes she had written across the page. "Women are just as capable of murder as men and sometimes more so. And she has a good motive; power."

"My aunt doesn't want power," Dark denied but Luca cut her off.

"Well what about her tantrum on our mating night? She would have killed you to prevent this marriage from taking place. Hell, she tried to kill me. Not that I'm complaining, mind you; I always loved aggressive women, but that woman is out for power. She tried to appoint herself our liaison. Oh yes, she has the hunger."

"But not enough of it to kill my father, her brother," Dark argued.

"Power-hungry people are capable of anything, Dark. It is best you remember that and stay on guard."

"I know my aunt, Luca. And she could never do a thing like that. She's not that selfish."

Before Luca could reply, the door slammed open and a furious Nubius filled the doorway.

"This is getting to be a habit, this barging in," Luca said to himself. Then to Dark, "Remind me to put the shield up next time. It's a damn shame that a man needs to shield himself in his own home."

"And speaking of selfish..." Dark drawled as Nubius stormed forward, a furious expression on his face.

"Okay, where is she?" he growled as he flipped his heavy mass of hair over his shoulder and slammed both hands on his waist. "What have you done with her?"

Saying nothing, Luca leaned back in his chair and lazily slung one leg over the arm; his favorite position for confrontation, Dark decided as she observed the cold mask of the Ruler slip into place.

Luca let his gaze travel over his irate "cousin" and he noted his agitation, his anger, and his closeness to his mate.

Again, Nubius was dressed in stark black, tight black leather pants, a sheer black shirt that exposed the planes of muscles in his chest, and a pair of short black boots.

"Something troubles you, Nubius?" he asked calmly as he steepled his fingers under his chin, his lethally sharp pinkie nails with their pierced bangles clicking softly together. Luca was lethally calm and the air around them chilled with his growing temper.

"You are damned right, Lucavarious," he growled as he slammed both fists on the desk and leaned onto them, bringing his stormy green eyes close to those of his cousin. "B.B. Where is she?"

"And I am supposed to know the whereabouts of my Blood Bank, Nubius?" he asked, still and controlled in the face of Omnubius' anger.

"She serves you, Luca," Nubius ground out as he continued to glare. "She was last seen entering your chambers, so yeah, I would assume that you would know the whereabouts of your body servant."

"Why so interested, cousin?" Luca asked, still clicking his nails lightly. "Been breaking into my bank?"

"We were supposed to talk this evening, Luca," Nubius said as he again rose to his full height and turned away to glare at Dark. "She had some information to tell me about a certain young Wolfen in our midst, and she was a bit frightened."

He began to pace the floor in his agitation. Nothing was going right this evening.

"What could she have told you about a Wolfen, Nubius?" Dark asked, sitting up as she took in his state. This could be a clue. Did that bubble-headed woman know something that they did not? It could happen. Humans were so non-threatening that most forgot that they were even around.

"Nothing to worry your pretty little head over, cousin," he said as he again looked at Dark. Funny, she didn't look like a cold-blooded killer.

"Then why barge into my office and disrupt my night, Nubius, if there is nothing to be concerned about?" Luca asked, drawing Nubius' attention back to him once again.

"She missed our rendezvous, Luca. And no, I was not sampling your supply, nor was I screwing her. She just wanted to tell me something important and now I can't find her. Nobody can. I assumed now that you were mated..."

"You assumed that she was killed off quietly and discreetly. Am I right?" Dark growled, as she stood in front of her chair. Her deep brown eyes were beginning to turn black with her mounting anger. *Nobody* impugned the honor of her mate and lived, not even dubious family members with more hair than sense.

The temperature in the room abruptly shot back to normal as Luca was startled out of his temper by her defense. His face still showing no emotion, he sat back to observe this event. The more he saw her flip out over someone insulting him, the more hope it gave him of making her love him back, if it was actually love that he felt, and not heartburn.

"I didn't say that," Nubius snarled as he again began to pace.

"No, but you implied it," Dark snarled back before turning to face Luca. "I think we should all go and look for Miss Blood Bank of the Year, and find out what she has to say, especially if it is about Wolfen."

"You don't...." Nubius began, but Luca cut him off.

"That is an excellent idea, Dark," Luca said as he dropped his leg and came to his feet. "I think we should all go and look for our B.B. Suddenly, I share your concern. If Nubius thinks something might have happened to her, we must intervene. Nothing is above the welfare of our people."

"Well said," Dark concurred as she turned a nasty smile onto Nubius. "If the Vampire is concerned, then we must also show caring in the like. By all means, let us search for her."

"Oh, hell. Just great. Just absolutely wonderful," Nubius growled as he started towards the door. "Let's just go look for her, but leave the Lady and Lord of the manor bit here, if you don't mind? That much sweetness is making me sick."

"Sweet? How dare you call us sweet?!" Dark snarled in her most nasty tone, the one usually reserved for Luca. "We are mean, murderous tyrants that would stop at nothing to have our way. Even doing away with an insignificant human who poses no threat whatsoever."

"Point taken," Nubius growled as he turned at the door to glare at his cousin's mate. "Now if we can leave the theatrics behind, we might find the woman and I can get on with my night."

"Wild party in the village to attend?" Luca asked, sarcasm dripping from his every word.

"Wild murder to solve," Nubius retorted as he held the door open for Dark and Luca to pass.

"Anyone we know?" Dark snorted as she passed with her nose in the air. She doubted that the peacock Omnubius could solve the mystery of how much oil it took to ease himself into those leather pants he was so fond of.

"How bad is it?" Luca asked quietly, placing a restraining hand on his cousin's shoulder as Dark stormed ahead of them.

"From what I have found out," Nubius said as he looked down at his cousin, "very bad. Watch your back."

Luca nodded and released Nubius to precede him into that hall.

If Omnubius was warning him to stay on guard at all times, it had to be serious.

* * * * *

"Well, she was definitely here," Dark said as she lifted her nose in the air and sniffed. "As usual, this room is saturated with her smell. You would think that she would get a life now that you are mated." she said as she turned to Luca.

They were all standing in the last place that B.B. had been seen, their bedchambers, looking for any clues to her disappearance, and thus far they were able to confirm that she had been there.

"Well, your grasp of the obvious always seems to impress me more and more, Dark," Luca drawled in retaliation for her small insult to his human. "I mean, with the fresh sheets on the bed and the place straightened up, how did you ever determine that she was here, performing her duties? You are amazing, with your Wolfen powers and all. Is there nothing that you can't do?"

"Oh shut up," she growled as she turned to scent the rest of the room. His sarcasm was amusing when they were alone, but she refused to be baited with the Vampire in the room.

"What else can you find, Dark?" Nubius asked, growing more concerned with each second. While they bickered like an old mated couple, B.B. could be in grave danger.

"There was someone else here with her, a man, or was it two men?"

"Let me check," Luca said as he stepped forward and closed his eyes in concentration.

"You don't have the tracking ability, Luca," Dark began but Nubius shushed her.

"He knows what he is doing," he said in a firm voice. "Let him do his job."

Dark subsided into silence as she watched her mate. As he stepped into the center of the room, he tossed back his head and slowly inhaled the scents in the room.

There was his Dark, smelling wild and sweet, the strong yet complex smell of the Vampire, his own spicy scent that he rarely thought about, the almost tangy smell of B.B., and the cool smell of Vincent.

"Vincent?" he asked out loud as he continued to scent the area.

"Yes, that's who it was," Dark cried excitedly. "That's the scent that I couldn't place. I knew I smelled someone familiar."

"And flowers?" Luca again spoke. Yes, he smelled the flowers from the garden room.

"Flowers?" Dark asked as she again began to circle the room. "Yes, flowers. It's coming from the bath."

She disappeared into that cavernous room, leaving the men to puzzle the mystery as to why lovable Vincent was in their sleeping chambers.

"Vincent? The human butler for this place?" Nubius asked as he looked at his cousin. "Are you sure?"

"One and the same," Luca assured as he inhaled deeply trying to place the flowery scent that he smelled.

"And the flowers?" he asked nervously.

"Found it," Dark cried from the bath. "I found the source of the flowers and it has Vincent's smell all over it."

Dark emerged with a glass in one hand and a bottle in the other.

"Looks like Vincent left us a mating present, well, me a mating present. It's a special wine, I think. That's where the flower smell is coming from.

"Flowers? In wine?" Luca asked as he again tried to decide what the unusual flower smell was. It had come from the garden, that much he was sure of, but what *was* it?

"Yes, Luca." Dark laughed as she watched him trying to puzzle out the herb. "Flowers are used for flavorings, to enhance the flavor of the drink."

She poured herself a small glass of the wine before lifting the glass to her nose to sample the bouquet.

"And this smells delightful. Do you know that half of the flavor comes from the smell?"

"Herbs for wine?" Luca mused as he watched her lift the glass to her lips. "I don't have many herbs there. But I do have some potent...Dark, no."

In a flash, Luca was across the room, knocking the glass from her hand, splattering her white tunic with the red wine, shattering the glass with his swipe.

"Luca? What that hell!" Dark cried as she reflexively jumped back, letting go of the bottle.

"The bottle," he roared to Nubius as his momentum carried him away from the falling bottle.

"On it," Nubius cried as he, with catlike skill and grace, dove forward. With one lunge, he hit the ground, catching the bottle seconds before it slammed into the marble flooring of the room, saving it from shattering on impact. A little wine sloshed over the tiny rim of the bottle, but nothing else spilled out.

"Did you drink any of it?" Luca cried as he regained his balance and grabbed Dark by the shoulders, shaking her a bit with his intensity. "Did you swallow any of it?"

"Take your hands off of me, Lucavarious," Dark growled back and she raised both hands to push at his chest. He was crowding her and manhandling her and she didn't like it. "Are you out of your tiny little Vampesi mind?"

"Poison!" he shouted as he shook her again for emphasis. "That flower smell was poison and I need to know if you ingested any of it."

"Poison?" she muttered, suddenly feeling a bit weak in the knees. "There was poison in that glass? Someone tried to poison me?"

"Did you drink any of it?" Luca again demanded as his grip tightened on her shoulders.

"No, Luca. I didn't. You saved me. Are you sure it was poison?"

"Pretty sure, Dark," he sighed as he pulled her to his chest and hugged her to his heart. "Pretty sure, Dark."

Someone had tried to kill her in her own home. She was feeling safe here, but now that feeling was gone. Someone had tried to kill her.

"You saved me then?" she breathed against his chest.

"I will always save you, Dark. If there is life in my body, I will come for you." His arms trembled as he held her, quivering with the fear of a lonely, endless existence without her. This had to be love. "I will always keep you safe."

He would keep her safe, she realized. Yes, there was safety in his arms. "I just realized something, Luca," she said as she pulled back a bit to look up at him. "Safety isn't with a place; it's with you. You keep me safe."

Suddenly, his trembling stopped just as quickly as it started. *Bingo.* Her declaration had to mean that she loved him. But did she know it yet? A slow smile took over the concerned look upon his face as he realized what he had here. He knew something that she didn't know. She was falling in love with him. Good. That would make his job a whole lot easier. Soon he would make her admit to loving him, then his life would return to something that resembled normal once again.

"I will always keep you safe," he again vowed as he looked deeply into her dark, luminous eyes. He was lowering his head for a thank-you-for-saving-my-life-kiss, when the clearing of a throat interrupted him.

"If we are done with the sentiment and the lovey-dovey mumbo jumbo, can we get back to the matter at hand? Someone tried to kill Dark and all roads lead to Vincent."

Pulling away from Dark, Luca suddenly realized that he was angry, mad, pissed even. "Someone tried to kill my mate."

The temperature in the room suddenly dropped so low that even Nubius began to shiver and cautiously backed away from Luca. Dark stepped forward, but the force of his anger even held her at bay.

"Luca?" she began, but suddenly his anger exploded into a shattering of purple ice.

The forces of the explosion almost knocked her off of her feet, but by sheer will, both she and Nubius remained standing.

"That ungrateful sack of blood and guts tried to murder my mate, my woman."

"Luca?" Nubius said carefully as he approached the enraged man. He had seen this kind of anger only once before, when Luca found that his parents had been murdered, and then it wasn't a pretty sight. But now that Luca had had about four hundred more years to grow into his power, who knew what could happen?

"I took him in, gave him a job, something to live for."

"Yes, you did," Nubius agreed, hoping to calm his anger a bit.

"I took care of his family, treated him like a brother."

"Yes, you did, but you are not really sure, Luca, that it was him."

"And this is the thanks I get? He tried to murder the woman that I love?"

"Love?" Dark cried out, something between joyous surprise and out-right disgust in her voice. *Love?* Who needed love? This was an arrangement of mutual sexual satisfaction with the benefits of rulership thrown in. There was no love here. She liked the guy, and he was cute, in a boorish arrogant master-of-all-I-survey kind of way. But that's all it was. Love was not here.

"Be sure, cousin, before you go and start splattering people all over the place," Nubius soothed after shooting Dark a, uh, *dark* look.

"Yes, we must first make sure," Luca chanted, almost in a fury of anger as he stalked forward and out of the room. "I have a few questions to ask Vincent, then the bloodletting shall began. This castle will know wrath that has never before been felt in all the years of my rulership. No one flaunts my authority, attempts to murder anyone that belongs to me, and lives through the night."

"Oh, dear." Dark ran out of the room, following a man who was so angry he glowed purple, and trying to think of ways to defuse the situation. She had liked Vincent, too. She would hate to have to order someone to scrub him off of the walls. "Oh, Lord."

"Oh, shit," Nubius agreed as he, still carrying the incriminating bottle of wine, raced after them, trying to come up with ideas about how to prevent Luca from murdering Vincent until he found out more about B.B. This thing was beginning to get out of control.

Chapter Fifteen

"Vincent!"

Luca's bellow almost caused the castle to shake.

"Vincent, I want a word with you."

No one had ever seen Lucavarious so angry in recent memory. His eyes glittered silver and black and the very air around him snapped and sparkled with purple flashes of energy. Ice coated the walls where he passed, chilling every person who was near, causing many to scramble away to their private corners and cower in fear and uncertainty.

Dark raced just behind her mate, trying in vain to calm his anger while Omnubius brought up the rear, quiet and thoughtful as he carried the glass bottle of wine with great care.

A strange procession they made as they crossed the halls of the castle and made their way unerringly to the kitchen where a subdued Vincent stood waiting.

"Master?" he asked as he looked up from the large kitchen table and caught his breath. Never a more fearful apparition had he ever seen. The master looked about ready to explode with rage, and the new mistress had a warning in her lovely dark eyes.

"Vincent, come here," Luca ground out. "I want a word with you."

"Luca," Dark began, but he cut her off.

"I want to know about some wine," Luca growled. "I want to know all about it."

"Wine?" Vincent gasped as he lost what little color he had left in his face.

"The wine in this bottle, human," Nubius added as he deftly placed the bottle down on the table. "Tell us all about it."

"Oh, that wine," he gulped as looked at the bottle with some fear and confusion.

"What did you put in it?" Luca asked as he reached out and almost lovingly caressed the bottle top. "What herbs did you use?"

"Nothing harmful, Master. I swear," he stammered as he tried to rub some warmth into his now freezing arms. The temperature in the room had begun to plummet, coating the room in a deep chill as the man looked fearfully towards his master.

"What is in it?" Luca asked again, calmer this time, and the cold began to burn.

"Uh, *dantura,* but just a little for relaxation, lemon-grass to balance out the flavor, wolfsbane for contrast, elderberry to…"

"Wolfsbane?" Luca snarled all of a sudden.

"Oh my God," Dark sighed. "I think I'm going to be sick."

She slid rather limply into a chair and dropped her head onto the table.

"Have you lost you mind, man? Dear God. Don't you know what wolfsbane does to the Wolfen?" Luca growled.

"Wolfsbane?" Vincent asked again. "But the women said that the spices were okay, that no harm would befall anyone?"

"Wolfsbane is a poison, Vincent," Luca growled. "It may not affect the Vampesi, but it is deadly to the Wolfen. When it enters the blood, it latches onto any red blood cells, seizing them and preventing transfer of oxygen to the organs. If Dark had taken one sip of that wine, she would have stood there and suffocated in front of me."

He then went on to describe what would happen in concise detail so that Vincent would be aware of what he had almost caused.

"First she would get dizzy and lightheaded. Then her lips would turn blue and she would feel great pain in her chest and back. Soon after that, the strokes would start. The blood vessels in her brain would pop one by one, until blood ran red from every orifice of her body, but she would still be alive and feeling pain, for that's when the convulsions would start."

"Stop." Vincent panted as beads of sweat beaded up on his forehead.

"Thanks for the graphic description," Dark muttered as she dropped her head back onto the warm kitchen table with a groan of disgust.

"I didn't know," Vincent breathed and he looked rather green in the face as he weakly lifted one hand. "I swear I didn't know. She said that they would just relax her."

"Who?" Luca asked as he calmed a bit upon seeing Vincent's reaction. "Who told you that?"

"The woman," Vincent muttered as he pressed the heels of his hands into his eyes.

"What woman?" Nubius asked. "B.B.?"

"B.B.?" Vincent asked. "What does she have to do with anything?"

"Where is she?" Nubius asked as he stepped forward.

"B.B.? I don't know. I saw her last changing the linens and I offered her a bit of the wine. I thought that it was delicious and so did she. I left her there completing her job. I swear."

"Who gave you the herbs?" Luca demanded again, causing Vincent to look at him with fearful eyes.

"The woman in the cloak. She said that she was one of them."

"One of whom?" Dark asked as he regained her composure and lifted her head.

"Wolfen. She said that she was Wolfen."

"Zinia," Dark breathed as she turned large betrayed eyes onto her mate. "It had to be Zinia."

"We don't know that," Nubius said suddenly as he looked at his cousin and his mate. "Anyone dressed up in a cloak can claim to be Wolfen. Humans don't have the senses to detect such a thing."

The temperature in the room began to warm up a bit as the cold fury left Luca and he started concentrating on what was being said.

"Just because you have a thing for the daughter doesn't mean that the mother is innocent, Nubius," Luca finally said as the anger abated but did not totally leave his voice.

"I don't believe that my aunt would do such a thing, Luca," Dark stated sadly as she stood up. "I know that she has more than enough motive, but I have to ask her to be sure."

"Then send for her," Nubius said in the sudden silence that filled the room. "Send for her and ask her."

"And what's to stop her from running?" Vincent suddenly said, and fury entered his voice.

"Anger, Vincent?" Luca asked as he turned his eyes back to the smaller man.

"Yes, anger. She used me. I could have killed my mistress, could have caused…Lord knows what would have happened if my mistress had died."

"You still don't know what's going to happen, human," Luca drawled as he glared at the man who had almost taken his love away from him.

Vincent visibly shrank as he stood in front of his master, shaking yet determined to take his punishment.

"Whatever you wish, Master," he said as he stood fast in preparation for what was about to happen.

Dark held her breath as she waited to see what her mate would do. This was a true test of honor, how he dealt with this unknowing pawn.

"You will take the message to the village, Vincent. You will tell them that they are invited to a ceremony tomorrow at dusk. You will tell them that they must be here to represent the Wolfen people and to show respect to my mate."

"What ceremony?" Nubius asked.

"Go with him, Nubius," Luca ordered. "Go with him and see that the message is sent. Ensure that he makes it back here in one piece. I am not done with you yet, human."

"What ceremony?" Nubius asked again, looking puzzled. "It can't be an official celebration, which would make them suspicious. You need to invent these events carefully so they won't suspect."

"Tell them that I am seeking a personal vision and that I want them present. I have a few truths to impart."

"Not again, Luca," Nubius sighed as he shook his head at his cousin. "You know this is unnecessary."

"I have been contemplating this for quite some time actually," Luca said with a grin at his cousin. "You are welcome to join me."

"When donkeys fly out of my butt," Nubius returned with a snort.

"What are you talking about?" Dark asked, puzzled as she glanced at the two men between her. "What is going on?"

"He's talking about becoming the human pin cushion again," Nubius sighed as he shook his head.

"You want pleasure/pain now?" Dark asked, incredulous as she examined her mate. Did he drink some of that wine when she wasn't looking? Did it affect Vampesi brains?

"It kills two cats in the bush with one stone," he waved away her concern.

"What?" Everyone in the room looked at him as if he had gone completely mad.

"It serves two purposes," he explained. "It will get them willingly to the castle and possibly force a confession out of them. Plus, I will get the new piercing I was thinking about."

"What?" Vincent looked at Luca as if he'd grown another head.

"Leave us, human; go prepare the message, and Nubius, go with him. I want him protected. I will speak with you before you leave."

Dark remained silent as the two exited, then she stood up to face her mate.

"What are you doing?" she asked. "What are you planning? All the time that I have known you, you have never put your desires in front of those you serve. What's the plan here? Let me in on it."

"Not here," he whispered before he took her hand and led her from the kitchen.

Again the halls were conspicuously quiet as he led her through the castle to his study. Once there, he closed his eyes and a purple glow surrounded the room.

"I don't want anyone else to hear this, Dark. This is between you and me. There is someone else involved in this thing. I smelled him in the room and I need to be sure it is him before I perform any executions."

"Executions?" Dark cried out, her eyes growing wide in fright.

"Did you think I would take this assault lightly, Dark?" he asked, his voice filling with authority. "An attack upon you is an attack upon me. And I take that very seriously."

"But, Luca," she said, her eyes growing dark with worry, "they are my family. I don't know if I can stand seeing them killed."

"They would have killed you, Dark. And if it is who I think it is, we are in more danger than we thought."

"Luca?" she asked as she stepped forward and placed her hand on his chest. "What is going on?"

* * * * *

"Did you hear?" the first voice asked as they traveled down the empty halls.

"Yes I did. All of our plans are coming to fruition. Tomorrow night will be the beginning of the end.

"And the beginning of a new order."

"As I spoke it, it will be," the voice uttered.

"But what about the girl?"

"She is useless after this. Kill her when we rid our house of the rest of them."

"It will be done"

Chapter Sixteen

"I hate woods," Nubius complained as he and Vincent trekked across the tree-filled valley that separated Vampesi and Wolfen land. Without the usual protective glow of Luca's shield, the forest suddenly looked very intimidating indeed.

"What is wrong with the forest?" Vincent asked as he tried to keep pace with the swiftly moving Vampire.

The sound of the leaves crunching beneath their boots filled the almost deathly silence that had descended upon them from the moment that they exited the castle and made their way towards Dark's former home.

"Ticks, fleas, sneaky Wolfen hiding in the shadows, murderers running about. Take your pick. Also these branches are hell on my clothes. Do you know how much it costs to get a leather coat of this quality repaired? You humans charge an arm and a leg for services. And I'm not speaking of gold either."

"So who did you have to kill to get that coat?" Vincent asked jokingly.

"Farmer. He was beating up on his wife and kids, not to mention what he did to that poor milkmaid. I would have done it for free, but the relieved lady insisted that I take this coat as payment for services."

"What?" Vincent stopped and stared at Nubius as if he had grown another head.

"You should check out this lining too. Real silk. Nowadays, silk is very hard to come by. I mean, it's not like the year 2025 when people were practically giving this stuff away. No sir. This was some gift."

"You killed a man for a coat?"

Nubius stopped walking and looked over his shoulder. Poor Vincent stood there, pale in the face, as he tried to hide the disgusted look on his face.

"You think I value life so little, human?" Nubius narrowed his green eyes as he stared at the pale human who stood there judging him.

"You just said that you killed for a coat," Vincent shouted, forgetting for a moment that this man, this Vampire, could easily sentence him to death and carry it out in a way that no one would ever find the body.

"You misheard me, mortal," Nubius snapped out, wondering why he even bothered to try and defend himself to this man, this human. "I said that I killed him for nothing. His wife insisted that I take the coat."

Vincent was shocked. This man was an animal. He killed for less than a supreme purpose and yet he still declared that he valued life.

"And how can you appreciate life, Vampire, if you so easily take it away?"

"Why don't you ask that farmer's wife, Human? When I happened upon them, she was nearly dead from the beatings she had received at his hands. The milkmaid was already gone. Dead from being repeatedly raped and beaten by the man who had hired her to work so that she could afford to help her parents with food and necessities. Ask his children, who will bear the scars of their father's," he snorted derisively, "*love,* for the rest of their lives."

His eyes glowed with his passionate beliefs as he dared the human to question him further. "I would have killed him for the sheer joy it would have given me to twist his puny little head off of his neck. The coat was an added bonus." For a moment his eyes bore into Vincent's before the human looked away.

"But he was human," Vincent said as he began walking beside the Vampire again.

"Was he?" Nubius asked as he turned away, disgusted, from the pitiful little man. "If that is what a human is, I am damn grateful that I drank that Vampesi blood all those years ago."

"We are not all wicked, Omnubius," Vincent sighed as he realized that maybe he took his comments too far.

"No," Nubius agreed. "Not all, but don't make the mistake of condemning my people out of hand, human. I was once where you are and I made the decision to change my life. So here is what we shall do for the remainder of this trip. You won't call me a murderer and a scourge on humankind everywhere, and I won't call you an overly pious, weak-minded, irritating, very lucky little prick. Sound good to you?"

He turned back to see Vincent's face flame red with embarrassment and anger before turning again and forging a path through the trees.

"Yup," he sighed as he let go of a particularly low swinging branch, not even checking to see if it hit the human, and tromped further in the earth-smelling darkness. "I really hate the woods."

* * * * *

"What are you telling me, Luca?" Dark asked as she looked up at her mate.

"I am telling you that there is more here than meets the eye, Dark. There is something going on here that I have never comprehended."

"And what is that, Luca?" Dark asked as she stepped closer to him, wanting to find reassurance that this was all some grave misunderstanding, that this was some sort of heat-induced dream, but finding none.

"I mean that your aunt very well may have tried to kill you, but there is a snake in my garden, Dark."

"Who?" Dark demanded. She would not let this unknown person or persons interfere with what she had with Luca. Good sex, she had heard, was hard to come by. And when you coupled that with a man who actually cared about you, who would die to protect you, it was priceless.

"I smelled him, Dark. I smelled him."

"Who, Luca? Who did you smell? Not that I would trust a Vampesi interpretation on any situation where they had to use their noses," she added.

"Oh, I am quite sure who this person is, Dark. But I can't tell you. If I do, your reactions will let him know that you are on to him."

"How can you be so sure that you smelled a traitor, Luca?" Dark asked, a bit miffed that he wouldn't let her in on his suspicions. Like she couldn't control her emotions. "Who in the hell are you keeping me in the dark about?" Her eyes began to grow black with her anger.

"Trust me, Dark. I know, the same way that I knew that you were in heat, and the same way I can identify the scents of your relatives as they tried to kill me in my rooms. I have a very good sense of smell."

"Not as good as mine," she argued, as if anyone would trust Vampesi senses. "It is common knowledge that the Vampesi excel in strategy and planning, and the Wolfen are best when it comes to using our senses."

"That is true, Dark. But let's just assume that I know what I am talking about here. Okay?"

He sounded a bit exasperated, but still he looked down at Dark with serious eyes.

"I need to depend on you, Dark. This ceremony will draw them out, but I need to know that you will be there to defend me, if need be. There will be a time when I won't be able to do much for myself, and I will need blood, human blood, to recover."

"What are you planning on doing, Luca?" Dark asked, finally understanding how serious this problem was if Luca was willing to make himself vulnerable.

"Remember I once told you that I needed a mate who would sacrifice anything to protect her people?"

She nodded, remembering those words that he'd spoken to her such a short time ago, yet seemed like forever.

"I would not ask anything of my mate that I would not ask of myself. I will do anything to protect my people, Dark. Anything at all. And if the betrayer is who I believe it to be, then we are all in a lot of danger."

"Who is it, Luca?" she asked again. "Tell me so that I can put an end to his miserable life right now. There is no need for all of this pomp and circumstance."

"I have to know if it is only this one person, Dark. Someone murdered your parents; someone tried to poison you, and suddenly my Blood Bank up and disappears. Is it the humans, the Wolfen, the Vampesi, all of them? I have to get rid of them in one fell swoop, Dark. Or they will retreat, regroup, and return at a later date, a day, perhaps, when we are occupied with our offspring. Can you imagine something happening to a child we created together?"

As Dark stared into his earnest black eyes, she could picture a child. Not just any child, a child with a mane of long, curly black locks, black-brown eyes, and an engaging smile. She could see him, a silver bangle around his wrist so that he could be just like Daddy. She could see him leap and pounce in the garden as she played a chasing game with him, see him assume wolf shape for the first time at puberty and grow long fangs to drink blood from his very own simulated supply sack? Uh, that would require a bit more thought, she sighed, but she knew in her heart that her child, *their child*, would be protected and loved. She could not see anything happen to him. She would go mad.

"I understand your point, Luca, but does it have to be done with so much drama?" She turned and walked away from him to perch on the edge of his desk. To her way of thinking, it would be easier to flush out the would-be murderers, betrayers, and Wolfen slaughterers, explode their brains, and get on with life.

The thought of that little boy pouncing around and laughing happily was making her want to give in to the constant urge to go and practice conception with her mate. Near-death experiences heightened the senses, and with Luca standing over there looking so masterful and asking her for her help, well, it did things to her.

"Can you get your mind off of carnal delights for a moment or two, Dark?" Luca finally growled, recognizing the sudden gleam in her eyes. This was not the time to indulge. He was possibly setting himself up for the kill to protect the woman that he loved, and all she wanted to do was screw.

"I'm paying attention, Luca," she said with a small wicked grin. "I don't want anything to happen to you."

"I can imagine why," he groused as he looked up at the sky for enlightenment.

"It's more than sex, Luca," she assured him.

"Really?" he asked, his eyes lighting up a bit. Maybe she was ready to start loving him so that they could suffer this hell together.

"Yeah," she laughed. "I need you whole because I think you'll make cute kids. Do you have any, by the way?"

"*Argh*," Luca growled as he turned away from her in disgust. *Easy*, he told himself. *Love takes time to recognize. I mean, it took you a few days and look at the superior creature that you are. She is just a female Wolfen, newly turned at that. She will figure out that she loves you and can't live without you soon enough.*

"So, what happens during this ceremony anyway?" she asked, amused by his reactions.

"I'll show you," he sighed. "Come with me."

With a wave, he banished the shield and led her from his study. He would explain his plan further once they reached the Garden room.

* * * * *

"Hello, the wood hovel to my right," Nubius called out as he and Vincent made their way into the Wolfen village. "Anybody home?"

"Can you not be so insulting?" Vincent asked, suddenly very nervous.

"What?" Nubius asked as he shrugged his shoulders and turned in a full circle. "How am I insulting?"

"Forget it," Vincent sighed as he too looked around the area.

The large house to their right looked empty, no lights shining from the glass windows. Further up and starting a small circle, the other smaller houses appeared also empty and deserted. The cobblestones looked damp in the glow of the rising moon, and the stars appeared a bit brighter than usual.

"Hey, you never told me what happened to B.B.," Nubius reminded Vincent as they walked around in what appeared to be an abandoned village.

"I have no idea," Vincent said, but his eyes shifted a bit away from the keen intelligence in Nubius' eyes.

"I'll bet," Nubius returned as he raised one eyebrow in suspicion.

"Hello? Is anybody here?" Vincent called.

"What do you want, Human?" a low, gravelly voice called out.

"I, uh, we extend an invitation to the castle tomorrow," Vincent called out as he stepped closer to Nubius.

He may despise me, Nubius thought as he felt Vincent press closer to him. *But he knows who to come running to when he feels he is in danger.*

"To the castle?" the voice asked as a shape suddenly emerged from shadows that surrounded the large house to the right.

"Yes, you are all invited. Compliments of Lucavarious and his utterly charming and amazingly alive mate, Dark," Nubius added, rolling his eyes as Vincent pinched him on the arm.

"She had better be," Zinia said as she stepped forward, looking up at Nubius with disgust.

"What could happen to her, Mother?" a voice cried from behind as Puaua rushed forward to smile at the tall dark stranger.

"What indeed," Nubius breathed as he went still, taking in her great beauty.

Puaua blushed as she observed the close attention Nubius was paying her.

"Tell him that we will consider it, and get off of my land, Vampire. One freak in the family is quite enough."

She turned on her heel and stalked away, her long robes swishing behind her.

"Puaua, you have less than five minutes," she called without looking back as she again disappeared into the shadows that surrounded the village.

"Freak?" Nubius laughed as he took Puaua's small hand within his. "You do know what Old World connotations that word holds, Lady?" he asked as he placed a gentle kiss on her palm.

"I have an idea," Puaua breathed, entranced by the handsome vampire.

"Let us be off," Vincent said suddenly, tugging at Nubius' sleeve. "We have to report to the master."

"I wish I had spoken to him before we sojourned to this lovely hovel, Lady," he purred at Puaua.

"You didn't speak with him?" Vincent asked quietly.

"I had not the chance, but knowing that I could have spent some time with this beauty makes me regret not taking the time," he sighed dramatically as he pulled her close into the shelter of his arms, nibbling softly at her arm, trailing kisses to her neck.

"Oh, be not alarmed about our short time, Omnubius," Puaua purred as she stepped even closer to the vampire. "I find that we will be spending a lot of time together."

"Really," he asked as he fingered a lock of her hair, her long, gorgeous dark hair.

"Really," she answered as she lifted her head to nip at his chin.

"Do tell?" he asked, ignoring Vincent's sharp indrawn breath.

"Because you will not be leaving this area," she said.

"Why is that?" he asked as he ran one dark-tinged pinkie nail over her throat, lightly abrading her skin.

"Because you will be buried here."

Nubius sighed as he pulled back from her.

"I thought as much," he groaned as he took a deep bracing breath. "And I suppose you have a knife at my back, ready to plunge it in for the kill, and that Vincent knew all along."

"Quite right, my love," Puaua laughed as her hand struck with supernatural strength, slicing through the leather of his coat and burying itself deep into his back.

"Damn. I really love this coat." he gurgled, as blood welled up in his throat and ran in small rivers down the sides of his mouth. Blinding pain exploded just beneath his shoulder, causing his breath to catch and tears to fill his eyes.

"This coat will be the least of your worries," Vincent added as he shoved Nubius from behind, knocking him on his face into the leaves and dirt.

"And this is for the farmer who you dispensed justice, Vampire justice, to."

Nubius said nothing but grunted in anticipation as he felt Vincent's foot connect sharply with his side. The pain was enough to make him want to beg for mercy, but he would not give this lunatic the satisfaction. Besides, he had questions that he needed answers to.

"B.B.?" he groaned as he rolled painfully to his side.

"Oh, I have plans for that bitch," Vincent crowed as he landed another kick, this time to Nubius's face.

"Not the nose," Nubius joked weakly as he rolled again, barely avoiding the lash, but feeling the hot leather as it passed inches from his face, only to be stopped with a strongly swung branch to the back of his head.

"Oh, that's not all, lover boy," Puaua added as she swung the branch again. "You will be the first to go, nothing personal. Soon there will be no more abominations of the flesh running around. And to make sure that you die a painful death, you bloodsucking octopus, I am going to leave you with a parting gift. If the beating you are about to get won't kill you, the silver in your back will."

Then the blows began to fall steadily and rapidly. His whole reality became the next painful kick, the next agonizing lash with a stick, the next cruel taunt thrown at him.

"Why?" he managed to gasp as a few others joined in the beating, their laughs taunting him as he tried to brace himself for further abuse.

"For my mother," Puaua cried as she lifted the branch and let it fall across his face.

He looked up at Vincent, seeing the unholy light of a fanatic glowing in his eyes, at Puaua, who thought all her plans were about to come to fruition, to the others who had joined in her cause with her, and smiled.

This game was not at an end yet.

Chapter Seventeen

"Why are we here, Luca?" Dark asked as she looked up at her husband as they entered the threshold of the Garden room. "What do you intend to do and how?"

Luca almost smiled as he inhaled the familiar smell of the earth, of rebirth, of growth. This room had always calmed him and did not fail to do so now. Confidently, he clasped Dark's hand and led her into his sanctuary.

"I will show you, Dark," he said as he stepped onto the lush green grass, savoring the feel of it against his bare feet. "Just follow me, and I will let you know what will happen."

With an almost reverent silence, Luca led Dark to a far corner of the Garden room, a corner overlooked because of its abundance of tangled greenery and vines.

There, centered in a circle of irises, stephanotis, and rose hips, sat a large stone altar.

"What do you worship here?" Dark breathed as she took in the dimensions of the solid stone table.

There was an indentation in the center near what she assumed was the top. But other than that, the large slab of stone remained undecorated. It was a golden red color; a color so mellow it almost glowed in the faint moonlight, and almost breathed of power.

"So what do you worship here?" she asked again, looking up at the apprehension and acceptance that she saw on his face. Was it demons of old? Did he worship some blood-drinking creature from her nightmares? A benevolent goddess? An evil...

"Me," he said shortly.

"Uh, excuse me?" Dark asked as she narrowed her eyes on her mate. Did he think he was some kind of deity? Even if he had a god complex, there was no way in hell that she would drop to her knees and…

"Not what you are thinking," he sighed as he shook his head in sudden amusement. "There never is any worship done here, Dark. That's the place I will be strapped for the ceremony."

He even had the nerve to chuckle at that last bit.

"We have to strap you to this? And do what?" she demanded, arms akimbo. She was now curious — that strapping thing sounded intriguing. Did they use metal or leather?

"Usually we try to gag him, but if all else fails, we pierce a part of his body and hope for the best," laughed a low voice from behind them.

"Sage," Dark gasped as she turned to face the robed figure.

"Indeed it is I, child," he chortled as he stepped from the shadows.

"I didn't even notice you, you smell so much like the plants here," Dark laughed in delight. "Every time I see you, you are in this place."

"It gives me joy in my old age, child," he answered softly as he turned towards Luca. "Going under the needle again, boy?" he asked.

"I am not a boy," Luca sighed as he shook his head in futility. The Sage would continue to call him boy until his dying day. "But yes, I feel the need to center and balance my understanding of things. Besides, not only will it represent a new beginning for all of us here, it will look damn good."

If anything, Luca was arrogance at its best.

"But the pain," the Sage began, but stopped as he read the certainty in Luca's eyes. "Very well. I assume you want it done by tomorrow evening?"

"Yes."

"Then you have the day to prepare."

"And how does one prepare for a hole being drilled into their body? Oops. Excuse me. *A piercing,*" Dark drawled as she rolled her eyes at her mate, still not quite understanding his preoccupation with the whole thing, even though the strapping down part appealed. She would never understand that man. And this professed love thing. Boy, was he getting in over his head.

"Well, one must be perfectly relaxed," the Sage began.

"How?" Dark asked, her interest growing.. She wondered if they used special herbs or scents. She already knew that he didn't approve of drugs in his body, so the process had to involve natural supplements.

"There are many ways to obtain perfect relaxation," the Sage began. "There is meditation and chanting to reach a certain level of awareness. Then there are more physical ways of releasing the tension from one's mind and body."

"Which I will certainly take care of when you leave," Luca sing-sang to the old wise one.

"Oh? *Oh.*" If voices could blush, the Sage's would have been blood red. "I will leave you to it then. You must, after all, fulfill the contract and give us the pitter-patter of little feet around the castle."

"Two legs or four?" Luca drawled and this time, Dark was the one to wear a blush, an annoyed one.

"Does it really matter, you miscreant?" the Sage laughed as he backed away from the couple. "The signs are right this evening for conception. Don't let me down, boy," his voice commanded as he disappeared from view.

"Physical ways, huh?" Dark asked as all awareness of the Sage vanished into thin air.

"Well, I had to tell him something to make him leave, and he is gone," Luca assured her as he closed his eyes and focused his attention.

As Dark watched, a deep, almost solid purple shield bubbled around the area that held the stone altar.

"I have put a heavy shield around the entire room, but I have put an extra one here in this section, to make sure no one can interrupt us."

"What about Omnubius," Dark asked as she felt her blood begin to race. They were locked down in this small area with a table and restraints that could hold Luca immobile. Oh, the possibilities...

"I believe he has gone on without seeking any conference with me, as I expected."

"Then why did you ask?" Dark was curious, despite her rising ardor.

"To give him an out, if he needed it." Luca looked, for a moment, concerned about his cousin. "I believe that he knows more than he is telling, and probably for a good reason."

"Afraid that he will hurt your feelings?" Dark joked as she stepped back and threw her arms over her head in a long slow stretch.

The sensuality of that move was not lost on Luca, whose body tightened in response. "Probably afraid that he would hurt yours," he nearly crooned as he watched the thin material stretch over her full breasts. He had to find a thicker shirt, he thought as he watched her dark berry-colored nipples harden against the soft/rough material of that tunic.

Or maybe a breast binder.

"I don't even think that he likes me much, Luca," Dark purred as she noticed him noticing her. "In fact, I don't believe that he even considers my feelings in what he does. He is too busy trying to get into Puaua's pants."

She turned from him and tossed him a pouty look over her shoulder, pursing her full lips for a moment before lazily letting her eyes travel over his body. The loose material of his pants gave rise in her mind to a new condition—'Tent Pole Syndrome.'

"He protects you because you belong to me," Luca choked out as he watched her slither across the few feet that separated her from the table. He groaned silently as she turned her back to it and lightly leapt onto the broad flat surface.

"Tell me more about this ceremony, Luca. What material can they make to hold a powerful, strong Vampesi male like yourself?" Now she was openly flirting with him as she licked her full lips and languidly ran her hands along the length of her body.

Down boy, he commanded his swelling member. *Remember who controls the body here*. His answer came as a hot rush of blood to his cock, bringing pleasure as well as a bit of misery, as his body's new master took up residence.

A knowing grin spread across Dark's face as she noticed the ever-increasing size of his tent support. "Well, Luca? What do they use to tie you down?"

"Uh," he choked, then cleared his throat. "They use — I use restraints made of silver and leather."

Move forward, dummy, his body demanded, and against his will, his feet carried him closer to the tempting vixen who now sat there and delicately chewed on her bottom lip as she spread her pant-clad legs in an unmistakable invitation.

No, his mind cried. *Not until we make her love us so she can be just as confused as we are*. But his body only obeyed its new master. Every step he took toward her filled his senses with the taste, the feel, the smell of her, and it made him hunger for more.

"And just where are these restraints kept?" she asked as he moved close enough for her to ruffle her fingers through his thick curls. She bent forward and slowly ran her tongue around the outer shell of his ear.

His body shuddered as if shocked by electricity.

"They are connected to the table," he breathed as his large hands gripped her waist and pulled her against his hard body.

The thin material left no doubt to the force of his sudden desire. Every taut sinew of him was pressed against her feminine opening, teasing her as well as pushing his passion to another level.

"They hang down the sides, I suppose?" she asked as she deftly slid her behind back on the table and pulled her feet up and under her, rising to a squat position.

"Yes."

Not liking her sudden avoidance of him, he too climbed up on the table, but instead of jumping, he placed one knee on the altar and pulled his body towards her in a slow, even crawl.

"And your head would go here?" she purred as she backed away from him, playing an innate game of chase with the alpha male, and pointing to the indentation at the head of the table.

"Yes." He crawled closer, the muscles of his body shifting smoothly under the cover of sin and material.

"Show me."

Dark stopped backing away, openly daring him, challenging him to position himself on the table.

"As my lady wishes," he murmured before lying prone on his back and smiling at her.

It was a smooth smile, a smile designed to shatter the resistance of any willing female present. A pheromone-exploding smile that hinted at danger, at sensuality, and at the unbelievable heights of pleasure promised and delivered. It was pure Luca.

"Anything I wish?" she purred as she dropped to her hands and crawled across the small space that separated them, dragging her softness along his steely hardness, small gasps of pleasure escaping her throat.

"Within reason," he responded, his mind taking over for a moment before his body ruthlessly gagged and bound that unnecessary device.

"Anything?" she asked again as she slowly pulled herself astride his slim hips and pressed her tender womanhood against his aching hardness.

She eased back on her haunches as she crossed her arms in front of her and untied the ends of her tunic.

The temperature in the room became sultry and humid as she slowly eased the material up and over her stomach, exposing her small, sunken navel and the soft flesh that surrounded it.

"*Anything?*" she asked again as the shirt inched higher and higher.

Just as it reached a point that exposed the bottom fold of flesh that made up her full breasts, she stopped and looked down at him from beneath long dark lashes.

"*Anything?*"

She leaned down and ran a moist hot tongue along the exposed skin of his neck, making him shudder and buck underneath her.

Her hands left their striptease act and almost gently her nails scraped a small trail along the tunic-covered nipples on his chest and down across his arms, hitting every pressure point that they could.

"*Anything?*" she breathed as she took a small delicate bite out of his chin, teasing him with the small pleasure/pain.

"Yes," he nearly screamed as his hands reached up and gripped her waist to slam her down onto his masculine heat.

"Oh!" they both gasped as the sharp contact sent waves of tickling desire through their bodies, igniting their blood.

"Then," Dark gasped, fighting for control. Luca's lust was hard to resist. "Then I want this."

Before he could move, Dark reached down and felt for the small chain that held the restraints. Still grinning wildly, she slowly pulled on it until the leather cuff rested in her palm.

Running her fingers across his strong hard hand, she turned his wrist over and in an instant, slipped the leather cuff over his hand. With a few pulls, the band tightened snugly around his wrist, leaving just enough room for circulation, but not enough play for him to escape.

For a moment, still lost in a drugged haze of desire, Luca lightly pulled against the restraint as he shivered at the sparks her touch ignited, his black eyes shot silver with lust, before he gave a questioning look at his wrist. Still not really understanding what had happened, his eyes traveled to Dark, then widened with the sudden realization that he couldn't move his arm.

She used that moment of confusion to slam the second cuff around his other wrist and pull the restraint tight.

It dawned on him slowly, as he reached up and found that he couldn't. He was semi-trapped and at her mercy.

It was a sobering thought. It made him feel exposed and vulnerable. He liked it.

"What are you doing, Wolfen-woman?" he asked, his voice low and gravelly with his suddenly spiking passion.

"I'm going to relax you, baby," she purred. "But in my way and in my own time."

"Oh, hell," he muttered as another hot spear of desire pierced his already overworked libido

You were warned, his mind screamed.

All right, his body screamed.

He was in trouble.

"Uh, Dark, love, sweetheart?"

But Dark paid him no heed. She was too busy stroking along his chest and coming teasingly closer to the center of his explosive desire.

"Not now, Luca," she growled, her eyes growing dark and wide as she toyed with his immobile body. "I'm not done playing."

And that was that.

Luca groaned as he felt her caressing touch ease down his sides, hitting a place that he would have never connected with sexual stimuli. He tried to control the shuddering of his body, but failed miserably. A thin sheen of sweat began to coat his body and his clothes felt like another form of bondage.

"I like playing with you," she purred as those deliciously lethal talons appeared from her fingers.

With a mischievous smile, she began to trace the tight clothing around his penis slowly, teasingly, drawing out the anticipation.

"Then play with me, damn it," he growled, his breathing labored as he watched the erotic picture of his love straddling his thighs and almost licking her chops in hunger as she examined the proof of his desire for her.

"All in good time, mate," she purred as she watched his muscles tense against the restraints. "I am having fun."

After saying that, she reached up and gripped a fistful of his tunic at the collar, teasing the thick muscles of his neck with her fingers.

"Dark," he growled in warning, his eyes narrowing at her.

"Hush," she snapped as she tightened her fist and pulled.

The delicate cotton of his tunic rent easily, parting down the center and falling to expose his glistening, heaving chest. This was pure torture. He couldn't reach her to return the favor.

Dark smiled triumphantly down at her mate. He looked so deliciously helpless, so uncharacteristically defenseless, yet she knew that with a wave of his hand, he could end her little game at any time.

He wanted this as badly as she did. His tightly aroused body gave him away, and as usual, her desire rose sharply when faced with the undeniable heat of his excitement.

A few more pulls tore his arms free of their cloth confinement, leaving his upper body free to tease and torment.

"You have a beautiful body, Luca," Dark purred as she ran her fingers slowly over his knotted pecs and lightly over his nipples, grinning with delight as he sucked in a deep breath at the light contact.

"So do you, Dark. When are you going to show me?"

"Later," she purred as she began to tease the drawstring of his pants.

But soon, that wasn't enough. Soon she was nearly panting in excitement as she ran her fingers over the hard bulging ridge of flesh that comprised his desire for her and for this mating.

Luca hissed as her heated touch traveled over his sensitive skin. His body was on fire; his mind was set ablaze with the wonder of this creature that now belonged to him. Even though bound and at her mercy, he knew that the ultimate pleasure of their joining was based on their willingness to please the other. Never before had he been in a relationship like this. It had to be love.

"Dark," Luca warned then hissed as her fingers brushed against the taut skin of his stomach. Apparently, Dark had grown tired of playing the touch-and-not-be-touched, poor-man-at-my-mercy game. With reckless abandon, she ripped and tore at the pants that hid him from her view.

The sound of the rending material mixed with his heavy pants and her excited breaths and swirled over their heads, creating an aura of excitement.

The humidity in the room became almost oppressive and Dark freed his heavy love tool and hungrily examined every inch with her eyes.

"You are amazing, Luca," she breathed as she reached out one trembling finger to run along his heavy fullness. "Absolutely amazing."

Luca gritted his teeth as her gentle touch contrasted sharply with his raging lust. Her touch set off bombs in his bloodstream and sweat peppered his forehead. He felt his control slipping as he focused all of his intense passion on the fine woman perched above him.

"I am drawing dangerously close to the end of my patience, Dark," he growled as she bent over him and inhaled his spicy aroma.

"You have control, my mate."

Ever so gently, she lowered her head and began to lap a wet trail of heat across his chest, making sure she stopped and lapped at his turgid nipples.

Luca shuddered and arched his back towards her, desperately wanting the touches and caresses to continue, but frustrated when he couldn't pull his hands free to force the issue.

Dark laughed—a low, gravelly sound that touched his every nerve ending—as she blew along the wet trail she left behind.

Luca began to curse under his breath as he pulled at the restraints, damning himself for making them so difficult to break.

"Lie back and enjoy it," Dark advised as she settled her mouth at the spot where shoulder and neck met. "I'm just warming up."

Then she bit him.

It wasn't a hard bite or a hurtful one, just the feel of her teeth grasping his skin, but Luca went perfectly still.

With a deep rumbling growl, he felt the sweet-sharp pain as his fangs exploded into his mouth. He arched his head back and nearly howled to the heavens, so much did her love bite affect him.

Dark gave an answering growl, her heated breath wafting over him as her fangs parted her gums and dropped into place.

Blood singing with desire, Dark began to nip and lick every bit of flesh on his chest, traveling lower and lower until she reached his navel.

"Yes," he moaned as she drove him hard against his control. "Don't stop."

"Never!" Dark cried as the fire in her blood settled low in her stomach at the taste of him. He was like some intoxicating drug and she craved more of him.

"Dark," he gasped as she ran her fangs over his skin, lightly scoring him in places, leaving a delicious sting that was rubbed away by the soft massage of her finger.

She looked up at him, her pupils dilated to black, her face flushed with the force of her passion, and Luca almost lost his control and rocketed into a climax, just because of the possessive way she regarded him.

When she was sure she had his undivided attention, she slowly lowered her eyes, stealing a teasing glimpse of his hardness, before returning her gaze to his silver-shot eyes.

"Mine," she snarled as she ran her fingers over the thin patch of soft hair that surrounded his erect pillar of flesh. "All mine."

"Mine," Luca tried to correct her even as the breath exploded from his lungs. "Mine."

"No, lover," Dark purred as she lay her head on his thigh, nestling into the hard muscles there as she lazily ran one finger up his length. "It's mine, tonight and always."

She smiled, her lips pulling back to expose her sharp fangs, just before she nipped at her lower lip, drawing his attention to their plump fullness.

"Uh, Dark?" Luca began, becoming a bit concerned.

If she was contemplating what he was secretly praying that she would do, she had to be very careful. And at the moment she looked anything but. She looked wild and lost in her body's desires.

"Do you trust me, Luca?" she asked as she licked her lips and tightened her hold around the base of his hardness.

"Yeah," he gritted out in a cross between a whine and a moan.

"How much?" she asked as she moved in close enough to bathe him with her hot breath.

"With my life," he groaned as his head dropped back to the altar, his body trembling with an excited fear.

"Good," Dark purred. "That's real good."

Before he could react, her hot mouth covered his length, sending lightning and fire shooting through his body from the place where she gently worshipped him to his brain, then back to his toes, stealing his breath and his reason.

"Dark," he gasped, his eyes closed as he savored the feel of her hot wet mouth surrounding him.

"You taste good," she pulled away long enough to assure him, before she again dropped her head and delicately lapped at his flesh.

Luca closed his eyes as he floated on a cloud of tingling excitement. He felt her lips surround him and heard her sighs of enjoyment as she pleasured them both.

Then he felt her teeth.

Inhaling sharply, Luca's eyes popped open and his whole body tensed.

"Dark," he said very carefully, but she just laughed a wicked laugh and nibbled at him.

"You trust me, remember?" she crooned then sent him spinning into oblivion.

"I...You...Please...Dark," he muttered as his head whipped back and forth. His second set of fangs exploded uncontrollably as he tossed his head, praying for release from this sweet torment, then praying for it to continue.

His whole body arched off of the table, nearly unseating her as she swallowed as much of him as she could. He was now in her power.

Rising up above him, she moaned at the sight he made, trembling and helpless at her hands. The aura of sexuality that surrounded him was multiplied a hundred fold, and it showed in the slick sheen that covered his body; the muscles that bulged and strained as if trying to contain the sensations that swamped his body; the utter sexual devastation that showed in the sensual set of his features.

Dark shuddered as her own passions began to overwhelm her. She had never performed such an act on anyone before and she found that she liked it. It gave her an intense sense of control while heightening her awareness of her mate. Now her body churned and begged for release. She could feel her own dampness as she carefully examined his erect flesh, his straining body, and his pleading eyes.

"Now, Lucavarious," she managed as sharp stabs of desire rocketed throughout her system. "Now, I am done playing."

Luca sucked in a deep breath as she leaned over him again, brushing her swollen nipples against his chest, swinging into position to drive them both through the gates of paradise.

With a few tears, her pants were gone and she trembled at the feel of the air caressing her hypersensitive body.

"Yes," he chanted as he felt himself at the portal of her womanhood, trying to urge her to move faster if only by force of sheer will. "Please."

But Dark paused as she gripped him firmly and positioned herself over his hardness.

"Say my name."

"What?"

Luca's surprise at her order did nothing to ease the pressure of the sexual tension that filled him. If anything it heightened it.

"Say my name, Luca. Say it and I will give us both what we want."

Luca tried to be strong. He bit his tongue and closed his eyes. If he could not see her, she could not tempt him. But boy, could he *feel* her.

He almost cried tears at the feel of her feminine heat and moisture, just out of reach.

"Say it," she urged in her deep throaty voice. "Say it, Luca."

Then suddenly, he couldn't hold back any more.

He wanted nothing more than to be buried within her hot, giving heat. He wanted to feel them joined as closely as two people could ever be. He wanted to use his body to express his love and desire for her. Nothing else mattered, nothing but this.

"Dark," he forced past his tight throat. "Dark, please. Take me."

Then he was encased within her.

"Luca!" Dark nearly screamed as she settled his full length inside. Her body was on fire; her nerves were stretched taut. Never had anything felt this good before! She felt as if she was the queen of this castle, of her man, of her life.

He filled her to overflowing, satisfying every need of her body, yet she craved more.

Slowly, she began to move, crying out at the feel of him making her desire spiral higher while satisfying the needs of her soul.

"Oh, Luca!" she cried out as she felt herself building. Tension tightened her body, sending tingling waves through her limbs, making her tighten her hold on her mate.

Bending forward, she offered her breasts to his open mouth and nearly screamed as he clamped onto her, sucking and nibbling, and moaning under his breath.

She began to move faster and faster, spiraling out of control, forcing him deeper and deeper until he touched the very heart of her womb.

Grunting her approval, she pulled back, braced her hands on his chest and began to slam herself down as hard and as fast as she could, relishing the bolts of lightning that streaked faster and faster through her body. The ache centered low in her belly began to churn and her stomach muscles tightened. She was going to implode.

"Luca!" she screamed as the force of her climax suddenly hit her. "Oh yes, Luca!"

It was too much. It was *way* too much. Luca began to thrust his hips upward as best as he could as he struggled to release himself from his leather bindings. His head thrown back and his heels pressed against the stone altar, he felt his muscles contract as he was pushed to unbelievable heights.

"Dark. Dark, how I love you!"

The words tore themselves from his heart as he felt the strong convulsions of her inner muscles milking him, demanding his surrender.

With a loud shout of completion, Luca felt himself break. His head felt as if it was about to explode, as wave after wave of satisfaction coursed through him. He felt his world explode as he felt himself release deep within her, mingling their essences, fulfilling nature's purpose for the two of them.

He bit down on his bottom lip, drawing blood, as an amazingly strong climax tore through him, leaving him shuddering and sputtering, lost in a daze of pleasured contentment.

The feel of her soft body as it settled against his only seemed right and perfect. The feeling just added to his satisfaction. His whole body hummed in relief and he struggled in vain to free his hands, to hold her, to touch her, to comfort and love her.

Dark lay, amazed, on her mate's chest. When she had started this game, she had not actually known what to expect. She had never expected this type of response from herself or from him. If anything, she'd expected him to use that shield of his and lift her away or to hold her hostage until they found a way to end their standoff. She never expected, or even dared to dream of his capitulation.

"You trust me," she managed as she struggled to catch her breath and fight off the lethargy that now had taken hostage of her body after such an extreme orgasm. "You really trust me."

I love you, he thought, but only said, "Release me, baby."

It took some doing, but Dark finally managed to build up the strength to grope for the restraint at his wrist.

"You are not mad?" she questioned as she toyed with the release.

What's the point of leaving herself open to revenge if she didn't have to? He might not let her leave this room, but he damn well wasn't going to be set free to make it easier to catch his prey.

"No," he sighed, his eyes still closed as he enjoyed the afterglow, the time when his senses slowly sharpened into focus and he returned to his own body from somewhere out in the cosmos that she'd hurled him. "Should I be?"

"I know I'm not," she giggled as she slowly freed one wrist. "Are you relaxed?"

"Boneless," he laughed, loving the feel of her firm flesh pressed closely against his.

He opened his eyes and stared, utterly entranced by the soft glow that suffused her person. Her eyes were once again deep brown, but filled with a soft contentment that he had never seen before. He had to kiss her.

Raising his head, he captured her mouth in a long, slow, drugging kiss, running his tongue over her retreating fangs and enjoying the pricks of her sharp teeth.

"Mmm," Dark purred as she returned the favor, discovering both sets of his fangs and delighting in the difference.

"Mmm, is right," he agreed as he lifted his free hand to bury it in her soft hair, loving the feel of her thick shiny curls. "You taste divine."

"Why two?" she asked as she reached for his restrained hand and quickly did away with the cuff. She wanted to feel both of his arms around her, gentling her. She didn't know why, but she was beginning to crave the comfort of his touch and his presence. He was growing on her. She could picture a future with the two of them together, sharing...sharing whatever the rulers of two powerful peoples who despised each other, did.

"Two?" he asked as he cupped her head with his now-freed hands and pulled her down for another deep drugging kiss.

"Fangs," she answered, as she flicked her tongue out and tasted the poor lips that he had been abusing with said fangs. "Why two sets."

"It's because of what I am," he answered as he placed little nipping kisses along her chin, before tasting the skin on her neck, delicately nipping her with his fangs.

"Ruler of the Vampesi?" she asked. "Cousin to a Vampire? Arrogant bastard?"

Then she groaned a bit and snuggled into his grasp, settling her body more comfortably against his.

"Part Wolfen," he replied.

"Oh," she purred as his kisses traveled to her ear. "Part Wolfen...*Part Wolfen*?"

"Surprise," he chuckled as she rose up in shock, her eyes widening as his words sunk in, her face going a bit pale. "Aren't you happy? Now we can sit out on the front porch and collect fleas together in our old age."

"My God," Dark whispered as she stared at him in growing understanding.

"*Bark, bark,* baby."

Chapter Eighteen

There was nothing more alluring that the scent of a female.

A woman's contours were unique, special, something to be cherished, and did he appreciate every hill and valley of the female form.

Pressed as tightly to him as she was, there was no way for him to mistake her full breasts for anything other than nature's bountiful playground that they were.

Her skin, so soft, begged to be caressed. The small shivers that she gave only made her seem more sensual, aware of her body's own desires, and in his opinion, more desirable.

The feel of her soft skin pressed so closely to his almost caused him to moan in the agony of hot sharp desire...or was it pain?

She whimpered softly, and he tried to make a place for himself between her lush thighs; he was about to enter paradise, or was this hell?

He shifted his weight, but something seemed to be holding him back.

Kinky. Had the little minx tied him up? It wouldn't be the first time.

But he tried to shift his weight, left arm numb, when the pain and her voice hit him at the same time.

"Oh, God. Nubius, stop that."

Stop? But it was just getting interesting. Nubius forced his eyes open a touch to discover that he was not where he thought himself to be.

"Nubius?" the rough voice rasped in his ear. "What is happening?"

"B.B.?" he managed as he forced his eye to open wider.

"Nubius?"

With a groan, Nubius attempted to shift his weight again, only to find that he was really immobilized. But it was the warm welcome of the earth that bound him to this woman. He was buried alive, so to speak.

"It's okay, B.B.," he assured her as he tried to clear his thoughts.

What had happened?

Oh, yes, now he remembered.

It was the dark-haired Wolfen bitch that had done it to him. But why? She did not know of his purpose. He was sure of that. So what had caused her to turn so swiftly?

"Nubius, I feel funny," a small voice intruded on his thoughts. "I can't move and I'm scared."

Her voice sounded like she had screamed for hours, but if that was the case, she should be dead. Unless...

"Can you see me, B.B?" he asked urgently. "Can you see me?"

"Yes," her broken voice whispered, "I can see you Nubius, and my head hurts from the owls. What is happening?"

"I think you have been turned, my dear." He tried to soothe her as he again attempted to move his arm. Damn, but his back hurt.

Her breathing noticeably quickened as she absorbed his words.

"Turned into what?" she panted, her sudden fear drenching her blood with adrenaline and filling the small confines of their space with the sharp smell of fear. "What did they do to me?"

"B.B.? Calm down," he urged as he tried to judge how he was positioned on top of her. Not very comfortably, that was for damn sure. And the constant pressure from the earth seemed to agitate the knife, pushing it in deeper.

"What, Nubius? What did they do?"

She was crying now, her body wasting precious moisture that she couldn't afford to lose, her whole body trembling and quaking.

"B.B.," he urged. "Keep calm."

"What the hell did they do to me?" She tried to sit up, fear giving her strength. She violently arched her body upwards, struggling to be free of this shallow grave, of this situation, of what her body was trying to tell her that her mind refused to accept.

"Damn it. Hold still," Nubius roared as her frightened movements jammed the blade even deeper into his back, painfully jolting his body.

"No!" she screamed, becoming hysterical. "What am I? What did they do?"

"They turned you, damn it!" he roared as she jerked again, giving him a bit of space to maneuver, but bringing intense pain to his abused body. "They turned you into a Vampire."

B.B. froze, as if the very life had been jerked from her body, and in a way, it had.

"Why?" she finally whispered, tears running unchecked down her face. "Why would they do that to me?"

"I don't know, B.B., but I will find out. What you risked for my blood kin will not be forgotten. Your changed life will be considered when all of this comes to a head. They will pay. This I promise you." His confident, determined words filled her with a small measure of peace, though she was still in shock about the changes that were taking place in her life. Besides, they ruined his coat. And he really loved this coat.

"I don't want this," she finally managed. "I don't want this. Nubius, change me back. I never wanted this."

"I can't."

"Please?"

"I cannot work miracles, B.B.," he growled. "I am what you are becoming, and nothing short of death will change that. I am sorry, little one, but you have to keep calm."

Then her sobs started.

"But, Nubius, I can feel my body…dying. It burns, Nubius. It doesn't feel right."

Right then, Nubius wished nothing more than to be able to wrap his arms around the scared woman, but it was now a physical impossibility.

"I am so sorry, B.B.," he whispered, his own throat growing tight at the force of her emotions. "I am so sorry."

"Nubius?" she whispered again, in her rough, gravelly voice.

"Yes, little one?" he answered, finally managing to work his left hand slightly above her head.

"I messed my pants."

For a moment, Nubius froze in his place.

"You did what?"

"I messed my pants," she wailed. "I messed my pants and I couldn't stop it from happening."

"*My coat.* Why did this have to happen when I was wearing the full length leather?" he wailed, just as loudly, before he noticed the shame and fear in her eyes.

"Okay, B.B.," he again soothed. "This is normal. You could not control that." Still, he cringed at the thought of what he was now lying in.

"But I tried, Nubius. I really tried."

She sounded like a scared little girl. "Your body is dying, B.B. It will expel whatever it cannot contain."

"It is normal?" she asked, a bit hesitant, but feeling reassured.

"I should know, B.B. Look who you are talking to. Am I not the king of the Vampires? And I will get us out of this, but not now."

"But, Nubius," B.B. stuttered as a curious humming filled her blood. "I can't stay here. I want to go home."

"We can't B.B., not now. Do you feel it?"

"What?" she whispered, scared to the tips of her toes as this new sensation began to overwhelm her.

"Sunrise, doll. We have to stay here a bit longer, but I promise you, we will be getting out of here, and soon."

There was silence for a moment, and Nubius' thoughts turned once again to the wardrobe desecration that had occurred as the dark-haired one and her friends tried to beat the stuffing out of him.

But B.B.'s tentative voice intruded again.

"How did they do it?"

"What did you drink?" he absently replied.

Someone else was involved, he thought, as he realized that the attack on him had to be to get him out of the way. But why? No one knew of his true purpose, unless it was to take away a layer of protection from Luca.

Puaua said that she was doing this thing for her mother, but she had nothing to do with B.B. Was B.B supposed to be dead? Was that why she was buried? But if she was going to die, why turn her into a Vampire?

"Wine."

"What?" he asked, wondering if she was referring to herself. It was a good thing that Vampires were so long lived; she needed the time to erase that annoying habit from her life. He understood that being turned was a difficult adjustment when you did not choose this life, but really. Have a cry and get over it.

"I drank wine," she explained. "Vincent gave me the wine."

"Vincent?" he nearly shouted as pieces began to fall into place. "Vincent gave you the wine? Out of the bottle or a flask."

"A flask," she answered. "I can't believe that Vincent would give me Vampire blood. Where would he get it?"

"There are ways, B.B.," he assured her as he assimilated this new piece of information. "Then he really didn't know that the wine was poisoned. But who did?"

"When will the paralysis wear off, Nubius?" B.B. suddenly asked. "Will I ever feel my legs again?"

"There is no paralysis involved, B.B., just the burning and the bladder and bowel evacuation."

"But I am just getting some movement back, Nubius," she assured him. "Otherwise I would have tried to dig myself out."

Who paralyzed her? How? There were two people working, or was it three?

Vincent, on the count that he hated Vampires. But why make one?

Puaua, because she wanted her mother's power or rights of ascension.

Then who would have more to gain by Dark's death? Or was Dark the target? Was she the bait?

The only person who would benefit by Luca's death and the destruction of Dark was…

"We are in some serious shit," Nubius breathed as the answer dawned on him. "We have to get out of here."

Chapter Nineteen

"*Bark, bark*? What the hell is that supposed to mean? *Bark, bark*? What kind of games are you playing Lucavarious?"

In her sudden complete and total confusion, Dark scrambled backwards off of the body of her mate. What he said made no sense and was scaring her.

"No games, Dark," he assured. "I am part Wolfen, somewhere in my considerably elite bloodline."

"Seriously?" she gasped, her eyes wide in amazement.

"Well, something has to be the cause of my small and insignificant faults, Dark."

"Insignificant…What else have you been keeping from me, you bastard? Are we related? Oh my God. Did I just screw my cousin?"

Her body began to shake in delayed reaction. This had to be a misunderstanding. This couldn't be true.

"We are definitely not related by blood, Dark," Luca sighed as he sat up. The look of her was beginning to bother him. He had not seen her this shook up since the first time that he had met her. "We just happen to have a similar genetic code. Otherwise, I would not be able to drink your blood and complete our mating ceremony." Then gently, he added, "You are a part of me, Dark, something that can never be taken away."

"Why are you telling me this now, Luca?" Dark calmed down a bit but still stared at him in horrified amazement. "Why are you telling me your secrets now?"

"You now have a need to know."

His answer was straight and to the point.

"Why?"

"Because, Dark, I don't know how this whole situation will resolve itself. There is a lot at stake and you need to know some things to protect yourself and our child."

"I'm not pregnant, Luca," Dark sighed. She settled herself comfortably, tailor–style, on the altar and got ready to have her questions answered. They were safe for the moment, inside Luca's protective shell, so they would not have a better time to sort some things out.

"Not yet, Dark, but if something were to happen to me and you found yourself…with child…"

"I believe 'knocked up is a term that suits you better, Luca," Dark tried to joke, to ease the tension a bit. She had just gotten him relaxed and she didn't want all of her hard work to go to waste.

"Okay. If you find yourself knocked up, you need to know a few things. Number one, a Vampesi cannot drink the blood of a Wolfen, not a pure Vampesi at any rate. It will make us ill. I have enough Wolfen in me to allow me to indulge," he leered at her. "But I'm not so sure how it will turn out in our child. The Wolfen gene that allows me to partake might be dormant in her. Take no chances; stick with the synthetic blood."

"Him," she corrected.

"What?"

"Our child. It will be a boy."

"But I want a girl, Dark. There are too many males running around this castle as is. I want a girl to dress in lace and ruffles and bounce on my knee. I will train her to respect her elders, unlike some people I could mention."

"Boy," Dark hissed. "If you give me girl children Luca, I will send them back the way they came, and I don't mean through me."

"No Vampire blood either." He rolled his eyes as he changed the subject.

"But Vampire and Vampesi are related," Dark objected. "They did start out Human and changed after having Vampesi blood."

"Yes, Dark, but the blood changed their DNA. It altered their blood as well as their bodies. A Vampire cannot drink Wolfen blood either. It kills them most painfully. A Vampire can feast on all the Vampesi blood they want, but if I were to try it, my head would explode."

"Off?" Dark asked, fascinated. Her eyes grew wide at the thought and she had to bite back a chuckle. "That's a lot of explosion for a head the size of yours."

"Very cute. But need I remind you that that very big head you are referring to is a genetic trait, and will be passed along to our daughter. A daughter that you have to push out through your birth canal."

The laughter ended abruptly.

Score one more for the Vampesi. Luca added another mental tally line to his inner scoreboard.

"So what else do I have to know?"

That I love you, he thought. *And that I think you love me a bit too.* But he kept his mouth shut. "Nothing else major," he answered. "But I suggest that you pierce our daughter as soon as possible. She might not like it, but it will help her out in the long run."

"But it's painful, Luca. Why else would I have to strap you down? I don't want my child in pain and I won't be the one to cause any distress to any child." Dark was determined in this. It went against everything that she believed in to harm a child. It was a crime against her Wolfen nature and punishable by death among her people.

"I know it hurts," Luca sighed as he ran a frustrated hand through his hair. "Believe me, I know that it hurts, but it must be done. It is the only way to protect her. I have my immunity to silver because of what my parents in their foresight started. I am immune to the sun because of the exposure I faced as a child. I am living proof that it works, Dark. And our child must be protected from both sides. There are many people who would spill innocent blood and take a child's life just to prove that their beliefs are right. Power is a heady and addictive thing, Dark. Just look at your aunt."

"We are not sure that it is her," Dark protested. "That's what tomorrow is all about. I refuse to believe it until after the ceremony tomorrow."

"That is another thing, Dark. Trust no one tomorrow. Go to no one tomorrow. I will protect you as much as I can, but I need you to protect yourself and my daughter."

"It's a boy, and you don't even know if I am pregnant, Luca," Dark countered, still a bit in limbo about all that was unfolding before her.

"Do you want to take the risk?" he asked.

Silence.

"Okay. Here is what will happen tomorrow. Omnubius will be present and a big help to you. He will stand behind you at all times. Trust him, for he has had a hand in raising me and can fill in any information gaps that I don't cover."

Dark nodded in understanding then prayed that the Vampire would soon return. She wanted people she could trust around her.

"I do not trust that Human, Vincent. Be wary of him, Dark. I still believe that he means us ill will. He will be allowed inside, though I will put up a shield like this one. You can tell a lot by a man's reactions. Pay close attention his."

"Got it."

"The Sage will do the actual ceremony, though. Keep your distance from him, Dark. He will do what needs to be done then fade into the background."

"But I have known the Sage all of my life, Luca. He wouldn't hurt me," Dark argued, her hands on her hips.

"Trust no one, Dark." He reiterated. "Trust no one but me."

"I trust you, Luca, to a point."

"Very good," he praised her, an amused smile turning up the corners of his lips. "You are finally learning something other than sexual positions from me."

Dark snorted, but the heated light began to fill her eyes as they became glazed as she eyed his naked form sitting before her.

"Not again," Luca muttered to himself, shuddering a bit, but managed to control himself. "Pay attention, Dark," he said in his most commanding voice. "Dawn approaches and we have much to discuss yet."

"Fine," she sighed but still eyed his body with a smirk. "But if you can't control yourself, I won't be held responsible for my actions."

Luca shook is head, but reminded his body that it had had its fun. Control was once again his. "All the key players will be here tomorrow, Dark. It ends after sundown, no matter what"

"That I understand clearly," Dark answered, all traces of amusement leaving her.

"I might not survive this, Dark. But I want you to know that I trust you to keep our people safe. We need to have understanding between us, or the wars will start anew."

"I understand," she replied, but inside she quaked at his words. Life without Lucavarious? No one to argue with, to tease, to learn from, to teach. Not to smell his special scent or to hear his voice change with his emotions. No one to make the room go hot with his ardor or cold with his rage. No more smartassed comments…

"Why you bastard," Dark snarled.

"What?" he asked. For a moment, he had been lost in contemplation of tomorrow's ceremony, but her words brought him back to the present.

"What? *What*. What about all of those stupid names that you have been calling me? Flea-bag, mangy mutt…you know?

All of those oh so cute slurs that you threw at my heritage. You are a bigger mutt than I could ever be, you Mongrel."

He actually had the audacity to blush. "Takes one to know one?" he offered lamely. Boy, he hated it when his own words caught him.

"Takes one...Lucavarious, you need help."

With that, she hopped off of the table and stalked around the perimeter of the shield.

"That doesn't look too good," he muttered under his breath as he watched her pace.

She was mumbling under her breath and every so often, she would look up at him and growl. Strange as it was, that growl, combined with her firm naked body, was actually beginning to have an effect on his body. He could actually feel his flesh start to harden again. This was going to kill him.

"And you claim to love me, too."

That made him go limp faster than seeing Omnubius naked. How did she know?

"I...I, uh...I."

"You told me when you lost your temper and made the room go cold."

"How did you know that it was me?" he asked, desperately trying to buy some time to come up with a reply. It was too soon for her to know that he held her within his heart. That would give her the advantage over him, and he did not like being vulnerable.

"Who else could make the temperature obey their commands, Lucavarious? Besides, it is a good gauge for your temperament. If you really don't want to give your enemies a clue to your thoughts, you would do better to learn how to control it than piercing your body with silver."

He blinked, before indignation took hold. "If you didn't make me lose my temper so often, I would have no need to learn that bit of control," he snarled back.

"Isn't that just like a man," she growled. "You blame me for your lack. Well, I refuse to take the blame for this one, you hypocrite."

"Hypocrite?" he wailed. "I am no more a hypocrite than you are a Vampire."

"That's right. You are something worse. You are a half-breed mongrel mutt with no manners. Just because tomorrow is going to determine our future is no reason for your sudden disclosure of the truth. You should have told me, Lucavarious. I should have been informed about your heritage. And then you tease me about being Wolfen, calling us stupid names, all the while you were hiding that part of yourself from us. Are you ashamed, Luca? Is that why you did that?"

Luca sighed as he again closed his eyes and ran his fingers through his hair. "No, Dark," he answered in a low voice. "I am not ashamed of what I am. That would be lying to myself and even I have my standards. It was just not important for you to know until now. How else could you believe me when I explained about the wine? Even an educated guess would not have been as accurate. I need you to trust my decisions; they are almost always based on fact."

"You claim to love me, then you hide these things from me, Luca. What kind of love is that?"

"Dark," he sighed. "I don't understand it all myself. But I know that I do love you, and the thought of that terrifies me to near death."

There was silence as his words touched her, but her anger was as yet too strong for forgiveness. She reached down and began to gather her clothing.

"What are you doing, Dark?" he asked, sitting up and trying to catch her eye. "It is almost dawn, and we still have things to discuss." *Like if you love me or not, or even if you will ever be capable of loving me.*

"I need some time to myself, Luca. I have to take this all in. Every time I think I understand you, you throw me another curve. Diamonds have less facets that you."

"But I need you here, Dark. With me."

His eyes showed a sincerity that they never shown before, that and a hint of fear, but Dark refused to be drawn in. She had some thinking to do. She wanted him, there was no doubt about that, but how was she supposed to act towards a man that had made her feel so inferior because of who and what she was? How could she trust him not to revert to the old Lucavarious, despite his avowals of love?

"I need to wash, Luca. As charming as the feel of you running down my leg actually is, I prefer to be clean." As if making love…no, having sex with him… would dirty her, she thought.

Luca reacted as if she punched him. He reeled back on the altar and his eyes filled with incredible pain, before the black orbs settled into a pale black gaze, the look he wore when she first met him.

Apparently, he didn't know her either. She was lethal in a fight; she bypassed his jugular and went straight for his heart. Score one more for the pureblood Wolfen. In fact, call it a game. She won, hands down.

"As you wish," he said in a low monotone as he collected the pieces of his breaking heart and gathered his dignity.

"Luca," Dark began, frightened by the sudden change in his demeanor. "I didn't mean…"

"You are free to go and cleanse yourself of my touch, Dark, my Wolfen-child."

"But Luca…"

But Luca wasn't listening anymore. He had to protect his inner self some way. His enemies were closing in on him, he was sacrificing his body for his people, newfound and old, and he was tired. He had no energy for battling with her. He could not stand to have his heart trampled further.

With a wave of his hand, the shields and all of their protection vanished as if it had never been. Funny, suddenly protecting himself didn't seem all that important anymore. But Dark still might be with his child. That he had to protect, no matter what the cost.

"Luca," Dark began, but he cut her off.

"I am giving you what you are asking for, Dark. Go and clean yourself up and spend your time alone. I realize now that you only want a child from me, and I shall do my best to see that you have your wish. The love I have urges me to make you happy, no matter the personal cost."

"That is not why…"

"Go, woman. I find that I suddenly need a few moments for myself as well. I will expect you here before sundown. Now leave me."

He lay down, naked and vulnerable, upon the stone altar and turned his back to her, protecting what was left of his inner self by hiding it away.

Dark took one look at him and didn't know whether to cry or to curse.

She had truly not meant to even insinuate that she found his touch dirty and repellent, especially now that she had found out that he had mixed blood. But the fact that he hid it from her while making those vile taunts heated her blood to boiling.

She truly found Lucavarious to be a very complex man. In fact, she enjoyed his complexity very much. Even in his sarcastic mode, Luca was a joy to be around. He never backed away from a fight and it seemed that whether he was insulting her or loving her like mad with his perfect body, he had always given himself wholly to her. This was the first time that he had cut her out.

"Luca," she began, but he flinched at the sound of her voice.

She turned and walked away, but the tears that she never thought to shed were slowly filling her eyes.

She couldn't imagine life without Luca there, annoying her, arguing with her, making her laugh, and making her want to blacken his black eyes. She didn't know how she felt about him, but she didn't want to lose him.

It would devastate her.

Wolfen mated for life.

* * * * *

Shadowed eyes observed Dark leaving the small corner of the Garden room, pulling on her tunic and looking as if she had been dealt some terrible blow.

This was not part of the plan. This could ruin things. There were a few hours left before dusk, so something had to be done before then. His plan would not fail.

The silent observer turned and walked away, thought of a new plan forming in his head.

Chapter Twenty

"I am so sleepy, Nubius," her low voice moaned. "And I can't breathe."

"You don't need to breathe," he snorted impatiently as he tried again to get his right hand above his head so that he could dislodge the blade buried there.

"Because our oxygen is carried through the blood, not the nose," she obediently repeated.

"Very good," he snapped. "Now if you can move enough to grip the hilt of that knife…"

"Why did he do it?" she asked.

"Who?" he sighed. He could not reach high enough to even brush against the knife, let alone get a grip on it. If this pudding-head would shut up and help him…

"Vincent. Why would he do this?"

"Force a change on you or stab me?"

"Bury us together."

Now why hadn't he thought of that? What was the purpose of burying them in the same grave, especially since he knew that she wasn't dead, or did he?

"I think he knew that you would get me out, Nubius," she sighed. "So now will you get me out?"

"As much as I would love to, toots," he answered, "we are stuck here until the sun goes down. That's what you are feeling, B.B., so you had just better lay back and get some sleep. We have a long day ahead of us and I don't want you to see me cry."

"Cry, Nubius?" Her voice raised with her surprise, as much as a near whisper could sound surprised. "What could make you cry? You chose this life. I didn't. I should be the one in tears."

"Well for one thing, you can't cry. Your body needs the moisture too badly. And you would cry too, if you had your lucky leather coat slashed to rags, was lying in a pile of someone else's excrement, and knew that your most favored boots, the ones that you had for centuries and pampered as if they were your only child, were now buried in common dirt. Never mind the crazy assassins, the governmental coup perpetrated by an obviously delusional Wolfen, or being betrayed by a human that you never trusted in the first place. My wardrobe has gone to hell in a hand basket. Who around here knows how to fix leather tears? Have you seen the way people around here dress? It's an abomination."

Then he glared at her, his green eyes sparkling even in their dark earthen womb. "You have no fashion sense, lady."

"Well," B.B. retorted, mystified by his reaction, "your lucky coat wasn't so lucky after all."

"If I wasn't wearing it, woman, I'd be dead now."

"I don't believe it." This argument was pushing the dark sleep away and she found herself feeling strangely comforted by this almost hostile exchange of words.

"It's lined with silk," he said slowly as if he was instructing a child…or a dimwitted human.

"So?" she said as she fought back a yawn. Her eyes were growing heavier by the second.

"So, if you knew anything other than to change the bed linens and try to seduce the master, you would know that a knife plunged through leather and silk with the force that she plunged it in, will not tear."

"What?' she asked as she absently forced her hand up to cover the yawn as it broke free.

"The knife parted my flesh, my dear, but the silver is not touching me. The silk is a barrier between it and its poisonous touch."

"Oh," she said as understanding bloomed. "That was smart of you, Nubius. And I know more than linens and seduction. I have stopped trying to sleep with the master. His wife is too crazy. I am happy to have him alive, as he saved my life, you know."

"Yes, I know." Nubius sighed as he grunted and shifted his weight again. Even though it seemed impossible, he would try to get a grip on that knife so that his body could heal. He would need both arms to dig them out.

"So it was a good thing that I called you in. That woman would have killed him and no one would have been the wiser, at least that's what I thought I overheard her say."

"Very smart, B.B.," he sighed as the attempt failed again.

He was glad that the earth piled over them was deep enough to protect them from the deadly rays of the sun, but he still longed to be free, to go to his rooms and have a hot bath and a quart of the good stuff, never mind that synthetic watery stuff that Luca insisted he consume while in residence.

"And she never overheard me listening in on her and that man, either," B.B. added as she brushed a few grains of dirt from her forehead.

An air pocket was formed when they tossed Nubius on top of her, but the loose soil was aggravating her. Air pockets. That reminded her that she couldn't breath and brought her back to her original point.

"I want out, Nubius."

"Not until sundown, woman," he shouted, his patience ending. "And not until I find a way to pull this knife out."

"So why didn't you say so earlier?" she asked as she worked her arm around his shoulder and gripped the protruding handle.

"You can move?" he growled low, a feral light flashing gold sparkles in his eyes.

"Uh huh," she said, fighting to stay alert enough to follow his words. "It came back a while ago. Is it that important? I mean, you said that we couldn't go anywhere anyway."

"Sudden flashes of intelligence," he muttered. "That has to be the answer."

"Do you want it out or not?" she snapped, wondering why he was questioning her intelligence. She was a very bright girl. Luca told her that when he rescued her from the pleasure house when she was a young girl. She was so smart that she had managed Luca's rooms and his household. Well, most of it by herself.

"Yes, I want it out," he growled. "Would you like to be skewered with a knife? I can show you how it feels if you are curious?"

B.B. sniffed, then taking a firm hold on the knife, yanked for all that she was worth.

"*Damn*," Nubius shouted, as stars filled his eyes and suddenly he was on a mystical magical journey of sight and sound.

The colors were beautiful, reds and yellows mostly, and the sound of his screech sounded quite melodious to his ears. Was that a high C he just hit, or was it a C sharp?

Either way, his head swam in a wondrous place filled with flowers and sunshine. He could feel the sunbeams caressing his skin, or was it dirt?

Yup, it was dirt, the color that he saw was B.B.'s auburn hair, and the squeaking sound he heard wasn't him at all. It was B.B. And her face was turning a nice shade of purple as his hands squeezed the afterlife out of her.

Reality returned with a bang.

"I am so sorry. B.B., talk to me."

His hands went from choking to shaking as he tried to get some signs of life out of her.

"I can't breathe," she managed as her eyes watered and her head swam. "And it's not from the Vampire blood."

"God, I am so sorry, B.B.," he rushed to explain. "I have a problem with pain. I don't like it."

"I wonder how I figured that out, Omnubius?" she grated as she tried to punch him in the jaw, a futile maneuver since they could each only move a few inches within their confines.

"Forgive me?" he asked, his green eyes filled with regret.

Omnubius had done a lot of things in his lifetime, but he had never purposely set out to hurt a woman. It wasn't his style.

"Forgiven," she sighed after examining his face for a moment. "Besides, I need you to get me out of here."

"I am glad that I have my uses," he chuckled, before relishing the movement he now had.

Already he could feel his flesh mending and repairing itself.

The knife that B.B. dropped lay against his back, a subtle reminder that it needed to be returned to its owner and soon.

"What can we do now?" she asked, the adrenaline rush ebbing and sleep threatening to overtake her again.

"Rest and heal," he answered. "In a few hours, I want you to feed from me, because when you awaken, that is all that will be on your mind. When you are safely fed, we will leave this place and make our way back to the castle. Luca has to be warned and protected. He is surrounded by danger and I can only hope that he will see my warning in time."

"Yes, Nubius," B.B. sighed as she gave in to the tiredness and closed her eyes. What did he mean by safely fed? Even though she was turned, she was no monster. Safely fed indeed, as if she could hurt anybody.

* * * * *

Dawn was just breaking as Vincent stealthy made his way back to the castle.

The plan was working and he was a genius.

Soon these fools, these oh so superior fools, would be chasing after their shadows as he stepped in and took command. His mother would have been proud. Soon, he would have the immortality that he longed for, and everyone would know the true power, the perfection of his Human brain. All would tremble with fear before him, and he would live on until time indefinite.

This he had been promised, but this he also ensured with a plan of his own.

Vincent was smiling as he entered that castle, so full of his own coming victory that he paid no attention to the person watching him, a knowing look on his face.

Chapter Twenty-One

Everywhere she stepped, memories haunted her thoughts

She could find no peace in the bedroom, their bedroom, where she had experienced a joy only imagined. There she had found a passion to eclipse any fantasy, any promised dream. She had discovered and accepted her true nature, became part of the Wolfen in more than name only, initiated by the most wild, yet gentlest of touches.

It was also here where someone tried to murder her, and where her mate, however unwittingly, had declared his love for her.

There were too many memories there for any unbiased thought.

There was no peace in the kitchen. How could there be peace when the human that her mate distrusted resided there? How could she think with the memories of those meals where they had acted so sweet and informative were still so close to the surface? She should have known that if a human dumped that much information on you, he had a purpose or a plan—yet he had seemed so harmless.

There was no way she could stay in the study. That room had so many encounters imprinted in its walls that she was quite thankful that they could not talk. Her first meeting with Lucavarious, their battles of wit and grit that intrigued and infuriated her at the same time, the picture of him lounging in his chair so commanding and aloof. Too many things had happened in that room for her to rest there.

So it was back to the Garden room or outside where she would be an easy target.

The Garden room, it was.

Stealthily, she slipped into the opening of the room, praying that Luca's senses would not detect her until she had some time to think about things. Things like his keeping secrets from her, and why his rejection of her hurt so much.

The sun shone brightly through the tall glass panels that made up the high ceiling, a mockery of her blue inner thoughts.

Still, it was a place that was not filled with too many memories. And as long as Luca stayed in the back, she would have the fountain to herself.

She knew he was still at the altar, she could sense his presence, but she felt that if she didn't intrude on his privacy, he would leave her alone. Besides, for some strange reason, she felt better, safer, and more complete with him around.

So with a heavy heart, Dark kicked off her shoes and tip-toed through the bright sunlight until she made her way to the stone bench with its frayed cushion that smelled of her mate.

"What is happening to me?" she breathed out loud as she settled on the bench. "What am I supposed to do now?"

She didn't mean to hurt her mate with her words. Hell, she had no idea that she *could* hurt him with words, but she had felt something inside her wither painfully as shock and horror replaced the usual arrogant, confident look that he usually wore on his face. His eyes, usually so vibrant and full of life, dulled into pale black orbs that radiated their pain for all to see. Then just as quickly, the shutter snapped into place. He shielded his heart and his mind as easily as he shielded the room. Nothing could escape and more importantly, no one could get in. Luca was protecting himself from her, from the pain she had unwittingly caused.

But how was she supposed to know that a few thoughtless words would tear at him so?

"Because he loves you," a low, gravelly voice intoned.

Startled, Dark looked up, eyes wide and claws unsheathing, as the Sage entered the area around the bench. The flowers seemed to bow to his majesty and the sunlight respectfully dimmed. Smiling, he knelt down to caress their moist petals, caressing them as he would a tender lover.

"Relax, child," he soothed. "I mean you no harm. I just happened to overhear your conversation with yourself and I found it interesting."

With a few grunts and groans, the Sage eased himself to his knees, then to his feet, his robe still hiding all but the slightest impression of his eyes.

"At my age, it is a bit difficult to maneuver theses old bones."

"Oh. Allow me to help," Dark said as she quickly rose up to assist the man by taking his arm, but he waved her away.

Dark gasped at the strength in that arm, before she released him and took her own seat again. The Sage probably did a lot of gardening in this room, which would account for the muscles that she felt beneath his robe.

"So what has my puppy done now?" he asked, in a resigned voice.

"Puppy? Suddenly that takes on a whole new meaning," she groused as she again began to lose herself in her dark thoughts.

"So now you know?" he asked, his attention focused wholly on her.

"Yes, I know, and it seems that I was the only one who didn't. What is that old saying? The mate is the last to know?"

"Hmm."

"What was that supposed to mean; that hmmm? I don't like it when people do that to me. It never bodes well." Her eyes narrowed as she glared at the Sage. He would not make her feel guilty, if that was his game. Lucavarious should have told her.

"Just *hmm*."

"It is never 'just *hmm*', Sage. That *hmm* has a meaning behind it." She glowered at the robed figure while guilt began to do a number on her insides.

Her stomach cramped as she thought of the expression on his face, and her heart felt raw and exposed.

"Look inside yourself for answers, Dark. You are no stupid, naïve youth with nothing but thoughts of going into heat and choosing your mate filling her head. Open your eyes, woman."

"You will not make me feel guilty," she insisted heatedly.

"You're right," came the calm response. "I can't make you anything. Only you have to do that, Dark. This you should know."

Dark took a deep breath and tried to maintain control. She realized she was looking for a fight; she was seeking confrontation, the confrontation that Luca would not allow.

She needed something or someone to release the pent-up frustration and guilt that had been building up since she uttered those dark words to Lucavarious.

Even now, she could feel the beast in her straining to break the bounds of humanity that tied it to her flesh. Her fangs fought to break through and her claws were beginning to tear into her palms, so tightly gripped were her fists.

With a deep breath she forced herself to calm down.

"He loves you, and only you have the power to hurt him, Dark," the Sage continued as if the battle she waged within herself meant nothing to him. And maybe it didn't.

"I never asked for his love," she growled, his words ripping fresh holes in her heart.

"But he has freely given it to you, something that I thought even I would not live to see."

"And why is that, old man?" Never had she been this disrespectful to her elders before and a part of her cringed even as she fought for control.

"How well do you think the Vampesi took to this mutt of a child, a part Wolfen child slated to rule while the Wolfen decimated what was left of our population? How do you think they accepted him or his first mistakes with his powers? And how well do you think he was accepted after his parents died?"

"He was an adult, Sage," Dark argued. "He was twenty-seven and capable of handling his emotions."

"Twenty-seven is mature for a Wolfen, Dark. But that is juvenile for a Vampesi. At twenty-seven he had not even fully come into his powers. He was made ruler through right of blood, but he had to hide part of himself to survive. There were no less than fifteen attempts on his life, Dark, the week he was made ruler. Who would back the dirty little Wolfen boy? If it wasn't for Omnubius and his parents' scheme to force immunity to silver and sunlight, he would be dead."

There was silence on Dark's end as she took in the Sage's words. No wonder her words wounded Luca so deeply. Being called *dirty* had to be a favorite taunt of those who opposed him.

"Luca had to keep private about himself, Dark, or others would have used it against him. You saw the Wolfen pelts he had in his room?"

She nodded, remembering the distaste and horror that she had felt.

"Well, those two are the ones who murdered his parents, Dark. They also found out that he was part Wolfen and tried to use that faint blood-claim to stake a hold on the Vampesi land. He withdrew into himself for almost a month after he executed them. It killed him to do that, Dark, but he had to. He had to avenge his parents' death and he had to protect his people, all of his people. And do you know why he kept those pelts, Dark?"

Numbly she shook her head. She couldn't fathom the strength it took to execute your own people, let alone know that they were responsible for your parent's' death. The again, maybe she could. The similarity there was almost eerie.

"He kept them to remind himself of what he could never become."

"But what does that have to do with him keeping something this important away from me, Sage?"

"He was protecting himself, Dark. And for him to share that truth with you proves that he loves and trusts you beyond all others. He has made himself vulnerable again, as vulnerable as that scared twenty-seven year old child who avenged his parents and garnered the respect of his people. He risked his soul in telling you this truth, Dark. He made himself vulnerable to you. You are his one weakness."

"I never chose to be his weakness," Dark nearly screamed. She was fighting against something that was bigger than her and she knew it. And the more she learned of her mate, the bigger it grew.

"He never chose to be part Wolfen, or Vampesi, or the leader of his people. Yet does he handle his responsibilities."

"I never asked him for his love."

"He never asked to fall in love."

"He lied to me."

"He omitted facts, Dark, yet he told you when he felt the time was right."

"I never asked for this love!" she screamed as she rose to her feet. "I never asked for that. I didn't want to fall in love."

The Sage said nothing.

"Oh…my…God. Did I just say what I think I did?"

"You love him."

Dark sank back into the bench, all the fight leaving her. She loved that man over there. That's why any thought of carrying on without him hurt. That was why the pain he now felt weighed heavily on her soul. "I can't tell him that," she whispered. "That would make me…"

"Vulnerable?" he asked as he struggled to his feet.

Dark fell silent. She just garnered more insight to what Luca was feeling, and she found it hard to deal with.

"You have things to think about, Dark," Sage soothed. "And I have incantations of the high ancients to review. You have time, child, but not much of it. The sun is now high in the sky, and in five hours the people will gather for the ceremony. It is best that you present a united front, but if that is impossible, let it not be open warfare. Never iron your dirty sheets in the public square, or something like that, the old saying goes. But why someone would want to iron dirty sheets is beyond me."

That broke the tension a little and Dark had to smile.

But soon her thoughts began to churn on what she had learned.

Was this how Luca felt? This fear mingled with excitement? How long had he carried this mixed up jumble of nerves and emotions around with him? What courage did it take for him to admit that he loved her, knowing how she felt about his...omission? Was she as strong as he?

Before she knew what she was doing, Dark rose to her feet and slowly made her way back to the place where the altar rested.

She peered into the dense greenery — noting that he had not put up a protective shield — and made her way to her mate's side.

Luca lay curled up in a ball, almost a fetal position, with his back to her, his arms wrapped protectively around himself. He was vulnerable, made vulnerable by her words, and now he sought to put together the pieces of his shattered soul.

"Luca?" she asked quietly as she reached out one trembling hand to touch him, then pulled back uncertainly. Her confusion and fear were plainly visible in her eyes, her own vulnerability made all the more real as she observed her devastated mate.

"Luca?"

"Yes, Dark," he sighed painfully as he stirred slowly into awareness. His shoulders tensed as if he waited for a further blow.

"Luca...Wolfen mate for life."

"That I know," he sighed again, as if counting the years of a loveless existence where his feelings amounted to nothing and he was chained by his own heart.

"Luca...can we start over? I mean, have we ruined it? Have *I*... ruined everything?"

Luca inhaled deeply and eased onto his back to look at his mate.

Her eyes were filled with knowledge that was not there before, but of what he didn't know. Maybe of her own heart, because nothing short of love could make someone that miserable. Her bottom lip was well chewed, and not by him. Her expression was between broken pride and all-out pleading. Her hands shook as she crossed them protectively in front herself. He was now quite familiar with that pose.

She was suffering.

He didn't even want to get his hopes up as he contemplated why. "Can we?" he asked, his voice made husky by expectation, even as he prepared himself for the worst.

Nothing else mattered to him, nothing but having the balm of her love to soothe his hurts. He wanted her beside him, beneath him, on top of him. He wanted her fighting with him, laughing with him, loving him, until the day his life ceased to be. She was a part of him now, the part that sustained his heart, that fueled the fire in his blood. He needed her, he needed her, and he needed her. And he would take her on any terms. If she didn't love him, they had years for her to learn how. But he needed his mate, his Wolfen-woman beside him now. Any pain was worth it.

She smiled at him. Sure it was tentative and trembling, but it was a smile.

He held out his hand, pretending that it wasn't quivering with anticipation and fear. He held his breath as he waited.

Then the touch finally came, his heart exploded in joy. There would be time to evaluate this situation later, but for now, he had his Wolfen-woman, his Dark, his mate, back where she belonged.

As he pulled her in his arms, all seemed right with the world.

Let the assassins come. Let the people revolt. Let the Wolfen and Vampesi tear themselves to bits. He didn't care. His Dark was back where she belonged.

Back in his arms.

Chapter Twenty-Two

"We still have to talk," Dark warned as she snuggled into Luca's touch. "I kind of understand what you did, but I still have issues about it."

"But you are here," he murmured into her hair, savoring the feel of her.

"Yes, I am here Lucavarious. And I hope we can work our problems out."

"Problems?" He froze for a moment, then snuggled her closer to his chest, his heart. They had problems?

"Yes, Luca, problems. And I mean problems other than people trying to kill us and disappearing B.B.'s."

Which brought his thoughts to Omnubius. Or more precisely, where was Omnubius. "Later, Dark," he sighed in her hair. "We can deal with us later. We have more pressing things to deal with now."

"More pressing than our relationship, Lucavarious?" Her words sounded ominous even to herself.

She had gotten herself in the mood to discuss this major problem that they were having, this major crisis, and he wanted to talk later? Was she the only person to see the wrong in that? What was more important than their relationship and these new feelings that she was having? She had finally made up her mind to tell him that she maybe, kind of, perhaps felt a tiny bit of love for him too, and he wanted to put their conversation on hold until a more convenient time? Love had to be blind – blind, deaf, dumb and stupid.

"Dark," he began on another sigh. It must be a woman thing to be argumentative. "Have you noticed? The sun is up."

"And it will be up tomorrow, and the day after that, and the day after that. It happens daily, Luca, even if the clouds cover its shine." Okay, that was just plain sarcastic, but she had built herself up to discuss this mating, and damn it, she was ready to discuss it.

"That is true, Dark," he began, tightening his hands in her hair and forcing her eyes up to meet his. "But have you noticed that certain nocturnal members of our family have not reported in yet?"

She blinked a few times, and then she remembered. Nubius hadn't checked in with them. She had heard nothing from either Vincent or Nubius, not that she was afraid that the Human had done something to the Vampire, but he was to have reported to them.

"Can't you check on him? Do a mental thing or something?"

"As powerful as I am, Dark, it is still beyond me to put out a mental call for Omnubius. Not that he would ever answer even if I called, but it is a physical impossibility."

Well, she should have expected that response. He might be part Wolfen, but the extent of her powers in that area was just communicating while in beast mode.

"So how can we check up on him?"

"We can't. But I know that he can take care of himself, unless someone has figured out that he is the family troubleshooter."

"Then what can we do?" She might not be all that crazy about Nubius, but he did have a hand in rearing Luca. And for that alone, she owed him.

"We can question the Human. And if Nubius found out something, you can be sure that he will find a way to let us know what is going on."

Dark was quiet for a moment, digesting this newest development. Then she realized how tense Luca was. It now felt as if she were lying against a slab of rock, so tightly drawn were his muscles. He was really beginning to worry, even though his expression remained passive.

"I can question him, Luca. You need to rest for this ceremony."

"I don't want you facing him alone, Dark. I still don't trust him."

"But I am capable of getting the answers I want out of him, Luca, and protecting myself too. He is only a human."

"And those thoughts have caused many a Vampesi's downfall. Never underestimate an opponent. Lives get lost that way."

With that said, he unwrapped himself from Dark and reached for what was left of his pants. He would face the Human, but he would do it in full regalia, kind of. He wanted to make an impression on him, to remind him what side his bagel was buttered on, as the human saying went.

"By the way, Luca," Dark interrupted his thoughts as she swung her feet over the side of the altar. Funny, but her back felt better for laying on it. "Have you decided where the next hole, I mean, piercing is going to be put? And it better not be below the waist either. That property is mine until the day you die."

A fiery blush filled his face at her words followed by a snort of amusement as she realized that she laid claim to his personal, uh, property. He peered over his shoulder at her, one black eyebrow raised in question.

"Well, it is." She stuck her chin out and dared him to say otherwise.

"Uh, how about my navel?" he asked, and she shook her head.

"Too close to the goods." And she leered at his crotch, causing him to jerk his pants up before the stir he felt there became apparent to her interested gaze.

"An eyebrow?"

"Maybe." She tilted her head to the side, trying to envision his stoic features with a frivolous silver hoop attached. Not a good look for him, she decided, and shook her head no.

Luca tightened the drawstrings on his pants and reached for his tunic, his bangles jingling merrily with his movements.

"A nipple?" he asked, almost jokingly as he lifted his arms to pull his shirt over his head.

"Let me see," she said, suddenly very interested in his chest.

"What?" he asked, his voice muffled by the remains of his shirt that swaddled his head. He shifted as he tried to untangle it and pull it down.

"Yes, your nipple, Luca. I like that idea. And make t the right one, the left is too close to your heart." And the only thing going to be next to that was her.

"You are serious?" he asked as his head popped through. "You wouldn't mind a ring there?"

"I get to play with it, Luca," she purred. "And I'm sure you remember how responsive your nipples are."

Luca gulped.

His lower extremities cheered.

His brain began to cloud over.

Dark sat perched on the altar staring at him, her eyes glowing with the beginnings of a new arousal, licking her lips like a hungry cat.

"Vincent," he managed as he felt his body respond to her invitation. "We have to go and question Vincent before the sun sets."

With that, and a jingle of silver, Luca disappeared into the dense foliage that lived in the room.

"Later, Luca," she called softly, knowing that his sensitive ears would pick up her voice. "Later, after we get some answers, I get to relax you again."

His faint, "Lord, help me!" was drowned out by her sudden burst of laughter.

* * * * *

"Tonight," he chanted. "It all ends and begins anew tonight."

Vincent sat in the center of the floor in his room just off of the kitchen. His blood-splattered clothing had been tossed into the furnace that heated up the massive cook- stoves of the castle.

There were, after all, over four hundred humans who depended on the food from the kitchens. Over four hundred, who would suddenly find themselves in need of leadership. Over four hundred to show his power to, to garner the respect of, to conquer.

"Tonight," he chanted. "Tonight is the beginning of the end, or the end to the beginning."

He had to chuckle at his own wit.

He was so clever, that he was not surprised by the knock at the door. He knew who would be there. After spending time with certain elements, you began to know how they thought. Ever the logical, Lucavarious would be at the door looking for answers. The wild card was his mate, but she would be dealt with soon enough. How she found out about the wine was beyond him, but he had planned for that eventuality as well.

"Enter, please," he called, ever polite and subservient.

He tried to feign surprise as Luca and Dark entered.

"Master," he stuttered, raising to his feet quickly. "I did not expect you. I was meditating."

"So I see." Luca kept his face devoid of emotion and his voice even.

"How may I serve?" he asked, looking anxious to please.

"You may tell me what has happened to the Vampire."

"Omnubius?" he asked brows lightly furled then a knowing look crossed his face. "He met with a young Wolfen woman and decided to stay there with her until this evening," he lied with a straight face.

"And he left no message for me?" Luca asked, face still devoid of expression.

"Which woman did he stay with?" Dark quickly added her own question. "And did you find B.B.?"

"No message master, other than that the invitation had been extended. I made no mention of the mistress or the attempt on her life." That much was true. "And I believe that he stayed with a young woman named Puaua."

Dark sucked in an annoyed breath and her eyes narrowed into dark slits. If that man messed with her young and innocent cousin, she would bleed him dry herself, before she removed certain parts of his anatomy that she was sure that he loved.

Yes, dear Puaua, the scapegoat, he thought. With her help, another obstacle was out of the way. Luca was losing his bodyguards at an alarming rate. What would he do, when the time came? What would he do?

"And the response, Vincent?" Luca asked, bringing the human's thoughts back to the conversation.

"The Wolfen, Zinia, said that they would possibly show up."

"Which means that Auntie will be here," Luca said, "if only to harass me and try once more to force her case." Luca allowed a little annoyance to show. "Oh, and of course, to finish you off, my dear," he said in an aside as he turned to Dark.

"Not funny, Vampesi," she said as she rolled her big brown eyes towards the ceiling.

"Thank you, Vincent," Luca suddenly said, bringing everyone's attentions back to the Human in their midst. "I appreciate having you on my side. You will of course attend the ceremony, to represent the Humans that I consider family? I would consider it an honor to have you there, the one who is watching out for me."

"It would be my pleasure," Vincent almost purred.

Checkmate. The game was nearly through.

"Oh, no," Luca answered back, his face showing sincerity. "The pleasure will be all mine."

* * * * *

It is time, thought the watcher. It is time to put the plan into action. No one double-crosses him and lives. Not that he would have allowed him to live anyway. But he had planned for this, oh yes. Always have a backup plan and expect the worse while hoping for the best.

The watcher observed as the couple exited the room, and he smiled. Time to upset the apple cart. There were only a few hours left, and then he would have it all.

Chapter Twenty-Three

"He did something to Nubius. I am sure of it."

"The only thing that I am sure of is that his libido is out of control. What is he doing messing around with my cousin?" Dark growled.

They had exited Vincent's room and were now headed for the privacy of their own bedroom.

"Hmm," Luca mused. "Maybe your cousin isn't as innocent as she appears."

"And just what is that supposed to mean?" she growled, baring her teeth at him a little. Her emotions were still in a jumble, both from being in heat and from the earlier incident with Luca, but she still sought to control them.

"It means that your cousin is a big girl. And that she won't let Nubius do anything unless she wants it."

"Lucavarious."

Luca grinned as he looked down at his mate. She was still touchy and he still had that ability to set her nerves on edge. There was still hope for him yet.

"Dark, the only thing I want to worry about right now is getting into a hot bath and relaxing my sore muscles. The sun will be going down soon and we need to be rested in body and mind. Tonight, it ends either way."

"You're thinking that there is more than one person involved?" she questioned.

"Ask me again when we are in the bath," he replied as he ushered her down the hall.

Once in the bedroom, Luca closed is eyes in concentration and in a flash a purple shield surrounded their rooms.

"Can anybody hear through this?" she asked, knowing that he had the ability to create barriers that sound couldn't penetrate.

"We are safe to speak openly," he replied as he moved wearily towards the bathroom. "Would you take a look at this?"

Luca stood in the entrance to his bath and shook his head that what awaited them.

Flower petals of all kinds floated in the tub, bringing a fresh floral smell to the room. Tall, unlit candles surrounded the tub, waiting for a match to bring about an intimate glow. The water was still hot, as steam drifted slowly over the surface.

"Why is it still hot?" Dark asked as she peered over his shoulder.

"It comes from the hot springs below the castle," he replied. "The bathtub is sunk into a pool. That way the water stays at a constant temperature and no cold porcelain at your back when you sit down."

"Ingenious," she breathed as she took in the air of romance that surrounded this large room. Even the towels seemed extra fluffy today. "Is it safe?"

Luca closed his eyes and inhaled deeply. He could detect no dangerous smells or fragrances. He opened his mouth and tasted the air, noting that nothing sent his senses into a state of panic.

"I believe we shall come to no harm from bathing here. The poison was in the wine."

"Great," Dark cried as she began to rip off her clothing. "After all that's happened, a bath seems perfect."

"Sore?" he asked as he observed the abandon in which she tossed her clothing to the side.

He also noted that she trusted his word without question. That too was telling.

"You have no idea," she drawled as she stripped off her pants. This day had left her battered and bruised mentally more than physically. They still had to have that conversation about their relationship, but she didn't want to take his mind off of the situation at hand. There would be plenty of time for that after those bad guys had been rounded up and put in their place. Then there would be time for her to rail at him, forgive him, and if he was a good boy, she might even admit that she had a little, tiny bit of love in her heart for him.

Yes, that was a good plan.

"A hot bath will help," he decided as he picked up a long pack of matches and struck one.

The hiss of the match as it began to blaze sent shivers through his body. He had her back but his body wanted affirmation that she wouldn't be going anywhere.

Focusing his attention, he floated the match across the tub, touching the flame to the wick of each candle, before snuffing out the light.

With another look, the lights dimmed and his growing excitement added to the humidity in the room.

"Neat trick," Dark laughed as she stepped up to the edge of the tub. "What else can you do?"

Without a word, he focused on her and she was lifted into the air and gently settled into the warm water.

She sighed as the wet heat seeped into her pores, easing the tension in her muscles, making her moan in delight.

"Is that sufficient?" he asked as he stepped to the side of the tub and trailed his fingers through the water.

"More than," she assured. "Join me?"

Luca grinned. He grinned as he nearly ripped the shirt from his body and he grinned as the pants shared the same fate. He even managed to grin as he settled himself into the deep tub, relishing the feel of the water against his skin.

"You are enjoying yourself?" she asked, still unable to find that perfect medium where she could tease him and still keep control of her emotions. Now that the dam had burst, it was kind of hard to keep her feelings concealed.

"Immensely," he sighed as he sank down to his neck across from her.

"Are you relaxed?" she asked, one eyebrow cocked to the side.

As always, she was having a reaction to his naked body, but now that she had accepted the fact that she had great affection for him—that sounded better than love—her body seemed to crave him more in a deeper way.

He was as relaxed as possible, seeing that he was still in limbo with her, his cousin was missing, his Blood Bank was still lost, her people were trying to take her out, a crazy human was running around in his castle, and there was still an unnamed murderer on the loose. "I am fine."

Dark opened her mouth to comment, but then her stomach growled, making its needs apparent.

"You need to eat," he said, eyes still closed, relishing the feel of the silky soft water.

"And what about you?" she asked, even though she made no move to exit the tub.

"I shall feed later," he replied.

"But, you are the one going to be stuck with poisonous metals, Luca. You need to feed."

"Later, Dark," he insisted. He didn't want to waste a moment of time separated from her.

As the sun drew closer to setting, the more he realized that this just might be the last time he had to spend with her. What mattered food when he needed this time with her more?

"Now, Luca. You will just have to feed from me."

"Dark," he began, sitting up his eyes opening at last.

His stomach began to crave her, the thought of taking her blood, real blood, hot from the vein, was doing things to his body.

"You need me, Lucavarious."

She was amazed at how much she wanted, *needed* this for him. It was her right to protect her mate and provide for him in times of need. It was part of her animalistic nature, but it was also an extension of her love for him. She wanted to see him whole and hale before he went off to battle. It was her right and her privilege.

"I would not hurt you, Dark," he admitted slowly, as if the words were painful. "If I have you with me, drinking your blood is not the only thing that I would want. I don't know if you are ready for that, Dark. It would...pain me...to see you hurt." *It would be like ripping out my own heart*, he added silently. Being in love sure did change a guy.

"You will not hurt me, Luca," Dark sighed in impatience. The more she thought about it, the more erotic the thought of having him feed on her became. "I want you to do it."

Before he could protest further, Dark moved through the water, slick as an otter, closer to the heat of his body, so much hotter than the water.

With a smile, she settled herself on his lap, facing him, and wrapped her arms around his neck.

"Dark," he warned, his eyes starting to glitter silver. "Be warned, woman. This is no time to play games."

Her answer was to glide even closer and nip at his neck.

"Dark," he growled, his whole body shuddering with delight.

"You know you want to, Luca," she purred as she lapped at crystal droplets of water that rested against the dark skin of his neck. "You know that I want you to."

Luca grabbed her hands and forcibly pushed her back, only to get a great view of...

He never before realized that breasts could float.

He shook his head as he fought to contain the hunger that was building within him at a rapid pace. He could almost smell her sweet rich blood, so much thicker than the watery, red, protein-filled sap that they fed off of now.

He began to sweat at the thought of lapping at the smooth skin of her neck, there, just where her pulse beat so strongly. She would arch her neck in welcome, just as she did before, and he would gorge himself on the sweetness that she offered.

"Luca," she urged as she tangled her fingers in his hair, pulling him closer to the source of life within her. In response, she groaned deeply as he pulled away from her and took her lips in a fiery kiss.

No, *kiss* was a word too shallow to describe the heat and intensity with which he devoured her.

Luca forced his tongue past the barrier of her lips and moaned as he tasted the sweetness of her mouth. He closed his eyes as he felt a part of himself sink deeply into her. Her flavor was as heady as ever, her scent intoxicating. He gratefully — like a thirsty man — drank in her essence.

She moaned deeply in her throat, the sound captured by his conquering mouth. With a tentative tongue, Dark began to explore her mate, sighing as she felt his first set of fangs began to release.

Luca stiffened as he felt his gums part and his Vampesi fangs slip into place. There was a sweet sharp pain followed by an all-consuming lust that caused him to clutch his mate closer to him. He shuddered at the feel of her hardened nipples pressing against his chest, the feel of her fingers locking into his hair, dragging him closer, the feel of her rounded thighs pressed against his.

He felt his manhood leap to sudden life, as if it knew her intimate parts were so close. Hunger and power surged through his body, making him feel masterful and dominant.

Yes, he would drink from her. It was his right. Dark was his mate, his light, and his love. She offered herself to him freely. Who was he to deny such a gift?

Dark felt the changes taking place in Luca's body. She felt his sudden surge into full erection and the hunger that began to claw at his body.

Yet, she felt no fear. This was Lucavarious, her Luca. He would cause her no harm. This was what she was made for, to protect and keep her Luca safe. It was her duty as a woman and his mate. He would surely perish without her. She would save him.

Dark tipped her head back, breaking the connection between them as she gripped his shoulders. She struggled to bring air into her oxygen-starved lungs as her whole body writhed in desire.

The heat of the room had increased, the humidity was almost stifling as Luca made known his want and need.

"Now, Luca," she panted. "Do it now."

"Soon," Luca moaned as his lips followed a trail up her neck and to the underside of her chin. "Soon, my dark, dark angel."

He could smell her acute arousal, a heady mixture of spices and Dark's unique scent. It went straight to his head and stroked his burning forge of lust into an inferno. She was ready. She would be soft and tight and wet, and Luca couldn't wait.

Without warning, Luca lifted Dark free of the water and slammed her down on his hardness, filling her to the hilt, burying himself as deep as he could go.

"*Yes!*" Dark screamed as she felt his hot hardness parting her, filling her beyond full.

This was her mate, her Luca, dominate, brash, handsome, arrogant, and completely under her power.

Luca whimpered as he felt scalded by her heat. This was growing out of control, and he wanted it that way. With one hand, he fisted his fingers through her short soft hair and pulled her head to the side,

"Yes," she whimpered as her fangs exploded into her mouth.

As he hesitated, licking at the vein that pumped excitedly, she closed her fangs around a small section of his skin, just below his ear.

Luca's whole body stiffened, then became wracked with great shudders. Her erotic bite was filling him with a hot urgency that he had never felt before, not even in the arms of his Dark.

"What are you doing to me?" he rasped as he clutched her body close to his and slammed his hips upwards, impaling her with his maleness.

"I am loving you." Dark shivered as she scraped her teeth over his skin.

"Dark," he moaned, just as she tightened her inner muscles around him, sending his head spinning and shutting down his mind. Now he was acting on pure instinct, the animal in him set free.

With a growl, he scraped his teeth, once, twice, then a third time as his tongue dragged across her now sensitized skin.

Dark moaned and tried to squirm closer to him, but his teeth clamped down on her neck and a warning growl, *his* warning growl, filled the air.

Dark's claws began to unsheathe in reaction to his dominant gesture, digging painfully into the skin of his shoulders, drawing blood.

The smell of his own blood was enough to break his last bonds with his control.

With a growl, Luca's second set of fangs exploded into his mouth just as he used his first set to pierce deeply into flesh of her neck.

"Luca!" Dark cried out as the sharp pain filled her being, just as quickly turning to pleasure as his hot mouth covered his puncture marks.

"Sweet, Dark. You are so sweet," Luca murmured almost mindlessly as his tongue lapped at the scarlet droplets that pearled up on her skin.

Then no words were exchanged as Luca placed his mouth over the wounds and began a pulling suction.

Dark moaned, stars careening behind her eyes as she felt Luca accept what she offered and begin to feed.

The universe seemed to spin on its axis as she felt her body clutch and tighten around him.

Mindlessly, she began to move upon his marble hardness, slowly sliding up a few inches and then down, making the head of him tease her womb. She was as hungry for him as he was for her.

Luca fell, losing himself inside of his mate as he fed from her. Never had any blood tasted this good, this engrossing. With every swallow, he felt a strength that he had never felt before. His hungry organs drank in nourishment as his equally hungry body relished the small moves that his mate made above him.

Slowly the haze began to clear from his head and a tension of another kind took its place.

He hungered for her body, for her movements. Soon he did not know what was more important—drinking her in or physically becoming one with her.

Then the desire to join her body became more important than any feeding.

Freeing her hair, he raised his wrist up as he tore his mouth away from her neck. With a snarl, he used his fangs to tear a wound in his arm so that his blood ran freely. Then taking his other hand, he gathered up a finger full of blood and rubbed it over the wounds in her neck, mixing their blood and closing the puncture marks at the same time.

Dark jumped as she felt his mouth leave her, and weakly tugged at his head in hopes of bringing his mouth right back where it belonged. Then she cried out as the wounds began to burn.

"Damn it, Lucavarious. Ever hear of a bandage?" she growled as the sharp pain pulled her from her fog of passion.

Looking up, she gasped at the sight of her mate. With her rich blood filling him, he had never looked more vibrant, more alive than he did then. And she was the reason for that.

A slow wicked smile spread across her face as she observed the changes that she had wrought within her mate.

His eyes were now basically silver and his breathing was slow and steady. She could feel the heat radiate off of his skin like never before. His nostrils flared as he scented the air around her, smelling her arousal combined with his, making his cheeks flush with his intensity.

"Dark," he purred, his voice gravelly and low.

"Luca," she breathed as his excitement fed her own.

Before she could move, Luca wrapped his arms around her hips; pulling her to him tightly, he rose up to his knees.

Dark gasped at his sudden movements, wrapping her leg around his waist as her arms went around his neck.

"Time for a little death," he purred, before he began to thrust his hips.

"Oh, hell. Oh, Luca!" Dark screamed as the first waves of fire hit her.

With every thrust, Luca touched the center of her womb, setting off nerve endings that she had not known that she possessed. With every pounding move, he ground his hips in a circular motion, stimulating the sensitive flesh of the mouth of her opening as well as her clitoris.

She groaned and threw back her head as she felt tension mount within her. Tighter and tighter her muscles gripped as her toes pointed and her thighs began to shake.

Luca was going to kill her.

There was a moment of absolute silence, of peace, where she could feel everything and yet nothing. The universe was hers and she sat atop it ready to plunge into the fiery heat of oblivion. Then it was upon her, a force that she had never felt before. She had no time to move, no time to think, no time to breathe, as she began to drown in waves of release.

"Lucccc," she panted as her body rhythmically began to stoke him, to milk him, to make her senses sing with delight.

"Dark," he hissed between clenched teeth and fangs as the passion became too much for his body to contain.

The temperature in the room spiked, hot and dry as he closed his eyes, threw back his head, and roared.

There was no help for it. The feeling that she wrung out of his body had to be released, or the tension would have broken his mind. Never had he ever felt anything so prolific, so astounding, and so damn good. Waves of his climax traveled from the straining muscles of his thighs, to his knotted stomach, to the top of his head, and finally expressed themselves in a spurting release that flooded the hot cavern of her body.

He moaned as he felt her body taking what he had to offer, demanding more, and giving untold pleasure.

Luca felt as if a part of him, a part of his life force had been transferred to her, making her the stronger one, the once chosen for a purpose…his soul mate.

Shakily he lowered them both back into the still steaming water as his head dropped to her shoulder.

Dark's breath was rough as she relaxed against her mate, craving the touch of his hot wet body.

Luca finally threw back his head and opened his eyes to view his only love.

Dark's hair stood on end from his fingers, her face was flushed bright red, her lips swollen from his kisses. He never thought that she looked finer. There was a glow about her, a soft purple shimmer that…

Purple shimmer?

"Dark?" he asked slowly, his voice still rough from his release.

Slowly, Dark opened her eyes and tried to lift her head to view her mate. What she saw astounded her.

Luca was pale, his black eyes wide with...fright?

Was he having a reaction to her blood? Was he going into shock because of what she forced him to do? Was he going to get ill? Was he going to die?

"Luca," she panted, as fear made her rise off of him, but his arms tightened around her and pulled her back down.

"Luca, what is it?"

"Pregnant," he breathed.

"What?" she asked, wondering if her blood had fried his brain instead of exploding it.

"You are pregnant," he whispered in awe as he ran his hands reverently over her body. "My baby is within you."

"You can't know that!" Dark exclaimed, angrily knocking his hands away. What was the big idea, scaring her like that? What a way to come down off of a magical release like that. "It's too soon." This man had issues.

"Purple, Dark. You are glowing purple," Luca breathed, tears filling his eyes.

"What?"

Dark scrunched up her face as she decided to humor him. It was wise to placate mad Humans and Vampesi, her parents always said. She would get some practice in now. Would 'Yes, Dear,' suit?

Holding in a snort, Dark looked down at her arm and...

Screamed.

"I'm glowing purple!" Dark cried as she leapt away from Luca, shock giving her strength.

"Purple, Dark. Purple!" he laughed.

"What did you do to me, Lucavarious, you bastard?" she screamed, leaping to her feel, almost tripping from her still-weakened muscles. "What did you put in me?" Was he rabid?

Could a Vampesi bite cause some horrible disease? Would she now become, (gulp), part Vampesi?

"A baby, Dark. I put a baby inside of you!" he exclaimed as he, too, leapt to his feet, only to grab her around the waist and lift her out of the water in a fierce hug. "Oh, my love, you are carrying my daughter."

"Baby?" she asked as she reached out to cup his cheeks, now glowing with pleasure. "A baby? Are you sure?"

"Yes, Dark," he laughed as he began to sway with her in his arms. "A baby. My baby. Our baby. Our child, born of love."

"Our baby," Dark mused, then she began to laugh. "We are having a baby? You are sure?"

"Yes, Dark," he assured yet again. "We are going to have a little girl of our own."

"Oh Luca," she breathed, then she laughed as a warm loving feeling began to fill her heart. It was now so full it felt as if it were going to explode. She had Luca, and now a baby of their own. Born of love. Love?

Did she let that little bit of information slip?

She tried to think back on what was said in the heat of the moment, but her brain was not paying attention to her words. The something else occurred to her.

"Damn it Luca," she cried as she raised one fist and bopped him on the shoulder. "What were you thinking?"

"Ouch," Luca let out as he let her go with amazing swiftness. "Why did you do that?"

"Why? Why? You noodle noggin. You get me knocked up while there are people out there trying to kill us. How am I supposed to protect you and a newborn too? You aren't leaving me to raise this kid alone, Lucavarious. You had better call off this ceremony thing until after this baby is born."

In a huff, she leapt off the edge of the tub and stormed into the bedroom, a disconcerted Luca following behind.

"I can't do that, Dark," he cried as he snatched up a towel before following her out.

"Yes, you can, you silver-eyed devil. And it is a boy."

"It's a girl," he countered as he reached out and grabbed her arm. Ignoring her struggles, he pulled her close to him and enveloped her in a big plush towel. "And I have to go through with it, now more than ever, Dark. Our child's life depends on it."

Dark stopped struggling and looked up into the eyes of her mate. He was right. If they waited until the child was born, he would be too vulnerable to attack. She had only known of this child's existence for a few moments, and already she was anxious over its safety. She already loved him.

Laying her head on his damp chest, Dark silently conceded his point.

"I'm gonna get big and fat and horny," she breathed against him, relishing the feel of his arms as they wrapped gently around her, his hands stroking her.

"Horny?" he asked, his hands pausing in their gently caressing of her back.

"I told you, we get highly sexed when we are pregnant. But don't worry, it only lasts until about a week before the child is born."

Luca froze, his mind screaming in terror, his body laughing with delight.

Third trimester?

"What have I done?" he breathed softly to himself.

"And the weird cravings don't start until the second. Is there any way to get anteater around here? My mother drove my father mad looking for fresh anteater, rare. Perhaps I'll crave something different. My mother said that her mother craved raw bats, but then she was a bit touched in the head. Luca?"

He was too still and quiet.

"Help," she thought she heard him whisper before he shook his head and led her to their bed.

"And another thing, how soon do Vampesi fangs come in? I want to breast feed our child, but he is going to suffer if he thinks that he can get away with teething on my boobs. I draw the line at that."

Chapter Twenty-Four

The sun was going down.

Nubius could feel it, feel the tingle in his blood that signaled the renewal of another Vampire night.

He sighed as he felt life return to his lethargic limbs, any trace of a wound, but for a small soreness, gone. He lifted his head and tried to listen to the area around him. There was the scurry of small animals as they ran for the cover of their nighttime burrows, the feel of the temperature as the sun released its heated grip on the land, the smell of another evening as the moon began to cool the land with its pale face.

It was now, in this twilight time, that the Vampesi and the Vampire stirred. It was now that he would come into his full power, a power that had been muted by pain, blood loss, and the bright rays of the sun. Now, it was time for action.

"Nubius?" the small voice whimpered from beneath him.

"B.B.?" he questioned. He had no time for her pitiful whining. He had things that needed be done. First order of business, feed her so that she wouldn't become a Vampire of legend.

"I feel funny."

"Of course you do," he began. "You died, kind of, and are reborn."

"Nubius?"

"Yes?" he sighed as be begun to work his hands around her, positioning her so that the fledgling would have easy access to his wrist. He was no fool. No one was going to take a bite out of his neck without proper training, of which she had none.

"Remember when you said that you were going to feed me?"

"Yes B.B."

"Then let's get on with it."

Nubius looked down into her green eyes; her glowing green eyes and almost chuckled. She was coming into her own at an alarming rate.

"And my name is Tamara."

"With an attitude like that, you expect me to invite you to dine on my blood? You had better start treating me nice."

"Nubius," she hissed and her hands gripped the sleeves of his coat, tearing holes with her sudden strength. "This is no time for games. I am in pain."

"My coat," he nearly wailed.

"Oh, hush up. It was ruined anyway. Feed me."

"Aren't we little Miss Demanding? I have a good mind to leave you here," he growled, offended by her lack of concern about his coat. He'd had this coat for ages and it was his favorite. And there was no telling what his boots looked like.

"Feed me, or I swear I will strangle you with the remains of this coat and feast on you cooling blood."

"Well," he harrumphed, "if you are going to put it that way."

"*Omnubius.*"

The tingling ache in her stomach that she had felt earlier had developed into a bone-deep hunger. Her body craved nutrients and protein. And only one thought sustained her. Nubius said that he was going to feed her, and he damn well would. Or she would rip his stupid head off.

"What is that smell?" she whispered lowly as her head whipped from side to side. Her senses, never acute, were exploding into full life. She could see Nubius clearly now, the disgruntled expression on his face and the condition of his clothes. She could also smell something rancid.

"You," he laughed, his eyes swirling colors and looking quite malicious. "You crapped your pants, little human. And now you get a small dose of what I had to go through these last few hours. It's amazing that I could sleep at all."

Her face would have flushed, if it had that much blood in it. But instead she managed to look shame-faced as she realized that his words were true. "I have to go wash," she breathed, tears starting to fill her eyes. "I don't feel clean."

Realizing that she was going through yet another phase of acceptance, Nubius made a vow not to tell the truth so bluntly next time. Women, whether they were Wolfen, Vampesi, Human, or Vampire, were too vain and sensitive by half.

"We will attend to that momentarily," he agreed. Even the rich smell of the earth could not completely blot out the smell of her waste. "But for now, let me introduce you to the age-old act of feeding."

"Feeding...yes," her tears dried up suddenly as the prospect of easing the ache in her stomach.

"First, have your fangs dropped?" he asked.

"Fangs?" she asked.

"Oh, great. A late bloomer," he sighed. "Okay. I will make the incision for you. You are to suck and sip, not gorge and gulp. Understand me? Suck and sip. And if I pull away from you, you had better let me go. We need my strength to get us out of here and if you take too much, I will kill you to take back what I need to save Lucavarious. Understand?"

"Yes, Omnubius," she breathed suddenly aware of their precarious situation. She could read the certainty in his face. He would kill her in order to meet his goals; she had no false hopes about that.

"Good, we understand each other. Suck and sip, Tamara."

So saying, he raised his left wrist to his mouth and closed his eyes.

He felt the sweet hot pain as his fangs parted his gums, exposing their sharp tips to his tender wrist. One bite was all it took for him to locate a vein and spear an opening for her first feeding.

"Damn, I taste good," he chuckled as the flavor of his own blood filled his mouth. "Are you ready?"

At the first smell of blood, Tamara felt all of her senses focus in on the source. Everything in her was concentrated on his wrist and the way it was held just out of her reach. "Give it to me," she growled, her voice low and urgent as the bright red droplets of blood filled their small tomb with the rich smell of life.

"Suck and sip," he reminded her as he held his wrist out to the right, making it easier for her to turn her head and latch on.

"Yes," she breathed as her hands flew up and gripped his wrist in a tight hold. Slowly she raised her head, her whole body tense and trembling, and lapped the thin trail of blood that ran down his arm.

"Today, Tamara," Nubius sighed at her slow movements. Now was not the time to savor. Now was the time to suck and sip.

Tamara said nothing, but quickly wrapped her lips around the puncture.

Nubius stiffened as he felt her began to suck slowly at his wrist. The sensations were so erotic to him he almost howled in delight while he fought to keep his manhood under control. He had forgotten how good it felt to have a woman sup at his flesh. He made a mental note to go and find one soon.

Tamara groaned in delight as his rich blood flowed over her tongue and was seemingly absorbed into her body. She tried to remember what Omnubius had told her, sip and suck, but it was a battle she had to fight fiercely. He tasted so hot and sweet, so alive, that it was hard not to gorge herself.

As she supped, she felt strength, strength never before felt, flood her body. She felt her senses, already acute, heighten even more. She could hear his heartbeat, hear the blood rushing through his veins, smell the dark-haired witch that had stabbed him and buried him alive with her. She felt power, power like she had never felt before flood through her body. It was because of this wonderful fluid that Nubius was pumping into her body. She wanted, needed, craved more, from any source.

"Enough," Omnubius said in his deep master Vampire voice as he tilted his wrist away.

"No," Tamara whimpered. "No please."

"More later Tamara," his voice boomed. "Don't make me kill you."

That's what he thought, she growled in her mind. This blood source was hers. She would kill if he tried to take it away. It was hers. She would drain him and then seek out another. There were so many humans running around, good prey for her. She would drink until she was sated. Then she would drink some more. She was higher up on the food chain. She was...

...going mad with power.

With a pop, she let his wrist go and stared up at him, horrified. "What have I become?" she asked shakily as tears filled her eyes. "What have they done to me?"

"Don't you dare waste my blood on your tears, Tamara," Nubius growled as he smeared his blood around the wound. He felt a bit faint, but still strong enough to do what had to be done. And he felt no pity for this former human.

"But I didn't ask for this. They have turned me into a monster."

"There are all kinds of monsters, Tamara," Nubius said in low ominous tones. "They come in every race, every species, every walk of life. The trick is not becoming what you loathe most. If you suddenly find yourself craving blood from the unwilling, tempted to take and steal which was not offered to you, I suggest you make peace with your house and take a walk in the noonday sun. Because if you don't, Tamara, former B.B. and fed my blood at your birth, I will hunt you down and you will regret ever being conceived. I am the alternative to your lack of control, and I am quite dedicated to my job. Have I made myself clear?"

His little speech dried up her tears and she put thoughts of her flagging humanity behind her for later thought. "I understand," she answered, almost meekly.

"And it passes," he added. "The feeling that everyone you meet on the streets is fair game. And it had better pass in your case or else."

"Or else what?" she asked, curious and horrified at the same time.

Nubius said nothing, but closed his eyes and clenched his fists.

She felt the power in the air, felt it hum through his veins and fill his very being with white light. He opened his eyes, and his deep orbs glittered with a rainbow of colors. The air in their tomb seemed to evaporate and the small hairs on her body stood on end. A strange tension began to mount and soon she felt her own heart pound in her chest as her muscles became so tight she felt that she had to scream in order to stop the top of her head from exploding.

Just as she was about to give voice to her terror, Nubius opened his hands and the dirt that surrounded them, four feet of dirt, exploded up and away from them as if they were feathers.

Then in a feat of strength, Nubius rose, muscles tense and unbending, lifting backwards until he stood on booted feet, loomed on booted feet, above her.

White sparks fired and flashed around his form as an unseen wind whipped the loose dirt and debris from his hair and clothes. In a moment, the only signs of his attack and imprisonment in the bowels of the earth were the minute tears in his coat sleeves, and the unseen tear over his left shoulder.

The earth held its breath as Omnubius gained his bearings and pulled his power back under a tight control. "Or else, Tamara," he finally answered, "you meet up with me and I get a new pair of gloves out of your miserable, weak, pathetic Vampire hide."

Point taken.

Tamara nodded and lifted a hand for him to assist her from her would-be grave.

With one glance, Tamara floated out of the grave and landed on unsteady feet, unnerved that he lifted no hands and came in no contact with her to get her out of there.

"There is a river nearby," he said. "We have just enough time for you to wash off, then it is back to the castle. The game is coming to a close tonight and they can't end it without a key player. Namely, me. I intend to be there with Luca. He is warned about Puaua and he is too smart not to notice the threat of Vincent. But there is one other who will benefit from his joining and his demise. And I intend to stop him at all costs."

Chapter Twenty-Five

Luca's eyes opened with a snap and he sat straight up, dislodging his mate who was lying across his chest.

"Luca?" she mumbled sleepily as she struggled to right herself out of the tangle of bedsheets that she had tumbled into with his abrupt maneuver. "What is wrong?"

"It has begun. It is time."

Without a word, the dread lord of all Vampesi rose to his feet.

"Time?" Dark asked, looking down at her arms and scowling. Would this purple glow ever leave? How long did it last anyway?

"Time to bring this game to a close," he replied as he moved naked across the room.

Dark could not help but admire the twin globes of his bare behind as he strolled to the closet. Had any other man looked as good as he walking around in the raw? She felt her hormones jump and sighed with annoyance. Damned libido. At first, this constant craving thing was fun and educational, not to mention entertaining, but now it was just getting to be plain annoying.

"What do I wear?" she asked, tearing her gaze away from him and tossing the sheets aside.

Luca turned to look at her and mentally tallied the time it would take for him to convince her to stay here safe within their rooms with a shield around. Then he decided that it wasn't worth the effort. He could stand there and argue with her all night, but she would kill to be included in the ceremony.

"Anything you want," he decided, "as long as it covers up ninety percent of your body."

Her purple glow was very distracting and attractive. He only hoped that he could keep his protective instincts under control. It was his right as a male to see to her benefit, but he also knew that he had to let her make her own decisions and be strong enough to back her up.

With a heart-felt sigh, he longed for the olden days, when a woman knew her place — beneath her mate — and didn't involve herself in potentially life-threatening matters, especially when she was pregnant.

"Then I think I will wear one of your tunics, Luca. They are so very comfortable and more practical than those ultra oh-I-am-going-to-swoon-any-minute dresses that you prefer. Man, get out of the 2000's. Women no longer need to dress helplessly and rely on a man to protect her from the big bad Vampesi."

"Dark," Luca began with the patience of one who had lived many lives and learned quite a few things. "First off, by the 2000's, the women were protecting the men, doing the hunting, keeping house, and caring for their men. And for another thing, those dresses are beautiful and express your inward femininity outward."

"Outward?" she spat with narrowed eyes. "Are you saying that I am not feminine?"

Her breathing noticeably increased and Luca felt the small hairs at his nape stand on end as she released her claws.

They exited the room a half an hour later with Luca in his customary white tunic and drawstring pants, while Dark sported the exact same style glowing with purple delight, even though her tunic was tied high at one side and her pants were cuffed.

Hey, Luca thought as he escorted her to the Garden room. *I may be crazy but I'm not dumb.*

* * * * *

The guests began to arrive at the castle in droves. It had been quite some time since Lucavarious proved his powers and prowess by submitting to the silver.

Soon the halls were filled with Vampesi and their human counterparts; all eager to partake of the feast that always followed such an event.

Vincent was in his element, providing tempting food for the humans while his staff replenished goblets of the blood-substitute that Lucavarious insisted be served at all gatherings in his home.

The air was ripe with speculation. Had his marriage to a Wolfen weakened him? Was that the reason for this ceremony? Did he intend to prove his worthiness to his mate, her people and the Vampesi as a whole? Was it true that the Vampire Omnubius, the wise trickster, the midnight hunter, was present at the castle? Why was he there?

The question circulated quickly around the room, almost as fast as the answers were rejected.

Luca was showing his mate who was boss. Luca was invoking the rite to ensure that he was still man enough to control two clans that were so obviously different. It was a statement of power. Their leader was showing off.

Vincent paid scant attention to the rumors and speculation, but instead kept his eye on the robed figure who stood in the background.

When he began to exit the room, to follow the halls that led to the Garden room, Vincent signaled his assistant and quietly exited behind him. Time to play.

* * * * *

Luca reclined upon his stone bed, Dark glowing happily at his side, and waited for the assembled players to…assemble.

"Trust no one, Dark," he urged. "Stay behind me at all times. I know that your emotions aren't quite stable now, but it is important that you listen to me."

"Unstable? Who are you calling unstable you Wolfen/Vampesi pincushion?" she hissed as she glared down at him. "I am not the one about to have a deadly substance forced through my skin, so you just lay there. Humph. Unstable indeed."

Humor the pregnant woman, he sighed to himself, as he watched her eyes go wide with her anger. This was worse than when she was just in heat. Who knew that her hormones would react so quickly?

"All I meant to say, Dark, is that I wish you to come to no harm while I am otherwise engaged. Nubius should have been here to guard you, but I have a feeling that he will turn up later. But until he does, please listen to reason."

"I can take care of myself, Lucavarious," she hissed through clenched teeth. "Just because I am now carrying your son does not give you the right to…"

"You will listen, mate," Luca commanded in his Master-of-All tone of voice. It was the authority that Dark recognized and respected. "You will stand behind me at all times, keeping this altar between you and those who would enter. You will obey me in this. And no matter what happens, you will maintain this barrier, even if you think that I am in danger. Do I make myself clear?"

Black eyes bored into her deep brown ones; cowing her momentarily and forcing her to not only listen, but to heed his words.

"I can hear just fine," she conceded wryly, trying to save a little face. "And I understand."

"You had better, Dark," he growled, still holding her eyes. "Because if you don't, when I have put an end to this situation, I will spank your tight little bottom until you are unable to sit for a month."

"Yes, Lucavarious," she meekly replied, the animal in her recognizing the dominant male in him.

After one more hard look to make sure that his words had the desired effect, Luca rested again calmly on the stone table. "Thank you, my mate. You have no idea how my heart sings to have you pay attention to my words."

Even though she tried to hide it, Dark couldn't keep the flush of pleasure off of her face, which only made the purple glow more prominent.

I love you, she whispered to him in her mind. But she replied, "You have the greater power, Vampesi. I have to listen to you, so the contract states."

For a moment, Luca glowered at her, but then his face relaxed itself from its tensions. He had a secret. Much like he had spouted out his feelings in an intense moment of shared passion, Dark had let her true feeling become known to him. She loved him. She said so herself. She loved him and that took the sting out of all of her words.

Dark eyed the strange smile on her mate's lips with trepidation. What did he know that he wasn't telling?

The Sage was the first to enter the room.

With his usual stealthy gait, he stepped into the prepared area, head bowed and chanting under his breath, until he raised his head and looked at Dark.

"Child," he gasped as he looked at her purple tinted countenance. "You heeded my words after all."

"What?" Luca asked as he lifted his head and his eyes shot from Dark to the Sage.

"And you have at last proved to be a growing boy," the Sage chuckled as he observed Luca's brows drawing down in displeasure. "Is there a problem, boy?"

"I told her to stay with me, to avoid all others, begging your pardon Sage, including yourself."

Dark narrowed her eyes at her mate before she answered. "If it wasn't for him, I would still be angry with you for your omission, Lucavarious."

He only glared harder.

"Now children," the Sage said, laughing at the little spat taking place before him. "All was said and done for a good cause. Don't look a gift donkey in the mouth, as the humans say. Or are the means so important to a perfect ending?"

That caused Luca to almost blush as he thought about the satisfying ends that had followed Dark's return. And Dark blushed because the results of those ends were written plainly on her face.

"Now children, we must wait for the others to arrive. The hall is fair bursting at the seams, and I am quite sure that the arrival of the Wolfen will no doubt make this another memorable occasion."

The Sage stepped closer to the couple.

"Allow me to congratulate you." He opened his arms wide.

At first, Dark started to walk around the altar and embrace the man that she had always known, but then her mate's warning reasserted itself. So instead of walking around with raised hands, she gasped and clutched at her stomach.

"Dark, what is it?" Immediately, Luca was off of the altar, taking her into his arms. Even the Sage looked suddenly concerned.

"Nothing, nothing," she assured as she waved the Sage away and took Luca's hands. "My hormones, you understand." She gave Luca's hands a gentle squeeze.

"Perhaps I could…" the Sage began, but stopped as he felt another presence enter the room.

"Vincent," the Sage said, his voice showing nothing but delight. "You are here."

"I was invited," he said, a huge smile on his face as he looked at the Sage. Then he did a doubletake as he saw Dark. "Mistress, uh, do you realize that your face is purple?"

"It's glowing," she growled in all her feminine dignity as she pulled away from her mate. "And it's temporary?"

"Yes, it is," Luca assured her. "It only will last for the next twelve hours or so."

"Very good," she replied as she assisted her mate in again taking his place on the altar.

"But, it's so purple," Vincent repeated again, amazed. "I have never seen anything so, uh, purple before. It's fascinating really," he added as Dark glared at him.

"Human," Dark growled low and dangerously. "If you know what is best for you, you had better change the subject."

* * * * *

In the hall, there was a sudden hush as a distinct smell filled the air, the smell of earth in its rawest, wildest form.. There was a light rustling of the trees and a wind blew and rattled the windows as a low growling filled the air.

Everyone gave an involuntary shudder as the sounds grew louder. The humans, known for avoiding trouble, sought protection next to their Vampesi counterparts.

There was a sudden silence, not unlike the quiet before the storm, then the main doors swung open with a *bang*.

The Wolfen had arrived.

"So where is the big event to take place?" Zinia growled as she stepped into the hall.

Then the grumbling started.

"Patience, Mother," Puaua said soothingly as she entered behind her mother. "I'm sure that one of these Humans will point us in the right direction." She gazed over the crowd as if searching for someone.

Both Wolfen females had come with the usual honor guard; the dark-haired, dark-eyed Wolfen males looked serious and dangerous as they observed the crowd with barely contained disgust. They remembered that last gathering, and not favorably, either.

Puaua and Zinia were both dressed in traditional ceremonial robes that befitted their stature in the Wolfen chain-of-command. Both had ceremonial daggers made of silver in their belts, which gave the robes some shape. Both were dressed in traditional greens, as befitted people of the land.

"They have adjourned to the Garden room," a helpful servant bearing a tray of rare meats got up the nerve to say. As the two glared at her, she lifted the tray with a trembling smile. "Hors d'oeuvre?" she asked, wondering if they would think that she had meant herself.

"See to my men," Zinia said shortly as she turned and surveyed the many hallways.

"Which direction?" Puaua asked as she nodded to one of the guards in the back.

"Use your senses, Daughter," Zinia snapped. "That is, if the stench of all these bloodsuckers hasn't dulled them."

"Mother," she scolded as several Vampesi glared the small group. "Remember, we are among family."

There were several Vampesi snorts at that. Even Zinia herself wondered silently when her strong independent daughter had become such a pudding-head.

"Never mind that," she sighed. "Follow me."

Closely following her mother, Puaua nodded again to the rear guard as they exited the main hall and followed the route to the Garden room.

"Now how the hell am I supposed to find anyone in this mess?" Zinia declared as she stepped into the Garden room, so named because it was an overgrown weed bed. "Everything smells like flowers."

"Concentrate on Dark, Mama," Puaua urged. "I'm sure that you can still smell her."

"But we can hear you just fine," a low voice called from the shadows in the back of the room.

"Sage?" Zinia called.

"Auntie," a cheerful voice rang out.

"Back this way," Dark added.

Shaking her head in almost amusement, Zinia followed the voices to the furthest recesses of the room.

"Aunt Zinia," Dark said with extreme politeness as she observed her aunt's entrance. "Puaua."

"Your face is purple," Puaua pointed out and then shrugged at the strange looks she was getting.

"Auntie," Luca crowed from his supine position. "You came."

"Lucavarious," she groaned.

"And dear sweet Puaua. Step closer. What have you done with my cousin? Have you addled his brains so much that he is now baying at the moon?"

Puaua stepped closer and glared at the man on the slab of stone. "I have no idea where he is. Maybe he is out playing cavalier instead of representing the Vampires."

Luca starred at her for a moment, then drawled, "Yes. You know how Vampires are. Popping up when you least expect it and laying waste to well-laid plans."

"I'm sure that he'll be here," Vincent assured, smiling up at the small group. "So, what happens next?"

"I ensure that no one will...interrupt us," Luca said, his voice low and deep.

With an audible crack, a large purple shield surrounded them. This was no ordinary shield either. It had a thick, almost viscous feel to it. It pulsed with the beating of his heart, proving that it was an extension of himself.

"What is this?" Puaua demanded, voicing the thoughts of the others.

"Protection," Luca said as he closed his eyes and made himself ready for the ordeal at hand.

"Protection?" Zinia asked,

"No one can get in," Dark said quietly. "And no one can get out."

Chapter Twenty-Six

"We are gathered here today for a renewal," Sage intoned as he positioned the observers around the altar. "A renewal of strength, of power, of might."

There was silence as the observers leaned forward, listening to the almost hypnotic voice of the robed figure as he made his way to the head of the stone.

"It is a test of strength and courage, what we do here. It is also life affirming. No other Vampesi is greater than this man, Lucavarious, and yet again he proves his worth."

There was a slight mumbling from the ranks, but one silencing look from out of that dark hood was enough to quiet even the slightest complaint.

"What he does is not for show, nor for selfish reasons; it is done to prove to our enemies that the Vampesi will never be eliminated. That we can and will adapt. That even in the darkest hours, under the most trying conditions, we will persevere."

Vincent stiffened slightly and glanced at Puaua. She too was silent and tight-lipped.

"But with this occasion comes special meaning today. This is also to stand for the next generation, as of yet unborn. So that this child may know the strength of its sire, the courage of its mother, and diligence of its people."

"Child?" choked Puaua as her lips tightened in annoyance.

"You are pregnant this soon?" Zinia all but wailed. "But what will it look like?"

"Congratulations, Master and Mistress," Vincent choked out. "This is unexpected but joyous news."

"Have you selected an area?" the Sage continued, ignoring the shocked outbursts from the observers.

"I...we have," Luca answered.

All through the little speech, Luca had been concentrating his breathing, slowing it down and balancing himself from within. He knew the agony that was to come, and he also knew that this was the perfect time for his enemies to strike.

He looked over at Dark, and she nodded slightly, just enough to let him know that she understood the danger and would take no chances.

"Where shall the next mark of honor be placed?"

"Mark of honor?" Zinia scoffed. "More like piece of unnecessary adornment. What are you getting, Lucavarious? Another toe ring?"

"Mother, please," hissed Puaua anxiously. "Don't interrupt."

"It's a piercing," Vincent hissed at the woman while anxiously keeping his eye on the action. He didn't want to miss his mark.

"If there are no more questions, we shall begin. Where is the mark to be placed?"

"The nipple," Dark said, an odd quirk to her lips. "The right one."

Vincent, the Sage, and even Luca winced a bit as the location was revealed. Dark looked curious, Zinia horrified, and Puaua mildly...aroused?

"I think that is going to hurt a bit," the Sage said as he looked down on the boy that he had known for a lifetime. "Are you sure you don't want it in the ear again?"

"Where?" snorted Puaua. "Both of his ears are covered in silver."

"I think you pay too much attention to my mate," Dark growled.

"Whatever do you mean?" Puaua asked, all innocence and light.

"I think that you are developing a taste for bloodsuckers, Puaua," Dark growled as her eyes darkened to the deepest black and her claws unsheathed. "Be forewarned that this one is mine."

"Ladies," Vincent tried to soothe as he shot a chilling look at Puaua. "This is not the time. And Mistress, I am sure that your cousin meant no disrespect."

"I'm sure I don't know what you are speaking of, Dark," Puaua added, looking up at her mother. "I think maybe it's hormones."

"I'll show you hormones," Dark began, but a hand on her arm stopped her.

She looked down and saw Luca shake his head no. He didn't care one way or the other if she bit off her cousin's head and used it as a play toy, he just didn't want her to cross the barrier of his body and the stone altar.

"All right, fine," Dark growled. She raised her clawed hands to the neck of his tunic. "I'll show you where to stick it."

A loud rip filled the air as she tore the front of Luca's tunic right off, her sharp claws making short work of the thin material.

"Thank you, I think," Luca growled as he saw the mess that his tunic had become. "With you wearing all of my clothes and destroying the ones that you let me keep, I'll be running around naked within a week."

"Don't you start," Dark growled then turned her eyes to her cousin. "And don't you get any ideas about peeking through windows, either."

Puaua started to comment, but was hushed by her mother.

"Can we please get on with this?"

"If you are ready to proceed?" the Sage asked, still as patient as ever.

"Yes," Luca said as he tossed what was left of his shirt to the floor. "The wait is abominable."

From within the deep folds of his robe, Sage produced two things, a clamp and a needle. The clamp was rather small and made of silver with ornate engravings. It was old and had probably been used in the past only for this occasion. The needle, on the other hand, was about four inches long and hollow, with a wickedly sharp point. It was enough to send shivers through all those who watched.

Then from another hidden pocket, he produced a tiny silver hoop. It was as small as his little finger, but solidly built and even attractive to the eye. All admired its delicate beauty.

"I thought you were going to get one down below, so I made the tiniest hoop that I could," he said in an aside to Luca, which caused him to glare up at his old mentor.

"I'm not that stupid," he hissed back and rolled his eyes as the Sage let out a dry cackle.

"First, the clamp," he explained as he ran his fingers over Luca's chest.

Within seconds, he had the clamp tightened around his dark copper nipple, holding it steady.

"Now the needle. Are you ready, my boy?" he asked.

Luca nodded as he inhaled deeply.

Dark tensed, trying not to eye her aunt to gauge her reactions. She also kept a wary eye on Vincent, but almost lost her concentration at Luca's deep inhalation.

"Show your strength, boy," Sage growled, before the needle cleanly slid through his flesh.

Luca didn't flinch.

Everyone else gasped in sympathy for the pain.

"Luca?" Dark asked, her eyes growing wide with concern.

"I am fine," he assured her. "The hard part is still yet to come."

"It is time," the Sage intoned as he held the silver hoop aloft. "And with the addition of this silver hoop, so deadly to those of our kind, I again reaffirm your strength and courage, Lucavarious. May your reign, your legacy…never end."

The end of the hoop was quickly inserted into the hollow needle and drawn down through his flesh. Quickly the metal was threaded through and the needle withdrawn. A small silver ball used as a connector was put into place and then it was done.

All grew quiet as they watched Luca for his reaction; all breath was held suspended as they all eagerly waited what would happen next.

Luca, his face rapidly paling and going totally blank, lay stark still. There was an eerie quiet as his body recognized the poisonous substance that was now a part of his body. His face tightened slightly as his body first warned of the dangerous intruder, then tried to expel it from his flesh.

"Luca?" Dark asked quietly as she felt his whole body began to tremble. "Luca?"

His eyes snapped open, his gaze blank, and the whole room began to tremble.

That's when all hell broke loose.

* * * * *

"Where is that bitch and her consort?" the voice bellowed as again the doors to the castle were flung open, this time by power unseen and never before felt.

Omnubius had arrived. And he was flaming mad.

Standing in the doorway, an unseen wind whipped his long dark hair around his leather-clad body. Standing with boots braced apart, the Vampire exuded fear and menace, from his tightly clenched fists to the set expression on his face. Small sparks of white energy zipped around his powerful frame.

His bare chest gleamed damply in the glowing lights of his energy bursts. His leather pants tightly caressed and held the power of his long muscular legs, drawing attention to their strength. His long leather coat, one that had not often been seen in this age of cloaks, strained at the seams as the expanding muscles in his arms threatened its ability to sheath them. The air crackled with his power, power that had only been felt when Lucavarious unleashed, power that intrigued as well as frightened the masses as they stared at the spectacle before them.

And standing just behind him was small, red-haired woman, whose eyes spat venom and hunger at every person, Wolfen, Vampesi, and Human alike, in the hall.

"Bitch?" a servant asked in a trembling voice as she stepped forward. She had no idea who he was speaking of, but she would find the woman and turn her over, before this mad man killed them all.

"The Wolfen Bitch," he demanded as he plowed a course through the gathered people, only to be stopped short by a tall dark man.

"You speak of my Lady Zinia with such disrespect?" he growled, his fingers lengthening to shredding claws and his fangs dropping in his mouth.

"Why does everyone have to be a hero?" Nubius growled before he thrust up his right hand and a powerful burst of white light slammed into the man, knocking him backwards into a table set up with food and drink. His was unconscious before he hit the floor. "Anyone else?" he asked, the colors in his eyes swirling madly as he observed the room.

The Vampesi grinned collectively, glad that the insane Vampire, Lucavarious' blood kin, was not after them. The humans looked around, planning their escape and defense, as they watched the body settle uncomfortably onto what was once a very healthy spread.

"The Lady Zinia is no...." another voice piped in before Omnubius could walk away, but silenced as he turned to face his next attacker.

"I was referring to that bitch, Puaua." he roared, tendons straining in his neck, his face turning almost purple in his rage.

"Puaua?" the assembled Wolfen guard murmured, one man looking very nervous.

"Yes, Puaua," he bellowed. "The flea-bitten mutt who ruined my coat and my boots. Real hand-worked leather is impossible to find these days. And my damn boots are scuffed beyond repair. How dare she bury me, *me* in the dirt? Plus she made me bleed my own blood. My blood. The bitch has to die."

There was a moment of silence before two of the remaining rear guard rushed the Vampire, desperate to stop him. And they just as quickly met the same fate as their companion as Omnubius lifted his hands and power bolts of energy exploded from his palms. The third guard bolted down the passageway to the Garden room.

"Follow that bastard," Omnubius bellowed as he gave chase, a stunned and weary Tamara pulled behind him. He recognized the man who had kicked him in the face. Oh, this one had to die.

"Mistress!" the guard panted as he raced through the lush green grass of the internal garden. "The Vampire is here." He counted on the Wolfen's superior hearing to warn his mistress.

"Mistress?" he called softly again as he reached forward...and slammed into a purple wall.

The impact sent him careening backwards into a pile of fragrant flowers, flowers that on any other occasion he might have enjoyed.

"Hell," he muttered as the pulled himself to his feet and staggered toward the large barrier. He reached out one hand and was immediately zapped back by the strength held within. What was this...thing?

"Leaving so soon?" a low voice purred from behind.

The frightened guard turned and felt his mouth dry out in fear as an eerie white glow announced the arrival of the Vampire.

"You are dead," he whispered as his breath rasped in his throat. "We killed you. We buried you. You should be dead." His eyes widened in terror and cold shivers traveled down his spine as he looked his own death full in the face.

"Do I look dead?" Omnubius taunted as he walked towards the skittish man, each step snapping and scorching the grass beneath his ruined boots.

"No," the man hissed as he felt his fangs explode and his claws drop. "Stay away from me."

Like the wolf blood that flowed through their veins, this man was essentially a pack animal. Take away his leader, and the pack crumbled into fear and disorder. This man, this guard, knew that he had nowhere to run, nowhere to hide. His end was approaching, and it was wearing torn leather.

"Observe, Tamara," Omnubius ordered and the red-haired woman stepped forward, fascinated and disgusted by the smell of fear and adrenaline that now cloaked the floral smell of the room. "Observe how the expendable underlings always fall apart when they are not given direct orders by their fearless leader. Note how he is trying to change, but fear won't let him. He is young to die, but then, we all have to go sometimes."

"Stop it!" the man screamed as he made a desperate decision. He lunged for the Vampire's throat.

"Observe, Tamara," Omnubius continued as he watched the man gather himself for a leap. "Never give in to desperation. It's a guaranteed way to get you killed."

He caught the man's head in one hand, halting him in mid-air. There was a sickening crack, like the sound of old dead limbs cracking beneath the weight of a mighty blow, then the Wolfen dropped heavily to the ground, lifeless.

"Observe Tamara," Omnubius continued. "Life is too precious to waste and easily destroyed. You didn't want this life, but you are still alive. It is a gift. Don't waste it."

Solemnly, Tamara nodded.

Nubius, still angered and glowing, stepped up to the barrier and lay one hand upon it. The combined energies from Luca and Nubius snapped and cracked, feeding off of each other.

"Now let us see if we can even the playing field a bit."

Then he closed his eyes and focused his strength.

* * * * *

Luca groaned as his body lifted a few feet off of the table, trembling and sweating. Never before had he felt a pain this intense, this all consuming. Not even as a child when he was first pierced had the pain seemed this incapacitating. White-hot heat flashed along his veins and he felt his whole body encased in a block of agony.

He closed his eyes and tried to contain the sensations that burned like fire in his chest, tried to focus in on his control, striving to find the balance.

Slowly, his mind began to clear; his thoughts stopped their mad rush through his head. He felt his breath, fast and furious, but under his control. His clenched his teeth, both sets of his fangs dropping to add to his torture even as the familiar feel comforted him.

He could feel beads of sweat pearl up on his body and run in rivers to drop to the table below; he could feel the tiny hairs at the base of his neck stand on end; he could feel the energy pattern that flowed through his body disrupt then realign themselves, becoming accustomed to the new silver inserted into his skin.

Soon, he was able to distance himself from the pain, though he hid it. The pain was still there, ravaging his body, but there was also a sense of peace, a sense that he had struggled and fought a great battle, and that he was winning. He opened his eyes; his mind cleared.

Now was the time for them to make their move.

They didn't disappoint.

Chapter Twenty-Seven

"Now!" screamed Puaua as she clutched the silver dagger at her side. "Do it now, Vincent."

"What?" Zinia got no further as her daughter shoveled her to the side.

In her headlong flight to reach Luca, Puaua knocked the Sage backwards and into a tangle of thick ferns. Vincent stood there, shocked as the screaming woman took a few steps towards the altar.

"Die, bitch!" she yelled as she placed one foot on the table and dove towards her target.

Dark, stunned into silence at her cousin's outburst, stood there, paralyzed. All this time she had been actively watching her aunt for any signs of a coming attack. She had never suspected Puaua.

Before anyone could move, there was a blast of purple light and a sudden heat filled the room. Then the silver blade buried itself into its victim.

There was a loud crack as Luca dropped to the table as the silver blade buried itself in his side. For a moment, silence reigned, as everyone regarded the battle-crazed woman. Luca's groan of pain broke the tense quiet.

"No," she wailed as she realized that Dark still stood unscathed, that the Vampesi had protected her somehow. "I need you dead."

"You made a calculated error," Luca panted as Dark's sudden stillness began to evaporate at the speed of light.

"Luca," Dark growled her voice deep and dangerous. "Are you dead?" She could smell his blood as it pooled beneath him, could sense his new pain.

"Not as such, no." he replied as he reached down to touch the handle of the blade, felt his blood attempting to clot around that blade and failing. "Calm down. I've had worse."

"There is a knife sticking out of your side," she growled, as her breath became loud and raspy. "My cousin stuck you with a knife. A damn *silver* knife." She was screaming as the last words slipped past her lips. "How dare you hurt my things, Puaua? You were warned not to touch him, now you die."

With an invisible wave that was not seen but felt by all, Dark began to change. Audible clicks and snaps were heard as her bones began to shift and elongate. Short dark hairs began to sprout out across her face and arms. Her clothes began to tear at the seams.

"Vincent," Puaua nearly whimpered as she backed away from the thing that her cousin was becoming. "Vincent?"

The human stood to the side, silent.

Seeing no help for her there, she turned to Zinia.

"Mother?" she began to plead, the heat of the room adding to the cold sweat that began to build up under her robe. "I did it for you, for us."

Zinia stood and stared at her child, the baby that had sprung forth from the seeds of love between her and her long dead mate—may he rest in peace. She stood there and stared at her, eyes filling with bitter, salty tears, her body refusing to bend under this terrible blow. Breathing was almost too painful as she watched her child, her precious baby girl, become the monster of Vampesi legends.

"Get away from me," she said in a low growl. "I have no daughter. I never knew you."

"Mother!" Puaua screamed as she tugged frantically at Zinia's robes. "Mother, I beg you do not forsake me."

But Zinia turned away from her, as if she didn't see her.

Puaua backed up against the purple shield as she frantically tried to meld her mind into that of a leader, to try and decide what to do next.

"Mine."

"No."

Dark and Luca's voices sounded almost simultaneously as she, partially transformed, leapt over the altar, reaching for her cousin, the one who would murder her true love in cold blood.

"Vincent!" Puaua shrieked desperately, her eyes wide with fear as Dark lunged for her throat, deadly claws extended, a promise of death in her eyes.

Before Dark could reach her target, Vincent reached out and wrapped his arm around her stomach, dragging her against his body, ducking the flailing hands and feet. Before the struggling beast could turn and maul him, his other hand flashed out and rested against her stomach.

"No, no, no," he sighed as he looked over to make sure that Luca was still on the table struggling with the silver. "We wouldn't want anything to happen to Junior, now, would we? I can carve that brat out of you without killing you, my dear mistress, and won't regret not letting that abomination live."

Dark subsided.

"Yes, Vincent," Puaua chanted. "Kill her. Kill them all. That was the plan."

"The plan?" intoned the Sage as he rose to his feet and staggered towards the action. "What plan?"

"My plan to rid the earth of all of you...freaks of nature," Vincent crowed as he cupped Dark's still flat stomach and grinned. "My plan to cleanse the planet of this filth that pollutes it now."

"But, Vincent," Puaua gasped. "We were going to rid ourselves of Dark and lead the Wolfen in a glorious battle against the Vampesi? What are you talking about?"

"I think you have been had, as the humans say," Luca gurgled, his voice amused despite the pain that was ravaging his body.

"Luca, you are injured," Dark breathed worriedly as Luca struggled to his feet, ignoring the thin trail of blood that flowed freely from his wound.

"Your constant grasp of the obvious always amazes me, my mate," he joked as he looked at her with silver-shot eyes, trying to tell her with his very gaze that things were well in hand.

"You don't look surprised?" Vincent taunted as he watched Luca struggle to his feet as he fought the urge to wipe away the sweat that was building up on his forehead.

"I am not. I was warned," he replied as he pushed back the assisting hands of the Sage and gripped the knife with both hands.

"I want out of here," Vincent added as he began to walk Dark backwards towards the door. Puaua watched as her partner in crime approached, but with weariness on her face.

"By all means, go through the shield."

"What trick is this?" the man muttered as he quickly turned to the side where Zinia was making ready to lunge. "Don't do it, Grandma," he warned as he held Dark tighter. "She and that brat of hers will be dealt with before you take another step."

"No trick," Luca gasped as he gave one mighty heave and the blade was free of his body. "No trick at all. Just keep walking."

"Luca," Dark warned as she felt the human calculating his next move.

It was clear that he didn't trust Puaua enough to pass her or her mother, for that matter. He was also keeping Dark between himself and Luca. They were at a standoff. So as any hunter, he decided to get rid of the least dangerous target first.

"Puaua," he crooned. "Go and touch the shield. We have a hostage and we can escape to start again."

"Vincent?" she asked, still unsure of their alliance.

"Go on. Touch the shield and let us leave this place. The Vampesi will do nothing to endanger his mate. We can be free of this place to start again.

"Start again?" she breathed as she reached out a trembling hand towards Vincent. "Truly?"

"Truly," he assured.

"Don't trust him," Dark breathed. "He'll turn..." but her words were cut off by a gasp of pain as Vincent pressed the knife into the skin of her stomach.

Luca growled low as her blood, her precious blood, began to flow and stain her tunic red.

"Yes," Puaua breathed. The site of Vincent harming that spoiled little bitch was the deciding factor for her. Dark, everyone always talked about Dark, the one to bring lasting peace between the people. Dark, who was so very unworthy, yet destined for greatness because of who her parents were.

"Yes, Vincent. Let's away with ourselves. The stench of this place turns my stomach."

"Puaua," Zinia cried out in an agony of the soul as she watched her daughter stride towards her certain death. Did she not know that Lucavarious would never let her escape these halls? That she and the Human were already dead?

"No Zinia," she shouted as she turned maddened eyes towards the horrified woman. "No. I am nothing to you, less than nothing. You disowned me, cast me aside. Well, I have news for you, *Mother*," she sneered the word. "I had every intention of ridding myself of you as well. It's easy when people trust you. It is so easy. Darkir never questioned the drinks that I brought for him and his mate. My God, I had to bite my lips to keep from laughing as they sucked down that Wolfsbane and thanked me for it. They thanked me, those pitiful fools. Would you have thanked me, Mother? Would you have licked your lips and pled for seconds?" Her laughter rang out, terrifying and truly fear inspiring to hear.

"Enough of this," Vincent called in his sing-song voice. "We must leave and now."

"Yes, Vincent," Puaua cried, tears running down her face as she regarded her mother, maybe regret filling her eyes, before the madness took hold once again. "Watch your back, old woman," she hissed in parting to her mother. "I am coming back for you."

"Not quite," Luca breathed just as her hand touched the purple shield.

A loud droning sound began to fill the small space, causing Dark and Zinia to cup their ears in agony. A bright purple flash filled the room as thin tendrils of purple power began to ooze from the walls and reach towards Puaua.

"What is this?" she shrieked as a tendrils lashed around her wrist to hold her in place, as the other slow waves of power reached hungrily for her. A powerful wind whipped around her, forcing her closer to the shield as the noise threatened to drive her to her knees in pain.

"What the hell?" Vincent cried as the light exploded, causing him to lose his grip on Dark and clap both hands over his burning eyes.

"Silver only hurts when it's forced to stay in," Luca sang as he stepped forward and thrust Dark behind him.

"But you were powerless," Puaua shrieked as she struggled to pull against the purple snakes that were slowly wrapping around her body, encasing her in a writhing cold power.

"Oh, but I knew about you, Puaua," he sneered as he watched in cold satisfaction as the tendrils of power began to mummify her, the room increasing in temperature.

"How?" she shrieked as she was slowly encased up to her neck.

"Omnubius warned me." He chuckled a bit at that.

"But he is dead," she shrieked. "I killed him myself. I killed your bodyguard."

"No, not my bodyguard, my enforcer," Luca openly laughed. "He marked you, baby. I knew about you from the moment you walked into this room. I knew and keyed this shield especially for you."

"What is happening?" she screamed and sobbed as the winding threads finally hushed her as they covered her mouth.

"Well, now you have to decide," Luca grinned as he looked down at his knife wound and nodded as it sealed itself. "Explosion or implosion. Take your pick, but you had best decide fast before the worms make that decision for you."

"No," Zinia wailed as she ran towards Luca and fell to her knees. "No, please Lucavarious. She is my only child."

"And she killed herself the moment she went for Dark's throat, Auntie," Luca explained as he reached down and took the woman's hands to urge her to her feet. "She brought this down upon her own self."

By now, Puaua was a writhing purple mummy, rolling across the grass, struggling and whimpering as she felt her death approach. The sounds that emerged from the cocoon were nauseating at best; her fearful cries were muffled as the worms of power slid down her throat, in her ears, and filled every orifice of her body.

"I think they have decided on explosion," Luca drawled as suddenly a solid purple shield covered the heaving woman, hiding her from view.

"God," Zinia sobbed as the last horrifying view of her child was taken away and a muffled boom echoed in the area.

"Shit," Vincent breathed, his breath panting as his vision returned, just in time for him to catch a glimpse of his accomplice and her demise as the shield encasing her melted away to show a small scorched patch of grass. "You tried to fucking kill me."

"Oh no, you were perfectly safe," Luca explained as he turned to gather his mate in his arms. Dark was silent through the execution, but now bowed her head against her mate for strength as her body stopped its transformation and the Wolfen blood was contained once more "It was keyed for Puaua. I have a much better punishment in mind for you, Human."

Safe was all that Vincent needed to hear. He shot to his feet and lunged towards the shield. He would pass through and try to mend fences with his original partner.

But again, fate intervened.

* * * * *

You are going to kill yourself," Tamara said quietly as Omnubius pushed against the purple barrier in front of him. "No one can break the master's shields."

"Don't believe everything you hear," Omnubius gasped as he leaned into the power he was applying to the shield. "I am not planning on breaking this bubble. I am just parting it."

As Tamara watched, Nubius' white energy began to surround him like an aura. Slowly he pushed and grunted, sweat beading and rolling down his face as he struggled.

Suddenly he was rewarded as his hand slipped through the breach that he had forged.

"Give me your hand, Tamara," he ordered as he removed one hand from the vibrating purple wall, reaching out for her.

Without a word, Tamara reached for Nubius and gasped as he forced her through the small opening. She was propelled through the shield like a pea popping from its pod.

She took a deep breath to orient herself, then automatically jumped back as a body came flying towards her.

"What the hell?" Vincent cried as she tried to skid to a halt. "Tamara?" he cried. Then with delight, "*Tamara!*"

"Human," Omnubius growled as he stepped neatly through the breach, fangs bared and hopping mad.

"My surprise," Luca drawled as he held Dark tighter to his chest. "I'm not sure you should watch this," he muttered to her as she looked up in amazement at her mate. "It might not be good for the baby."

Whatever she was about to say was drowned out by a loud slap, as Tamara used all her strength to lay one right across Vincent's cheek.

"You asshole," she yelled. "My name is Tamara. Look what you have done to me!"

Her eyes were glowing an unholy green and her hair began to fly wildly around her head.

Slowly, Vincent picked himself out of the ferns and wiped away a thin ribbon of blood that trailed down his face.

Instantly, her eyes were drawn to that spot, her hunger a palatable thing as she gazed upon fresh warm blood.

"You know, B.B., you are supposed to be dead. In a panic, you were supposed to dig yourself out and wander around for a while in the sun. Why didn't you dig yourself out? You are such a coward, B.B. First you sell yourself by slaving for that bastard over there, and now you are too much of a coward to even try and save yourself." He sniffed as he pulled himself to his feet, blood dripping from his nose now, too.

"The plan was so simple, too. All you had to do was start digging and you and the murdering Vampire would be at eternal peace. Looks like you fucked up again, B.B."

With a laugh he pulled a silver flask out of his pocket and held it up for his observers to see, slightly surprised as no one made a move to stop him.

"Vampesi blood," he stated as he pulled the cork from the bottle.

"Do tell?" Luca asked as the man lifted the flask to his lips.

"Given to me by my secret friend. Oh, I have been planning this for a long time, Lucavarious."

"How quickly they forget," Luca drawled to Dark as the man chugged down a huge gulp of stored blood.

"Oh I forget nothing, Master," he drawled sarcastically as he felt the change began to happen. "This is undiluted Vampesi blood, so there will be no hours of pain before a change. Sorry, B.B., you didn't rate that privilege," he breathed before he clutched his stomach and bent double in pain.

"I hope he craps his pants," Tamara said, remembering the agony and pain that she had dealt with as she observed her one-time friend and confidant. She unconsciously tugged that the shirt she wore, Nubius' shirt. He let her bathe but had refused to let her wash her clothes. Nor would he give up his coat for her to wear.

"You will be incapacitated for a time, you know?" Omnubius informed him as he leaned against the purple shield, unconcerned, and crossed his arms.

"But only if I don't get an immediate infusion of blood," he managed.

"Stop him," Zinia cried suddenly as she looked at the unconcerned faces that surrounded her and pulled herself together. Even the Sage, a man that she knew and trusted, seemed to be mute and frozen in place. Didn't they see that they would lose their opportunity to kill this monster?

"Well, if you won't do something..." she cried as she released her claws and dove for the transforming human, the one that she blamed for the madness of her only living child.

"No," screamed Dark, but again Luca pushed her behind him as the new Vampire reached out and grabbed the Wolfen woman. "Zinia." She struggled to free herself from her mate and reach her distraught aunt.

"Remember," Luca said to her as he held her behind him. "Remember what we spoke of."

With a crow of delight, Vincent neatly sidestepped her claws and tripped Zinia to the ground. Before she could gather her wits, he reached down, and ignoring the pain that was ripping at his insides, jerked her to her feet and locked her back against his chest.

"Let me go," hissed Zinia as she felt her muscles tense and her fangs unleash. Could she make a fast change before he drained her dry?

"How convenient," Vincent taunted, "fresh blood on command."

Luca and Nubius said nothing as the man lowered his head to Zinia's neck. She gave one sharp cry as his teeth, not yet fangs, savaged and tore at her neck. Her struggles ceased as pain rode over her in waves.

With a moan of delight, Vincent managed to tear her skin then he began to sate himself with the first few drops of fresh Wolfen blood.

"That should do it," Omnubius said finally as he uncurled his form from the wall and lazily approached Vincent.

"Stay back," the man hissed, lifting his face, lips dripping red from the injured woman's neck, and faced this threat. "I am as powerful as you."

"Not quite," Dark drawled in amazement as she realized what Luca was trying to tell her. She stopped trying to struggle and rested her hands upon her mate's back, drawing comfort from his solid warmth.

"You see, Tamara," Omnubius explained as he reached out and lightly tossed Zinia in Luca's direction, not stopping to see if she was caught. "You were right to suspect Puaua from her conversations with this, shall we say, nefarious character. *Ooooh.*" He shook his shoulders in mock fear.

"And because I helped rear that scamp over there, I always kept tabs on him. I knew that it was about time for the contract to be fulfilled, so your request fit right into my plans. You are a bright girl. I commend you for that. Next lesson." He took another step towards Vincent, who by this time was wondering where that sudden rush of magnificent energy had flown, and was now feeling quite human again. "There are rules in which we live by, for our own protection, mind you. A Vampesi can drink the blood of another Vampesi, human or the blood of another Vampire, since we come from the same stock, so to speak. A Vampire can drink the blood of a human, a Vampesi, or as you already know, another Vampire. One big cosmic no-no is that a Vampire or a Vampesi must never drink from a Wolfen. It explodes their heads."

"Heads!" Vincent screamed as he looked wildly around the room for help, his eyes settling on the Sage.

"Heads," the robed figure assured.

"Explodes," Luca said with some delight from his place now on the floor.

He had caught Zinia as Nubius intended, and then proceeded to open a wound on his wrist to smear his blood over the torn flesh of her neck. He knelt beside the woman to ensure that she was breathing and that the treatment was taking effect, then nodded to Dark that Auntie would be okay.

"But you are a Vampire, Vincent," Omnubius said, the white halo of his energy once again growing to surround him. "Wolfen blood will only make a Vampire deathly ill, a slow lingering death, a slow, lingering, painful death."

"Shit," Vincent breathed as he saw death approaching in black leather. He knew that his time on this plane of existence had come to a bitter end. He now had nowhere to turn, he had no allies left. There was only him and death.

"Consider this a mercy killing," Luca informed him as he watched the proceedings with flat black eyes. The room began to chill as his cold rage banished the previous heat of the room. With quiet detachment, he observed the Human who would have tried to exterminate them all.

But Vincent knew that there was no place to run or hide. He stood and faced Omnubius with all the courage that his hatred could lend.

"For my coat," Nubius suddenly cried out as the back of his hand sent Vincent sprawling towards Tamara; she stepped back and calmly watched his body bounce on the ground a few inches from her bare feet.

"For my cousin's mate!" he cried as with a wave of his hand, he lifted the human and sent him careening into the purple shield, which bounced him off to land at his feet.

"For B.B.!" he cried as he reached down and lifted the human for a strong punch that caved his stomach in and snapped a few vertebrae. Vincent whimpered in pain, his heightened senses making the pain a thousand times worse. He curled into a heap on the grass.

"For my boots," Omnubius grated out as he stepped back and delivered a stunning kick to the man's chest, lifting him a few feet off of the ground and cracking ribs with a loud *snap*.

"And this is for all of humanity that you would have destroyed if you had succeeded in your plans—for every Wolfen, every Vampesi, every Human that you would have destroyed. *Vincent, breathe no more.*"

Loud blood-curdling screams erupted as Omnubius lifted his hands to the level of his eyes and shot two solid streams of concentrated white light into the broken body that lay before him.

Vincent jerked and choked on his own blood and felt as his internal organs began to pop and burn. His blood turned to dust within him as his eyes rolled to the back of his head. His hair caught fire and his bowels and bladder released as his clothes began to smoke.

There was a loud hiss, then the burning heap that was Vincent erupted into light gray ash, then that too disintegrated away, taking with it every trace of the man that had been.

"And he crapped his pants," Omnubius said calmly to Tamara as the last of the smoke cleared.

"Now for his special friend," Luca said as he rose to his feet and turned around to face the true villain in this peace.

"Make no move, boy," the voice commanded as Dark gave a sudden loud shriek.

"Sage," Luca commented, unsurprised as the temperature began to chill in the room. "How could you?"

Chapter Twenty-Eight

"Oh it was quite easy, my boy," the Sage said as he got a tighter grip on Dark. "Then again, all things are easy when you want them badly enough."

"And what is it that you want?" Luca asked, as the temperature in the room grew uncomfortably cold. "What makes a man want his own death?"

"No need to be so dramatic, boy," the Sage sighed as he made sure the arm wrapped around Dark's neck would cut off her breath if she made any sudden movements. "Death is such a permanent thing."

"You paralyzed B.B.," Nubius stated quietly. "I wondered why you didn't want her dead."

"I never trusted that fool, Vincent. He was a few Wolfen shy of a pack, if you know what I mean," he chuckled. "But he served his purpose."

"Which was?" Luca asked as he gauged the distance between himself and his old mentor.

"Don't even think about it," Sage tutted as he easily read Luca's intentions. "And before you can send out one of those energy blasts at me, the woman will be dead."

"All of this to see me dead?" Luca suddenly cried out in frustration. "Why?"

"Oh don't be so self-centered," Sage sighed. "Not everything is about you, boy. And to think that I had a hand in raising you. When did you become such an arrogant brat?"

Luca stiffened and narrowed his silver-shot eyes at the man who had indeed had a hand in rearing him. Damn, even looking at him hurt.

"What do you want?" Nubius asked as he eyed his old friend carefully.

"Oh, I'm not going to tell you everything," the Sage laughed. "Too predictable. Besides, what man would brag when he is holding all of the cards?"

"Because you owe me an explanation!" Luca roared as he read true fright on Dark's face.

As the Sage spoke, he was steadily moving backwards, dragging Dark as easily as one would carry a child. Her feet barely touched the grass. Everyone present knew that he could easily snap her neck and would not hesitate to do so.

"An explanation? Okay. I never wanted you to die, boy. I love you, I truly do. It's just that you have grown mad with power."

"Mad with power?" Both Luca and Nubius looked at the Sage as if he had just grown another head.

"Mad with power. And do so try to control your temper, Lucavarious. It is becoming unbearably cool in here, even for me."

"How is he mad with power?" Nubius asked as he helplessly watched Dark's eyes widen even more as she realized that he was pulling her away from her only chance. Her face, still glowing purple, was beginning to pale.

"I'll tell you how," the Sage sighed as he halted in his movements. "Fake blood. Fake blood and alliances with humans. No one of our supernatural natures was meant to live like that. Who is Lucavarious to tell us how we should live and who we should dine upon?"

"Well, he is the oldest living Vampesi," Nubius drawled as he struggled to understand the motive behind the Sage's madness.

"Not quite," the Sage said with a smile in his voice. "And he is not the only living Wolfen/Vampesi mixture either."

"What are you saying?" Luca asked, his eyes widening as he began to piece together the story.

"Well boy, do you think that you are the first experiment to survive the mix? Where do you think your Wolfen blood comes from, boy?"

"You?" Dark managed to gasp as she gripped his arm with both hands, again feeling the muscular strength that belittled the bent over posture that the man had always affected.

"Me," he laughed. "Say hello to your direct ancestor, boy. I always thought that I looked good in you."

"No," Luca breathed as shock made his senses reel.

"Yes, boy. Why did you think I took such an interest in your upbringing? You were to have ruled it all and I would have been right there beside you, behind you, pulling your strings. But that damn Vampire had to stick his nose in and disrupt your education."

"Thank you," Nubius said as he buffed his nails against the leather of his coat. "I do my best work under pressure."

"Always the kidder," the Sage sneered. "But that is why your kind, parasites ,each and every one of you, will never amount to anything more than pale shadows of what I am, of what he was supposed to become."

"Of what I am?" Luca asked, drawing the attention back to himself again. "What am I?"

"You are an experiment, the ultimate experiment, boy. When your parents gave birth to you, the Wolfen in your mother's blood was kept a secret from the clans. You see, long ago before the Wars started, both parties wanted peace. But you and I both know that that is impossible. Vampesi are the thinkers, boy. We have the brainpower and the intelligence to make decisions. Wolfen are dullards, present company excluded," he nodded to Dark.

"Thanks, I appreciate it," she growled, then choked a bit as he tightened his hold, making both Nubius and Luca jump in agitation.

"Bright girl, clever girl, now keep your mouth shut." The Sage shook her a bit to make his point before turning his attention again to Luca.

"The Wolfen may lack intelligence, but have you ever seen such graceful hunters in all of your life? Have you ever seen people who grab onto a scent and never let it go, even years after it has been identified? Can you imagine Vampesi with those gifts?"

"Perfect solider?" Nubius asked, one eyebrow arched.

"Perfect *weapon*," the Sage countered. "And all that was left was to decide who would master the weapon."

"A weapon like that can never be mastered," Luca argued. "They would kill those foolish enough to try it."

"And that is why the Wars started, Luca. Use what little Vampesi brains that you still have. The Wars were never about Humans and their useless attacks against us. It was for control of you, boy. You and the others like you."

Luca staggered back as if someone had delivered a physical blow to him. His wild eyes sought Dark's but now the Sage was supporting her more than holding her.

"For me?" he breathed as he tried to find his inner balance again. "There are more like me?"

"Not anymore. Why don't you ask the Vampire what happened? Or better yet, ask him why your parents had to die."

"Nubius?" Luca forced through a shock-frozen throat. "What do you know, Vampire?"

"I would love to stay and chat, but you have fulfilled my purposes admirably, boy. In matters of lust, at least you haven't failed me."

"Let Dark go," Luca growled, his voice suddenly low and dangerous again. The other matters could wait until later. What was important now was his mate. The single-mindedness of the Wolfen in him took over, the urge to fight and protect overran all thought, and instinct began to rule.

"Oh no, dear boy," the Sage laughed as he backed almost to Luca's shield. "She was the whole reason for this exercise in futility. The crazed Wolfen and the double-crossing human were just unexpected yet entertaining side-shows before the real finale." Then the voice grew dark and cold. "Remove the shield, boy. Or the woman dies and I start my master plan again in the years to come. Time is nothing to me, Lucavarious. I can wait."

"Dark," Luca cried out, anguish showing in every taut line of his body, in every crease in his face.

"Do it, boy," the Sage urged. "Or you will never save your mate."

"Let it go, Lucavarious," Omnubius urged. "We can find Dark later. If he wanted her dead, she would be dead by now."

"Very astute, Vampire," the Sage laughed. "Now the shield, boy. And be quick about it."

"Dark," he began again, but then Dark smiled.

"I'll be fine, Luca," she whispered. "I told you before I can take care of myself."

"Feisty little thing," Sage laughed, then growled, "The shield, Lucavarious. I don't have all day."

With a snarl that would have done any Wolfen warrior proud, Luca turned and waved his hand in the air. Almost immediately a humid heat began to fill the area, banishing the cold of his rage to nonexistence. Luca had dissolved the shield and the natural elements in the Garden room again claimed the preserved area.

"Thank you," the Sage chortled as he pulled Dark into the thick foliage. "No hard feelings, boy?"

"You will never make it out of here," Nubius called after him. "This castle is crawling with Vampesi and they should all start to feel Luca's rage at any moment now."

"I know that, Vampire. I am no fool. Believe me, I have my ways. It was never my intention to waltz out the front door. An ostentatious display like that, all flamboyant and unnecessary, is, I believe, your department."

Then he was gone, melded in with the shadows.

"Dark!" Luca roared, and the castle began to shake, its inhabitants began to quake with fear.

* * * * *

"Where are we going?" Dark gasped as the man pulled her along behind him. "Where are you taking me?"

"We are going on a little trip, Dark. Be assured that I mean you no harm. I just want the child."

That made Dark's stomach clench in fear and her purple glow began to look a bit green.

"My child?"

"Yes, Dark. And if you behave, I might even allow you to look after him until his training begins."

"Training?" she squeaked, then sighed as he released his hold on her neck and instead gripped her arm.

"Why, yes, Dark. Training. A perfect weapon takes time and patience to build."

"My child will not be a tool for you to use and destroy," she cried out as she dug her heels into the grass and tried to pull free of his hold. "Let me go."

Surprisingly enough, he let her go. Unfortunately, she was still pulling against him at the time. With a squeak, Dark flew backwards to land on her bottom in a thick clump of tall stringy grass.

"Well, you did ask," the Sage drawled as he turned away from her to face the far wall.

"You are trapped now, old man," Dark stated with confidence that she didn't feel. "Let me go and forget this nonsense."

"Never trapped, my dear," he assured her as he touched different parts of the wall. "I always plan for every eventuality."

Even as he spoke, the wall began to separate and a huge chunk of it pulled away to reveal a dark humid maw.

"Where…" she began, but cried out as the Sage, moving as fast as lightning, scooped her up in his arms and ducked into the dark hole.

"There are hot springs beneath this castle, Dark," the Sage told her. "I could hide in here for years and your Lucavarious would never find me."

"He can scent you, Sage. And he will find me."

"Ah, young love," he sighed dramatically. "But you are not as bright as I thought you were, Wolfen. What nose can track through running water, Dark? Even as highly developed as the Wolfen senses are combined with Luca's near perfect Vampesi brain, how could he find me here?"

"He will find *me*," Dark countered as even her specialized vision was having a hard time cutting through the all-encompassing dark in this cave. She shivered in fear and then contemplated jumping from his arms and hiding.

"Don't even think about it," the Sage warned, easily reading her thoughts. "You don't know your way around here and some of these hidden pools are over three hundred degrees in temperature. One misstep and you would be boiled Wolfen."

"How did you know…?" she began, terrified all over again. Could he read her mind? Were his powers so advanced that he could pull the thoughts out of her head?"

"I can easily second-guess you, Dark. My Vampesi brain, remember? Oh, do try to keep up."

Dark crossed her arms and snorted, all the while trying to make herself heavier, if only by thought. Anything to slow the monster down.

But with a strength that turned his claims of old age into so may lies, the Sage plowed forward, not even breathing hard in the hot sticky air.

"What did you do to B.B.?" Dark asked after a few moments of silence.

"I saved her life," he replied shortly, but kept moving.

"Are you going to tell me the details of this wondrous plan of yours?" she asked as the loud silence began to throb in her head. Her hormones were jumping again and she was feeling a bit irritable.

"Well," he started as they continued to go deeper into the earth, "I guess I can tell you, since you are the mother of the future," he replied.

"Gee, thanks," she drawled as she purposely wiggled her bottom, trying to get him off balance.

"Hold still or I will drop you on your little Wolfen ass," he growled in retaliation as he squeezed her a bit painfully.

Dark subsided, for now.

"As I was saying before I was so rudely interrupted, you will bear the perfect weapon. He will have enough of Luca's Vampesi intellect to stop him from going completely power hungry, plus he will have the added benefits of your Wolfen strength, agility, and transforming capabilities."

"To what end?" Dark asked sarcastically. "I mean you are part Wolfen and Vampesi and you are mad as a loony bird. What's to say that this kid won't be just as mad under your care?"

"I am not insane," the Sage growled as they suddenly entered a cavern lit by several torches. "I am a genius."

That said, he dumped Dark onto a pile of blankets like she was so much unwanted baggage that he was glad to be rid of.

Dark fought the urge to yell as she was dropped, but then quickly gathered her wits as her gaze took in the large stone room.

"One man's genius is another man's insanity, I always say," she drawled as she noted that he stood in front of the only entrance and exit.

"How true," Sage snorted as he reached up and grasped the hood of his robe. "But then, I always said you were a bright girl."

Dark bit back a scream as the hood was tossed back as she saw, for the first time, the face of the Sage.

* * * * *

"What was that all about?" Tamara asked quietly, breaking the tension that had jumped to incredible levels the moment Luca's roar of rage had disintegrated into the faintest of echoes.

"Tamara…" Nubius began but was cut off as Luca turned towards them.

Both gasped in shock at the changes that had taken place on his handsome visage. Gone were the patrician features of the controlled man that they both knew. In its place was a face filled with anguish, fear and soul-deep anger.

Luca's eyes were totally silver in the narrowed slits that dropped his brows to the bridge of his nose. Impotent blood-tears rolled down his face as his nostrils flared wide in his rage. His lips, so full and perfect, were small, tight lines pulled back to expose both sets of fangs. His chest heaved with each forced breath of air that he savagely stole from the atmosphere.

"What do you know of this, Vampire?" he growled as he took a step towards his blood cousin. "Where do you fit in? Tell me?"

"You don't look so good, Luca," Nubius said with all the confidence he could muster. "Maybe you should lie down."

"*Grrr.*" He roared as he rushed the Vampire and lifted him two feet off of the ground by the lapels of his leather coat. "Tell me."

"If you are going to be rude about it," Omnubius said, face bland, and tapped Luca's fisted hands with his fingertips. "But first…"

Snarling under his breath, Lucavarious slammed Nubius back down on his feet, in the process, sinking him a few inches into the lush grass.

"That's going to ruin those boots more," Tamara added shakily as she observed the power that she was facing. Fear made people say stupid things, she decided, as those violent silver eyes pierced her.

"And what does she have to do with it?"

Tamara gulped, feeling more and more like B.B. every second. She retreated a step, then another as her fight or flight instinct kicked into overdrive.

"Well, you'll have to ask the Sage that," Omnubius said, catching Luca's sole attention once more. "And if it's about your parents, they were killed for trying to turn you into a Wolfen killing machine."

"Did you…"

"Perish the thought," Omnubius threw in, interrupting the questioning accusation. "The Wolfen killed your parents. I just killed the four other hybrids like yourself."

"My brothers, sister?" Luca growled, his sudden shock giving way to the need to do violence to someone. "My family?"

"No, Luca. Not direct members of your line. They were insane little monsters that the Wolfen hoped to pit against Vampesi. They were so malformed and brain dead that they ate anything that crossed their path, including their mothers, who were fed to them as a 'welcome to life' treat. Oh, they were nasty little buggers."

"Are you telling me," Luca began as he backed away from his blood cousin, "are you saying…?"

"That your parents bred you to counter those monsters? Then the answer is yes. You were an experiment, Lucavarious, but you were the only one of your kind not to be born insane."

"And the Sage?"

"You call that sane?" he asked, an incredulous look on his face as he pointed out the way that the mad man had disappeared.

"I don't believe this," Luca breathed; the blood tears began to dry up, leaving dark lines on his face as his breathing decreased.

"Believe it. And your father wanted you to be in top fighting form, too. Your mother continued after he was killed by the Wolfen scientists after a game of 'my creation's better than yours.'"

"Father," Luca breathed as he dropped his head in, pain...anger? What was he supposed to feel?

"When your mother decided that it was time for the Wars to end, she met with the Sage and the leaders of the Wolfen clan. They came up with the contract, Luca. It was the only way to save us all. They wanted peace."

"And the Sage?" he asked, not wanting to think on the past just then.

"Oh, I believe he is one of the original half-breeds that was spared. The original plan, if memory serves, was to unite our peoples as one. But then there are always power-hungry bastards running around. This side wanted power, then that side wanted more power, then *bam*, you have a war. The other original experiments went insane and killed themselves, were destroyed, or died off. The Sage, your mother told me, was the only one to keep his sanity, thus was allowed to deal as a go-between for the two clans. He was even allowed to take a mate. That would make him your, great, great, great...great, great grandfather. Or something like that."

"I am related to that monster?" Luca cried, his head snapping up to gaze wide-eyed at Nubius.

"Well, maybe it's senility finally kicking in?" Nubius offered, a slight grin tugging at his mouth. "A case of, what do humans call it, Old Timers disease?"

For a moment everyone stared at each other, at a loss for words, then Luca began to speak.

"Okay, I have the history. But what does he want with Dark?"

"How did you know that it was him?" Nubius asked avoiding the question as he pulled himself out of the bootprint ditch Luca had plowed him into.

"I could smell him," he said, as he ran one hand across his neck. "At least I thought that I smelled him."

"Where?"

"The flowers in my bedroom. The Sage spends so much time here in this room he began to smell like it. I never really noticed it, because the flowers in here are so strong, but his scent didn't match those in the flask of wine."

"Very good, puppy," Nubius praised as he stepped past Luca and peered into the shadows where the Sage had disappeared with Dark. "I figured that he was the only person to benefit by my disappearance and the contract."

"What do you mean?" Luca asked, suddenly alert. He began to pay close attention to what Omnubius said and did. The Vampire was on to something.

"Simple. The only thing that you two could make that he couldn't acquire was a child. With your blood being mainly Vampesi with a little diluted Wolfen thrown in for flavor, you should provide the right genetic mixture for a fully transforming Wolfen child that won't bay at the moon, but don't quote me on this."

"What?" Luca nearly shrieked, making Tamara rush past him beside Nubius. She was taking no chances. Omnubius seemed better able to calm that particular Vampesi down, and she was going where the safety was.

Nubius looked down at Tamara as she not so subtly sidled up to him, and held in his laughter. The he turned to face Luca again.

"I mean your child may be nuttier than Vincent or Puaua. But I seriously doubt it. The Sage planned this well. He was there for each new generation and he just loved to play in that lab that you have upstairs."

"So that's where Vincent got the Vampesi blood," Luca breathed, the whole picture becoming clear to him.

"Yup, Vincent's special friend. I'm sure that he promised all kinds of glory to the Human if he helped him in his cause, never knowing that Vinny boy had plans of his own."

"Like sludge, filth seeks its own kind," Luca snarled then stepped past Tamara and Nubius. "So that answers the 'who' and the 'what', but I need to know the 'why'," he growled as he lifted his head and began to scent for his mate.

"I guess we ask the freak show when we meet up with him," Nubius said as he carefully watched the man that he helped raise.

"How old?" Luca asked suddenly as he lowered his head and pierced Omnubius with a look.

"You have to ask him," he replied.

"I'm speaking of you," Luca said, his silver eyes curious despite the drama taking place.

"Old enough to fuck without getting stuck," he replied calmly, before he pointed into the darkness beyond them. "The caves?"

"The caves," Luca agreed and then they were on their way, stalking the creatures of the night.

What have I gotten myself into? Tamara thought as she took one look back at the unconscious Wolfen lying on the crumpled and scorched grass, the only signs of the battle that had taken place. Then she turned and raced after the suddenly running men, not wanting to be left behind to explain.

Dark, I am coming, Luca thought as he raced into the shadows. *Upon my life, I swear it.*

Chapter Twenty-Nine

"Oh...my...God," Dark breathed as she gazed upon the monster that had just taken her away from everything that she held dear. She felt as if the breath had been knocked from her body, that the walls had closed in, that the spotlight of his black eyes trapped her within the spotlight of their gaze. "You...you...look,"

"Like Lucavarious, yes I know," laughed the Sage, as piercing black eyes bore into hers, holding her paralyzed in shock. But the major difference between her beloved and the twisted creature that stood before her was the glint of insanity that circled those black orbs, swirling like so many vultures circling carrion.

"But..."

"And do you know how painful it was to me to have to look at my face all of these years? My face, Dark, nurtured our people until they are just a bunch of watery, blood- colored sap-drinkers that they are today. Do you know how many lifetimes I spent looking at my descendants and watching them descend into madness? All of my great genius withered and died away because the genes used to propagate them were substandard and inferior."

"I definitely think insanity is heredity," Dark murmured as she watched a change began to overtake the Sage. She backed away from him, as far as she could go with her back pressed against hard stone.

"You think me insane?" he asked through narrowed eyes. "Insane is forcing our superior people to become impotent. Insane is allowing that watered-down version of myself to assume a role that he is clearly not capable of handling." The more he ranted, the wilder his eyes became. She watched, amazed, as a large, misshaped set of fangs dropped into place, causing a burst of blood-stained spittle to dribble down the corner of his mouth.

"He would have been perfect, Dark. The perfect weapon to rule, a perfect iron fist. But then that Vampire showed up and twisted Sumna's head. She gave birth to the ultimate Vampesi, and let that fool Vampire interfere."

"Luca's mother?" Dark breathed in horror as she realized that she just found herself in a similar position as Luca's mother. Only this abomination would see to it that she would never influence her child.

"But through that baby, Dark…" he gestured with a finger that, even as Dark watched, began to change. A wave of dark black hair exploded on the surface only to be drawn back internally as she watched with horrified eyes. "…I will have my chance for greatness."

"You are changing," Dark breathed in fear. She knew the struggle to maintain humanity when that change was upon you and instincts ruled your every move, attempted to control your every thought. "You are changing and you can't control it."

"You are wrong, Wolfen," he snapped as a loud cracking of bone filled the damp air of the cave. With painful intensity, a large wolf-shaped muzzle erupted from the place where just moments before his nose and mouth had been. Then with a sickeningly snap, they retreated, leaving only the odd fangs to fill his mouth. "If I were out of control, you'd be dead."

"You are anyway," Dark growled. His changes were starting to affect her and in a negative way. Her purple-tinted skin grew dark and the pupils of her eyes began to widen and darken. "You are not the alpha male in this pack, evil one, and I am definitely not the low-status bitch that you think I am. Lucavarious leads this pack, and he is going to kill you."

The Sage reeled back as if struck as he gazed upon her cold features. Her expression was filled with supreme confidence and glowed with an inner light that hinted that she knew something that he did not.

"What makes you so sure, Dark?" he growled as his hunched-over form began to shudder and tremble. The wolf was fighting to free itself and was battling an inner barrier. He was at his weakest point, but the girl didn't know this, did she?

"Easy, you old senile fool," Dark grated as her eyes lit up with unholy amusement. "He loves me."

The Sage blinked large black eyes at her, then again. "Love? And you call me a fool?" He threw back his head and began to roar with laughter. "Love? Love. A stupid human emotion created so that the men could screw the women without complaint."

Dark's laughter was even louder than this. "Keep thinking that, old man. Luca will kill you, or if I get the chance, I will. My love makes me want to protect him from bothersome roaches like you."

His laugher ended abruptly.

Dark laughed on.

"Keep laughing," he suddenly growled as he threw his hood back over his head.

"Oh, I intend to, you pathetic old creature. And I promise I'll laugh as I tear your throat from your miserable neck. Just give me that chance."

"You talk big, girl," he growled from the depths of his hooded robe. "You talk very big for someone who is in my control."

"Space and opportunity, you old shadow of a man. I just need space and opportunity."

The Sage backed away from this girl, as if he was suddenly confused about his captive. Why wasn't she crying and screaming in fear? Why wasn't she begging him to free her? He had to rethink this sudden development. Sage never underestimated anybody. That's why he had gotten as far as he had and was still alive.

* * * * *

"Do you hear that?" Luca asked as he stopped near the cave entrance and cocked his head to the side.

"I hear not as well as you do and you know it, puppy," Omnubius drawled as he too paused and observed the younger man. A panting Tamara brought up the rear.

"Laughter," Luca decided, his eyes still sparkling with the silver of his contained rage. "I hear laughter. How dare he mock us?"

"At least he didn't say *me*," Nubius said to Tamara as she leaned against him. "Obviously he is not as self-centered as the Sage thought."

"Shut up," Luca snapped as he ran his hands over the wall before him. There had to be a way inside. He was sure of it. It would lead to the hot springs, he was sure. Now how to open it?

"Maybe I was wrong," Nubius said to anyone that would listen. Then with a sigh, he urged the other man aside. "Out of the way, man. Let me show you how to do this with style. It's kissing cousins with class, you know?" he asked. "You have class, but believe me, baby, I have style."

With a huff to let Nubius know that he was standing down because he wished, Luca stepped back beside Tamara, who scooted back from him and eyed him strangely.

"What?" he snapped. Luca always hated being stared at. It took him back to the pleasant days of his youth, he thought with heavy sarcasm.

"You look different, Master," she finally forced past her pale lips.

"Hey," Omnubius turned from his inspection of the wall to glare at Tamara. "Why is he Master and you address me with such disrespect?"

"He's scarier," Tamara said, sounding a bit like the B.B. of old.

"Damn," muttered Nubius as he turned again to face the wall. "Save a woman's life and you get no respect. Cock her head to the side and drink from her veins anytime you want and you are called Master. Is there no justice in this world?" he cried out as he glared at the ceiling.

"Just open it," Luca groused, as he tried to glare at his blood cousin. One thing about Omnubius, he always had a way to make Luca forget his cold irrational anger and force him to think. That was reason enough to keep him around.

"Just watch," Nubius said as he placed his hands upon the stone. In a few seconds, his whole body began to glow with the white energy of his inner being. The glow seemed to flow from him into the rock, making it pulse with his heartbeat. Then it appeared to breathe as its molecules rapidly began to expand and contract. Dust and smoke began to fill the air, creating a thick, heavy ash that coated their skin and hair.

"Watch this," he grinned from beneath his mud mask and the rock began to pulsate.

With a sharp crack, the wall exploded, showering them with small sharp bits of rock and gravel.

"Oh," Tamara breathed, then coughed as dust began to fill her lungs.

"Way to announce our presence." Luca cut his eyes to Omnubius who shrugged his shoulders with indifference as he dusted off the tattered remains of his coat.

"Sneakiness is not my style," Nubius drawled as he stepped forward and glared at the hole left in the stone wall of the Garden room. "But is it hard on the clothes," he sighed. "My coat is a complete loss now and I can just kiss these boots good-bye. I wonder if another farmwife needs some killing done?"

"Let's just move, okay?" Luca sighed as he brushed past Nubius and entered the tunnel entrance. "We are trying to save a life here," he reminded them.

"Two lives, actually," Tamara piped in, then gasped as she gingerly walked across the newly strewn gravel path.

Heightened senses may work well in some situations, but when walking across sharp stones, it was a bitch.

"Here," Nubius sighed as he picked Tamara up and slung her onto his back.

"I didn't know you cared," she drawled as she tightened her legs around his waist and her arms around her neck. The leather of his coat felt sensual and exciting to her as it rubbed against her skin, picking up her heat and sending it back to her. There may be something to this leather wardrobe after all.

"I don't," Nubius said as he took off after Luca who was moving at a rapid clip. "I just don't want to have to come back and look for you after the hard work is done. And don't get any ideas about my clothing, woman. I know that the leather feels good, but it is my statement, my trademark. Go find your own."

Tamara said nothing, but settled back to enjoy the feel of his sleek muscles and hard tendons shifting beneath the buttery soft leather. It was like riding on the back of some wild jungle cat. Already she was planning her own wardrobe; although she had no idea what she would be doing when this mess was done. Maybe she would become a detective. Yeah, a real Sherlock Jones.

* * * * *

The loud boom reverberated throughout the caves and reached the Sage's cavern room, alerting the waiting woman and the pacing man to their presence.

"They are here," Dark drawled as she observed the man's pacing with a hunter's eye. He was becoming agitated, and that was good. Agitated men made mistakes.

"It doesn't matter," Sage growled as he ceased his pacing before her. "They will never find this cave, and if they do, I'll kill them."

"And you said that you loved Luca," Dark argued hotly, her eyes glowing with her rage as her claws silently dropped into place.

"And have I not screwed him?" he asked, laughter filling his voice. "They can search for an eternity, but I will still have you, Dark. I suppose I will have to go back and find B.B. I saved her when I saw Vincent slip her the tainted wine. She would have been the perfect nanny for my new child, and probably still will be. But Luca must die now. He is too worthy an opponent. I trust you won't grieve too badly, my dear?" he questioned. "I hear that it's not good for the baby."

Dark's face broke out into a grin, then into a wide smile. She was still smiling as her fangs dropped into place, straight and sharp, and as her eyes became wide pools of dark night.

"As I said before, he is coming, and he will kill you if I don't. Time to prepare, old man. Death is at hand. Your end is near."

* * * * *

There was a loud splash and Tamara began to shriek as if her death was imminent. It echoed around the many caverns and bounced off of the stone, magnified and showering down upon them like hail in a storm.

"Will you please shut up?" Luca growled as his sensitive ears were battered, clamping his hands over his ears.

"But that bat almost got me," she shrieked with less volume, treble and base. "It was creepy."

"But you just batted it out of the sky and into the boiling water," growled Nubius as he lifted his own hands from his ears.

"There are worse things in these caverns, B.B.," Luca growled as he turned to face her. "Like me. So keep your lips buttoned, Blood Bank. We would like to maintain some sense of surprise here."

"Not to mention decorum," Nubius added as they began to make their way again through the maze of tunnels. "Hey," he called to Luca who was again in front of them and moving rapidly. "Do you know where you are going?"

"Yes, I do," Luca called back quietly as he picked his way over hot stones and slippery rock.

"How?" demanded Omnubius as he slipped again on the smooth surface of the stones. He was tired, he was nearly drained, he was hungry, and he was dirty. He hated being dirty. It smudged his image and ruined his clothing.

"Part of her is within me." Luca stopped and looked at Omnubius, stared him straight in the eyes, the silver sparks contained within parting the darkness and letting his every emotion show. "And part of me is with her. I will always find her, Nubius. No matter what, I will always find my way back to her. She is the second half of my soul."

And for a moment, Omnubius envied the Vampesi cub that he had helped rear. The awe he felt just listening to the truth of his words and the force that moved him silenced even Tamara.

"The let's go get her," Nubius said finally, breaking contact with those soul-burning eyes that glittered with the assurances that he was right. "Let's go get Dark."

* * * * *

"I think there went the nanny," Sage sighed as he sat on a bolder across from Dark. "Pity, but it's good for you. I guess I'll have to keep you around a bit longer than I expected."

Instead of cringing in fear or pleading for mercy, Dark just smiled wider, small hairs beginning to sprout out along the surface of her exposed skin. Her muscles began to tighten and grow dense. She seemed to expand where she sat, without moving an inch.

"You're going to die," she grinned as muffled clicks filled the room, the sound of her body growing to accommodate her inner spirit. Or the sounds of the cage holding the beast at bay, snapping like twigs, Sage couldn't decide. But he grew weary as he sat and watched her slowly change. "You're going to die."

* * * * *

"Are we there yet?" Tamara asked, breaking the tense silence that had surrounded the two men since the bat incident.

"We are almost there," Luca answered as the rest of him was swallowed up by darkness.

"Well, I hope that we are," complained Nubius. "This coat is damnably hot in this humidity. No wonder you have no trouble keeping this mausoleum warm in the winter months."

"Planning and intelligence," Luca shot back. "You might want to try it sometimes."

Omnubius opened his mouth to deliver sharp retort, but Luca hushed them into silence.

"We are here."

"Well, what do we do?" Nubius asked as he lowered Tamara to the ground. "How do we get him before he hurts her?"

"I'm thinking," Luca snarled.

"So much for planning and intelligence,"

"Will you..."

"Hush," Tamara suddenly demanded. "Can't you hear them? They are speaking."

* * * * *

"If you don't learn a bit of control, Dark, I'll just go and find a replacement for that B.B. Luca had. Too bad she had to be boiled alive, but that's the chance you take when you run with rogues."

"The only rogue I see is the pitiful, sick, twisted excuse for a Vampesi or Wolfen who can't seem to keep both halves of himself in line," Dark taunted as her breathing began to increase. Now her ears were beginning to stretch into the triangle-shaped appendages that served her wolf form so well. She could scent the man-thing before her, smell his confusion and his growing worry. He was rogue, unclean, something to be driven from the pack. And since the alpha male wasn't present, it fell to her as alpha female to see that it was done.

"You go too far, Wolfen," the Sage growled as he leapt to his feet. And Dark realized that his aged voice was not due to the time he spent alive — and a considerable time it was too — but because it was partially Wolfen, partially Vampesi, trapped between the two.

"And I still pity you, old fool, trapped between two worlds and not belonging to either. That plus your so gracious social skills must have made you a popular child."

"I was popular because I didn't eat my dam," he snapped back. "A mistake I will be sure to rectify with your child."

"You won't live to see that day," Dark snarled as she allowed the change to slip a bit more, allowed the beast within to gain an inch more leeway, let the animal within a bit more free rein. "Your time is coming, old man. Make peace with your creator."

* * * * *

"*No way,*" hissed Tamara. "I ain't going in there alone."

"You will," growled Luca as he grabbed her by the arms and got right up into her face. "This is the chance that we need and you will damn sure provide it."

"I can't walk in there and demand that he release Dark." Tamara shook her head in denial. "That thing will kill me."

"Tamara," Omnubius broke Luca's hold on the woman and glared at him. He wasn't hurting her, but trying to intimidate her wasn't working either, because worse than her fear of Luca was her fear of the unknown. "You just have to distract him for three seconds. From the sound of their voices, his full attention is on Dark. We need to draw his attention away from her so we can save her and the baby." He took her arms in his hands and rubbed them gently, trying to be reassuring.

It didn't work.

"He will tear me into shreds, then feed me to the mistress. No way am I going in there."

"Please."

There was a shocked silence and Tamara and Nubius looked around to see who had joined them. Had Zinia recovered and found her way to them?

"Please, Tamara,"

"Luca?" Both Tamara and Nubius wore incredulous looks as they turned to the man standing a few steps back from them.

"Please, Tamara. I have only one chance of rescuing Dark from Sage, and it is a slim one at that. He can easily kill me or Dark and our child before I can do anything to save us. With all of the screaming you did, he has to think you are dead. That will throw him for a moment. The Sage thinks that he is never wrong. He is prepared for Omnubius and me. You are the unexpected element. I ask you again, as I have never asked of anyone, not even Dark, please, Tamara."

There was urgency in his hushed whispers and he stood alone, his stomach twisting in knots as he awaited her answer. Being so close to Dark and not being able to touch her, not being able to go to her, to hold her, to ease her fears, was driving him to the brink of madness. He had never begged anything from anyone in his life, yet he was prepared to go on his knees and humble himself before this newly turned Vampire who had been his blood servant just a few hours ago. He would give anything for his Dark, his pride, his will, his life.

"Please."

* * * * *

The crumbling of rock made both parties in the cavern room turn towards the entrance.

"Is anybody home?" a small, frightened voice called out. "I am really lost and I need…help?"

Out of the shadows, a bedraggled, barefoot redheaded woman stumbled, cursing and muttering under her breath.

"B.B.?" called Dark as she took in the scent and the view of the woman.

"You're alive?" called the voice from the depths of the robe. "How?"

He took one step towards the red-haired woman who was suddenly struck mute, turning his attention away from the pregnant Wolfen.

It was what she was looking for.

"Time to die," she cried as she let the manacles holding back the beast…*snap*.

"Now," cried two voices as the men stormed the cavern, but they were struck mute by what they saw.

In slow motion, Tamara dodged to the side, hugging a wall of stone. The Sage, torn between the two voices yelling in his direction, turned to face the doorway, then towards the frightening cry that sounded like something out of his worst nightmares.

Still partially human, the fur-covered form of Dark erupted from her supine position on the floor. Even as she flew through the air, her body began to elongate, to burst out of her clothing, to take on the form and characteristics of her wolfish brethren. A snarl more than a voice filled the air as the body hurtled towards him, leaving behind a shower of white cloth and humanity.

Knowing that he was backed into a corner, the Sage too let go of the remaining bits of his humanity, and sanity, and let the urge to kill overcome him.

Even before Dark's enormous front paws touched the front of his robe, the change that had been threatening took hold.

As the momentum of Dark's body propelled the Sage backwards, the material of his dark robes began to shred. When his back hit the hard stone floor with a crack, he exploded from his clothing, a horrific caricature of a Wolfen and Vampesi, something out of a human's worst nightmare.

There was a loud yelp, and Dark was shoved aside as the man-beast rose to his crooked hind legs.

Covered in patches of black fur, the Sage now stood seven feet tall, even in his hunched-over state.

Lethal black claws emerged from where his fingernails should have been, a gross mixture of a wolf's paw and a human hand. His groin was covered in thick, matted fur while his chest was a patchwork of long hair and Vampesi flesh. His legs were twisted and misshapen, with long thick thighs and short twisted calves. A small stub tail flickered rapidly at the end of his hairy back, an indication of his irritation. His long ears were laid back flat against his skull, while his black lips outlined yellowing and twisted fangs. But most horrifying of all, was the remainder of his face.

Black eyes, so like Luca's, were sunken into a large misshapen head. Fur sprang from his face in odd patches while his nose and mouth had the cone-shaped mouth that showed clearly his Wolfen heritage in the most frightening way. The long muzzle, the stretched-back, flaring, triangle-shaped nose, the short whiskers that twitched in the breeze, the thick, cloudy saliva that dribbled down his chest as if he were a mad dog, he was neither man nor beast, yet he was both.

"Get away from him," Luca bellowed, the first to break the hypnotic creature's hold on his senses. "Get back, Dark." He raced towards the creature, eyes narrowed as the heat of battle overtook him. Seeing Dark, his Dark, his powerful and vital mate tossed aside like unwanted garbage caused something inside him to snap.

"Lucavarious!" called Omnubius as he too raced towards the man-beast. Luca could not transform, and, therefore, maybe was a bit out of his league. He needed help, even if he was too hotheaded to ask for it.

But Dark paid no attention to either of the men. This was her fight, her duty to drive out the rogue who would weaken and ultimately destroy her pack. It was her right to defend those that she loved. Gathering her feet underneath herself, she bunched the powerful muscles of her Wolfen body and lunged for the creature, noting the weakness in his legs as she leapt.

Luca reached the creature first, sending out a purple blast of energy, aiming for the face and eyes, and diving for his chest.

But the Sage was part Vampesi too, and much older than Luca. He easily deflected the blast and swatted Luca away like an annoying gnat. Luca hit the wall with a muffled plop, the pain that he still held in control breaking free momentarily and blinding him with its searing white-hot heat.

Omnubius hit the creature around the waist, hoping to unbalance him, but the Sage, so long used to this ungainly figure, didn't topple or even budge.

"Hell," Nubius muttered before a large fist came crashing down upon his head, driving him straight into the ground.

By now, Dark had calculated her move and leapt, while the Sage was distracted.

"Die," she bellowed, her voice echoing around the room, as the Sage turned to meet her attack.

He never expected her to go for his knees.

With her cry still reverberating around the room, Dark pulled her leap short and skidded into the monster's legs, clamping her massive jaws around his right knee, delighting at the crunch of his bones.

"*No!*," the strangled voice shrieked in rage and pain as he collapsed to the side, striking his head on the floor, dazed. But Sage was not through yet. He still possessed powerful weapons and was well versed in using them.

With a calculating glint in his eyes, he glared at Dark. Glared, until a green aura surrounded her body. "Damn the baby," he growled, "I will begin anew."

"Shit," Luca gasped as he gained some control and saw what was happening to his mate. The Sage was trying to trap her in a force box, where he could fill the air with pressure or suck the oxygen right out if he so chose.

Thinking quickly, before the green completely surrounded her, Luca launched his own shield at Dark, easily and quickly encasing her in his warm purple shield, protecting her from the evil force that would do her harm.

"You can't hold that for long, puppy," the Sage growled as he saw what his former pupil had done. "Her death is inevitable, as is yours."

He increased the amount of energy he was tossing into the green shield, trying to squeeze and break the purple, to squeeze and break the Wolfen inside.

Luca doubled over in pain, clutching his head as he felt a terrific and horrifying pressure build up in his head. In all of his days, he had never felt a force such as this. It felt slimy and cold, cold as ice, and was trying to break his sanity.

But he had to concentrate. Blood droplets began forming on his forehead as he strained, blood tears ran down his face and his dark skin blanched, yet he maintained the shield.

"He's killing him," Tamara screamed as she broke through the barriers of her fear and raced towards Nubius. "Wake up. Wake up!" she screamed as she roughly shook his shoulders, before jerking him to his back. "I said get up, you worthless Vampire." She reached back, flattened her hand and let it fly. The crack of her hand on his cheek sounded loudly in the still room, but it had the desired results. Omnubius' eyes snapped open.

"Now get it," she screamed as she pointed down towards the fragmented creature who lay on the ground, a purple glow beginning to cover his body.

"Lucavarious, you bastard," screamed Omnubius as he struggled to his fee. "Don't you dare give up. Keep fighting."

Concentrating his energy, he raised his hands and shot a pure white energy beam at the creature's mangled knee, his weakest point.

"Arghhhh," The Sage screamed as pain exploded throughout his body. For a moment his concentration slipped and the green surrounding Dark lightened.

It was what Luca was waiting for.

"Now!" he bellowed, lurching to his feet, his body streaked with rivers of dark blood.

Spreading his arms out, he expanded his shield, steadily and rapidly pouring more of his life energy into it, until the green began to shudder and crack.

"What?" the Sage bellowed before a different pain attacked him, a pain that was in his head as the cracks in his mind began to expand.

"Yes!" Omnubius shouted as he poured more energy into the creature, giving him more pain to contend with, making it impossible for the doubly attacked creature to concentrate. "Keep at it, Luca."

The green was now a thin sheath that was dulled by the brilliance of the purple that stretched it. It pulsed again, flaring before growing faint, then began to splinter. With a popping sound, Sage's green shield exploded, sending shards of green force energy flying about the room.

"Die!" Dark's voice echoed around the room as she gathered herself and leapt through the purple barrier without fear. The purple would never hurt her.

Omnubius stepped back, his concentration broken, and Luca collapsed to his knees as Dark brushed past his protective barriers and went for the kill.

The Sage's eyes opened in real fear as he beheld his death, in the form of a sturdy, large black wolf, descended upon him.

Large paws, claws extended, landed upon, then tore through the muscles and bones that made up his chest. The crack was loud in the silent room, blood spurting out to coat Dark's furry paws in dark stickiness as they buried themselves in the opening she had made.

The Sage's eyes widened in pain and shock; he arched his neck back and a howl of pure rage and agony escaped his tight throat.

"For that pain and misery you caused, for the suffering you caused my family," Dark's disembodied voice echoed throughout the cavern, clear and succinct. "For the misery that your existence has created, I, Dark, co-Leader of the Wolfen Clan, condemn you to death."

In a flash, Dark's muzzle, lips pulled back to bear her teeth, dropped low over his exposed neck; then there was a loud *crunch.*

A wet gurgly sound bubbled up from his torn throat as Dark's fangs sank deep, severing arteries and tearing cartilage. Blood erupted from the torn flesh, coating her muzzle as she gave a low growl and began to shake his limp head violently. The Sage's body arched and spasmed, but the weight of the true Wolfen held him in place, held him until his death throes were ending, until the life force seeped from his body, until death met him and carried him straight to hell.

Dark released the mangled neck with a shiver, and the transformation began to take hold. The beast was satisfied that vengeance had taken place, satisfied that justice had been served.

Her fur receded, withdrawing beneath her skin as her body began to quiver and reform. A low moan punctuated the return of her muscles and bone to their corporeal shape, her body looking feminine and small once more.

"I killed him," she gasped as in a blinding instant, she returned from being Wolfen, to being Dark. She shuddered as she pulled her hands from his chest, her right still clutching pieces of his mashed heart. "I killed him."

Her naked body began to spasm and shake, then she was off the shell of that body and racing to a corner, where the meager contents of her stomach spewed, rejected from her stomach.

Luca, watching with pride and awe, struggled to his feet and staggered to her side, wrapping her in the comforting touch of his arms, murmuring into her hair until the spasms stopped.

"You saved me," she muttered as she drew a hand across her mouth, grimacing when she realized she had used her right arm, moaning at the blood that now covered her face.

"Didn't you know, Dark?" he asked as he reached down with one hand and tore a hank of material from his blood-stained dirty pants and gently began to blot her face, understanding her revulsion and loving her all the more for it. "Didn't you know that the most handsome, good-looking guy always wins out against the ugly bad guys? He was dead from the moment that he touched you." His chest puffed up as he eyed her reaction from beneath his lowered lashes.

"Right," Dark snorted as she gathered her strength and pulled herself upright.

"Hey, it was inevitable," Omnubius added as he pulled himself together and stepped forward towards the couple. "I am, after all, the best looking creature in this whole dump."

"Stop," Luca growled, pulling Dark behind him.

"What is it now, puppy?" Nubius sighed. He was tired, he was nearly drained, he was hungry, and he was dirty. He hated being dirty. It smudged his image and ruined his clothing.

"She is naked, Omnubius," Luca grated out, as if the man standing before him was a complete imbecile.

"Well, she don't have anything that I haven't seen before," Nubius declared, exasperated.

"Yeah," Dark growled with scowl in his direction. "A hole is a hole, right? Or in your estimation, at least."

"Tight, lubricated, hot…"

"All right," Luca shouted over Nubius, glaring him into laughter, which Dark joined in. "But she is my woman, and if I'm not allowed to ogle her naked, no one will."

Dark took one look at the fierce expression on his pain-etched bloody face, and broke into fresh peals of laughter.

"Give up the coat," Luca growled as he gazed up into the ceiling, looking for answers to the cosmic question that would allow him to understand women.

"My coat," Nubius wailed, then glanced at Luca's determined face. "Okay," he sighed. "I don't feel like wrestling you for it."

He slung the battered garment off of his shoulders and tossed it over to Luca.

After Dark was properly covered, he strode forward and took her into his arms. "Glad that you are safe, Cousin. But next time, let us deal with the trash, please? You will give me gray hairs."

"Omnubius," Dark began, wanting to thank the man for what he had done, but he waved her off.

"I know, dear heart, I know. Just make me the godfather and we will call it even. I always wanted a nephew to train,"

"It's a girl," Luca called out, scowling at the couple as Omnubius led them out of the cavern, shielding her from the sight of what Wolfen justice demanded of her.

"Coming, Tamara?" Nubius called back as he raised one arm in invitation. "I do have two arms and it does my reputation good to be seen with two such lovely ladies."

Tamara was still frozen, standing where she had forced Omnubius to awaken. She had never contemplated that such things could happen in this dark world. But there stood Lucavarious, growling after his blood cousin, Omnubius the Vampire, as they passed the corpse of the monster Sage, leading a Wolfen woman out of a series of dark caves deep in the bowels of the earth. This was the stuff that the legends of old told of. And this was her new life. She was going to enjoy being a

Vampire, although she never thought that those words would ever occur to her.

"I'm coming," she called and she raced to Omnubius' side. "Wait for me to catch up."

"Got about a thousand years?" Nubius asked, cocking one eyebrow up at her.

"Oh, Lord. Another one," Luca groaned as he followed the two out of the cave, keeping an intense watch over his mate.

"And if what that creature said is true, also of your blood line, our blood line. Know that, Cousin?" he asked as he gave Tamara a squeeze.

"Oh, hell," Luca muttered as he raced forward and pulled Dark into his arms.

"Look at it this way," Nubius continued. "It's a great way to increase the family stock. And you do know that you can't kick family out? Tamara and I must now discuss training and adjustment to her new life. Once the rush is over, she will probably start regretting her life and all of that. We have to keep a close eye on her." He winked at Tamara.

"You bet," she returned. "I might just become unstable and kill myself or something. You don't want that on your hands."

But Lucavarious and Dark were paying no attention. They were lost in each other's eyes, merging their souls.

"Life is good," Omnubius laughed as he began to lead the way back towards the castle. Dawn would be breaking soon and he had to get Tamara settled before the sun was high.

"So very good," Dark murmured as she gazed at the face of her beloved. "Luca I—" but he placed a finger over her lips to silence her.

"I know, Dark." He felt her love envelope him, cover him with its healing touch. "The words aren't necessary. I can feel you inside me."

"Where you keep me safe," she sighed and lifted her face for a slow, deep, painfully tender kiss.

"Always," he breathed as he broke away from the kiss to lead her back to the light, the castle, to their lives. "Always."

When Lucavarious and Omnubius went back the next night to take care of disposing of the shell of the Sage, they discovered that the body was gone, just vanished.

"If he's not dead, we can search these caverns for years and wouldn't find him." Omnubius said with a concerned look. "He probably dragged his carcass off somewhere to die."

"Just to be sure, I am sealing off the entrance to these caves, Nubius. I don't trust him. He survived too long for me to take this lightly."

"Seal the cavern off and warn the people, Luca," Omnubius decided. "If it is fated for him to return, nothing you do will make a difference. We will just be prepared for the next time."

"The next time," Luca agreed, a fierce look on his face.

And if that day ever arose, Lucavarious and his family would be prepared.

Epilogue

"Push, Dark," Luca urged, looking pale underneath his dark skin. "We're almost there."

"What do you mean *we?*" Dark roared as the next contraction hit her; tearing at her back and moving like octopus arms around to her stomach. "Luca, you are a bastard."

"Why do people persist in believing that my parents weren't mated?" Luca groaned, then gritted his teeth as Dark's extended claws pierced the flesh of his hands.

"If you two would stop bickering for a moment, maybe we can proceed to deliver the wonder-child," Zinia admonished from her position between Dark's widespread knees.

The thin white tunic that Dark wore was covered in sweat as she labored to bring forth her child. The air in the room was scented by waves of flowery smoke and dim candlelight, all placed to make the new mother feel comfortable as she struggled to bring new life into the world. Beside their big bed, Luca panted out the rhythms that she was supposed to copy, to help take her mind away from her body. Low music played in the background, compliments of a string quartet that Omnubius had trained for the blessed event, music that was supposed to help her relax.

None of it was working.

"You will never touch me again, Lucavarious," Dark growled through gritted fangs as sweat beaded up and poured down her face.

"I touch you, madam? I think you need to turn that statement around."

"And you can't control yourself, Mr. Big Bad Vampesi? This…really…*hurts.*"

Luca paled even more as Dark began to lose control. In a panic, he looked to Zinia and demanded answers.

"Why is she hurting like this? Is this normal? How long will this take? Can't you see it's killing her?"

"Lucavarious, nephew," Zinia soothed. "It hurts because she is labor, it will take as long as it takes, this is perfectly normal, and she's not dying. She is pissed at you and regretting all of those hot evenings that you two spent together. You are really potent, young man," Zinia giggled as the blush spread across his face.

"Something's happening," Dark panted, breaking the silence that had sprung up between her two midwives. Her body began to quake uncontrollably. "Something dropped. I have to push."

Zinia peered between her legs and nodded her agreement.

"All right, Mom. You know what to do. Give me a slow easy push. I don't want you to tear."

"Tear?" Luca whimpered, before his face turned green. He began shaking worse than Dark.

"Like the nausea, and the shakes, and the teeth marks that are on your arm, Dark will handle this too, Luca. Stop being so concerned. The women in my family have been birthing litters for years."

"Litters?" Dark shrieked, drowning out the sound of Luca's tortured moan.

"I see the head," Zinia called out, turning Dark's attention back to the matter at hand. "I need a push, girl."

Dark released her grip on Luca and curled her hands around her thighs. Pushing her chin down to her chest, she grunted and heaved until her face was purple with exertion.

Luca, trying to help, positioned himself behind her, bracketing her with his legs, holding her back against his chest, as he wrapped his arms around hers, urging her silently onward.

"That felt good," Dark moaned as the urge to push waned, but before she could catch her breath, the need to push was back. "But this hurts."

"Almost there," Zinia urged.

"Almost there, my Wolfen-woman," Luca echoed.

"I don't want to do this anymore," Dark gasped as she lost her breath and felt her body shutting down. "I'll do it tomorrow. Stop everything here; I'll finish later."

"*No*," Zinia growled, her own deep brown eyes going dark. "You will push now, young lady, and that is an order."

"Yeah," Luca frantically agreed, looking torn and seriously frightened as Dark attempted to give in to lethargy that was trying to claim her body. "You heard her. *Push* Dark. I want my daughter now. Do you hear me?"

"Daughter?" Dark snarled, her body using her sudden anger to fuel her energy resources. "Daughter? You fang-faced fool, it is a boy. You hear me? *A boy.*"

With a mighty heave, Dark again bore down and was rewarded with a tearing pain as the child's head pushed free of her body.

"I see the head," Zinia called to Dark excitedly. "Come on, Dark. Almost there."

"I see...hair," Luca cried. "And more hair. Dark, we are having a *puppy.*"

"Puppy," she shrieked, and with one more heave, the baby came screaming into the world, his sudden loud wails forcing the world to know of his displeasure.

"A boy," Zinia called out. "It's a boy. You have a son, Luca. You actually are a man."

"Thanks, I think," Luca snorted as he turned his attention to Dark.

She was trembling, she was a sweaty mess, but she had never looked more beautiful. With large, liquid-filled eyes, she eyed the squirmy hot bundle that was placed upon her stomach.

With trembling lips and hands, she reached for her child, the creation of hers and Luca's love.

"A boy?" she asked in a small, quivering voice.

"A boy," Luca whispered as he wrapped his arms around his mate, lost in unexplainable emotions that flooded through his body. "Thank you, Dark," he breathed as he pressed his lips against her brow. "Thank you for my son."

"Give me another push for the afterbirth," Zinia commanded, her voice cracking suspiciously as she gazed at the two leaders of her people as they lost themselves in a love so new and tender, it was heart-wrenching to behold. "Before I start crying and make a fool of myself."

Soon, the not-so-little, little boy was bathed and diapered, his mother cleansed and made comfortable. The new parents basked in the joy of their creation, who lay sleeping in his mother's arms, oblivious to the world.

"What shall we call him?" Luca asked as he carefully snuggled his wife and child to his side. "He has to have a good name, a great name. A name that befits his status as my son."

"I thought you wanted a daughter?" Dark asked over a yawn. She had never been so sleepy in her life, but she didn't want to miss a moment of this new mommy thing, this parental bonding.

"Daughter, son, as long as it is from my bloodline, it will be great." He stuck his nose in the air and preened like a peacock, as if he himself performed some magical feat.

"So long as he doesn't have your ego," Dark yawned and giggled as Luca squeezed her a bit for her impertinence.

"So what do we call him?" Luca asked again.

But before she could answer, Omnubius slammed into the room, posed dramatically in the doorway, before entering the room with flourish. Around his shoulders was a long leather cloak lined in the most brilliant scarlet silk. His pants were leather, tight and black, his shirt a long black poets blouse with a loose string closure on the front. The shirt was positioned just to show off enough of his tanned muscular flesh to make women drool, but not so much as to appear to vainglorious.

"The godfather," he announced with pomp and circumstance, "is here."

"Ego?" Luca asked as he stuck his thumb in his cousin's direction.

Dark rolled her eyes at him before addressing the Vampire, who stood with great pomposity at the foot of her bed,

"Omnubius," she called then jerked her eyes to her son as he began to squirm in her arms. "Want a peek?" she asked, fighting back another yawn. She had never been so tired in all of her life.

"Does a Vampire outsmart a Vampesi?" he asked, snickering at Luca before turning his full attention to his new charge.

"Why, the darling is positively gorgeous, Dark. I see little of his father in him."

Luca snorted and rolled his eyes yet refused to comment.

"We are trying to pick a name," Dark laughed as the fierce Vampire melted at one look of her precious baby boy.

"And he won't be named after you," Luca drawled. "If you want progeny and namesakes, go make them yourself."

"Me, a father?" Nubius snorted. "Dear boy, labor has warped your brain. But because we are in a sense related, I will do the honor of naming this Vampesi cub. His name is Lucavarian."

"Lucavarian?" Luca tasted the name on his tongue and found it pleasing to his pallet. "Yes, I like it. Lucavarian he is."

"What a beautiful name, Nubius," Dark agreed. "Lucavarian it is. We will call him Varian." Then she spoke to her sleeping child, "Hello Varian. Mommy loves you very much."

"Now I must take the child and introduce him to his family," Nubius declared as he deftly lifted the bundle from Dark's arms.

"Hey," Luca protested, but the Vampire was swift and knowing, having planned his attack beforehand.

"Hey nothing. Dark is about to collapse, you look like Vincent after the change, and the whole castle is waiting to see the new heir. We will be back before his next meal time, which is, if he is anything like you were, puppy, will be in fifteen minutes."

Nubius turned and added, "Besides, I have so much to teach him."

Luca actually whimpered as Omnubius exited the room.

Dark and Luca stared at the closed door from which their child and his self- proclaimed godfather just passed through.

"Can you believe that?" he asked, still not quite sure how he'd lost possession of his only and newly named son.

"Luca, when it comes to your family, nothing surprises me," she laughed as she snuggled down against his warm side and let the soreness of her body fade, along with her consciousness.

The last thing she heard and felt before she gave in to the deep void calling her, was the feel of Luca gently running his hands through her cropped hair, and murmuring in her ear, "I love you, woman. You make my soul sing. But we will have to discuss Lucavarian's tail later."

Dark chuckled as she forced her eyes open one last time.

"Luca, I..."

I know, Dark," he murmured as he lowered his head to brush a tender kiss upon her forehead. "You don't have to say the words. I know."

He fell asleep, holding his heart in his hands.

Life was good.

About the author:

Stephanie is married to the most wonderfully maddening Irish Viking ever created and has given birth to two children, affectionately known as The Viking kittens.

Stephanie's main support in her writing career has been her wonderful parents who are always willing to take her spawns, uh, children for a weekend so that she can work, her older sister Teresa, the stuffed chicken, and of course, her Irish Viking, Dennis.

Stephanie loves to write paranormal and fantasy characters with a lot of humor, because there is no such thing as enough laughter in the world. She also loves to write erotica, just to shock people, but in her heart she is a romance fanatic...

Stephanie Burke welcomes mail from readers. You can write to her c/o Ellora's Cave Publishing at P.O. Box 787, Hudson, Ohio 44236-0787.

Also by STEPHANIE BURKE:

- Keeper of the Flame
- Dangerous Heat
- The Slayer
- Seascape
- Merlin's Kiss
- Hidden Passions Volume 1
- Hidden Passions Volume 2
- Wicked Wishes anthology with Marly Chance & Joanna Wylde
- Threshold anthology with Shelby Morgen

Why an electronic book?

We live in the Information Age—an exciting time in the history of human civilization in which technology rules supreme and continues to progress in leaps and bounds every minute of every hour of every day. For a multitude of reasons, more and more avid literary fans are opting to purchase e-books instead of paperbacks. The question to those not yet initiated to the world of electronic reading is simply: why?

1. *Price.* An electronic title at Ellora's Cave Publishing runs anywhere from 40-75% less than the cover price of the <u>exact same title</u> in paperback format. Why? Cold mathematics. It is less expensive to publish an e-book than it is to publish a paperback, so the savings are passed along to the consumer.

2. *Space.* Running out of room to house your paperback books? That is one worry you will never have with electronic novels. For a low one-time cost, you can purchase a handheld computer designed specifically for e-reading purposes. Many e-readers are larger than the average handheld, giving you plenty of screen room. Better yet, hundreds of titles can be stored within your new library—a single microchip. (Please note that Ellora's Cave does not endorse any specific brands. You can check our website at www.ellorascave.com for customer recommendations we make available to new consumers.)

3. *Mobility.* Because your new library now consists of only a microchip, your entire cache of books can be taken with you wherever you go.

4. *Personal preferences are accounted for.* Are the words you are currently reading too small? Too large? Too...**ANNOYING**? Paperback books cannot be modified according to personal preferences, but e-books can.

5. *Innovation.* The *way* you read a book is not the only advancement the Information Age has gifted the literary community with. There is also the factor of what you can read. Ellora's Cave Publishing will be introducing a new line of interactive titles that are available in e-book format only.

6. *Instant gratification.* Is it the middle of the night and all the bookstores are closed? Are you tired of waiting days — sometimes weeks — for online and offline bookstores to ship the novels you bought? Ellora's Cave Publishing sells instantaneous downloads 24 hours a day, 7 days a week, 365 days a year. Our e-book delivery system is 100% automated, meaning your order is filled as soon as you pay for it.

Those are a few of the top reasons why electronic novels are displacing paperbacks for many an avid reader. As always, Ellora's Cave Publishing welcomes your questions and comments. We invite you to email us at service@ellorascave.com or write to us directly at: P.O. Box 787, Hudson, Ohio 44236-0787.

Printed in the United States
24642LVS00001B/46-708

9 781843 604464